GOODIVA'S SECRET

First edition. May 8, 2020.

Copyright © 2020 Sienna Mynx.

ISBN: 978-0-9999078-0-1

Written by Sienna Mynx.

I0678131

Dedication

What is a Sigma?

Bye, bye, Alpha male....

A Sigma male is a man who lives outside of the hierarchy tropes of male heroes in romance novels. He is always so mysterious, obsessively private about the possessions and passions in his life. The Sigma male is a different side of the Alpha. He does his own thing until fate or natural selection makes him the leader. The Sigma doesn't respect the rules of any game, which could include courtship, love, marriage, and all that comes with it. He bends societal rules to fit the life he wants to have as a way of survival. Though women are drawn to him they mistake his pursuit of them for love and devotion. It is not. The Sigma does not fall in love easily, but when he falls he falls permanently. Unlike the Alpha male the Sigma male is never predictably controlling without good reason, or tamed by just submission, you must resist. You must prove yourself trustworthy to be his, not the other way around. The Sigma male waits, not with patience but with an unyielding focus to learn you, to understand you, to convince you that he has earned you, to make you permanently his. Then the world he builds a new world for you and him from that day forward. He is at the top of the socio-sexual hierarchy scale not beneath the Alpha but at his side. Do you like to read about the Sigma male? Have you read of him in the past? Goodiva's Secret will help you decide.

Welcome to Goodiva's Secret. The first installment in a three-book anthology focused on the twisted love of a Sigma, Zeta, and Gamma males. Each book is a standalone. However, the thread that binds the three is unbreakable.

I am Sienna Mynx, and this is the first installment of different love.

Goodiva's PlayList

1. How can I ease the pain - Lisa Fischer
2. Baby Be Mine - Miki Howard
3. Do you still love me - Meli'sa Morgan
4. Unbreak My heart - Toni Braxton
5. We've Only Just Begun - Glen Jones
6. Tender Kisses - Tracie Spencer
7. There you Go - By Johnnie Gill
8. Just be a Man About it - Toni Braxton
9. We Can't Be Friends - Deborah Cox
10. Adorn - Miguel
11. In My Mind - Heather Headley
12. Alexander O'Neal - Never knew love like this
13. Baby Be Mine - Mikki Howard
14. All I want is Forever - Regina Belle - JT Taylor
15. Show Me - Glenn Jones
16. Love Makes Things Happen - Babyface
17. I Call Your Name - Switch
18. Just Once - James Ingram
19. Moments in Love
20 Love Ballad - LTD featuring Jeffery Osborne
21. Forever My Lady - Jodeci
22. Until the End of Time - Justin Timberlake / Beyonce
23. Love Me In A Special Way - Debarge
24 After All - Al Jarreau
25. Make Me Say It Again Girl - The Isley Brothers
26. Don't Say Goodnight - Isley Brothers
27. Share My Life - Kem
28. Love on the Brain - Rhianna
29. Talk - Khalid
30. Best Part - H.E.R. & Daniel Caesar
31. Sativa - Jhene Aiko - Rae Sermund
32. Soul Capsule - Lady Science

Prologue

June 25, 2016, 2:22 a.m.

When darkness prowled, so did he. Jaxon preferred the night. Since he was a kid he had found solace in between the hours when most people slept. He drove to his studio alone, determined to meet with his team and get his answers. A fifty-million-dollar film project he had funded was now another ten million over budget. No matter the hour, when he wanted answers, everyone was present to give them.

He'd not make the meeting.

She was in trouble. She had run from him, now she was running to him for protection. The boyfriend was a mouse. He'd done his research. Rejection wasn't expected with her, she seemed so amicable to his desires. Was he wrong? Jaxon smiled to himself as his fingers gripped the steering wheel and his foot lay heavy on the gas pedal. Of course he wasn't. She was his, sweetheart just didn't know it. Apparently, the mouse did.

The BMW burned asphalt, hugged the winding curves of the road. Recovered nicely and gained speed.

"Listen to me," he said through clenched teeth as he squinted at the darkness.

"You have to stay calm," he shouted over her screams.

"I can't! He's behind me, he's ramming my car. He's going to run me off the road. Oh my God! He's going to kill me!"

"I'm coming. I'm coming," he mumbled, to himself rather than to her. Maybe the boyfriend wasn't a mouse after all. Jaxon sent her down the cliffside road, headed directly for him. After a few dangerous curves he saw the speeding vehicle headed his way. He flashed his lights at her to slow her down. She was either too panicked or too reckless to agree. Instead, she accelerated.

"Fuck!"

For her life, and for leverage over the car chase, he swerved left between the charging Range Rover and the pursuing Ferrari just in time, to keep them both from crashing off the side of the road. The mouse travelled far too fast to be stopped. The only good defense Jaxon could summon was a strong offense. He took the danger upon himself and blew out his gear shift to send his BMW into a spin. The impending crash followed bright beams of lightheaded straight for a collision he narrowly avoided. The Ferrari slammed into the back passenger door and they both spun dangerously close to the mountain side. The Ferrari missed the mountainside and avoided a double flip that would certainly have killed the driver and passenger by a double flip down the middle of the road. Jaxon wasn't as lucky. The collision sent his BMW into a car-to-street roll, with sparks flying from under the hood as he slid nearly a quarter of a mile down the slant of the road. The windshield shattered. His passenger door window was blown out as well. The airbag suffocated him.

His BMW rested on its roof. The engine burst into flames. Jaxon initially lost consciousness, but the heat of the fire that spread fast woke him. Dazed, bleeding, he counted down the broken bones: his wrist, his knee, and there had to be something wrong with his shoulder. The shock rendered the trauma to his body numb. He gagged on fumes of motor oil and cooking engine parts. Everything burned around him. The black smoke inside the car and the darkness outside of twisted his reality. He fumbled with the seatbelt. It was locked so tight to his chest he choked down whatever clean air he could grasp. A constant pressing on the button eventually freed him. It was then, just as the fire ignited his feet and pants legs, that he began to crawl out of the window using the good arm, elbow and shoulder for leverage. He felt the fire spread like the devil's forked tongue licking slowly up his leg. He felt his trousers melt and his skin burn.

"HELP HIM!"

Goodiva rushed from her car, down the slanted road covered in glass and motor oil. Jaxon Price crawled out of the car window with part of him on fire. He rolled and tried to put himself out. Before she reached him, Twixt, her boyfriend, grabbed her by the waist and threw her away from the scene so forcefully she spun before she landed on her hands and knees.

"Kill him!" Twixt shouted at his brother.

"No!" she pleaded. She could see Twixt's brother drag Jaxon away from the burning car before he began to kick and stomp on his body.

"Are you insane! He's hurt! You're killing him you assholes!"

She got to her feet and fought Twixt with her fists, swinging them like her best friend had taught her. She had used the pepper spray on him earlier—his eyes were red and glassy from the blast. Where was it now? She felt so desperate she was almost incapacitated by her breathless fear.

Twixt grabbed her by both arms and shook her violently. He threw her again, and she landed on her back. From what she could see, Jaxon Price fought back against his attacker. He caught Kumar by the leg, and Twixt's brother went down on the pavement as hard as she had. Twixt's attention turned toward the fight scene. He raced over to help his brother. She needed to find a weapon, anything. They were going to kill him. What else could she do?

Jaxon heard her screams. He felt the kicks and bone crunching stomps from his attacker foot, and his first instinct was to get past him to her crazed boyfriend. But his vision was impaired. One of his eyes didn't open. The car fire illuminated the road. It must have been her peril that surged his strength. He had little else to fight back for. He felt no pain as he went for the idiot kicking him, while only half of his body worked. A fast grip of his attacker's ankle caused the bastard to fall close enough for him to gain the advantage with his one good arm. What he didn't expect was the second attacker. He received another hard kick to the back and felt the force go straight through his spine. He flipped to his side and took a gut kick that sent him rolling closer to the burning car. The heat was extreme. The men then proceeded to stomp and kick him together in some macabre dance of death.

Jaxon folded, unable to overcome the repeated blows in time to fight back. From his good eye he could see her. She stood frozen and watched his beating. When the beatings got worse, he knew his fate was closer to death than rescue. She knew it too. Instead of trying to help him, she turned and fled. She ran from them all. The last thing he could remember was her white Range Rover drive away. One last hard kick, and he was gone.

Chapter One

Malibu, June 22, 2016

Another smile pushed up the corners of his lips. He peeked at her from under a typical glazed, droopy lidded stare. Not only was he guilty, but she saw a different truth in his eyes. A truth her best friends had warned her about the moment she brought him around and bragged over her new-found happiness. Twixt didn't love her.

His birth name was Vihaan Arjun. He was British, of East Indian descent. The moment he crossed over into pop music, Vihann was gone and Twixt was born. A five-foot-eight, popular, handsome, sweet dream of a man with deep brown skin and dark piercing eyes under lashes longer than any natural man woman or child. Women from all over the world listened to his hypnotic, thick-accented, rhyming voice and were seduced. Somewhere between becoming his black American deejay, lover and then girlfriend for clout, she'd fallen for the jerk. It wasn't difficult to do. What 24-year-old women living in the City of Angels hadn't fallen for the celebrity, wealth or popularity in the world she lived in?

"Play some music babe, that always chills you out," he said in a dull tone. "I'm not in the mood to argue tonight. I just got home."

He laughed into his fist at something on the television. He then picked up the bong and took another hit, causing the water in the glass bauble to boil with bubbles. Up went a smoke cloud through the pipe after his last deep inhale. Twixt held the marijuana deep in his lungs before he released a long exhalation of satisfaction.

"You're not going anywhere. I just got home."

"My stuff is packed Twixt. Pay attention. I'm leaving you."

At this, his eyes nearly opened to their wakened state. But awareness was fleeting when he fogged his braincells in marijuana. His lids drooped once more and he took another drag from the bong.

"Did you hear me?"

"Yea, yea. You're leaving because of some bra you found? C'mon! I wouldn't bring any thot here." He coughed out a cloud of smoke. "That belongs to one of my mates."

"Your mates? Here? Where we sleep?"

"You know the one." Twixt snapped his finger, pretending to try to remember. "Damn, you know him. What's his name? He stayed a few days back—uh, you remember? Kumar brought him by to meet you last month. Gave him a key."

"Briggs?"

"Yea. Yea. That's him. Briggs."

"You gave Briggs and Kumar access to our home to party with girls?" she frowned.

"It would be our home if you finally moved all the way in," Twixt scoffed. "You keep your condo when I've told you I need you here for me."

"Because I'm not stupid. Because I'll never be dependent on you in that way. Never mind it. I'm done with this clown show. Here's your key"

"Goodie, chill. It's not that deep. It could be from one of the girls my brothers' banging around with," Twixt shrugged. "Or it's yours, you have a million of those things."

"I don't care anymore. It's just lame to be caught up in this mess," she said.

"Lame? Did you just say lame?" Twixt laughed.

"I'm done."

"With who? Me? Are you taking the piss?" he scoffed.

"I'm serious—"

"Pop a Xan sweetheart, and sleep it off. Go to your condo if you want. I'll come through later tonight and we'll talk it out." He stood and patted down his saggy leather jeans with the chain links that hung from his belt and looped down to connect with his pocket. He was in search of his marijuana pouch. Smoking weed was as normal as chewing gum in their life. As a disc jockey to some of the hottest hip-hop musicians in the country, she walked through clouds of smoke daily. But marijuana could get really strange in LA. More and more people she knew and respected were becoming addicted to the casual smoking of potent strains of it. Twixt always kept his laced with something. She feared it eroded what was left of his brain and dead heart.

The door opened.

Goodiva turned and watched in disbelief as Twixt's older brother Kumar walked in with a leggy brunette.

"What are you doing here?" Goodiva tossed at his brother.

"I live here," Kumar barked back.

"The hell you do. Twixt gave you the keys to his place in Calabasas. You stay there. This is our home."

"He's my brother. What's his is mine and vice versa," Kumar said, and rubbed his woman friend's ass in a suggestive manner.

Twixt laughed.

"That's a joke, since you don't have anything that isn't his," she shot back.

Kumar sneered at her.

"Stick to spinning records that no one wants to listen to. Last I checked your name isn't on the deed." He walked off with his date holding his hand.

Goodiva shot him her middle finger, then turned back to Twixt. "This is what I'm talking about."

Twixt groaned. "He's just kidding."

"Are you going to let him talk to me like that? I don't let you talk to me like that. The blatant disrespect has to stop."

"You started it. You need to be less bitchy."

"Did you just call me a bitch?" she asked.

Twixt got up from his sofa and threw his hands up in defeat. He began to speak rapidly in Hindi as he paced and then walked away. She was sure there were more insults he muttered. He disappeared into the kitchen to fix himself something to eat or drink. She didn't know and didn't care. She should have just left. Delilah told her to send him a text after she was 300 miles away. But she wanted the closure. And she wanted out of his damn contract.

Why had he even chosen her? He never cheated with women that looked like her. In fact, she'd never seen him give a second glance to a woman who resembled her. Her Sudanese mother and African American father had blessed her with regal features, height, and a slim yet curvy figure that required no artificial additives. She knew she was more than surface beauty. Her beauty came from the heart. It was all wasted on a poser like him.

She kept the secret from her friends and family as to why she chose him. Goodiva's career had shifted into overdrive after the first public appearance with the UK musician who started the craze for Hindi hip-hop. It was a blend of rap beats with Hindi lyrics. Together they'd turned his creative flow and her musical mixing genius into a global sensation. First, she got selected by Twixt to be his personal DJ for his tour. That put her in the sights of several big-name acts who requested her services. And then Twixt's brother and manager negotiated a supporting role in her first film. She had both worlds, a chance to be a musician and act in a major film all bundled together as one. It was the only thing Kumar did for her that didn't come with a snide criticism or remark.

Now she wanted out. Out of the contract, out of his life, out of this life.

Twixt walked back into the sunken living room with the sectional white sofa, pearl marble floor and crystal glass coffee table. He had a sandwich he had fixed for himself and a beer. He plopped down on the section of the sofa that faced the large flat screen television. She watched him with mounting resentment as he chewed and stared at the television program.

"Well. I guess that's it. I'll have my lawyer call you."

"Your lawyer is my lawyer," he said after swallowing a mouthful. He picked up the remote and flipped through the channels. Goodiva couldn't believe his audacity. She got up and walked right over to him. She snatched the remote from his hand and turned off the television.

"You never deal with anything. It's all a game to you! Everything about you and your reputation is fake."

"You crazy? You want to talk about being fake? Look at you. Bloody hell, who names themselves Goo-diva? You couldn't even spell it right," he tossed back

"It's my birth name you idiot, not a box of chocolates!"

"It's stupid!" he said.

"You're stupid!" she shouted back. "And a racist!"

"Whaaaaaat?" he nearly choked on his sandwich. "Now I'm a racist? You're going to play the race card on me because you think I cheat on you?"

"Yes, you're a racist cheater," she said, crossing her arms in defiance.

Twixt sat forward. He set his food on the coffee table next to his drink. "Why? Because you're black? You're the fucking racist! Putting that shit on me."

"Isn't race the reason why you still won't tell your mother about me?" she asked. He stood. She took a step back. He took a step forward.

"Isn't my skin color and connection to the culture the reason why you insisted on hiring me in the first place?"

She was stopped from retreating by the opposite sofa bumping the back of her legs. Now he was face to face with her. "That was your play. How you got down."

"The culture. Are you mad? I am the culture. The new culture. Hindi rap is the culture, and I created that. You came along for the ride on my wave."

"Okay, we're done," she said. "I'm done. I'm seriously, done."

"Well crack-on!" he flipped her off with the toss of his hand. He picked up his plate and settled back down in front of the television. To be this angry with him was the biggest joke. She had signed up for the circus and let the fame become the ringmaster of her life. She sold her soul for celebrity. Whose fault was it that she fell in love with the pretending? There were deals between them that could take away her earnings and destroy her reputation if she walked away. In the age of social media and the paparazzi, most Hollywood couples had one. The answer to her problems was in her purse. Wiping her tears, she reached over to it. Twixt didn't notice. He laughed at the television show he was watching. She pulled out her phone and called her friend Jena.

"Hi Goodie!" Goodiva could hear loud explicit rap music blare in the background. "Sorry, I'm at a shoot. W'sup?"

"You tell me. You left a voicemail for me earlier. Returning your call."

Jena chuckled. "I got plans."

"You always have plans," Goodiva sighed.

"Want to have some fun?"

"The kind that makes you erase your asshole ex-boyfriend from your memory. Sure. I'm listening," Goodiva said while she stared at Twixt. If he was listening to her conversation, he didn't show it.

"How about a private party?" Jena chuckled.

"Oh?"

"Yeah, do you know that actor...uhm, Ali Jabar? He was in the latest James Bond movie?"

"Yep, I loved him in that. He's Arabian or Pakistani right?"

Twixt cut his eyes over at her. Now she had his attention. He then glanced back at the television.

"I dunno. I guess. Pool party. Lots going on."

"How old is he? Thirty?" she asked. She'd deejayed a birthday party for him a year ago, and the most popular female rapper in the industry performed. He paid over seventy-five grand for her time.

Jena laughed.

"What's funny?"

"Age ain't nothing but a number... when your boyfriend ain't nothing but a pain," Jena began to sing.

"Very funny," Goodiva said.

"Meet me at my house. Eleven?" said Jena.

"Yes. Sure." Goodiva got up and walked over to the door. She could hear Kumar and his lady friend laughing somewhere in the house. Her stomach soured at the thought of spending another minute with him and Twixt. If she went to her condo, then Twixt would show up on her doorstep. She had been stupid enough to give him a key. She opened the door and stepped outside.

"I want to come. I was calling for another reason," she said and closed the door.

"W'sup?"

"Can I stay with you for a few days? Need to clear my head. Give this asshole time to accept the fact that we are done and get him to agree to...never mind. I just need a place."

"You know my gate code. Andrea is there to let you in."

"Thanks Jena. I owe you."

"No worries. See you soon."

Goodiva hung up. She looked up at the sky. No clouds, no sun, just blue clear sky. She exhaled. Why was she constantly making her life complicated? Her best friends constantly probed her for the answer to the question. It was time for her to grow the hell up and stand on her own. She turned and went back inside.

"Got a date?" Twixt asked. He met her at the door. Was he trying to listen to her?

Goodiva ignored him. She walked around him to her luggage and things. She put her purse on her shoulder and headed for the door with all she could drag and carry.

"Goodie!" Twixt called out.

She paused and glanced at him.

"Have fun. Cool off. We'll figure it out."

"Bye Twixt."

"Don't do anything I wouldn't I do," he said and winked then closed the door on her.

"Go to hell."

Chapter Two

Calabasas, California, June 22, 2016

"What's her name?" he asked. Jaxon Price leaned forward with his arms and elbows pressed against the third-floor railing of the balcony. He stared down at the guests. Though it was well past midnight, he wore dark sunglasses to cover tired overworked eyes. And thanks to the dancing lights placed all over the property, he had a clear view of a strikingly beautiful woman up in the DJ booth. She laughed and sipped from a martini glass while talking to the guy who kept spinning up dance tunes to entertain the partiers.

"Who?" his cousin replied. When he didn't respond his cousin walked out to join him on the balcony.

"The one in the pink dress. See? Her. She's stepping down from the DJ booth," he said with a nod in her direction.

"Oh? Yeah, I remember her. She's that party-girl turntablist."

"Turn what?" he frowned.

"She performs with hip-hop bands, acts, mixing and remixing their songs during performances but using turntables not that electronic shit on a laptop. Think her name is Goodtime...or Goddess...don't remember what she called herself. Trust me. She's not your type."

"Goodtime. Interesting? I'd call her Kitten."

"Because you like young pussy?"

"Yea, wait, no, fuck? How young?"

Armand chuckled. "She's legal."

"How legal?" Jaxon asked now frowning.

"I don't know! I didn't check her I.D."

Jaxon returned his attention the party. She was gone. "I'm not opposed to some purring tonight," he mumbled as he searched the guests for a sight of her.

Armand Ali Jabar turned away from the scene and put his back to the balcony.

"Can we finish our talk inside?" Armand asked.

"She's leaving."

"Huh? Who?"

"Kitten," Jaxon said and sipped his whiskey.

"I told you she's not your type. She's too young, industry, risky," Armand said.

"I take risks," Jaxon said.

"You pay other people to take risks," Armand scoffed.

"She's my type tonight," he replied as he tracked Goodiva's movements across the lawn until she disappeared into the tent where many went to refresh their drinks.

"What about Leigh? She's out there purring for you."

"Boring," Jaxon groaned.

"I don't give a shit who sucks your dick tonight Jax. You know who I want to talk about," Armand said.

Jaxon sipped his drink.

"Jin," Jaxon said after swallow.

"Yes, *Jin*. You going to see him this time? He's only in the country for a few more days. He told me personally to invite you to meet with him at the polo lounge tomorrow. If you go, I go. If you don't, fuck him."

"*Jin. Jin. Jin. Jin.* Tell him you couldn't reach me."

"Not smart," his cousin replied.

"You just said fuck him," Jaxon chuckled.

"He was the one that called today about your father. He was there in Colorado in the end. In Mayfair when it happened."

"Don't give a fuck." Jaxon tossed back the last of his drink and swallowed a few cubes of ice. He walked off the balcony crunching them on his molars and thirsting for a new pour.

"I'm sick of this. You don't want to deal with the old man then just tell him. I'm tired of being your message boy," Armand yelled after him. "Pay somebody else to take your risks!"

"Why should I? You were born to do it," Jaxon chuckled.

IT WAS A LITTLE LATER that night. He was in charge. From the very beginning she was enchanted by his height, masculinity, and forwardness. All of it rolled up together in deep olive—swag packaging. Aggressive men often turned her stomach, thanks to years of Twixt pretending to be tough. She found them shallow and insecure underneath the bravado. But confidence, the genuine kind that was accompanied by unchecked power, could be an aphrodisiac. And he had confidence in abundance. Seasoned by his reputation, he moved through the partiers on cruise control.

The music's beat thumped steadily. The vibrations moving through her grew stronger the closer they got to the outdoor speakers. The best part of being a DJ were the vibrations. Sure she wanted to be an actress, an Oscar winning movie star, but she'd never give up her love for music to pursue it full time. In fact, if he wanted to stay at the party and dance with her until the heels on her shoes broke off, that would be the ultimate dream. He had a different plan. He walked her away from the loud laughter and conversation that mixed in over the melody. "Hotline Bling" by Drake serenaded the night and the bodies of at least four hundred people gyrated.

Goodiva giggled. She glanced back behind her once more for Jena. She saw her friend twerking against a rapper's groin, and shook her head, smiling. Those dancing around the eternity pool with blue, red and purple lights beneath the calm clear waters didn't notice her either. The DJ, an ex-lover and colleague, was the center of the attention. Raised on a platform with twirling lights, she envied his prominence most of all. She'd asked him for a battle last summer. She knew a promoter who could arrange it and her studio loved the idea of them doing it before the release of her first film.

"Wait, wait," she tried to stop him. Again, he paid her no mind. He walked too determined to notice. Her heeled shoes were at least six inches high, and she'd had plenty to drink before she ever laid eyes on him.

"Hey! Slow down," she said.

Mr. Romeo paused, and she crashed into his tall frame when he did. Embarrassed, she quickly recovered with his help. He looked back at her from over his shoulder with a furrowed brow and she flashed him the sexiest smile she could summon. The smile worked. His gaze lowered to her feet.

"Are you okay walking in those?" he asked.

"What? Oh, yea, I'm okay. Do it all the time. Kind of an expert, really," she said. "And it's better than the alternative, walking barefoot in grass. You know?"

After a few seconds he seemed reassured of her state of mind. His gaze switched to the gardens, in search of something, or perhaps some place. She stepped to his side, to be his partner rather than his captive. For a brief uninterrupted moment she could see his face and his handsomeness. His lashes were long for a man. He had thick, dark, silky brows with a flat squared forehead and chiseled jawline. His skin looked golden in the moonlight. A rich tawny brown. He kept glancing back at her. Did he know how excited she was? She felt her stomach muscles flutter over the question. He was more than a foot taller than her, and handsome in every way. She did her best to walk like a seductress at his side but stumbled more than once in the grass.

"Are you drunk?" he asked as they left the lawn and started down a sidewalk that headed south, off the property.

"Are you?" she asked.

"You sure? I can take you back to the party?" he said with staid calmness.

"That's weird," she replied.

"What's weird?"

"You didn't seem to care what I wanted before, when you pulled me out of the party?"

"True," he mumbled. "Maybe I'm the one that's drunk."

"I'm interested in walking around the mansion with you in circles, because I'm interested. Haven't you noticed?" she asked in a final attempt to lighten the mood.

"I've noticed," he said. "We've met before."

"No we haven't," she laughed.

"You deejayed a party for me last year."

"Uhm, no I didn't," she said.

"It was for my production company. Crown Entertainment. After the Golden Globes wins my production company won the Oscar for *A Man of Distinction*. Remember now?"

"I do. I don't remember meeting you though," she said.

"Guess I didn't leave an impression," he chuckled.

He knew she remembered. Most women in Hollywood would when they encountered a man of his influence. The moment she looked up from the DJ booth where her friend DJ Damage jammed and saw him staring down at her from the third-story balcony of the mansion she remembered him.

"Don't take it personal. I meet a lot of people," she said.

"Right," he said. She glanced back to where the party raged. She could hear the fun, but saw little of it. They were alone.

"Either you come with me, or you can take that path right there," he pointed left. "It'll take you back."

"And where will you go?"

"Some place quiet," he replied.

She'd only drunk two martinis. She'd never cheated on Twixt. Not once in the two years they'd been together. She had plenty of chances. Even his bandmates had tried to seduce her behind his back by giving her inside information on how much he screwed around on her.

"I'm looking for some place quiet too," she smiled.

"It's over there," he said with a nod of his head to the left.

She could see the shingled roof of another house. It was smaller than any house on the grounds, a guest cottage surrounded by tall hedges. In his free hand was the bottle of vodka he had swiped from the bar. He wore a dark silk shirt, possibly black or blue. It was unbuttoned at the top to reveal wisps of chest hair and a platinum Cuban-link neck chain that glistened like stars against his collarbone.

Don't do it Goodiva. Two wrongs don't make it right. This could blow up in your face. Who in the party saw you leave with him? A blogger? Another actor, maybe a person in the industry that can name you? Who? Nothing you do in this town goes unseen. Twixt will find out. And no matter what he's done to you in the past, you'll be labeled the slut. Screwing this stranger after drinking could make that title stick.

The door was opened for her. She froze within her indecision. Go inside or run away? Turn and leave, or stay and do the deed? Go in and get revenge, or go back and be the better person? What should a girl like her do?

He was behind her now. His face went into her hair, causing his nose to brush her scalp. Her breathing slowed and steadied to match the subdued rate of her heart. She relaxed, and the world around her began to swirl into colors dissolving all solids. Her head dropped back to rest upon his chest and she let his touch—a flattened palm with spread fingers pressed firm to her lower abdomen—relax her. His lips traced a faint touch from her earlobe to her jugular. Everything he did felt faint, just enough to be felt but not enough to convince her of his intentions. So she gave her answer and leaned her head to the left to find a position that accommodated the sweet glide of his lips now pressed to her skin. She only hesitated for a second more before the imprint of his stiff erection pressed hard against her backside and temptation won her over.

"I'll go inside."

"You sure?" he whispered.

She smiled. She entered the cottage. Inside they were locked in darkness. However, her eyes soon adjusted to discern shapes from shadows. And when he was close to her again, she knew it. She turned to face him. The bottle was gone. There was no barrier between them. His hands, large enough to palm a basketball, were slow to move down the curve of her frequently celebrated ass.

Men loved to see her leave a room because of her womanly figure. And Mr. Price was no different. Her lips parted in an attempt to say something clever. He didn't allow it. Instead his tongue slipped into her mouth. The ease of it across her own softened any resistance she may have carried. It was hard to think of breathing after the first taste, touch and feel of the man. But she did her best.

He released her first, or had she let go? She wasn't sure. The loss of intimacy was so profound she laughed a little instead of a protest. She knew her expression and eyes reflected the disappointment. He walked away. Dejected, she could do nothing but remain still and silent.

At first, he inspected the place he'd selected for them. Had he been there before? It appeared he had. Goodiva's self-imposed trance burst. She too began to walk around a bit to look things over. When he secured the locks to both doors, she knew he had. It was her turn to be decisive. When his eyes landed on her again, she lowered the side zipper to her sparkling pink mini-dress. It held so snug to her breasts, waist, and hips that she had to push it down and off her curves. All she wore underneath was a thin gossamer thong that disappeared between her butt cheeks.

"Beautiful," he commented.

"I'm far from perfect," she replied. Immediately she regretted the slip of tongue. Why did she do that? Every time she received a compliment, she pushed it away with an excuse.

"No one is looking for perfection. But if I were, I'd say you were the model I'd choose."

"That's nice of you to say," she said.

"Nice?" he frowned.

"Yes," she smiled. "The way you speak. Kind of poetic like a songwriter. If you start talking metaphors I'm going to give you a microphone and put your words to music."

"That's right you like music, eh?" he asked.

"All I had growing up was two best friends and a record player."

"Record player?"

"I know right. It's all vintage and hip now. But it wasn't the most popular thing for a kid. My father loved his blues and funk classics, and they were all on vinyl. We literally travelled with crates of them. When he left, I cried so hard he left them behind. For me. I played them as much as I could to keep him with me. My mother started feed my little obsession. She felt guilty too. My issues were the end of their marriage. So, she ordered albums of all kinds of music."

"That's understandable. A young girl needs her father and blames herself because her parents split." he mumbled.

"It's not the blame game that kids play. I was the reason they split. But that's another story," she sighed.

It was the right thing to say, but she detected a hint of disinterest. After all he wasn't with her to know her—he wanted what she came to offer. And if this would be her one night of rebellion, she needed to commit. He reached to the left and adjusted the dial on the wall. The ceiling lights dimmed. She looked up at them and then back to him with questioning eyes.

"Over there is music. Why don't you select a vibe for us?" he asked.

She laughed. "Vibe," she mumbled. "Yea, okay. If you want my skills to set the mood, it comes at a price."

"How much?" he asked.

She realized how what she had said might be interpreted, and frowned. "Uh, never mind, bad joke." She waved off the comment.

"I always leave music to the professionals," he winked.

She winked back. Goodiva walked over to the panel he had nodded to. She glanced back and could see he was again staring at her ass. It was a boost her confidence and take longer in her selection.

"How old are you?" he asked, recognizing the first song she had put on to play.

"Older than legal," she said. "You should listen to my playlist some time, you'd see I have all kinds of classical tastes."

"That doesn't sound like the classics to me," he frowned.

"'70s and '80s rhythm and blues is as classical as Mozart," she replied.

"How old?" he asked again, this time in a stern manner.

"Twenty-four. How old are you?"

"Thirty-two," he replied.

"Really? I thought you were closer to forty," she teased.

"I look that much older?"

"Uh yea, definitely," she smiled. "Kind of stiff."

His smile faded. Did he not find her funny, or did the lie mixed with a dash of truth hurt?

"I feel older. This town ages you," he admitted.

"Town?" she shook her head. "You definitely speak like a 32-year-old. But yeah, it ages you," she agreed.

"Who is this? Singing?" she quizzed him.

"I don't know," he shrugged.

"I have a lot to teach you," she said. "Isley Brothers? How could you not know the Isley Brothers. 'Don't Say Goodnight.' A real panty dropper in the early '80s. Part of what my dad called the 'Quiet Storm.'"

"I've heard of them," he said, but she wasn't sure if he had. "Quiet Storm? Yea. I know all about it. Maybe you can share your playlist with me sometime?"

"No," she replied.

"No?"

"Private. I can give lessons, and now that I've met you I'd suggest you take some. It'll help with your swagger; help you keep up with what ladies like. Ladies like me."

"Ladies like you, huh?"

She dropped her hand to her hips. "Am I your type?"

His gaze dipped to her feet and slowly swept up to her face. "Yes. You're my type. What else are you offering besides music lessons?" he asked.

She crossed her arms over her bare breasts. "You really are going to drag this out, aren't you? All this back and forth."

"I enjoy talking to you," he reasoned. "Are you in a hurry?"

"No. We're wasting a really good song by talking." She rubbed her arms. "Cold?"

"No," she said. "I do this sometimes. Rub my arms when standing in front of a man I don't know in just my panties waiting for him to come closer. Don't know why. Guess it's just the girl in me."

He laughed.

She watched as he began to unbutton his shirt. He revealed a broad chest with dark hairs smoothed like silk over his pecs. She didn't notice any tattoos. That was uncommon in LA. It was the first difference she noticed between him and Twixt. Before the night was over, she'd notice more.

Chapter Three

His cousin had tried guessing her name earlier. Later he learned her name was actually something even sweeter: Goodiva. It was fitting: out of all the beautiful women that had tempted him that night, she was easily in a category of her own. There was an authenticity to her sensuality. He liked the way her breasts bounced gently behind the bodice of her strapless dress when she danced with her friends. Her long dark silky extensions to her hair parted at the center and cascaded down to her waist like a Goddess', and swayed with the timing of her hips. Standing before her now, he tucked the strands behind her ears so he could see her clearly.

Her beauty was a unique contrast of a full nose, walnut-shaped, long-lashed eyes, lips slicked in a bronze gloss, and high cheekbones to sculpt the regal beauty of her oval face. The deep-dark rich unmarred beauty of her skin with her enchanting eyes softened her features. It was as if she belonged to another time. Her legs were slender, her body untouched by plastic surgery, unlike that of eighty percent of the women in LA. She possessed a rare authenticity to her that made knowing her all the more pleasing. He considered himself a connoisseur of finer things—sexy women, pleasure, pain. He'd passed on plenty of pussy in search of the best. The night was destined to be hell or heaven, depending on the first move he made and her acceptance.

There was just one problem. Nothing so sweet ever came to him without a price. He wouldn't put it past his *jin* to send him a goddess to lure him back into the den. His *jin* had tried before with women, business associates, and money. Tonight, however, he didn't care. He was less careful, greedy. If he hadn't been drinking he might have summoned will-power not to choose any woman at all. Out of respect for the dead. Out of respect for his mother. Out of respect for his girlfriend who was somewhere close looking for him in the party. He could not deny the basic instinct in him to bury his trauma and hide away from his pain between another woman's thighs. He wanted her. He needed a 'her'. He felt almost desperate about it.

Another song began to play.

He extended his hand to her. She approached him. He'd never know if it was his seduction of her that reeled her in. With her arms lowered he couldn't look away from her nipples. She stopped before him. His hand went to her hip to draw her closer. He'd never heard the song before. But the lyrics began to harmonize in a way that he could follow.

"You inspire me," he whispered, almost in timing with the lyrics. She lifted her arms to his neck and together they moved slow and in harmony. Their bodies, hers naked, his clothed, pressed to each other. In her stilettos, she was almost as tall as him. He liked that. He kissed her nose without having to fold himself to reach her. He kissed her slender brow and then kissed her closed eyelids.

"Who is this singing now?" he asked in her ear.

"A prize if you can guess," she answered.

He closed his eyes and tried. He really tried. The best guess he had was based off his limited knowledge of the music.

"I'll take Jeffery Osborne for $200?"

She giggled. "No! You're not even close. Teddy Pendergrass, silly."

"Oh?"

"You never heard of him, have you?"

He smiled and shook his head slowly. He found himself comfortable with confessing his ignorance, something men like him never did.

"It's called, 'You're My Greatest Inspiration,'" she said.

"Hmm, like a painter? I get it. You do inspire me," he said in time with Teddy's lyrics.

"Not a painter. Boring," she yawned. "Come up with something sexier. You're not that old. This kind of R&B is timeless."

"I get it. Timeless. Why are you so beautiful?" he asked, loving the smell of her breath as his face remained close to hers.

"I was born this way," she teased.

"And you will have beautiful kids," he said, studying her.

"Eww?" she frowned.

"I say something wrong?" he asked.

"Ah yea, before sex with a stranger it's impolite to mention making babies," she said.

"Is it?"

"How old are you again?" she frowned.

"Old enough to know better," he admitted. "But everyone wants kids. It's an honest mistake."

"Not everyone. Not twenty-four-year-olds. I don't want kids, I don't like kids, I don't need kids," she answered. It wasn't a response foreign to him. Most women he'd been involved with had the same temperament. Tonight of all nights he thought more on the subject than he had any other time. His father's obsession with a male heir. And his father's disappointment in the son he did get.

"Someday you'll change your mind," he said. "Every woman wants to be a mother."

"Not true. Not every woman. And I won't," she said. "Can we change the subject?"

"I should shut up and just dance?" he asked.

"Yes," she said, and rested her arms on his shoulders. He swayed with her and the lyrics. When the singer hit a very high-pitched note, she kissed him first. This time he returned her passion with restraint. If he moved to fast or said something wrong, he could ruin the moment. Her tongue swept inside of his mouth and he welcomed her. Their connection was forged. Her kiss made him fall apart and feel stronger in the same instance. He lifted her by the hips and pressed her up against him as he bit her bottom lip playfully. She giggled. *Where? Where should he take her?* For a brief moment he couldn't discern if he was laying or standing. No kiss had ever left him, so mind fucked. He sighed against her mouth. She tasted like sweet, fruity, forbidden desire.

Jaxon breathed harder and faster. He put her down on the sofa with unintentional force. Their eyes met. Her pupils were large under her long lashes. Her mouth quivered on the edge of a smile that she tried to stifle. He'd like to slip his dick between her pearly white teeth and down her slender throat until those lovely eyes of hers rolled back in her head. He smirked but didn't dare. The muscles beneath his pelvis and above his knees strained and tensed with pressure to fuck hard and savage. He did not. Those eyes tamed him, just enough for him to behave—barely enough.

"Goodiva," he said, letting her name roll off his tongue, as he took the time to gaze upon her physical beauty.

"Tell me you want this," he said and stoked his fingers over the lips of her sex. She was so wet he carried the drip of her arousal in the bed of his fingertips when he withdrew.

"I don't know what I want," she confessed.

Oh, yes, she inspired him. He slid his middle finger into her tightness once more. Her torso arched and her nipples peaked. He noticed everything, from the tiny pearls of sweat on her brow to the drops that peppered to the tip of her nose, to her tongue between her perfect white teeth. He withdrew his middle finger and then let it slip into her tightness once again. Then he repeated his finger-fuck twice more before he pulled the digit out and let it rest at the opening of her sex to give it a single pat. He watched how she fought against her wicked desires to beg for more. It amused and frustrated him. Typically, he did his research on the women he took to bed. Those women often could be bought to remain silent. Those women would never fold at the pressure of the press and fleeting celebrity that came with confessing an affair with him. Those knew how to keep a secret. Did she? It was the unknown about her that had his loins aching. His head lowered and he teased her right nipple with the tip of his tongue before sucking it into his mouth. All the while he pushed his erection trapped behind his zipper hard against soft lips of her pussy. She was beneath him. Nowhere to go. And he could feel all of her. In particular curves that were a twisting writhing example of any grown man's fantasy. He'd break her back and fuck her to hard if she didn't stop fucking his mind, and lust for her with the sweet way she purred and moved beneath her. He had to get himself under control.

To tame his inner lion, he released her nipple and traced her tongue south. Down her stomach it went bringing his face between her thighs. She inhaled sharply the moment he slipped his tongue inside of her. She stammered incoherent protests, so he pleasured her with a darting tongue to soothe any sexual ache he may have caused by nipping her love button too hard. The flicker of his tongue had her panting from desperation to a terminal state. Wait until he fucked her. He intended to make her scream.

"Stop, please," she shot upright with an alarmed cry.

He paused. The lower part of his face and mouth remained pressed against her pussy. He peered up at her with a deep scowl beneath his thick brows that connected.

"Sorry, excuse me," she said and tried to scoot back from his reaching tongue.

The way she pleaded sounded familiar. He supposed it was her attempt to reach the inner hero in him. A damsel in distress is what came to mind. Her beautiful large brown eyes reflected a deep concern. He was no fucking hero. But he'd play them game if it needed.

"We have to use protection," she said. "I never have sex without protection. You know? It's the golden rule."

He pulled back. He stared at her curiously before he spoke. "I was only kissing you."

"Yeah, uh, yes, but you know how that turns. It turns into, you know," she shut her thighs.

He nodded, and kissed her a final time before he completely abandoned the pleasure he enjoyed so much. He wiped her essence from his mouth with the back of his hand and sat back on the sofa with his arm stretched over the top of it. The liquor had turned his common senses to mush.

"I...I...I think—" she stammered and looked around embarrassed. She scooted away from him. "There might be some in my purse."

That was a surprise. Here he thought she was there because of his selection of her. Turns out she came prepared. His body remained feverish and his dick pained him so bad his mood began to sour over the delay. If she didn't find a condom in her purse, he was certain he'd cross the line. For her sake and his, he prayed that there was one in her purse. Two-seconds into the search of her bag, she came up empty.

"I thought I brought one," she mumbled in disbelief. "I know I did—oh shoot. Jena. Damnit. She must have taken them. Damn her!" She was up and walking around checking the drawers for them, and her distress had his dick growing harder instead of deflating.

"There's nothing," she finally said.

He dropped his head back and let go a deep groan of defeat.

"Want to get in the jacuzzi?" she half-joked. "It'll ease the pain."

He looked down at his upturned cock and then at her. There was only one cure for the torment he suffered. But he kept that truth to himself.

"No. Party has to end sometime. Might as well be now," he sighed in defeat and put his dick back into his pants. She stood before him in nothing but those sexy pink pumps of hers, with her arms crossed over her breasts.

"What's your name again?" he asked.

"Goodiva," she said. "I told you twice."

"Really?" he frowned. "Stage name?"

"Birth name asshole!" she shot back.

"Sorry," he shrugged. "That's right, you DJs are actors too."

Music continued to play. Classic R&B tunes he didn't know, but were as seductive as her body and the taste of her. He would definitely have to listen to more of this music.

"And you're Jaxon Price," she said. "King Asshole."

"So you heard of me?" he chuckled.

"We call you 'Romeo the Asshole,'" she said.

"We?" he asked.

"A few of my friends. You have a reputation."

"Really? Let me guess, my reputation is that I'm an asshole?" he asked, mocking her tone. He swiped his zipper up. She picked up her thong and slipped it back on, then put on her dress. She sat on the wicker chair across from him, while he sat on the sofa.

"What's my reputation?"

"That you love 'em and leave 'em."

"That's Casanova, not Romeo," he said.

She smiled. "I know. But from what I hear you're a nice guy at first. Charming. Attentive. At first. Only an asshole when it's time for it to end. On second thought it does sound like Casanova. Nope. Not you. You're no Casanova."

"Casanova is a better man?"

"Casanova was a scam artist, and a spy, and...hmmm...a church cleric. He wrote satires, fought duels, and he also escaped from prison more than once. Maybe you're somewhere in between. On second thought 'Romeo the Asshole' is the direct definition of Casanova," she laughed.

He shook his head, but smiled in agreement. "This conversation is weird."

Jaxon expected some damn good sex, and a warm body for the night. He didn't expect a disc jockey in a tight pink dress who loved music that was in style before she was born and read the classics. The woman had a brain to match her beauty. "How do you know so much about a lothario like Casanova?"

"I read. I read his biography *Histoire de ma vie*, the story of his life. It's kind of my thing."

"What else is your thing?" he asked.

"Why?"

"Curious," he said and closed his eyes. He liked to listen to the music and hear her talk. It was a soothing combination.

"Well. I'm an actress now. Got my first role in a good film. I play myself, a DJ, but I got a lot of acting parts. I want to be a full-time movie star."

His eyes opened. The mystery was solved. There was nothing special about this one. She wanted to ride his dick to get some kind of hookup from his studio. He was about to say something to that effect, but she stopped him cold.

"I think after tonight I plan to quit acting altogether. Stick to what I'm good at."

"You said you wanted it."

"I want chocolate ice-cream, but that's not good for me either," she smiled.

"What's the movie?"

She shrugged.

"You'll have to wait until it's on the big screen. Uhm, television screen. It's for Netflix."

He chuckled.

"Any more of that?" she asked.

He lifted the bottle he had brought in with them from the party. There was only enough for a swallow. He handed it to her and she came over and sat on the sofa next to him. She took the bottle and drank down the last of it. She gagged on the kick back, but took it down like a professional. She wiped her mouth with the back of her hand.

"If you have a boyfriend, why are you with me?" he asked.

"What makes you think I have a boyfriend?"

"All beautiful girls do," he said.

"And that doesn't bother you?" she asked.

"Nope, I'm 'Romeo the Asshole'," he replied.

"Well, to answer your question I don't really have a boyfriend anymore—technically. I'm no cheater. But he is. A very good one too."

"Sounds fresh, this revelation of yours," he said.

"It is. That's why I'm here with you. And because you're Jaxon Price, and I'm shallow, I decided to treat you to a taste of my newfound freedom. Before it expires."

"Now I'm confused," he said.

"Life's complicated. We have a business arrangement. I'm sure pretty soon I'll be back with him, at least publicly. It's pathetic," she sighed. "It's a business thing more than a love thing. I see that now."

"You're not shallow," he said and took the empty bottle. "Shallow people aren't so introspective."

"That's nice of you to say."

"It's just a compliment. Don't read too much into it."

She nodded that she wouldn't. He sighed as if bored. He looked over to her, ready to call it a night, but something stilled him in the way she waited for him to give her his attention.

"I'm sorry Romeo. I'm not going to sleep with you. Guess I should go now," she said and tried to move away. He grabbed her arm.

"Stay. No sex. Romeo the Asshole needs the company tonight."

"What about stranger danger?" she kidded.

"How are you dangerous?" he asked.

"All vulnerable rich men in this town who have been drinking with a strange woman is in danger."

"True," he agreed.

"What's wrong?" she asked.

"Can't explain."

"You're the strange one. Maybe the dangerous one," she said and then her hand went to his thigh. She rested it there.

"You can tell me. I know how to keep a secret," Goodiva said.

"That's what everyone says, until someone offers them enough money to buy the secret," he mumbled.

"Then I'll tell you a secret."

"Non-fiction I hope," he replied.

"Very funny. True story."

"Tell me a secret," he said.

"I saw a man die once. I was ten. And I never told an adult."

"You saw a man die?" he repeated.

She nodded.

"That's pretty young to see something like that."

"I know. That's why it's a secret," she said. "What's yours?"

"My father died today," he confessed.

"You have a father?" she frowned.

"It's typically how it's done. You know, man and woman make baby?"

She put her hand to her mouth. "I'm sorry. I didn't mean it that way." Everyone knew Jaxon Price and the infamous story of his being orphaned and self-made until adopted into a family as a teenager. She shouldn't be surprised that his infamous reputation was built on a lie. "Your history. It's like part of your legend. You've done interviews about never knowing who your real parents were."

"He died today," Jaxon repeated.

"That's terrible. Why is your father a secret?"

"That's another secret."

Jaxon hadn't said the truth aloud since he heard the news. Fikrit was dead. He lowered his head to her lap. He buried his face into the crease between her soft thighs. He held her waist and released the small amount of emotion he had left in him.

"I'm sorry for your loss."

"It's not a loss," he said.

"What happened to him?"

"Death. Karma. Justice. Pick one," he said.

"Don't worry. I won't say anything about this. I'm pretty good at keeping secrets."

Jaxon let go of her waist and sat up again. He ran his hand back over his head and released another deep sigh. "Why do you keep the secret of that man's death you saw as a kid?" he asked.

"Secrets are better than the truth," she said.

He glanced over at her. The music played in the background, filling the silence between them. Toni Braxton's "Un-break My Heart" spun a different kind of web around them. A protective one.

"Want to know another secret?" she asked.

He smiled. Her voice was as sweet and sultry as Toni Braxton's in that moment.

"Sure. I'm listening."

"I have six toes," she whispered.

Jaxon let go a deep gust of laughter that hadn't escaped him in weeks. He opened one eye to peek at a smiling Goodiva. She nodded. "It's true. I have six toes on one foot and five on the other." She took off her shoe. Though it was barely lit in the guesthouse, he saw her pretty foot with the pink toe polish. And next to the pinky toe was an even smaller one pressed flat.

"I'll be damned," he said. "You have eleven toes."

"Yep," she laughed. "Most people think it's gross. But Delilah said it was my superpower when we were ten years old."

"Delilah?" he asked.

"My best friend. We've been friends since we were kids."

She wiggled her toes and all but the sixth one moved.

"Does it freak you out?" she asked. "It freaks Twixt out. He's made so many comments about it I wear socks around him."

"Twixt is the boyfriend we're cheating on tonight?" he asked.

"I'm not cheating. We're done, sort of. I mean he's not done with me, well, yep, he's the asshole."

"Wait, I'm Romeo the Asshole," Jaxon reminded her.

"Okay, he's the bitch."

Jaxon nodded in appreciation of the description.

"And my partner in crime," she added.

"Well sweetheart, I like your sixth toe. But if it embarrasses you, why don't you have it removed? I got a good plastic surgeon I give all my girls."

"First of all, I'm not one of your girls. And I told you. It's my little secret. It just gets on my nerves. I don't get to wear sandals or some of the shoes I want. That sucks."

He smiled until he couldn't. He thought about all the secrets he carried. And there were many. Telling her even one of them could put his entire identity in jeopardy. He'd spent a fortune covering up the past. And he still paid a few blackmailers from time to time.

"I have to pee. Too many martinis," she squirmed.

He pointed to the closed door. She went in that direction.

She was gone for no longer than a minute before he got up and followed. He heard the toilet flush. He heard her humming to the music playing, and washing her hands. The sound system had speakers throughout the guest house. The sultry songbird lyrics sounded much sweeter from her. He dropped his head on the door and listened to her sing. She wasn't bad, but she wasn't good either. She was just perfectly imperfect. Without thinking, he turned the knob and the door opened. The singing stopped. He walked in to find her at the sink. She stared at him in the mirror. It was an invasion of privacy, but she didn't object. He wondered if her tolerance would change when he touched her.

Jaxon stepped right behind Goodiva. She continued to stare at him in the mirror as his hands swept down her hips. He kissed her shoulder and drew the hem of her dress up to her waist. When his eyes lifted to the mirror to see her reflection, he found her eyes closed. Jaxon lowered his zipper with one hand as his other went around her waist, then up to squeeze her breast. She leaned into the sink with a gasp. Her hands went to the basin and her back dipped. He kicked her feet apart and used his cock to slam into pure tight sweetness.

He grunted.

She groaned and moved her hips, causing him to go deeper, and deeper. Jaxon's hand went to her pussy and he rubbed her clit while moving in and out of her. A repeated upward thrust and tease of her love button made her ass cheeks bounce in rhythm with his thrusts. His body folded over hers and he forgot her comfort as he lost control and continued to pump his hips until he suffered a cataclysmic release. It came and went but he kept moving, refusing to let go of her. When he was done he was sorry immediately. She didn't deserve the ambush. She was worthy of much more respect.

"There's a bed in the room," he wheezed. "Want to lay down? For a while. Talk?"

"Mmhmm," she said softly as he pulled out of her. His semen slipped down her thighs.

"Excuse me," she said and got tissue to wipe. Jaxon shook his head. He never went in bare. If she was pregnant it would be a bigger event in his life than she could ever understand.

"Don't worry. I have an IUD. I'm not going to get pregnant," she said, and flushed the tissues.

Jaxon stared at her. "I didn't mean...to come in here."

"Yes you did," she said. "Have you been tested? AIDs, herpes, anything I need to know? Herpes is everywhere in this town. I don't want it."

"No one wants it," he laughed.

"Answer the question please," she said.

"I'm clean."

"You said you needed the company tonight. So it's okay. It happened; I'm not upset." she said.

It was her turn to extend her hand to him. He accepted. She took his hand and led him to the bed. Before he knew it, they were both undressed and she was in his arms sleeping. Strange. But he fell asleep with her pressed to him and his foot rubbing against her sixth toe.

HE FELT MOVEMENT. HE knew it was her, but he pretended to sleep. They used protection—he found a condom in a drawer after sleeping next to her for only forty-five minutes. She gave him her body in the sweetest way. And he fucked her until he collapsed in exhaustion with tears guarded behind his closed eyes. Afterwards he truly slept. The best sleep he had in years.

He peeked at her backside as she tried to slip on her dress. She had an ass that wars were fought over. He thought to himself how nice it would to be fuck her in it. And then he pushed the lust down before an erection revealed his deceptive snoozing.

He was tired of one-night stands. Leigh Ann was his steady woman, but they both screwed around so much on each other it was a joke to consider any commitment they shared real. He was tired of fucking actresses who wanted compensation in the form of the celebrity he could give them. He wanted a woman like her, with six toes and a boyfriend she couldn't leave. He wanted the normalcy of her complicated life instead of the constant danger of his own. Young, fresh, different, with timeless beauty, she could be a woman he could take away from the world to give him what he needed the most. The heir his family demanded of him. There wasn't enough pussy in the world to satisfy his hunger for sex—an addiction he'd spent many years with a therapist trying to exorcise. But maybe, with a woman that belonged to him and only him, he'd find the cure.

Of course, she didn't stop to say goodbye. She tipped-toed away from the bed with her shame leaving him without a single word. At least she didn't ask him for payment, or for a part in his upcoming musical. At least she spared him the grief. He closed his eyes and inhaled the sweet perfume she left on the sheets. And then he tried to sleep without any memories except the one they shared.

JAXON LEFT THE GUESTHOUSE barefoot, with his shoes in his hands and his shirt open. Armand was up on his balcony in a Versace robe and sunglasses. His cousin surveyed his property as a troop of cleaners restored it to its original immaculate state. These parties were expected of Armand. Jaxon had grown tired of the scene.

"There you are!" his cousin said.

Jaxon squinted when he looked up.

"Saw your little kitty-cat sneak away over an hour ago to a waiting Uber."

"Do you know how I can reach her?" he asked as he approached the house.

"Why ask me? You fucked her. Don't you know?" Armand asked.

"Funny. What's her name? Goodiva...what?" Jaxon asked.

"Don't know. I'll have Ahmed get the info on her. What did she do? Rob you?"

He glanced back at the guesthouse. She slipped away with his vulnerability. That could be considered a threat. "Something like that."

Chapter Four

"Goodie! Hey Goodie, wake up!"

Goodiva rolled over to her back. She put the pillow over her face. Two hours. She'd had just two measly hours of alone time to nap. She should have just gone back to her condo.

"Goooddiieeee!" yelled Jena.

"Yes!" she shouted back. She had been on an interview run for a straight twenty-four hours. This was the first nap she was allowed to indulge before she had to leave for the production studio. Jena opened the door and peeked inside. "Telephone."

"Huh? My phone didn't ring?" Goodiva sat up on her elbows.

"House phone. Twixt. He's found you and he's pissed. I suggest you take it," Jena said and slammed the door.

Goodiva sat up in confusion. She had blocked Twixt on her cellphone. And for the past two days she had managed to think about him even less.

"Hello?"

"When are you coming home?" Twixt asked. "You haven't been to your condo."

"You own the house, remember? And leave the key for my condo with management. You aren't welcome there either."

"Come home now. I'm not fucking kidding," Twixt said.

"No."

"I'm serious. We need to talk," Twixt insisted.

She sighed.

"I spoke to your manager. There's a way for us to end this that could work in both our favor. We'll meet with her next week."

"Goodiva..."

"We're over. I'm staying with Jena for a few days and then I leave to do the tour, so I'll be traveling—"

"Fuck your film. You disrespected me. Get your ass here now!"

"What did you just say?"

"Why the hell do you have men sending you flowers to my fucking house!" Twixt shouted. "Kumar said you fucked—."

"I didn't—"

"Jaxon Price?" Twixt asked. "Know him? Huh? You don't have an answer now, do you? Huh? Huh? Do you know him? Because Kumar said you do. Kumar said you were in Calabasas fucking him on the dance floor two nights ago."

"Kumar doesn't know anything about what I do. He's lying to you."

Behind every lie was a truth. Two days ago she met Jaxon Price. Since then she couldn't stop thinking of him. But she wasn't stupid enough to contact him. She didn't even tell him her last name. How did he track her down so fast?

"You're just going to deny it when I'm standing here looking at the fucking evidence?" Twixt said.

Goodiva frowned. Twixt wasn't prone to anger. His brother was always the instigator to get Twixt even the slightest bit riled. Goodiva could hear his brother shouting at him in the background and calling her names.

"Leave me alone. We aren't together. I can do whatever I want!" she said and hung up the phone. Goodiva scrambled out of the room to the top of the stairs. She saw Jena pick up her purse and head for the door.

"Jena! Did you tell anyone about the party? About what I told you? About Jaxon Price?"

Jena gave her a wink and then left. Goodiva sat on the top of the stairs in disbelief. The last thing she needed was this. What about her movie? It would be a nightmare if the scandal broke. It would be embarrassing for her co-stars, who would have to sit through the interrogating interviews. Even worse, she didn't know how to contact Jaxon Price to tell him about the storm brewing. What was she going to do?

Malibu, June 25, 2016

Goodiva tried her key, unsure of what to expect. The security system at the Malibu house was high-tech. The lights flashed the moment she arrived on the front step. Two cameras turned to focus on her. It had been over three days since she was last there, and she hated returning so soon. When the lock disengaged, she let go a sigh of relief. Twixt's car wasn't in the drive. And neither was his brother's. He was hosting a party at a club in San Jose. At least that's what his social media said. This was the perfect time to get in and out of the house and not have to deal with him or his accusations. However, she needed to remain cautious. There was no real guarantee that no one was home. He had a large enough entourage of bums to pose a risk. She pressed down on the doorknob handle and pushed it open slowly. The security alarm beeped. She went inside and hurried to turn it off.

Nothing human greeted her. The house, however, welcomed her. The temperature was adjusted to what she liked and three of her favorite rooms had the lights turned on. Twixt had made no changes.

All her fears were alleviated. Goodiva hurried. The automatic lights flipped on as she passed through one part of the beach house to the next. She didn't see much on Twixt's social media except for the promo for the party. He had to be gone. But even if he was at the party, he'd know from the security system that she'd returned. And he'd be home eventually. She'd been in a panicked state since she found out that Jena sold her secret affair with Jaxon Price to a gossip site. She expected it to be all over everywhere by now. The internet was savage over something scandalous. Yet, there was nothing. And that scared her even more. Her only hope was reaching Jaxon Price.

She went inside the kitchen first. She saw the smashed glass vase and the yellow roses in the sink. She stared at the evidence of their time together and felt nothing. Before her one-night stand, she was so hopelessly addicted to Twixt and his terrible treatment of her she'd grown used to settling for drama. The yellow flowers reminded her that she needed to be free. Goodiva searched the counters and everywhere for what she came for. It wasn't until she got to the trash can that she found the small white envelope, ripped in half. She picked up both pieces and pulled out the card that was inside. She put them side by side on the white marble countertop. And just as she had hoped, it had a single message on it.

Call Me.

Jax – 615-555-2392

Goodiva smiled. She used her cell phone to dial him and held her breath, hoping he answered and not some answering service.

"Hello."

Goodiva let go a sigh of relief.

"Who is this?" he asked.

"Goodiva. Ah, hi, it's me," she said. "Sorry to call so late."

"Hi, you," he replied. "Not late at all. I'm headed home."

"Oh, okay. You sent me flowers?"

"That was two days ago," he said.

"Why did you send me flowers?" she asked.

"Friendship," he replied.

"Roses aren't something you send to a friend."

"Yellow roses mean friendship. I need a friend," he answered. "You were a good friend to me the other night."

"Do they? The roses, I mean," she said, and glanced back to the wilting yellow rose petals.

"Google it. It's innocent. Totally," he said.

"Like the sex we had? That was platonic?" she asked.

"Well the sex definitely felt like more," he said. "I just wanted to finish our talk. Tell you my secrets. I never really got a chance."

"We did more than talk," she mumbled.

"Yes, I'd like to do that again too."

Goodiva put her hand to her head and paced. "Glad you liked it, because we have a problem. My boyfriend—uh, ex-boyfriend got the flowers. Not me."

"I'll send him pink roses," he said without a hint of remorse in his voice.

"What do pink roses mean?" she asked.

"Gratitude. I'm grateful he broke up with you permanently so I can have a new friend."

"It's serious. He said the blogs have found out about us, what happened at that party. They are going to run a story."

"They won't run it," Jaxon said.

"Are you insane? You're big in this city. And Twixt. He's getting a Grammy this year. It'll be on CNN after TMZ gets through trashing me. The internet will slaughter me."

"TMZ won't trash you because it never left the blogs. I've already handled it," he replied.

"Wait, you did?"

"I want to see you again. Where are you?"

"How did you handle it—"

"Tonight, now, can you meet me?"

"You handled it? Nothing can be handled on social media! Ever."

"I can come pick you up. I got a meeting at the studio that you can come to."

"This late?"

"Sure. I'll explain. Where are you calling from?"

"Stop!" she said. "How did you handle the blogs?"

"Information can be bought. Everyone has a price."

"Money can't buy everything," she scoffed.

"Sure it can. Your friends, the gossip sites, even your ex-boyfriend."

"What does that mean? How did you find me? And Twixt. Did you know who he was when we met? Who I was? Did you send these flowers to him on purpose?"

"If I can't come to you, then can you come to me?"

"I'm not meeting you anywhere. You blow up my life for what? You think this is a game?"

"Blow up your life?" he laughed. "How can I do that when you said you were no longer with him?"

"I mean...I told you it's complicated."

"Let me take you to a late dinner."

"No. Do you understand the word no? I'm not ready for that. Stop. Okay?"

"Then let me take you back to Armand's guesthouse and play with your pinky toe."

"Very funny," she sighed. "You do think this is a joke?"

"No more jokes. I'm sorry about sending the flowers there. It was out of line. Does that make it better?"

"Give me a minute to think about it," she said. "Don't rush me into a friendship or anything. It's not cool."

"It's called courtship. Has a man ever bought you flowers before?"

Before she responded, she heard the door open and slam shut. She nearly jumped out of her skin in surprise.

Twixt was home.

"Goodiva?"

"I have to call you back!"

"Wait—"

She hung up.

"I know you're here," yelled Twixt.

Goodiva shoved the ripped card pieces into the back pocket of her jeans and picked up her purse just as Twixt walked into the kitchen. To her dismay, his brother was with him.

"I just came to get some of my stuff and then I'm leaving," she said.

His bother Kumar walked past her and went straight to the trashcan. Goodiva walked out of the kitchen. Twixt tried to grab her arm but she side stepped his touch. "Where the fuck are you going? We have to talk!"

"The card is gone, bro. She must have taken it," Kumar said.

Goodiva looked back at Twixt to explain, but received a hard slap across the face. It knocked her to the ground. Twixt stood over her shouting, with both fists clenched. He'd never even raised his voice at her. Ever. In fact, she was the violent one. Throwing things at him when he cheated. Attacking him over text messages in his phone. Shoving him when his lies weren't enough. Never before had he shown any evidence he was capable of hurting her or any woman. His brother, however, was a different story. The shock of his violent outburst left her frozen on the floor and unable to comprehend the nasty accusations and insults he was shouting over her. He called her a whore. Yelled at her for having her fuck-buddy meddle in his life. She didn't anticipate any of his actions. But her best friends Delilah and Queen always told her that he was a punk, a fraud, a coward. And Queen taught her long ago how to defend herself.

"You bitch!" he seethed. She could see his brother pacing and egging him on with filthy compliments of Twixt's manhood for finally having the balls to put his fist to her. Was Twixt on something? The rage was all over his face, but extremely exaggerated, considering the hundreds of times he had done to her what she was now guilty of.

"Fucking cunt! Throw her out!" his brother said.

"I knew you'd sneak back in!" Twixt was going to attack her again. She fumbled for her purse and scooted back away from him across the floor. She found what she was looking for in seconds, just as he reached down to violently grab her by the throat. She flipped the switch on her weapon and caught him the face with a full blast of pepper spray. Twixt howled in pain. He fell back gagging and coughing. Goodiva got to her feet and stumped on his groin with the pointed heel of her shoe. Twixt folded. When he reached for her foot, she kicked him in the face. All of it happened in seconds. She looked up. His brother came charging after her. She hit him with another blast. But she didn't stop. The men were both on the ground writhing in pain as she ran for the door.

Adrenaline was all she had, and it proved to be all she needed. She hurried to her Range Rover and got behind the wheel. As she sped in reverse out of the driveway into the street, Twixt and his brother were staggering out of the house. In her rearview mirror, she saw them jumping in their car to chase her.

"Bastards!"

They'd catch her. She was certain of it. She gassed the Range Rover as best she could and put distance between them, with her needle pushing a speed limit of 90mph. Twixt was behind the wheel in his red Ferrari, swerving in and out of his lane and around traffic to get closer to her. She knew his vision had to be impaired, but still he chased her after, gaining on her within seconds. She fought to maintain speed and navigate around the oncoming traffic while she fumbled with her phone.

She wanted to dial 911. The best she could do was call back her last caller.

"Hi—" Jaxon Price answered.

"Jaxon? Jaxon I need your help," she sobbed, driving with one hand. She looked up to her rearview mirror. She didn't see Twixt yet, or maybe she did see him. She couldn't be sure. The headlights on her and the darkness covering the road made it very hard to decipher.

"What's wrong?"

"I'm in trouble," she sobbed. "Twixt is crazy. He's gone insane. He hit me!"

"He what?" Jaxon asked.

"Twixt, he attacked me. He's chasing me!"

"Chasing you how? Where are you?"

"I don't know. I don't. I'm uh, oh God! He's behind me!" she said. "It's him. I need to call the police! He hit me in the face! That bastard is going to jail. I don't care what his manager says! I'm pressing charges," she wept and swerved around a car going over 80 mph. The Ferrari didn't slip behind. In fact, it kept up speed, bumping her bumper.

"Where are you?" Jaxon shouted over her weeping rambles.

"Malibu. Uhm, PCH," she said. "Headed north."

"Can you get to Winding Way? I'm close. I'm on Portendale now."

"Yes, yes," she saw, the turn coming and up and made it fast. The Ferrari turned with her, causing two cars to spin out of control and crash into each other.

"Oh my God!" she screamed.

"Calm down," he said. "Stay calm. Bring them to me."

"I can't! He's acting crazy. He's going to run me off the road. He keeps hitting my car! I think he's on something. He took something. I'm sure of it."

"Is he following you now?"

"Yes, I'm on Winding Way and he is too!"

"Make the first left turn you see. It's a road that will take you to Murphy's Way. I'm cutting over to it. We can meet there."

"And then what?"

"I'll handle him."

"I need to call the police!"

"But you called me. Trust me. Did you make the turn?"

"Yes, but—oh God Jaxon, he's still coming. He won't stop!"

THEY WERE GOING TO kill him. She knew it. He'd come to her rescue and he'd die for it. What could she do? She'd seen someone die before. She'd seen the very worst happen to a person before. The only thing that awful act taught her was to run. Safety meant that she should run and keep running. So she did. She got back in the truck and she pulled out into the road and drove dangerously fast away. One glance to her rearview mirror and she saw Jaxon Price being beaten and stomped on next to his burning car. He was dead. She was sure of it. She drove for an hour. She drove for as long as she could while crying and cursing her cowardice. Not once did she think to call the police. Maybe she was in shock. Maybe it was the dying plea in his eyes when she watched Twixt and his brother attack him. The same look as Mr. Collins had when he knew he was going to die.

It wasn't until she was behind a locked door in a room at the Hyatt Regency that it all came crashing down on her. She'd done it again. She'd done the one thing she swore on her soul would never happen. She let someone die to save herself.

Goodiva dug out her cell phone and with a shaking hand called the only person in the world she trusted.

"Hello?" Delilah answered after a deep yawn.

"Dee? Dee? It happened. It happened again. He's dead."

"Shelly?" Delilah asked. "Is that you? Who's dead?! Shelly?"

"I killed a man," she said through her sobs. "I killed another man, Dee."

Chapter Five

Los Angeles, July 9, 2016

It hurt for Jaxon to swallow. The inside of his throat felt as if it were shredded with razorblades. He burned with inexplicable pain that radiated from every cell within. His eyes felt as if they were open, but there was nothing but darkness no matter how many times he tried to blink.

Am I dead?

His memory had been emptied. He didn't remember the past, or who he was in the present. He remembered nothing of the accident.

I am dead.

Jaxon Price had rarely experienced the vulnerability he suffered since he was a tot. This darkness felt different. It was complete, bottomless, a void for him and him alone. He inhaled a deep breath and his lungs expanded...this he knew, not felt. It was hard to explain, but he was aware of himself and lost in the shadows of his empty mind at the same time. Jaxon wasn't a man prone to fear, but this dark numbness that trapped him scared him to his core.

"I don't understand...it's been over two weeks. You're his doctor, and you haven't done anything to help besides stitch him up! When will he wake up and be my Jaxon again?"

"Would you just calm down? The doctor is doing the best he can."

"Don't tell me to calm down! My God! Look at him! Look at what's left of him!"

"I understand. All I can say is his recovery will be a long one. His hip is broken, his left leg was crushed, his chest and spine are all going to heal, eventually. But his blood work says something strange—"

"I don't care about broken bones! What about his face! I can't even see him? He's unrecognizable."

45

Jaxon heard her clearly. And through the sound of her voice his memory crystallized. Her name was Leigh Anne. She was an actress. She was...his wife? No...girlfriend? The word "girlfriend" didn't feel right. He couldn't remember much else about her. What he didn't need his memory to confirm was the distress he heard in her voice. Leigh Anne was distraught. There were two male voices. One was that of Armand Al Jabaar, and the other he assumed must be the doctor.

Wait! What did she mean about *his face*? What was wrong with his face?

"You will call every specialist, every doctor, everyone! You will fix him damn it! Fix him. Jaxon...oh Jaxon honey I'm here. I'm right here—"

And then the memory of her, the sound of her, the feel of her touch slipped away. His brain would only shift from one thought to another memory, and then back and forth. The numb emptiness that sat upon his chest felt heavier than a cinderblock. He was paralyzed under the weight. Breathing felt useless. The darkness lifted then descended. It was like being submerged in tar and then pulled only to the surface of it. The darkness spread over him until there was no him and his mind once again went blank.

A touch of old boyhood fear never promised to be good. Sleeping pills kept the devil away. But now he was trapped. He knew it the moment he couldn't find himself in the dark fog of what was left of his mind. Then he heard him, the devil. Jaxon panicked. He wanted to hide. Under the bed would be best. The steps, authoritative and concise, grew closer and closer. He had an urge to pee on himself, as he was prone to do when he was four or five and trapped as he was then. He felt another chill chase down his spine when the door opened. The premonition of disaster gripped his heart like a cold hand when his father spoke.

"Pathetic. Weak. Amcık." "Amcık" meant "little pussy" in Turkish. A name his father often called him.

Jaxon opened his eyes. He wasn't a man anymore. He was a boy of no more than four years old. Locked inside a room the size of a closet. The devil was with him. The Master of Mayfair stepped out of the shadows. The only light in the darkness was that on his face and his tall erect form. The devil leaned in from the shadows, swallowing all space around Jaxon.

"Come home boy. Where you belong."

The hideous cold element of the truth settled in. No matter how far he ran, no matter how much he achieved as Jaxon Price, he was still trapped in Mayfair.

"YOU HAVE TO EAT SOMETHING, Shelly?" Delilah said.

"Shelly" was the name her friends called her since grade school—short for her middle name Michelle. It was better than being teased by the name "Goodiva" that her mother gave her at birth. Goodiva's two best friends in the world had arrived to support her. She'd called them a week ago and confessed her crime. From that moment forward she hid from the world in a hotel room while watching the 24-hour news report on the accident that nearly killed Jaxon Price. Her best friend Delilah Montgomery had returned to the hotel with a bag of goodies from the vegan food truck in front of the hotel.

Delilah was married to Charles Montgomery. The Montgomery family were famously known as African American elite in Colorado. They were traditionalist and conservatives. They tended to marry people from their social circle only. Charles broke from tradition and married a very uncultured woman from the poorer side of the Cove—her best friend. It wasn't just her beauty that captured Charles' heart, it was her brilliance. Since they were kids everyone knew Delilah was destined to be someone great. She had a Mensa score of 160. She graduated from college at the age of seventeen and had a law degree two years later. She was everything Goodiva wasn't.

"I'm not hungry," Goodiva said.

The smell of the food did make her stomach muscles cinch into a tightening knot. However, nothing quelled her nervousness. And Goodiva noticed the sideways glances Delilah shot in the direction of Queen, her other best friend from home who stood near the window as if on guard. Queen could only look at her for a few minutes, then she would glance away. Queen was never good with emotion. Queen was a cop. She was a by the books all the way kind of cop. The Governor of Colorado awarded her with a medal of valor for her work in saving lives during a bank robbery. The FBI was actively recruiting her.

"Well, you don't want to eat sweetie, but you need to," Delilah kissed her brow.

"Queen, can you call your friend again? Please?" Goodiva asked.

"No Shelly," Queen said. "I've already told you. Jaxon Price is out of his coma, but there is no way I can get you into that hospital. I shouldn't even be involved."

"Queen, stop," Delilah said. "This isn't about your job. This is about Shelly. We made a pact and we've never broken it. She needs our help."

"She needs a good lawyer. You know better. You're encouraging her. You two covered up a crime then called me to fix it. By the law, I'm aiding and abetting for not reporting you."

"And you won't!" Delilah said. "LA isn't your jurisdiction. Jaxon Price is alive. He survived the crash. He's going to live. What crime did *she* commit? Those assholes would have killed her if she didn't run away."

"You mean the same assholes who are now taking credit for saving his life? The ones that are telling the press that he flipped his car and they pulled him out of it in the nick of time?" Queen asked.

"It's true. Jaxon did hit their car. It was an accident, at first," Goodiva protested weakly.

"No one has connected them with a crime. Only Goodiva and Jaxon Price know what really happened after that car flipped," Delilah said.

"And how long do you think he's going to lay in that bed before he spills the real tea on them both?" Queen countered.

"You told us yourself that they are covering up his medical file in this accident. They haven't mentioned anything else. Why should we destroy her life for a mistake?"

"A mistake? A hit and run is a mistake now? For the record, that's the press, not the facts. If Shelly had called the cops she could have intervened when Twixt and his brother attacked him."

"He's alive!" Delilah shouted.

"For now!" Queen yelled.

"Guys please stop!" Goodiva stood and put her hands up between her friends. "I know what I did was wrong. She's right, Delilah. I should turn myself in. Twixt's lie will be exposed."

"But where is the lie? Jaxon hit his car. You said it flipped after. They may have kicked his ass, but they didn't kill him. They got him help. Where is the lie!" Delilah said.

"I will be named. It's only a matter time before the world finds out about my role in all of this."

Queen sat down in defeat. "Listen to her Dee, she has to confess."

"There's something else you don't know Queen," Goodiva said.

"Don't do it Shelly!" Delilah warned.

"We don't keep secrets from each other. That was our pact. Queen deserves to know the entire story."

"The less I know the better," Queen shook her head and put her hands to ears. "Don't tell me anything."

"Please, Queen. Listen." Goodiva stooped before her. "I told you when you came to town it was road rage. That Twixt overreacted because Jaxon Price clipped his car. That was a lie. I was afraid to tell you the truth."

Queen lowered her hands and looked at Goodiva with grave concern. "What else happened?"

"I knew him. Jaxon Price. I broke up with Twixt and hooked up with Jaxon over three weeks ago. Jaxon was on his way to save me."

"Save you from what?" Queen frowned.

"Twixt hit me. He attacked me. It's the real reason I called Jaxon. Twixt and I weren't in the car together either. Twixt was chasing me with his car at first. Jaxon was on the same road to help me. Twixt and his brother tried to run me off the road. Jaxon risked his life to put his car in between us. And that's what caused the accident. He pulled himself out of that wreckage to put out the flames on his body, not us. None of us helped him. And when he was on the ground, Queen, they beat him. He looked at me for help. I couldn't. I just couldn't. I froze and then...then I left him. I left him to die. He knows it."

"She did what she had to do," Delilah added.

"Are you filling her head with this nonsense?" Queen asked Delilah.

"She is a victim of a violent crime. You and Jaxon Price are both victims. They can arrest Twixt and his brother. They should be in jail," Queen reasoned.

"Everyone needs to calm down. I'm the only lawyer in this room," Delilah said. "Things are complicated. They just are. Yes, Queen, you're right. Shelly should have turned herself in. And if you had called me right after the accident, Shelly, I would have told you to go to the police and report it. But you waited a week."

Goodiva frowned. She called Delilah right after the accident. Delilah was the one that told her to stay put until she and Queen got to her. Why was she lying now?

"Now we are another week into this lie and I'm telling you both, they have nothing. Queen has confirmed it. Jaxon Price is awake. He hasn't told them anything. He's a celebrity himself. A private man. He doesn't want the public intrusion in his life. He won't say anything."

"I know what you're doing," Queen said.

Delilah glared at her.

"This is fourth grade all over again," Queen sighed. "This is you convincing us that what I did to Mr. Collins was justified. Convincing us to bury another secret."

"We! We did it to Mr. Collins, not you alone. And this has nothing to do with that!" Delilah shuddered with rage. "How dare you throw Collins up in our face. I didn't want to come up with a lie for us at ten years old. I was as scared as the both of you."

"I'm a terrible person," Goodiva said, and put her hands to her ears to block out the shouting.

Queen rolled her eyes. "No honey, you're shallow, you're self-absorbed, you're spoiled and entitled. But you aren't a terrible person. You're like every other person on this planet nowadays."

Goodiva wept. "I saw him."

"Saw who?" Delilah huffed.

"Mr. Collins," she looked to her friends. "When Jaxon Price was on that ground bleeding I saw his eyes. They looked through me. The same way Mr. Collins did all those years ago before we did what we did. I saw him and I ran from him. That's the truth."

Delilah walked over to Goodiva and hugged her. She wept. "I need to confess. For all of it. For even Mr. Collins. I can't live with anymore secrets!"

"Confession is not good for your soul," Delilah cupped Goodiva's face to force her to look at her. "We learned that when we were ten. It may have been a terrible secret to keep, but we did what we had to do as kids. And right now, I'm doing what I have to do to protect us. I didn't make us evil or bad, I made us survivors." Delilah glanced back at Queen. "You're a decorated cop. I'm a soon to be mother, and you Shelly, you're the brightest start out of all of us. Mr. Collins almost destroyed what was left of your innocence. We fought back. Running that night from the accident saved your life. It did. Okay? Okay?"

Goodiva nodded in agreement.

"Whew!" Delilah said and clapped her hands. "Okay, now that's settled, we move forward with Plan B."

"Plan B?" Goodiva asked.

"Yes. Delilah has a plan. She always has a plan." Queen threw her hand up in the air. "If you want to survive this, then don't rent a room across from the hospital of the man you nearly got killed. We need to get you out of Los Angeles," Queen said.

"She can't leave. She has a life here? A movie? Hello?" Delilah said.

"I'm not leaving. I'm under contract with Twixt's management company. I can't walk away from it and keep my life."

"Contract? What kind of contract?" Delilah asked. "I manage you."

"It's an industry thing," she said.

"What did you do?" Delilah frowned.

"Never mind. Queen, please, make the call," Goodiva said.

"Not this again," Queen said.

"Maybe if she sees him it will help her. Let's try to get her inside the hospital," Delilah agreed.

"You're supposed to be some kind of genius Delilah! Where in your brain does it compute that sending her into a hospital to see this man makes any sense? Especially if he knows her. It's a terrible idea." Queen stood and removed her phone from the clip on her hip. She walked out of the hotel room into the hall.

"I shouldn't have dragged you two into this. I don't want you guys fighting because of me," Goodiva said. "What would Charles say if he knew you were mixed up in this? Queen could lose her badge. The scandal could destroy your marriage Delilah."

"We're sisters. We're in this together. No matter what."

"That was a pact we made in grade school, Dee. This isn't the same as what we did to Mr. Collins. We were children, we were frightened. I'm an adult now. I'm not going to hold you to this secret allegiance," Goodiva said.

"Mr. Collins was an evil pedophile freak. He got what he deserved," Delilah spat. "A monster."

"Maybe he is. But this? This feels wrong."

Delilah rolled her eyes.

"I have a question," Goodiva said.

"What?" Delilah asked.

"I want an honest answer."

"Fine. Say it. What is it?"

"Do you think I would have driven away and left Jaxon to die if we hadn't done what we did to Mr. Collins?"

"It's not that simple."

"Doing the right thing should be simple," Goodiva reasoned.

"Fine. Jaxon Price is a victim. I agree. But so are you. That's what you keep forgetting," Delilah reasoned.

"That's not an answer Dee," said Goodiva.

"Here's an answer," Delilah began. "We are what life makes us. And you are more than your mistakes. More than the past. Life made you a survivor, and that's what you did that night, you survived."

"I'm sick. Only a sick person would do what I did. Run from the scene of a crime? I'm sick," Goodiva said.

"The world is sick. Can we please focus on the present? I can't lose you. I love you," Delilah said and kissed her cheek. Goodiva smiled. She stared at her friend. Really looked at her.

"You're going to be a mom," Goodiva chuckled. "You'll have your own baby to mother, and not me."

"Very funny." Delilah stood upright from her kneeled position before Goodiva. She beamed with happiness. She and her husband Charles had been trying to have a baby for years. Now, through insemination, she was four months pregnant and growing.

"You're going to be a good mother Dee. I'm so happy for you."

"I told Charles you broke up with that stupid Twixt guy, and after you've promoted the film you were coming to stay with us to help me with the baby. He agrees. Said we need a DJ in the family."

"I can't do any more of this promotion tour. I can't go to these film festivals and stand in front of cameras smiling after what I've done. It'll make me a monster."

"You're legally bound to do it," Queen reminded her as she re-entered the room.

"But if I'm photographed and they find out the truth, no one will ever believe my story. They won't believe it was an accident. Think about it. How I first met Jaxon Price, the accident and everything after will work against me. Queen is right. We have one shot to fix this. Confession. It's the only way."

Delilah's eyes stretched. "I got it!"

"Got what?" the girls asked in unison.

"The perfect plan." Delilah grinned.

"You mean the perfect crime?" Queen groaned.

"Hear me out. You're right Shelly. Who you are to the world is everything. Give me your phone!"

"Huh?"

"Give it to me!" Delilah insisted. "You are going off all social media. Effective now."

"But why—?"

"And we are checking you into a mental health facility. I know a good one. I tried to get Charles's mom into one a year ago, so I know the perfect place."

"You did?" Goodiva asked.

"The witch deserved it. Of course, Charles didn't agree. But it's really a good place. I will call your agent and tell her about your breakdown."

"Wait Delilah—"

"You said it yourself. You need counseling. And after all of this I agree. I'll call that agent Cassidy whatever. Just to get the story out. Listen to this. We check you in and use my doctors back in Colorado to diagnose you. We say you had a mental breakdown. Hell, it's not too far off. Depression is real. The world will expect you to be missing. Plus, you can address this issue head on. Get yourself mentally well."

"There are business contracts that bind me."

"That can be changed. I'll represent you. Don't worry. This facility is where we send you."

"Have you forgotten my past. Yours?" she asked.

"You're strong. Like I said, I'll help. It's the perfect plan. We're going to fix this. Trust in me."

Queen shook her head. "And what about Jaxon Price?"

"She needs to see him. Talk to him. Explain. What did you learn?" Delilah asked.

In her usual dry tone, she shrugged as she shared the news. "He's awake. But they aren't sure of his medical state. I spoke to the detective on the case. They are still talking as if this was just a bad car accident. The investigation ruled that Jaxon Price was at fault, based on the impact marks on Twixt's car. So, it will take Jaxon Price to tell them the real truth."

"Why hasn't he?" Goodiva asked.

"I don't know. I can't make sense of it," Queen said.

"Help her Queen," Delilah insisted.

"Help how?" Queen frowned.

"You know how, damn it."

"Is that why you two called me into town? For this?!"

"Listen, you want her to confess, right? Take her to the hospital. Get her in to see Jaxon Price. If he demands that the entire truth comes out, then we do that. But if she can apologize and walk away, isn't that best? For everyone? Do you want them to make a public spectacle of her life? Dig into her past and ours? Pull out her juvenile file? Dig up Peter Collins from his grave?"

"Fine. Fine. We're going to meet my contact over at the hospital. I will get you on the floor where he is. Then after that, you got ten minutes before we're done. We're getting the hell out of this hotel and away from Jaxon Price."

Goodiva nodded to her friends that the plan would suffice. It was all she needed to be free of her guilt.

"The guilt trip is over." Queen pointed a finger at Goodiva, and then Delilah. "You two will stop holding what happened when we were ten over my head. You hear me?"

"Yes," Delilah said, and hugged Queen, who grimaced.

"Yes," Goodiva agreed.

Delilah cupped Goodiva's wet cheeks in her palms and looked her eye to eye. "It's a miracle that neither of you were killed. I saw the scene of that accident on the news. Shelly, this is a blessing. We have so much to be grateful for. You go with Queen and get your closure, and then we never mention Jaxon Price again. The past is behind us. All of it. After today, we're all free."

Goodiva understood. Deep inside she wished for gratitude, but she only found shame and guilt.

"C'mon," Queen said.

She was quick about changing clothes to look the part. She'd rented the hotel room and spent days with her friends trying to gain as much information as she could on Jaxon's suffering. It was safer than her condo. Even now she didn't trust Twixt to not come looking for her. Goodiva fixed her face and put on dark sunglasses to cover her eyes. She put on Queen's Colorado P.D. bomber jacket and a cap on her head. When she left the room and crossed the street to pass through the media camped out for news on Jaxon Price, she kept her head bowed. If she were caught on film, no one would get a clear shot of her. Queen flashed her badge. The officers let her through. Queen warned her to not speak. She wasn't even introduced. She kept her sunglasses on. If the officers thought that was weird, they didn't say so.

And Queen did what Queen always did. She was good at her job. She met with the contact who happened to be at the hospital waiting to interview Jaxon about the accident. The two detectives first met during a conference in Vegas a year ago. Queen contacted him regarding a case she had on Colorado before inquiring about Jaxon Price. Only as a courtesy did they share a few details. Then she shifted the conversation to the serial killer that was terrorizing Colorado by kidnapping and murdering young black girls no older than ten. Queen said she was having evidence tested in the labs for a victim in Santa Monica, which could mean the killer had crossed state lines more than once. It could turn into a federal case if proven.

Goodiva slipped away from the conversation with the mention of needing to use the bathroom. This was her chance. The other officers didn't seem to notice. Goodiva started down the hall and passed a few officers. With her police jacket on, she didn't look suspicious. She blended in with the cops. It didn't take her long to find his room. There were several officers outside of it. A woman in tears argued with a doctor. She recognized her as the actress in one of Jaxon Price's films. She couldn't remember her name, but she thought she'd been nominated for an Oscar.

One officer looked up at her approach and smiled. Goodiva broke the first rule Queen had insisted on and removed her sunglasses. She approached the second officer. "How is he? I hear he's awake and talking?"

"Don't know. I think he's the same. Excuse me," the officer said when his cell phone buzzed. He took the call and walked away.

Goodiva hesitated. Were she to be caught in this room, her life was over. No one stopped her. Jaxon Price's face was swollen beyond recognition. His scars and burns gave a scaly looking trauma to his face and his left eyelid was taped shut. She stared at him in disbelief. Surrounding this man were the signs of life beeping on the machines.

"I'm sorry, Jaxon. For everything."

Goodiva's hand moved over his. The touch of his scarred knuckles and limp fingers sent a cool wave of familiarity through her that she couldn't explain. It amazingly comforted her.

Her touch. Contact with another human being pulled on his memory from the dark torment where the devil controlled all of his misery. A voice so soft and gentle he was certain it was a whisper from an angel who had come to rescue him from hell.

Forgive me...

Forgive who?

Jaxon strained to hear the rest of the words, but could not. The dull pulsing heat of a headache throbbed in his skull and he struggled to remain conscious. He wanted to stay with the angel. The devil waited for him in the darkness. He tried hard to defeat the sedation dragging him back to hell. But once again he could not.

It was an accident, she said.

I was so afraid, she said.

I tried to help, but Twixt and his brother were crazy that night. I should have helped, she said.

It happened so fast, she said.

You switched lanes so fast, she said.

I should have called the police, she said.

I didn't mean to leave you like that, she said.

I'm so sorry. Can you hear me? It's Goodiva.

Did she say 'Goddess'?

"What the hell are you doing?"

Goodiva let go of Jaxon's hand and glanced behind her. One of Hollywood's most sought after actresses glared at her.

"I asked you a question bitch! What the hell are you doing in his room? Touching him!"

"I...I'm sorry, ma'am."

"Fucking cops. Now I have to protect him from you too!"

"What's the problem now?" another man asked as he walked in. He leveled his eyes on her and his brows shot up with surprise. She was caught. It was over. She knew him. It was Armand Al Jabar—the man who hosted the party where she and Jaxon first met. What if he recognized her?

"I'm sorry. I was just checking on him," she slipped on her sunglasses. "The machines were making noises."

"She was fucking touching him!" the actress said.

"Calm down. It's not a crime to touch Jax." The man extended his hand. "Hi. I'm Armand. And you are?"

"There you are!" Queen marched in. "What are you doing in here?"

Armand's questioning stare never left Goodiva.

"She's a rookie," Queen explained. "I hope she didn't disturb you too?"

Armand gaze swept over to Queen and then shifted to Goodiva, where it stayed. "And your name, officer?"

"Oh, I... ah... I'm Detective...Douglas. I'm not with CPD. We're...uhm... here visiting for a possible connection in the case," Queen answered for Goodiva and shoved her toward the door.

"Connection? You know the truth. That Jaxon wasn't at fault. A fake popstar nearly killed him and they are calling him a hero!" the actress shouted through her tears.

"We thought there were similarities to a case in Colorado. Too soon to tell."

"Colorado? What the hell? That makes no sense!" The actress huffed.

"Sorry, we shouldn't be on this floor. We won't disturb you any further," Queen said.

The actress wept and held Jaxon Price's hand. But Armand kept staring at them both. Queen grabbed Goodiva's arm and pulled her to the door before he could ask any other questions."

"I told you to be careful! Let's get out of here!"

"I'm sorry," Goodiva winced.

Goodiva glanced back. Armand stood in the hall staring after them. He caught her backward glance over the shoulder. She hurried to the elevator.

Chapter Six

Dubai, December 2017

"What time is the car coming?" Twixt asked.

Slumped over in an unbuttoned gold and black Versace designer shirt with diamonds around his neck and wrist, Twixt pulled the glass coffee table closer to him. He then ran a long line of the most primo cocaine he'd ever snorted up his nose. The first hit delivered a blast of crystalized sensations that exploded like fireworks in his skull. He stretched his eyes and rubbed his nose hard to calm the numbness that spread through every blood vessel in his face. Colors brightened for a moment, then his vision blurred, cleared and blurred again. All of it combined with the money and women thrown at him the past few days left him feeling like an emperor. Twixt dipped his finger in the powder and then rubbed the cocaine over his gums before taking a shot of tequila. He sagged back against the sofa cushion with a sagged smile. Through lowered lids his focus returned to his vision, and he noticed his brother remained on the phone with one leg thrown over a leather chair.

"I'm going to head downstairs, to find the driver. Give me a sec," Kumar said after ending his call.

"Hurry up," Twixt mumbled.

"Yea, I'll call you to come downstairs," Kumar tossed at him before walking out of the suite.

In the past four hours they'd found themselves trapped in their hotel room waiting on the driver to collect them. And he was bored. His band had performed the night before to a sold-out venue. A private chartered plane delivered him to the UK, and there he'd spent time with his mother.

"What time is the car coming!" he shouted over his own music that blared in the background. He was alone. The drugs made him act out his thoughts. He laughed at himself.

"Fuck, I'm ready to go," he continued.

The crown prince himself had requested they extended their stay an extra day. Kumar said the prince had the kind of money and power to make him an even bigger international star. He was ready.

Twixt laughed to himself as he thought of the Arabs. The way they danced around to his music drunk and celebrated with each other. They kept the women separate in the party. Except the ones they threw at his feet. He could really get used to it there. All the riches these men in this country had, and they didn't really know how to enjoy it. He'd show them a thing or two.

"I'd show ya! Yah!" he said and nodded his head. He spit a few rhymes and bobbed his head hearing a song form. "Yeah, yeah! Yah!"

His stream of thought was a gumbo mix of coked out delirium, over-boiled ego, and unsubstantiated bravado. He loved himself so much he could suck his own dick if his neck bent that far. He actually thought of trying it when the door to their hotel room was thrown open. He heard the noise. He didn't bother to open his eyes—not even when Kumar yelled for someone to release him. Instead Twixt thought of the next rhyme to follow the first rhyme as he created his beat by drumming his thumb against his thigh. Nothing could disturb the sweet euphoric delirium he drifted in. They were residents in one of the tall luxury buildings in Dubai with full butler service. He was certain his brother's quick return meant the driver had been summoned. That was his first thought, but then he heard shouting voices in Arabic.

Six mercenaries stormed the room. One dragged his brother inside. Two of the men were armed with large automatic rifles. All of the men wore long white traditional Muslim thobes. They had red and white checkered keffiyeh headdress secured by squared black bands on their heads. They looked no different to him than the sheikhs that welcomed them when they got off the plane. But he knew immediately they were indeed different.

Kumar shouted in Hindi for the man to explain themselves once freed from his captor. Twixt's brother Kumar was close to six feet tall, with a proud muscled build. He'd tried his hand at boxing one or twice. He feared no one. Kumar, paced. The men stared at him with no sign of retreat. Twixt tried to blink his way out of his drug state and couldn't. It was too late to warn his brother to stand down. Kumar charged the Arab with the gun but was caught mid swing with a swift karate chop to the back of his neck and dropped to his knees. Savagery was unleashed. The Arab yanked his hair back and another mercenary gave him hard punches to his face. Kumar's nose sprayed blood all over the Arab's thobe and two others started to stomp him nearly to death.

Twixt got to his feet. The effect of the beating of his brother sobered him with what felt like a bolt of lightning to his chest. He went after the Arabs in his hotel suite. The killer end of the gun aimed directly at his face stopped him cold. Slow and steady, he brought his hands up. His intoxicated state made focus hard, but Kumar's whimpers kept sobering him. The mercenary shouted in Arabic for Twixt to remain still and silent. Twixt nodded that he understood the threat. One of the Arabs went to the door of the hotel room. He opened it. Twixt's head did not turn, but his vision did. The first man to appear looked somewhat familiar. He too wore an all-white throbe, with an all-white keffiyeh. The fog shrouding Twixt's memory began to clear, and he soon recalled the name of visitor. It was Armand Al Jabar, the acclaimed American Muslim actor. *Was this a joke?*

Twixt opened his mouth to speak to him, but then he was stopped. The violent threat against Kumar was clear and present. His brother was placed into a headlock and forced to stand by the strong arm of the Arab. Kumar breathed blood bubbles through his nostrils. He was held so firmly he had no choice but to remain still. Another sheikh entered the hotel room. This one, taller than Armand, walked with the aid of a cane and wore a dark mask to cover only one side of his face. And this man was different. He was definitely the sheikh, the one in charge. Instead of wearing the all-white thobes the other men wore, his was black, including his keffiyeh. It took only seconds for Twixt to know who the man in black really was.

"Twixt? That is your name right?" the man in black asked as he balanced his weight on the cane before him with both hands.

Twixt couldn't speak. None one in the room spoke. The silence was only interrupted by the strangled gasps of his brother.

"Do you remember me Twixt?" the darkly dressed sheikh asked.

"I don't know you," Twixt said. "What is this about? We're guests of the crown prince. We're here by his request. Release him. Now!"

"You're not a guest of the House of Saud. You're here because of my request," the sheikh said. He took a step toward him. "Now. I'll ask again. Do you remember me Twixt?"

Twixt shook his head no for the answer. It was the safest response he could conjure.

"Has it been that long?" the man asked.

"I just want to leave. There's some misunderstanding here. We should just leave," Twixt said.

"Mmm," the man in black said. His gaze slipped to Kumar. He approached with the aid of his cane. "Is this your brother?" the sheikh asked.

Twixt nodded.

"Do you remember me, brother?"

Kumar's eyes stretched. He was either paralyzed by the chokehold to his neck or too terrified to try to respond. The sheikh's gaze lifted to the mercenary holding Kumar. The man squeezed Kumar's neck tighter and his brother gagged. A panic seized Twixt like he never felt before. What should he do? His mind overplayed escape scenarios and none of them ended with freedom. They were trapped.

The man in black pointed the cane at Twixt and then slowly he aimed the cane at the brother Kumar. He seemed to do a back and forth *eeny-mee-ny-miney-moe* between the two men before finally landing on Kumar.

"Make the brother remember," the darkly dressed sheikh said, and then stepped back.

The mercenary behind Twixt spoke and Twixt looked at him not sure what was said. The mercenary crossed his arms in a X formation before him then dropped them both in a downward swing that released long daggers from inside the sleeves of his thobe.

"Wait. Wait. Please. Wait!" Twixt said. Kumar looked to Twixt and then the sheikh with fear. He managed a weak and restrained nod to indicate that he did remember because he couldn't capture enough breath to breathe and speak.

"Good." The sheikh's gaze returned to Twixt. "Let's hear it?"

"Hear what?" Twixt asked.

"My name," The sheikh said.

"Jaxon. Jaxon Price."

The man in black gave a smile that was only seen on half of his face.

"Look brother, it was a long time ago. It was an accident man. You got in between me and my lady. It was all an accident."

"Brother? Am I in the family now?"

A few of the Arabs laughed.

"No. Fuck. You know what I mean. I don't know who you are now! I know who you were."

"He says it was all an accident, Armand." The sheikh said and began to walk away.

"I heard him," Armand replied. Twixt pleaded with Armand Al Jabar with his eyes. Afterall he was all Hollywood. *Not some assassin.* What was happening with these men? They were American.

"It's a shame. This all began with an accident." The sheikh stopped. He spoke with his back to Twixt. He was staring at Armand Al Jabar. They seem to have a silent wordless exchange. Then the sheikh gaze turned over his shoulder and what he could see in his eyes was a murderous threat. "It may have been an accident, this is intentional," the sheikh said. The mercenary shoved Twixt aside and rushed his brother. It all happened so fast. He attacked swifter than a ninja. From Twixt's limited view he saw the man stab, slash, cut, and disembowel his brother with the repeated swings of his knife wielding fists. He delivered hits harder than those of a prize fighting boxer.

"Stop!" Twixt yelled. Without thinking, he went after his brother's killer, and the assassin responded with unprecedented timing and in one deft move used the blades to slash a deep gash across Twixt chest. Twixt fell mid-counter strike to his side in more pain than he could ever imagine. He was alive, but blood poured like a river from his chest. His brother wasn't as lucky. Bloody all over, Kumar was tossed to the floor, his eyes frozen in a death stare.

Twixt held his chest and scooted away. He wept through his agony. The mercenary closest to him grabbed him by the left arm. The second mercenary came forward and took his other arm. The men dragged Twixt toward the windows. *Why are they dragging me? What were they going to do to me? Oh God, my brother is dead.* The hotel suite was sixty-five floors up. A tall window was actually a glass balcony door, and once opened by another, the two men holding him dragged him out into the night. The pain had numbed. Fear was now the only real thing he had felt. A hot searing fear that had him broken and crying like an infant. He wailed for his life and the life of his dead brother. He wasn't sure of how deep the Arab had cut him, but he knew it had to be a near-fatal wound, because he grew weaker and weaker in the struggle.

The men turned him so he could see his executioner. Armand Al Jabar walked out on the balcony. The sheikh with the mask in all black came out last. How could this man be the same Jaxon Price?

"Please, I need a doctor," Twixt begged.

The sheikh removed the mask from his face to reveal the horror of his deformity and confirm his identity. "I know doctors, I've seen plenty since we last met. I know pain. I live with every day. What I don't know is the answers I need. Answers you will give to me."

"What do you want man? What! I don't owe you anything man! You just killed my brother motherfucker! Fuck! What do you want?!"

"Where is she?" the sheikh asked.

"Huh?" Twixt said and nearly lost consciousness when he moved to sit further upright. He struggled to capture a needful breath. "I need help. I'm bleeding to death man."

"Where is she?" Jaxon Price demanded again.

"Who? Goodiva? Man, she left. I don't know where. She took off. Colorado. I guess? It's where her friends are."

"Who are her friends?" the sheikh asked.

"I'm going to bleed to death. Help me please!"

Jaxon lifted his gaze to the men nearest to Twixt. He grabbed Twixt. "No! Let me go! No!" He tried to fight back, but his chest pain made his arms weak. The men grabbed him by his belt and threw him over the balcony edge. "Wait! Wait! Wait! What are you doing? Oh God!" he screamed.

Twixt was flipped upside down. A rush of gravity joined with the whirlpool force of wind and gripped his flailing arms, trying to pull him to his death. But instead of falling, the assassins each held a leg and let him dangle, while he screamed madly. Twixt had to take several deep gasps for breath to keep from passing out.

"Please man! Please! I don't know what else you want!"

He felt himself slip in their grip and lost his voice to never-ending screams. He begged until his lungs deflated and no oxygen could be breathed. His brother was dead. And when he opened his eyes and saw the long drop to death, he knew he'd soon join him. He didn't want to die. *He didn't want to die like this.*

"Please man. I don't know anything. She left with her friends. They live in Colorado. Colorado! Delilah and Queen or something," he shouted because he feared they could not hear him over the wind. "It's a small town. A town called Falcon Cove."

"Bring him up!" the sheikh ordered.

Twixt felt himself being pulled back up and over the balcony. He nearly wept with relief.

"Did you say Falcon Cove?" the sheikh asked.

"He's fucking with you Jax. He's lying," Armand said. "Falcon Cove? Mayfair? Bullshit."

"I'm not," Twixt said. "She goes there, to see them. Falcon Cove. That's the name of the city."

The Arabs exchanged a look. For a brief moment Twixt felt a surge of hope. Though he'd never recover the loss of his brother, he still had enough strength of mind to want to hold on to his life.

"She can't be there. Can she?" the sheikh asked.

"What should we do with him?" Armand asked, ignoring the question.

The man in black looked back at Twixt with the side of his face that wasn't destroyed from the car accident.

"Please. I told you what I knew. We saved you. We did. You're alive because of us," Twixt said.

The sheikh smiled. He was right. Goodiva belonged to hi. What other proof did he need? How could she be in Falcon Cove of all places? He nodded to his men to finish the job and walked out. Twixt felt himself lifted, and then he was airborne. The men threw him like a bag of garbage over the balcony. He was sailing through the sky and clouds at maximum velocity. He didn't scream. He didn't have enough air in his lungs to do so. He closed his eyes and remembered a time when he wasn't the man he'd become. When he had a mother's love, a small village to support his dreams. A time when he and his brother lived simply. Life slipped away from him before every bone in his body shattered and his head exploded like a melon against the ground.

Chapter Seven

Falcon Cove had a population of 9,903 people. The small mountain town was situated between the Colorado Rockies in the Eagle Cliff valleys. The Cove, as local residents called it, was a winter paradise, surrounded by forested hills and snowcapped trees that often reminded tourists of a Christmas winter all year long. Goodiva moved with her family to the Cove when she was ten, but left again when she was fifteen.

"Shelly! Over here!"

Goodiva noticed a woman's arm wave above the heads of the sea of diners. Her heart filled with joy. After giving birth to her miracle baby, her best friend Delilah was more beautiful than ever. Goodiva knew she too had a captivating presence. It was how she made a fortune on the DJ circuit before Twixt. It was how she moved up fast in her acting class and landed her first movie. Still, no one compared to Delilah's beauty when standing next to her.

"I see you," Goodiva mouthed to her friend and started toward her. Time had pushed forward and Goodiva and her best friends went with it. She no longer used her birth name. She had it legally dropped. Now she was just Michelle Johnson.

"Wow, Shelly! You look great. Girl I like the ombre blonde touch to your curls!" Delilah got up from her chair and made such a scene with kisses and hugs even the wait staff and customers paused to stare at them.

"Stop, Dee, you're embarrassing me."

Noah began to whine over the loss of attention. Delilah grabbed Goodiva's face and stared into her eyes. "A year! It's been a whole freakin' year. Don't ever stay away from me that long. Promise?"

"I promise. Can we sit down now? Please?" Goodiva whispered.

"You hear that Noah? Auntie Shelly thinks I'm embarrassing her," Delilah chuckled.

"Mah-ma!" Noah stretched his hands up to Delilah. She let Goodiva go and kissed her baby before giving him a little tickle to make him giggle.

"I was hoping to slip into town unremembered. Thanks a lot for letting everyone know I'm here," Goodiva said.

"You left the Cove when you were fifteen. No one cares that you're back," Delilah scoffed.

"Me! Feed me," Noah said.

Noah was almost three and the center of her friend's universe.

"Me!" he repeated.

The women laughed. Delilah gave him a slice of buttered toast.

"I was wrong. Noah missed you too," she said.

"He's beautiful...but...my goodness, he's big," Goodiva said and ran her hand over Noah's curly hair. "What are you feeding him? Steroids?"

"Funny," Delilah rolled her eyes. "He's growing so fast. I don't know. Doctors say he's going to be tall."

Charles, Delilah's now dead husband, was barely five foot five. Most of the Montgomery men were short.

"I can't help but see it now, how different he is," Delilah said in a softer tone. She forced a smile, but Goodiva could hear sadness in her friends' voice. "Soon he'll be going to college."

After Noah was born his pale skin and hazel-brown eyes gave Delilah and Charles quite a shock. Goodiva and Queen were there for the delivery of course, and they all believed the newborn's skin would darken eventually. Though Charles' father did have lighter skin tone, the Montgomeries were all no lighter. In the African American community, it wasn't uncommon to have children born to brown skin parents of different complexions. Still, in a small town like the Cove, Noah's clearly Euro-ethnic features caused tongues to wag. He was, however, the sweetest and cutest baby any mother could dream of. Delilah was hopelessly in love.

Noah offered Goodiva a piece of his toast. She pretended to take a nibble. Delilah smiled and the mood shifted to joyous. She was home. It had been too long.

"How old was he when Charles died? Ten months, right?" Goodiva asked.

Delilah shook her head. "Almost twelve, remember? Charles died a week before Noah's second birthday. The best thing is he lived long enough to know his son, see him take his first steps and hear him say his first sentence. And Noah was such a little runner that day he walked. I took pictures on my phone I still can't look at." Delilah picked up her phone and searched for them. She found one and handed the phone over to Goodiva with tears in her eyes. "I miss Charles. It's been a full year and I miss him like it happened yesterday."

"I'm sorry hun," Goodiva said and smiled at the image of Charles with Noah on his lap. Charles looked hopelessly in love with his son.

"Ma-mah!" Noah said.

Delilah handed him his cup of juice. "I swear most days I still expect to see Charles come through the front door. Noah won't ever know how much his father loved him."

"Of course, he will. You'll show him. Tell him. We both will."

The waiter brought over a glass of water and offered Goodiva a menu. She declined with a smile.

"Not hungry?" Delilah asked.

"No, not really. So much unpacking left to do," she yawned.

"I really do like your hair like that," Delilah said.

"Thanks. The colorist lives in Ghana. I'm all natural now," she smiled.

"Wow. How was Africa? Spain? Europe? You've been everywhere, huh?"

"Africa was by far the best. I can't wait to go back," Goodiva said. "You would love it."

"Take me with you. I want some hair nurturing from the motherland."

Delilah's hair was thick and wavy with an addition of extensions that sent the dark curves to the middle of her back. Still, she could see her natural length mixed in with the waves.

"Enough about hair," Delilah waved the conversation off. "I gave you two days to get settled in. Queen said she was over at your new place helping you unpack yesterday. I still haven't seen this place!"

"I called you," Goodiva sighed.

"You called Queen first. You called me as an afterthought."

"Dee? I call you at least twice a week. Always. You knew I had landed, and I was dealing with the movers. We texted each other."

Delilah shrugged. Goodiva never understood why her friend always competed with Queen for her attention, but she rarely confronted the issue. The question often ended in an argument.

"Hey, I still got some more unpacking to do. You and Noah are welcome to come over and help."

"Have you spoken to Luvie?" Delilah shifted the conversation. "Does she know you moved back here?"

"No. She and the 'new boyfriend' refuse to leave Glendale. They made California their permanent residence. As long as my money keeps them comfortable, I guess it's okay."

"Shelly? Really? Are you still paying for everything? Can you afford it?"

"Of course, I can't. It's why I'm here. I've sold a few screenplays, but I need work, and a break from Luvie's constant needs. Besides, I don't mind them being in California. It keeps mom and her men from visiting me overseas."

"Got a new man for yourself?" Delilah asked.

"You know if I had a man I would tell you...I have male friends, but nothing serious."

"You'd probably tell Queen first," Delilah mumbled.

"Huh?"

"Nothing," Delilah said.

"I don't have a man. Twixt...his death in that plane crash. That was enough," Goodiva said.

"Yea, that was crazy. What was he doing in the Middle East?"

Goodiva shrugged. "I don't know. Performing, I guess. He and his brother both died in that crash. I was contacted to do a guest appearance at the festival to honor him in India," she looked down. "Of course, I said no."

"Contacted? By who? No one knows who you are and where you are now, I made sure of it," Delilah said.

"I reached out to his mother," she confessed.

"What! Why?" Delilah immediately lowered her voice. "We agreed."

"He's dead Dee. I know he was an asshole, but someone I once cared for died. I spoke to his sister, gave her my condolences and left my number. It was stupid, okay. When they asked me to come and perform at his event I said no. So drop it."

"Well I'm glad you didn't go to the funeral. It would have been too soon. And now I have to clean up this. If they asked you to perform some damn journalist or blogger will be looking for you."

"It's been two years," Goodiva sighed.

"That never matters."

She nodded. "I'm sorry. I felt bad about him dying that way."

"That's because you have a good heart," Delilah said. "No more sad talk. You're home. At last." Delilah picked up her glass. "Cheers to you moving back where you belong! No romance in Falcon Cove, I can guarantee you that."

Delilah toasted her.

Goodiva laughed and clinked her glass against her friend's. They both took a sip.

"I got a sweet surprise for you!" Delilah sang in her merry voice.

"Oh brother," Goodiva sighed.

"Here's the thing. I'm throwing a party. A huge one. Gonna shake things up in this town before winter covers us all with boredom. It'll be Christmas soon and I need the distraction."

"Okay?"

"You are the guest of honor. My own personal DJ. What you say? I still got your turntables in my storage."

"No thanks," Goodiva said. "I don't DJ. Hardly at all."

"No? Not even for fun?"

She shook her head in disagreement. "A little fun, but not much. I'm not an artist anymore. Just a writer."

"That's art."

She shrugged. "I guess."

"Well it's still a party. It'll be fantastic. On my ranch of course. I have so many people RSVPing. Celebrities too. A few NBA stars are coming. Tall, cho-co-late, available," she winked.

"I said no thanks, Dee."

"Why?" Delilah whined. "It's been three damn years Shelly. Live again. Please."

Goodiva dug down in her purse. She removed the folded paper she printed earlier that morning and handed it over to Delilah. "I need you to give me a recommendation. I want this job."

4315 Ansbury, Mayfair Landing, seeking Estate Manager to tend to all the home needs including: accounting, household budget, organizing and running a staff of 5. $55K. Start Immediately. 756-699-6455.

"Huh?" Delilah looked up at her with concern in her eyes. "Why would you want to work there?"

"I need a real job. It's why I had to get out of New York. I can't live off of you forever. And Luvie wants an upgrade in her life."

"This job won't pay for all of that. And what do you mean live off of me? You're trying to start your writing career. I support that," Delilah said. "I'm the prime investor in Michelle Johnson," Delilah said with pride.

"It's been too long. I want a place secluded, where I can work in peace and protect my privacy. And I have a better reason. I also want to be close to you. That's why I came home," Goodiva reasoned.

"Did something happen in Ghana? New York?"

"Something always happens. The internet never forgets. I go to dinner in Ghana of all places, the furthest point I could get from Los Angeles, and someone recognizes me from my Instagram days. It brought everything back. All they wanted to do was pound me with questions about Twixt's death. Why we broke up. Why I disappeared. Did I believe the rumors that he wasn't dead, since his body was never recovered for his family?"

"It wasn't?" Delilah frowned.

"Hell, it probably blew up in the plane crash. Who knows?" Goodiva shrugged.

"This little mountain town won't be any different than Ghana. It doesn't forget one of its own," Delilah reminded her.

"I've been gone from the Cove since I was fifteen, remember? Your family won't give me up. Who will? Queen? No. I can start over. And this job will help me save and not spend every dime. It's what my therapist recommended."

"Wait, what therapist?"

"Doesn't matter."

"Ah, yes it does. What therapist? I thought you were done with therapy. I mean, why are you meeting with therapists in Ghana?"

"One should never be done with therapy after one nearly kills a man," Goodiva said with evident bitterness.

"Lower your voice! It's too dangerous to even joke like that," Delilah said through clenched teeth. "And that was Twixt's crime. Not yours."

Goodiva sighed.

"I stayed a bit in New York before coming home. I started therapy there. To prepare me for living in the light. I'm ready to come out of the shadows."

"Shadows are safe."

"Shadows are never safe Dee. My therapist recommended I go someplace secluded. He mentioned Mayfair."

"Okay, now I'm really confused."

"I was shocked too."

"You never told him about Falcon Cove?" Delilah asked with a hint of disbelief in her tone."

"Yes. I told him about here. I grew up here. He said I always speak of feeling safest with you and Queen in Falcon Cove. He suggested I come home and apply for this job."

Delilah picked up the paper again. "How did he know about the job in Mayfair?"

"Who knows? A Google search. Does it matter?"

"Just strange. You know the history of that place. Before Charles was diagnosed, he started business with Yaşar Fikrit. He invested in the fertility clinic among other things I can't figure out. Charles' brothers keep the management of the Mayfair Trust under lock and key. They won't let me anywhere near these investments."

"Who is Yaşar Fikrit?" Goodiva asked.

"The Master of Mayfair. That's what they call the owners. That's why you don't know his name. He's been up at the mountain for decades. Rumor had it that he was Turkish, Muslim, billionaire with multiple wives. I dunno. The man I met with Charles was old, dying and alone."

"So it's Mr. Fikrit that's hiring?"

Delilah shook her head. "Yaşar Fikrit is dead. He's not the Mayfair of Master any longer."

"Then who is?"

"I don't know who moved in, because the estate is in a trust. Charles was on the board. His brother now holds the seat. Fikrit wasn't fond of women lawyers or women business partners. I wasn't allowed to touch the estate. I think Charles said that Fikrit has an heir. A son. I guess that's who lives there now."

"I really want this job. It's perfect for me."

"Hmm, too perfect," Delilah said.

"You are always so suspicious."

"No, I'm cautious. I don't like the coincidence. I mean Mayfair? And now? After Christmas the winter will lock you in up there. I won't be able to get to you," Delilah huffed.

Goodiva smiled. She shook her head. She missed her friend too.

"I needed you and Queen again too."

Delilah softened.

"I've wanted you to come back to the Cove for years. But I thought the memories of this place were too painful," she said.

"I have good memories here too. I can't keep running from my mistakes. I learned that in therapy. I need to face the past. I can possibly forgive myself for Jaxon—ah, you know who—if I can forgive myself for what we did."

"How much have you told this therapist about your past?"

"Nothing. Delilah, I swear. I wasn't stupid. I just told him I was abused as a kid and I was reckless as an adult. It was for my anxiety. I didn't tell him anything about the past. Not really."

"Come work for me. My ranch is so big you can stay in the guesthouse and we'll never see each other."

"No."

"Why not? Why go to this place?"

"There's more to it, I guess."

"What now?" Delilah asked.

"Happenstance."

"Oh brother."

"It means—"

"I know what happenstance means!" Delilah said.

"At a party in Ghana, a few months before I left, I was asked to DJ for a friend who had travelled in from New York. I didn't want to. I never do. I love my music, but I dunno, it's different for me now."

"What event is this? And who is this friend?" Delilah asked.

"It's called 'The Year of the Return'. The Ghanaian government opened its borders for blacks across the diaspora to return home after 400 years because of slavery. Big event. African Americans were coming and claiming citizenship."

"Too big and risky for you to surface. I thought you were staying in the shadows?" Delilah asked.

"That's why I didn't tell you," she mumbled.

"I don't want to hear anymore, do I?" Delilah asked.

Goodiva chuckled. "It was fine. Anyways, it was good money to be made. I didn't expect to see anyone I knew at the event."

"And?"

"I did. Well sorta. Leigh Anne Zanzible. The actress. Do you remember her?"

"What does she have to do with any of this?"

"She's his ex-lover. Jaxon Price," Goodiva whispered. "She was at the festival. High out of her mind on Percocet or coke and running her mouth. Someone asked her where Jaxon Price had disappeared too. The moment I heard his name my whole body went cold. I couldn't walk away."

"Wait. Wait. Leigh Anne is a French-Canadian actress, but she was at the migration of black people to Africa festival?"

"A party is a party, forget that part. I'm telling you something important."

Delilah sighed. "No. You're missing something important. That coincidence or happenstance is fantasy. This sounds weird to me."

"Let me finish. Leigh Anne knows Jaxon Price."

"She doesn't know where he is. No one does. The man had enough money to disappear. And he did, thank God,"

"I thought so too. But she said something. Something that sounded weird."

Delilah sighed. "Okay, fine. What did she say?"

"She said Jaxon went back to hell. She babbled about his being the devil now, the son of the devil, as deadly as a scorpion. No one took her serious. But I did. Because I feel like the devil for what I did to him. I didn't say much more to her. She could recognize me. For the next few months I researched him. Everything I could find about him—"

"Why would she recognize you?"

"She found me in the hospital room, remember? She's the actress that found me with Jaxon."

"Oh?"

"I started having nightmares again about the accident and Twixt. It all came back. I confided in someone. Just about how terrible my mistakes were, without revealing too much. I swear I will never reveal too much."

"I believe you," Delilah said.

Goodiva grabbed her napkin and dabbed under her eyes.

"That's not the end of the story, is it?" Delilah asked.

"No. I became obsessed. I've been tracking him like a private investigator. Pretended to be doctors and movie producers to get my hands on any information. Even hired a hacker to try to get into his medical records. Obsessed."

"Goodiva!" Delilah said.

"Don't worry. You're right. He's gone. He owns his production business, but he literally disappeared. My hacker said he's in the Middle East. Did you know he was Middle Eastern? And I found this," she went into her purse and pulled out an article. In it there was the crown prince, and all of his cousins. All of the wealth tied to the Saudi royal family.

"What am I looking at?"

"The name. There," she said and pointed. "It's Armand Al Jabar. He is the grandson of one of the royals. This is the man whose party I went to the night I met Jaxon. The man who is responsible for me meeting Jaxon."

"What does all of this mean?" Delilah frowned.

"It means he knows him, where he is."

"These Saudis are dangerous, did you even read this article?" Delilah frowned, scanning through it.

Goodiva snatched the article from her. "The point is, I went to New York to try to connect with Armand Al Jabar. He isn't in LA anymore. Lives in Manhattan. And that's when the trail went cold. No matter what I did I couldn't get close to him. I realized it's best it be left alone. So I went back into therapy. I needed to figure out what makes this such an obsession for me. It was in therapy that I realized my real problem. It's not Jaxon Price. It's not what I did. It's what happened to us when were ten. I'm home to face the past and bury it once and for all."

Delilah smiled.

"I will let this go. The past. All of it. A few months in Mayfair I can get back in touch with myself. With Falcon Cove. Accept what happened here. I'm done with my guilt. I just need to move on. Don't you see? I need to heal. I have to. By spring I want you and I to go back to Mr. Collins's place. It's still there, isn't it? His sister died several years ago, and his nephew owns it."

"No!" Delilah said. "Never."

"Fine, I just—"

"You can heal all you want, but Peter Collins is gone. The past is the past."

Goodiva nodded in agreement. "Baby steps. I'm here now. I'm not going anywhere."

"What would have happened if you found him?" Delilah whispered.

"Who?"

"Price. What would happen if your research uncovered where he was?"

"Nothing. I dunno. I mean, I barely knew him before it all went wrong. And he probably hates me now. It's just..."

"What?"

"Don't you ever wonder why he never exposed me and Twixt? Told the police what really happened that night? He's a cripple now, you know. In a wheelchair, and he has severe burns to his body. It's why he isn't seen in public. That's what his medical records my hacker unlocked said. Why did he not want vengeance or justice?"

"That is strange. If he's friends with those Saudi's in that article, we don't need to know."

"What do you have against Saudi's?"

"I'm not being racist. Charles had business deals in Saudi Arabia. He told me things. It's a messed up world," Delilah shook her head.

"Well we can't run from our past. Not really. I have to get over this. Mr. Collins—"

"Lower your voice!" Delilah warned her again.

"Sorry. We did the same thing to Mr. Collins. We had a good reason. But Jaxon Price was my mistake. My sin. I won't look for him, and I won't confess. I need closure. Closure starts with the Cove."

"Atonement won't come from being a maid in some funky old mausoleum. Mayfair Estates is ridiculously huge. I don't know what you will do with all that boredom—"

"You're not talking me out of this," Goodiva smiled.

"Fine. Sit the winter out on that mountain. But Shelly, please, please I'm begging. You have to let this Jaxon Price thing go. I support you doing this on your own, just let the past go. Really let it go. It's time for us all to move on."

"I know you're right. But after all this time I can't help but think about him. Me and Jaxon Price," Goodiva said.

Delilah picked up her son from the highchair and sat him on her lap. She fed him from her plate. "I love you Shelly, but you never see the big picture. I know men like Jaxon Price. I married one. He isn't some mystical figure in your life. If he's still rich then he's powerful, and probably a dangerous jerk."

"Jerks don't try to save other people's lives Dee—"

"He didn't disappear because he's been forced into hiding. Have you looked at the world? The #MeToo movement has Bill Cosby in jail and every other powerful predator running away. Leigh Anne Zanzible and slew of other actresses accused him and most of those Hollywood movie producers of sexual harassment. That sex you had with him that night was after he plied you with alcohol. It was barely consensual what you said he did to you in that bathroom."

"You're twisting my words," she sighed.

"I know these men! I'm not saying he deserved what happened to him that night, but he's no victim. Save your pity and get better. Stronger. I need my friend back. Not this bullshit! I've been going through things too!"

"I'm sorry. I'm sorry Dee. Of course. I'm here for you, and guess what?"

Delilah looked on with angry tears in her eyes.

"After the winter job is done. I'll move to your ranch. I want to be with you and Queen again. We can raise little man together."

"Why not now?"

"Because you're right about me. You warned me about Twixt. About signing that little relationship contract with him. Becoming his arm piece, his American trophy to get him into the hip-hop scene. You warned me about letting go of Jaxon and the mistakes I've made. I need to be solid. On my own two feet. I want this job so that I can have the time to work on me free from my bad habits. My therapist gave me some good tips for how the isolation can help me. And I'm close. Very close. I'll see you after winter, and maybe in between."

Delilah smiled. "You promise?"

"Yes."

Delilah sighed with relief.

"So you'll give me a recommendation? Help me get the job?"

"I can do more than that. I know the lady that owns the staffing agency."

"You do?"

"It's a small town, for goodness sake. Jobs like these are the best they can offer. If you are going to do this, then we have to be careful. Protect your privacy. Besides, I'm curious as to who is living up there now."

Chapter Eight

"*YOU ARE APPROACHING MAYFAIR ESTATES*"

Immediately she shifted her gears and decreased speed. The jeep slowed to a stop when she arrived before the 30-foot tall black iron gates with spear-pointed tips. No one ever ventured this far outside of Falcon Cove in the dead of winter, because most of the roads led to the old coal mines that were at the foothills of the mountain. The founding Mayfairs had built against the mountain over two hundred years ago. Since then, Mayfair had had three owners, not including the new resident. And every one of them took on the traditions of Mayfair protecting its dark legacy.

To her left was an intercom with a keypad. Beyond that a camera watched her from the trees. She hated to roll down her window. Even in her thick insulated jacket and gloves she felt unprepared for the icy winds storming down the mountain. She reached and pushed in the green button. The speaker box barked back with loud chimes like those of a doorbell.

"Mayfair Estates," answered the voice beyond the box.

"Ah hello, I'm Michelle. Michelle Johnson. You're expecting me?"

As if pulled by the hand of a giant, the two gates parted and opened. Michelle looked at the camera; the unknown stared back at her.

She shifted into gear and drove through.

JAXON PRICE STARED at the jeep traveling north on the monitor.

"She coming in?" Armand asked. He settled in his chair with crossed legs. "Never mind. Of course, she is. You spent three years casting this bait. She was bound to take a nibble eventually."

Jaxon dropped the side of his face against his index finger and thumb. The visitor drove along the curved drive that stretched for two miles before it circled the front of his home. Cameras and sensors remained trained on every angle of this property and they kept her in view. He waited and he watched.

Armand wasn't as patient. The ice in his whiskey clinked against the glass. Jaxon knew that was a sound of boredom. He'd prefer Armand not to visit, but he needed him to. Without the visits he couldn't trust himself to his lonely existence. The jeep, black with dark windows, parked. A woman, brown with a pink jacket and a pink matching knit cap, hopped out.

"She sure is bright!" Armand said as he peered over Jaxon's shoulder. He then turned and walked away, finishing his drink. The young woman plucked up her briefcase and purse, then hurried up the steps to the door.

"Did you hear me?" Armand asked.

"No," Jaxon mumbled.

"Storm should settle in within a week or two. I'm flying out now. Production begins in Egypt next week. I'm going to be a pharaoh."

"Good for you," Jaxon answered.

"This plan of yours is insane. It won't work. You're paranoid to think Jin cares enough about this when he has you right where he wants you."

"I know what I'm doing."

"Don't say I didn't warn you."

"Warn me?" Jaxon frowned.

"That's right. In some states they call this kidnapping, blackmail and a few other crimes. You wanted her, we could have taken her in Africa, or Spain. Yep, I would have preferred Spain."

"It's done best this way. She's home again, and so am I," Jaxon said.

"How can we be sure she won't be missed?" Armand pushed. "My name is all over this. And eventually you can be traced to me."

Jaxon didn't bother with an answer.

"Fine," Armand set the glass on the bar. "I'll do the interview; you can watch from here. Be a good boy and stay."

Jaxon Price wheeled his chair away from the monitor. He would go into the secret room situated off the hall to his bedroom. It was where he kept the video monitoring system and audio equipment. "I'll join you in the interview if I feel the need."

"Stick to the plan," Armand said before he left.

"MY NAME IS MICHELLE Johnson. Pleased to meet you," she said.

A tall, extremely thin woman with hair lighter than her skin ignored the handshake offered. "Welcome to Mayfair, Miss Johnson. This way please."

Goodiva hitched the strap to her attaché up on her shoulder and followed. Her steps echoed back in the tomb-like silence of the mega mansion. She tried not to be distracted by the interior architecture, gothic in nature with dark floors and walls.

"How many rooms?" she asked to the back of her guide.

The woman cast her a snobbish glance over her shoulder. "Twenty-two total on the property, two private cottages, a 12-stall barn, three recreational centers and two cafes that are only open for Master Mayfair during the spring and summer. Inside of Mayfair there are sixteen bedrooms and seven wine cellars that run the length of the property underground. Caves beneath us connected by bricked in tunnels that used to lead to the silver mines. One leads directly inside the mountain."

"Wow," Goodiva mumbled. "Delilah would love this place."

"Pardon?" the woman asked.

"Oh nothing, nothing."

"This way please." The escort turned on her heel and extended her arm to the open archway. It was a large carpeted room with walls just as dark as the others, a library or study of some sort. Big enough to park six Buicks, it was furnished in a masculine style, with Persian rugs, hardwood flooring, cranberry red draperies, and dead animals mounted as hunting trophies high on the walls. But it was the rows and rows of bookshelves that she loved the most. She was drawn to classic titles before her gaze drifted up to the lion's head. A real one. She stood under it in awe. The poor animal was frozen with a ferocious snarl.

"Mufasa?" She pointed at the lion. She turned to see if her reference had amused, only to find that her escort had gone.

"Well, nice to meet you too," Goodiva said to the empty room. She removed her knit cap and shoved it into the pocket of her puffy jacket. She did what she assumed was expected of her. She walked around the parlor running her hand over a few things: a floor model globe, Ming vase, Tiffany lamps, and statues carved out of marble. She touched everything out of habit. When she was on set for the movie she starred in, she'd watch the set designers make the most elaborate fakes. It always made her question lavish items and their real worth.

Goodiva's eyes wandered, as did her attention, until they lifted to the corner of the room. A camera was pointed down at her. If she moved, so did the camera. It tracked her in a silent unnerving way that made the threat clear. *Do something wrong and it will be seen.*

"There you are," a man's voice spoke through her thoughts. Armand Al Jabar greeted her. The sight of him made her drop her purse.

"Ah, hi," she stammered and picked up her belongings. Armand was every leading lady's leading man. He had movie star handsomeness that covered him, from his height to his chiseled features. She'd met him before, years ago when she snuck into Jaxon Price's hospital room, and before that his house party. She'd never forgotten that encounter. Why was he standing before her? She had searched almost all of Manhattan for him. Was he the new owner of Mayfair?

"Everything okay?" he asked.

"Ah, yeah, just clumsy," she said.

Armand's dark gaze swept over her as if she arrived for him. He had the same uncompromising look of seriousness on his face when he entered the room. His hair was tapered low around the sides and nape, but the top of his head was crowned in thick jet-black waves. He had tanned olive skin and deep set eyes that were black as coal. His handsomeness was kindled with a sort of masculine softness that could take him from a role of a hitman or secret agent to priest, then back to a dictator of a nation. He was that versatile.

"Frances deposited you here and didn't tell me. I get lost in this creepy old place. Forgive my tardiness. I'm Armand Al Jabar," he extended his hand.

"Ah...hi. Um...I'm Shelly. Michelle Johnson. We spoke on the phone."

"Oh yes. Michelle or Shelly. I remember. You look familiar. Have we met before?"

"No. I think I might remember that. You're one of my favorite actors," Goodiva gushed.

"شكرا," he gave her a curt nod.

"*Shukran?*" she repeated.

"Yes, شكرا means *thank you* in Arabic," he said.

"Oh, okay, *shukran*," she said with politeness in return.

His smile tipped the corner of his mouth and again his left brow arched as if amused. "Please join me," he gestured to the leather chairs near the fireplace. "How bad was the drive in? The weather getting worse?"

"It's not getting better."

He seemed concerned. It was another clue to her that he might not be the new owner of Mayfair. The first clue was his reference to Mayfair as being old and creepy.

"I guess you weren't quite expecting to meet with me," Armand asked.

"I wasn't sure who I was to meet. The agency didn't have much to say on the person I'd be working for. Other than that the job they recruited me for would be to manage his affairs."

"Yes, that's the job." Armand crossed his left leg over his right. He opened a slender mirrored compact case. He removed a thinly rolled white spliff as he stared at her. She tried to remain neutral to his celebrity and keep her interest in the conversation focused on the interview. Still, his unwavering stare felt like X-ray vision—both hot and penetrating. He didn't ask if she minded if he smoked marijuana in her presence. He used a sterling lighter and lit up as if it were nothing more than a cigarette. In Colorado, smoking weed was legal, so she wasn't too surprised by his lax behavior.

"Tell me a little about yourself, Michelle?"

"It's pretty simple. I'm a screenwriter and photographer. I'm looking for a domestic job where I can inspire my creativity."

"Domestic's inspire creativity?" Armand frowned.

She smiled. "Inspiration can come from anywhere. I've known about Mayfair since I was a kid. We had a few school trips here. I think it's a magnificent place. I'm not sure what's expected from the owner, but I've done some property management in the past. Are you the owner?"

"Me?" Armand chuckled. "Hell no. Not my style sweetheart."

"Oh, I know celebrities retreat to small midwestern towns."

"Interesting," Armand said. "You from LA?"

"No, Falcon Cove. I grew up here."

Armand paused. He took a drag and exhaled heavily as his eyes lowered with scrutiny.

"What the agency didn't tell you, what few people have learned, is that the person you will be working for is a very private man due to his 'celebrity'," Armand said with air-quotes. "Before you meet him, you will have to sign an NDA. And I have to warn you, even a whimper of his existence outside of Mayfair and you'll have to rise from death to finish working off payment after the lawsuit."

"He sounds intense."

"Oh, he is. Not fond of strangers, liars, schemers, grifters. Thinks every beautiful woman is a liar," Armand said as he held the joint like a cigarette between two fingers and flicked the ashes to the Persian rug.

"Why would he think so lowly of women?" she asked.

Armand stared at her for a pause without answering.

Stay calm Goodiva, he's testing you. Don't rush the conversation. Play his game, and then run the hell out of here the moment you can.

"Because they think so lowly of him. Add to that a touch of personal guilt maybe, after crushing many hearts? His own kink? Or maybe it's the business he's in. Celebrity makes for strange bedfellows, wouldn't you agree?"

"I wouldn't know," she replied.

"Right. You're a screenwriter from New York who has never visited the land of stars."

"I didn't say that," she half-smiled.

He stared at her for a moment before continuing: "He's had experience with people not being truthful with him in the past. In fact, he suffered a terrible car accident. Totally his fault. So said the police and the people who found him. He has some kind of brain damage. Really bad memory loss. Was in the Middle East to be treated for it. When we found that he could never be the man he once was, we relocated him here to protect his privacy and business investments. Mayfair is perfect for anonymity."

She felt faint.

"Are you okay?" Armand asked.

"He's an actor? Like you? The... ah...owner?"

Armand chuckled.

"You're funny," Armand said.

She stirred with unease in her chair.

"He's not an actor. He doesn't like actors. He only tolerates me." Armand smirked. "He has little sense of humor. His direct request of his staff is that you leave him alone."

"Sounds like a charmer. I don't think this job is for me—"

Armand nodded. "He used to be a charmer. A real lady's man. Heard he could seduce the panties off a nun, and probably did at some point. Some ladies called him Romeo the Asshole."

She coughed.

"You sure we haven't met before?" Armand pressed her as he smoked his weed and his eyes narrowed under a cloud of suspicion.

"I'm positive," she said, now ready to flee.

"Why not work for a publisher, something more in line with your career? Domestic work doesn't seem like a good fit for you."

"I...ah...I'm independent. I want to be. I think this job is good because it brings me closer to friends. Gives me focus."

"Feminist? Social justice warrior? Me-too gladiator? Times-up champion? Which are you? What type of writer are you?"

Goodiva didn't understand where he was leading her.

"Why do I have to be any of them?" she asked.

"Because today, most women are."

"You think women believing they have rights is some kind of gimmick?"

"No," Armand said. "I think women blaming men for not having enough rights is a trend. If you truly believe in correcting injustice, I respect it. If you use it as a means to cut a man's balls off to give yourself a pair, I don't."

She frowned. Suddenly he wasn't charming or handsome. Her dislike deepened when he taunted her with his sly smile. He knew her. She was certain.

"Well. Let's see it?" he said.

"I'm sorry?" she asked.

"Resume, references—?"

"Oh! Oh yes," Goodiva reached for her attaché. Delilah had gone through her employment record and resume. She made it positively bland. The resume exaggerated dates and details on the jobs she had in her early teens when she was a personal assistant for the Montgomeries.

"Seems like the only real estate management experience you have is working for the Montgomeries."

"I...ah...well I guess—"

"Nothing here about your screenplays?" Armand continued.

"Still working on my new project."

"Maybe I can read it? I know people who might be interested. Hollywood is going black lately, another trend," he said, and looked up to see if the comment generated a reaction. He was really trying to goad her into some kind of debate. She fought against it and kept her mouth shut. "Ever send anything to Tyler Perry? He's a friend of mine. I could pass it along."

"No. My work isn't the same as his. But thank you for offering," she smiled.

"Who are you?"

Goodiva's head whipped around. A masked man wheeled himself into the room with the aid of an electric chair. All of her nervousness and apprehension over being discovered slipped back into her at that moment. It was Jaxon Price in the flesh. He rolled deeper into the room. He didn't look natural in his chair. He was tall, yes, and well formed. However, he didn't appear feeble or unable to move his lower body. He was definitely in that chair by circumstance. The circumstances she knew she created. Twixt was dead and Jaxon was a cripple. Her heart and emotions sank to an even deeper level of self-loathing.

Jaxon's hair was longer than it should be; wisps of it shadowed his brow and fell just past his nape to his shoulder. And then came the mystery of his face. He wore a half-mask made of leather, the way a pirate would wear an eye patch. The left side of his face was hidden from his eye to part of his nose and around the side of his mouth to his chin. The leather strap went across his brow around his head, beneath his left ear to connect the mask in a perfectly crafted way. The amber beauty of his brown eyes made them almost golden beneath the mask. He wore a black turtleneck and dark blazer. A long thin platinum chain was around his neck with an oval shaped locket that had a black crest over it.

"I asked you a question," Jaxon Price repeated. "Who are you?"

"Michelle Johnson. I'm here...because...for...uhm, the interview."

Jaxon frowned. His piercing gaze cut to Armand. "I told you not to hire a nurse."

Armand not knowing her was one thing. But not even her hair color should prevent Jaxon from remembering her. Or had he really suffered some kind of brain damage and memory loss?

Goodiva stood. Armand ignored Jaxon and continued to read through her references. Jaxon wheeled his chair forward and stopped two feet in front of her.

Dear God, I can never atone for what I have done to this man. I deserve jail. I deserve worse. I should confess now. This is fate and karma all rolled up in one big serving.

"It's a pleasure to meet you Mr. Price. I've been a fan of your work for years," she said and extended her hand.

Jaxon Price was nothing like the world remembered, which explained why the world had not seen him in three years. He looked older than thirty, but younger than forty. He studied her with his good eye and made no attempt to accept her hand to shake. He reversed his chair and left the room.

Armand finished reading the references. He seemed amused. "He likes you. You're hired."

"But he thinks I'm his nurse—"

"Yes, he gets things confused at times. That was his greeting. If he wanted you gone, he wouldn't have made an appearance before I got you to sign the NDA." Armand tapped his temple. "I know him. You're the one. You'll

learn his signals in time. If he does make appearances. If he does not summon you, don't seek him out. That's the only rule."

The way Armand said 'the one' sent a sliver of curiosity through her.
She blinked and tried not to smile. *They didn't remember her. They didn't
know her!* Her obsession with Jaxon Price made her question her sanity at
times. He was all she thought about, read about, wrote about in her diaries.

"I have one final question," he said.

"Okay?"

"Why did you change your name? I thought Goodiva was quite exquis-
ite."

Armand stood. He clasped his hands behind his back. "Don't worry.
He doesn't know who you are."

"But you do?" she asked.

Armand nodded.

"I arranged this job just for you."

"Now I'm confused."

"Are you? Really? You've been snooping around Jaxon for years. My job
has been to protect him. I knew about the accident. He may not remember
it, but I remember Jaxon right before he met you."

"Then why did you bring me here? To offer me this job?" she asked.

"Because he needs someone to care for him. I can't keep this up in
this crypt he insists on living in. And after speaking with your therapist, I
learned your reasons for trying to reach him were based on guilt. A good
enough reason to trust you with his secrets."

"My therapist wouldn't share my personal—"

"Information can be bought. You paid a hacker to pry into Jaxon medical records. I only returned the favor."

There was so much truth in his statement she didn't bother to counter
it. He smiled. "Your secret is safe with me. He's not going to give you any
problems. Today he thinks you're a nurse, tomorrow he'll think you're his
wife. One of them," Armand gave a sly smile.

"I don't get the joke. If he's mentally ill then—"

"He's sane enough."

"I'm leaving," she said.

He stepped in front of her. "Apologies. I will admit I'm not found of you. You destroyed his life. But I protected that truth. Not for you or your rock star boyfriend, but for him. He isn't the same."

"I'm sorry for that."

"The media hunts him constantly. You're my last hope. Others I've hired have tried and failed. You do this, and in return maybe he can help you."

"How?"

"I don't know. You'll have to decide that for yourself."

"I can't do this. Not in a deceptive way."

"Take the job."

"It's wrong if he doesn't know me..."

"Take the job," Armand smiled. She stared into his eyes. "He needs your help now."

"Can I have time to think about it?"

Armand shook his head very slowly to say no.

"Really?"

"I'm on a flight in the morning. It's now or never beautiful."

She sighed. She put her hands to her face and tried to be reasonable. But all she could think of was the chance. "I will take the job."

"Word of advice: stay out of his way. Let it happen naturally. After a while, who knows? He may start to remember you again."

"The woman who greeted me, what was her name?"

"He calls her Frances, but her name is Francine."

"Yes. Frances. Why isn't she the estate manager?" Goodiva asked.

"She was. Mr. Cheerful fired her. Her last day is today now that we have decided. You have her job."

"Are you serious?"

"I am. It was quite a messy parting between the two of them. She's been here since long before his father died. This place is more of a home to her than it is to him. Frances and Andella, you'll meet her later, run this place. You'll have a problem proving you can manage the job without the dynamic duo's approval. So good luck with that."

"Can I ask why she was fired? I don't make the same mistakes."

Armand shrugged. "He found her in his room. Possibly she was cleaning it, but I suspect—"

"Bedroom?"

Armand smiled. "No. Not quite. Poor thing shouldn't be blamed. Her office is the only other inhabited room in those cellars."

"I don't understand. He fired her for being in a room when she is in charge of cleaning all the rooms?"

"Weird, isn't it?" Armand asked with a mocking chuckle. "Oh yes! I forgot. He has two rules, not one. First, you limit your presence around him, that is golden. He doesn't take well to the stares of strangers since the accident and all. Hates to be pitied and all that." Armand waved off the issue. "Not sure why he cares, he looks like Batman with his dark suits and mask. Women find that sexy. Don't they?"

"Not really," she said.

"You sure?" Armand teased. "I can call him back to test the theory."

"What is this other rule?"

"There's a room on the cellar floor. Not easy to find, but the door...well the door is hard to miss. You see it and you get curious. Don't. It's locked. It's always locked, but by chance if he forgets one day and the door is ajar, even an inch, pretend not to notice. Stay away from it."

"Why would I even bother to go to the cellar?" she frowned.

"That's where your office is. Like I just explained, you are taking on Frances' job. Lots of funky halls under this place. You will find yourself down there quite a bit, dealing with deliveries and managing this estate."

She glanced back to the door Jaxon left through and then her gaze lifted to the camera in the corners of the room angled toward them. "How does he get around, in his chair? I mean this place is four stories, right?"

"Two elevators on either side of the estate, and a lift in the center that takes you down to the cellars. The lift is the only way to get down there. I oversaw the technical upgrades of the elevators, but the lift has been here for over two centuries. Pretty old crank of a thing. He won't let me replace it with a more modern one. I have updated it so he can control it from his wheelchair. Still, if you get stuck in it, the only way to notify someone is the alarm button. Make sure to keep your finger on it. The alarm sometimes malfunctions too."

"Okay."

"He can be anywhere he wants when he wants. So don't think you can pull anything over on him because he's stuck in that chair." Armand pointed to the camera aimed at them. "The only place of privacy in Mayfair is the bathroom and the cellars. Every other inch of the property is under 24-hour surveillance. His father was quite the voyeur, and a bit paranoid."

"Anything else I should know? Are there ghosts?"

Armand smiled. "I would guess there are. Maybe. I try not to stay here too long. Not kidding about Devil Mountain, you locals call it Falcons Beak. But out here it's boring and drab. It's colder than hell no matter the season." He shrugged. "The place gives me the creeps."

"Yes, you've said that before."

He walked over to the table near the window. He pulled out the drawer and removed a contract and a pen. "Do you want the job or not? Either way, you have to sign the NDA. Sorry, but there is still a matter of trust between us. I'm leaving you with the biggest secret in Hollywood right now. I need to be sure you intend to protect his privacy. That means you aren't to tell your friends or anyone that he is here or why you accepted this job. Are we clear?"

She looked back to the entrance that Jaxon had left through. She glanced to Armand who stood there holding a contract and felt as if she were bargaining for her soul.

"Sign here, and he's yours."

"How much does it pay?"

"The agency didn't tell you. For this job you get $2300 a week. And overtime can be logged and submitted to Jaxon in writing if you need to be compensated."

Goodiva eyes stretched. The job posting said around $55k. The offer was considerably higher. "That's over 9000 a month?"

"So you're good at math too?" Armand smirked.

"I ah...uhm—"

"Do you want the job or not? Either way, you will have to sign. The ol' boy ruined the secrecy by showing up the way he did."

Goodiva sucked down a deep breath and considered the offer. She knew a hundred reasons why she should decline and not put her name on any contract associated with them. What could they do if she turned and walked away? Nothing. Right? She ignored the voice in her head and signed the NDA contract without reading it. She signed everything.

"There's one more thing."

"Okay?"

"Cellphones, you can't bring them here."

"Wait, why?"

"There's no internet, and he doesn't take the chance of pictures being taken of him. No cell phones. You have a phone in your room, and you can access one on the property at any time."

"I need the internet. Who survives in this world today without it?" she joked. "And my cellphone is—"

"It's non-negotiable. He finds you with it, and you're fired."

She chewed on her bottom lip.

Armand arched a brow. "You said domestic solitude would inspire you. This is domestic solitude at its finest."

"Okay, I'll take the job."

"Good luck, Ms. Goodiva Johnson. I do mean that."

Goodiva gathered her references and resume. She put them back in her attaché. She followed him to the door. "When do I start?"

"Today, tomorrow, next week, whenever. You work with the agency and they'll get you moved in."

JAXON WATCHED AS GOODIVA returned to her jeep. From his monitors he saw everything. Not long after her departure, Armand joined him.

"Does she think dyeing her hair changes anything?"

"I had her sign the documents. Stupid woman didn't even read them. You have all you need to teach the bitch a lesson."

"Did you see her face when she saw me?" Jaxon asked. "She looked like she'd seen a ghost."

"You almost ruined it. She could have run away before I reeled her in. If I were her, I would. You were right though. She took the bait."

"I wanted her to see me. I wanted to see what she would decide if she saw me, like this."

"And?"

"She made the right choice."

"If she had decided to bolt?" Armand asked.

"Then we would have done it the other way."

"Why go this far? Just have her arrested," Armand said.

"It wasn't her fault."

"Bullshit. She left a scene of a crime."

"You and I both know that I don't give a shit about the accident."

"Then what do you give a shit about? I saw what you've done in the cellar. You plan on taking up permanent residence below with her? Sex dungeon?"

"I have other plans for her. Not sex."

"Revenge? Yes. I know," Armand yawned.

"My father is dead. Charles Montgomery is dead. Twixt and his brother are dead. I don't need revenge. Jin wanted power and I've made sure that he's had it on three different continents. This game is mine," he said and took a sip of his drink.

GOODIVA STOPPED JUST outside of the closing gates. She squeezed her eyes shut and gripped the steering wheel until she ceased shaking. Her heart beat so fast she knew cardiac arrest was coming. The panic in her couldn't be calmed. She started heaving deep breaths as she fumbled with her phone. She'd call Delilah and tell her. She had to tell her. Jaxon Price was alive and well in Mayfair. He was the new Master of Mayfair. As soon as she dialed the number she stopped. She dropped her head back and closed her eyes again.

"Calm down. Just slow down."

She practiced breathing like her therapist had taught her. Deep inhalations through the mouth and long exhalations through her nose. She did it over and over. Finally, she felt the claustrophobic need to scream subside inside of her. It was him. And he didn't know her. Armand had arranged for them to be together again. She didn't care what his reasons were. She had her own. This was the healing she prayed for. She couldn't let Queen or Delilah know. They'd never agree to support her. If she took the job, she could possibly convince him of her sincerity, atone for her mistake.

Should she take the job?

No.

Shouldn't she try to fix him, help him, heal him?

No.

Could he forgive her for what she did when she told him the truth?

No.

Was this the only chance she'd ever get to try?

Yes.

Chapter Nine

Two days after her interview and two months before one of the biggest pandemic's in the history of the world was to arrive in Falcon Cove, Jaxon Price sent a personal driver and moving truck to bring Goodiva Michelle Johnson back to Mayfair Estates. She could have spared him the expense, since she had very little to take with her. She told Queen that she accepted the job and that the interview went fine. She said the same thing to Delilah. Neither of them expected the truth over her lies.

After a ride back to the mountain in the snow, she arrived mid-day. Frances wasn't there to greet her. Another equally intimidating woman stood in her place—all six feet of her. The dark-velvet floor-length coat she wore heightened the translucence of her milky white skin. Though it was cooler in the mountains at this time of year, Goodiva figured this woman and Frances both dressed stately every day of the year.

The older woman's face was arresting, and irregular. She had a long pointed nose, deep-set clear gray eyes, and chiseled cheekbones with a pointed chin and very thin lips. Her hair was pulled tightly to a ball of wiry jet-black strands at the center of her head.

"Welcome back to Mayfair, ma'am. I'm Andella. I run the kitchen."

"Nice to meet you," Goodiva said.

Andella had gathered the staff of about ten. She lined them up with military precision. Goodiva followed as the woman strolled down the line and nodded at every person Andella introduced, dropping names that Goodiva was sure to forget. The last person was a very nice older man named Hutch. In a checkered shirt and khaki pants, he was the tallest of the group, and his eyes were full of life despite his wrinkled skin. Hutch, she was told, was the groundskeeper and groom. He was also husband to Andella.

"Groom? So there are horses?" Goodiva asked.

Hutch winked. "There are, in heated barns that hold them through the winter."

"This way if you please. I'll give you the tour, then show you to your cottage," Andella spoke through her clenched teeth, taking hold of the front of her overly long coat that cinched tight at her waist as if it were a dress. Together they climbed the front stone steps of the manor. Goodiva glanced once more to the driver who was removing her luggage. He was not headed in the same direction as her.

"Please ma'am, come along," Andella insisted.

The place was drafty and dark thanks to the late afternoon hour. She'd expected some of the remaining light to seep through. Andella moved along the halls with her back straight and nose pointed north. Goodiva made valiant attempts to keep up with the instructional tour, but it was all too overwhelming. On the lower level, there were two of everything. There were two ballrooms, one for social events, and one for family festivities. Two studies, one with a complete library and the other with more personal works, some published by previous Masters of Mayfair. The place had two parlors for formal sittings and an open television room for casual entertaining that had a billiard table and small putting green. There was a solarium that opened into the exterior garden and then led to another solarium, of the same size and beauty, with a desk, computer, and small bar. It was here, she was told, that Jaxon Price preferred to spend his days working. He also spent many of the evenings in the gardens during the summer and spring.

"It is often where the master retires to smoke his pipe," Andella said.

Andella went on and on. All of the sitting rooms, dining rooms, bathrooms made Goodiva's head spin.

"Exactly what was expected of the last estate manager? I wasn't told in the interview," asked Goodiva.

Andella head snapped left and her beady slanted eyes narrowed with a mixture of disbelief and distrust. Her thin lips drew back to reveal stark white teeth as she spoke in a nasal tone, hands clasped in front of her. "You will be expected to do what is customary, of course. Francine always did more. Such as, keep care of the budget and staff. Work with the foresters and gamekeepers to keep them on schedule. And work with the house staff to keep them all on schedule, including me. You will have your own schedule with Master Mayfair, keeping him up to date on his varying priorities."

"You keep referring to him as Master Mayfair? I thought his name—"

"He is executive producer and director Jaxon Price to the outside world. Yes, I know. That title means nothing here. At Mayfair he is Master Fikrit Mayfair," Andella said.

"I will not call him master," Goodiva snipped.

Andella smiled. "It does not have the connotation you are thinking."

"I don't care. I'm not calling any white, black, yellow man—any man—master. Period."

"I'm not done," Andella continued. "You will also arrange all repairs, organize contractors or workers from the outside. Master Mayfair does not like visitors, so you must schedule them around his temperament, so he won't see or hear them. Oh yes, and make sure the health and safety rules are followed to a tee by the staff. We've had accidents in the past."

"What kind of accidents?"

Her smile grew snide, and her tone mocking, "Nothing to worry over, just please be careful. This place is quite old and some of the halls have not been refurnished. Our premium on our insurance is quite costly. Then there are the ski lodges. Master Mayfair was considering opening them up for private rentals after his father's death. But when he moved in, he decided against it. I believe he never intends too. He prefers the seclusion, as do we."

"Okay, okay, I get it," she mumbled. The job Andella outlined seemed to be fit for a small company not a struggling writer playing housekeeper. Besides, her plan required that she get close to Jaxon Price, and these duties would push her further away. Finally, they walked through the back of the manor and she was directed to a path cutting through the snow with iced-over paved sidewalks that led to a cottage bigger than any of the houses she grew up in as a child. The home was two stories with wide windows and a circling porch. It was fairytale beautiful in the snow. Goodiva couldn't imagine this would be her place rent free. Andella again cast her a backward glance. The hostility came off her like heat from a radiator. It was time to be assertive: if she was her boss, then she needed to act the role.

"That will be all Andella. I will get settled in and then speak with Mr. Price. Let's plan to meet at eight tomorrow morning so I can give you...um...instructions, yes, on how things will be done."

The tips of Andella mouth lifted in amusement. "As you wish ma'am."

LATER THAT DAY GOODIVA finished off her unpacking. She had dumped all of the clothes from her suitcases and settled on sorting out the mess. From her bed to the dresser she folded and placed her things methodically. Then her cellphone buzzed in her purse. She'd forgotten to turn the damn thing off. She didn't need to be caught with it so soon after her arrival.

"Hello."

"Shelly, it's me."

"Hey you," Goodiva smiled.

"All settled in?" Delilah asked.

"Almost. Why are you checking on me so soon? I said I'd call you before I go to bed."

"Can't I ring my friend to make sure she is okay?"

Goodiva paused.

"What's wrong?"

"Why do you think something is wrong?" Delilah said, but could barely hide the strain in her voice.

"Because you're whispering."

"Oh, hold on," Delilah said. For a few seconds Goodiva heard doors closing.

"Hey, I'm back," she said.

"W'sup?"

"I got a weird letter today," said Delilah.

"Okay," Goodiva said and sat on the floor.

"It's from the fertility clinic that Charles and I used."

"The one you both own?"

"We're shareholders, not owners. But yes."

"Okay?"

Delilah sighed. "They want to meet with me. They said they have concerns over some lab processes that are under review."

"Wait, I'm confused. You got pregnant. What processes?"

Delilah burst into tears. "Something is wrong Shelly. They won't explain it over the phone. I have to bring the attorneys. And all of Charles' brothers are here, having meetings without me. They...they are acting as if this was something they expected. They won't tell me what is going on."

"With your insemination? No. That's not it. You're a lawyer Dee. If some process was skipped or mishandled, then I'm sure his brothers need your professional help as a shareholder."

Delilah sniffed. "Right. Right. I dunno. The letter is weird. According to Henry, several shareholders got the letters. We are leaving in the morning for New York. I'm on edge. I'm going through Charles' stuff, and every month I find something else. He lied to me so much. He had dealings with all kinds of people. I don't know the man I married."

"How can I help?"

"Listening helps. Thank you. I'll let you get settled in. I'm going to New York, but I should be back in two days. I can come visit?"

"Sure. Call the house, not my personal phone. Remember, I told you. I'm not supposed to have it."

"Oh? Damn. Sorry. Did I get you in trouble?"

"No. I'm fine."

"Have you met the owner? Who is he?"

"He hasn't met with me yet. I'll tell you more when you come to visit. Okay?"

"Okay. Love you."

"Love you. And Dee?"

"Yes?"

"It'll be fine. I promise."

"Okay, bye," Delilah said.

She hung up. Goodiva got up from the floor and put her phone back in her purse. This time she turned it off. Delilah sounded distressed. And her friend wasn't the type to be easily worried. She considered calling Queen but stopped herself. She said a silent prayer for her friend that everything was okay.

JAXON'S MONITORS ALL began to switch feeds. He could see the west side of the estate, and he located the cameras in the cottages. He wasn't sure which one she'd taken, but it only took a few minutes to find her. Her back was to the camera. She spoke on her cellphone with a hand to her slender waist. Her backside in her tight leggings could not be ignored, and he didn't resist staring at her body. Her curly hair complimented her pretty face when she turned. She sat on the floor and appeared distressed. He focused on her treachery. She wasn't with them for more than twenty-four hours and already she was breaking the rules by bringing a cellphone on to his property. He knew she couldn't be trusted.

While she talked on the phone he opened the folder that he'd put together on her life over the years. She was born Goodiva Michelle Johnson in Heidelberg, Germany. Her mother Caroline 'Luvie' Andrews was enlisted when she became pregnant and had to return to North Carolina. After giving birth, her mother, who was of Sudanese descent, married her long-time enlisted boyfriend, Goodiva's father. The family moved to Falcon Cove when Goodiva was ten after he was discharged. There was interesting information on her time in Falcon Cove. An incident of aggravated sexual misconduct with a minor by a school counselor was reported soon after her enrollment in elementary school. A police report and complaint were filed, and then dropped shortly after the investigation began. However, the teacher was fired from Falcon County School District. There was another police report of Goodiva's father getting into a physical altercation with the teacher and being arrested for it. But those charges were dropped against the teacher and the father mutually. Armand also found a missing person's report filed on the teacher a few weeks later. He was discovered dead in a well on his sister's property. The toxicity report showed he'd been drinking. It was believed that, in an attempt to bring up well water, he fell in and hit his head. He drowned. Case closed.

After a few minutes of perusing the details of her past, Jaxon looked up once more. She sat on the edge of the bed with her face in her hands. Whoever had called had seemed to upset her. If she had heeded his warning and left the cellphone behind, the caller wouldn't have caused her the distress. He felt no pity for her.

She didn't move for quite some time. But when she did, she seemed to practice a deep breathing and relaxation exercise. She got up and paced back and forth in a ritualistic manner. Her mental health file stated that she suffered from panic attacks frequently, but who didn't nowadays. Her behavior must be the attempt to calm her nerves. Once the anxiety passed, she seemed to inspect her surroundings again. Her vision swept her room and then scaled up to where his camera was discreetly tucked in the corner. She stared for longer than a minute. Jaxon stared back. The camera couldn't be seen from a single glance, but if you looked hard and long enough, you would notice the pen camera no bigger than a cigarette only partially concealed. She walked toward it. Her head cocked left as she studied something she didn't understand.

She frowned.

He waited.

What would she do? What could she do? Complain? Threaten to quit because of invasion of privacy? He'd enjoy that. They could begin the game sooner. She walked out of the room and the second camera in her cottage showed her as she went to pick up a chair in the kitchen and bring it back upstairs to her bedroom. She stood on it. She grabbed the camera and yanked it from the wall.

"Well, I didn't expect that," he said.

WAS THAT A CAMERA? Was she being watched in her bedroom by Jaxon? Or was it some devious member of the staff peering into her life? She couldn't conceive the audacity of the intrusion. Besides the camera being creepy, it was damn disrespectful. Which was comical to her, considering all of his rules were to be respected.

"No the hell you won't!" she huffed.

She marched out of her room down the stairs and into her kitchen. She got a chair and brought it back up. She stood on it for balance and found the pen camera tucked into a drilled-in hole at the corner pocket of the ceiling. She yanked on it until the wire was ripped from the wall. It was then she searched every room for more of the things. All in all, she found a total of six. The only safe space was her closet and bathroom. It was criminal to be pried on in such a manner. She had a mind to call Queen and tell her. But she realized how ridiculous the thought was and dismissed it. So after her temper simmered, she went about folding and putting up her things.

She decided to fix herself dinner when the phone rang in her cottage. She wasn't even sure where it was. After locating it she sat down in the chair.

"MASTER MAYFAIR, YOU wanted to see me?"

"What is the plan for our new manager today?" he asked.

Andella frowned. "She just arrived. We assumed she would need to get settled and we'd begin tomorrow."

"Begin immediately. I want her in her office going over the budget and preparing a plan for the winter. I expect her to report to me on what she has tomorrow before lunch. Do you understand?"

"Yes sir."

Andella left. Jaxon drummed his fingers on the surface of his desk.

"HELLO?"

"Miss Johnson?"

"Yes," she said.

"Forgive me, but the staff is waiting for you. We must go over today's readout."

"Read what?"

"Read out, ma'am. You have to walk the grounds and sign off on the workers' tasks for the end of the day. It is customary we do so in the morning, around lunch and in the evening. Please join us in the picture room on the first level near the grand kitchen. Afterwards, you must tend to the budget report and your winter report to ensure they are ready to present to Master Mayfair tomorrow."

Before she could object, the call ended.

She was under the impression that she could relax, possibly unpack and make a small dinner, then call Queen and give her an update. She looked at her watch. She sighed in defeat and located her jacket then hurried back into the house.

Three hours later, Hutch approached Jaxon. "Sir?"

Jaxon looked up from his reading. He nodded for Hutch to enter. The 70-year-old groundskeeper was his closest ally in the new world he was building. Hutch was of Turkish descent but was raised as a British citizen. He was a very close friend of Jaxon's father and an ex-MI6 agent. Though he settled into the quiet life in Colorado, Hutch was not a man to turn your back on.

"The young lady's place has been tended too. She won't discover the new surveillance."

Jaxon glanced to his laptop. "I think I intend to move my plan forward sooner than you expected. Has Dr. Ten arrived?"

"Yes sir."

"Take care of it."

"Understood, I'll prepare," he said, then turned and walked out.

Jaxon continued to read.

Chapter Ten

The staff welcomed her, but the evening dragged on. She sat in an empty kitchen and ate alone. The quiet in the large estate was strange. It was a sound of its own. She could hear herself breathe at times. When she returned to her cottage she collapsed in exhaustion and slept until midnight. It was then she felt the uncanny sense of being watched. She spent the next hour searching every corner of her cottage and found two more cameras. She had half a mind to wake Jaxon Price and demand he stop the surveillance of her. He had rules. Well, she had a few of her own.

The next day was similar. She endured the watchful scrutiny of others as she moved through her tasks. With a clipboard in hand, she was able to inspect rooms one by one. Although no one visited Mayfair, fresh linen and tidiness were requirements to prevent dust and mites in the old estate. The cleaning of the rooms looked impeccable to her, but she pretended to notice little things that had the three maids assigned to the floor buzzing around. That seemed to impress Andella a bit.

Before his lunch was prepared, she visited the kitchens and was shown how to approve of Master Mayfair's meals. He had a specific diet and favorite dishes due to medical concerns. She wondered what other medical concerns these might be. She was given the liberty to switch his meals around on the schedule. For dinner he would have roasted chicken with risotto and asparagus. It was all so boring. When she was done, the staff that closed out the house was introduced to her again. She was informed they'd meet before dinner every weekday. There was one hour left in her schedule to get his budget prepared and presented. It was an unreasonable request, but she looked forward to their first meeting. It would be her time to really confront the past and get to know the man he'd become. A small part of her still wasn't convinced that he didn't remember her.

The cellar was eleven-thousand square feet beneath the estate and only five percent of it was accessible and wired with electricity. Dark halls with sharp maze-like corners that were drafty, and empty went on forever. There were six turns from the lift to her office door that she had put to memory. She found her office without incident. She dreaded being left alone. However, alone in her office she had the liberty to relax and be unseen. There were no cameras—she checked—and if there were some in the cellar corridors, the darkness made it hard for anyone to observe her. Maybe that was why Frances' curiosity got the best of her and she ventured into the 'forbidden' room.

The first thing Goodiva did when alone was kick off her shoes and plop down in her big chair. She fished out her cellphone and turned it on. She kept it tucked inside the pouch she wore belted around her waist. Goodiva wanted to see if Delilah had responded to her text she sent, since she hadn't answered her calls. Delilah told her last night that Delilah feared there was something wrong with the fertility clinic and Noah. Her friend needed support. To her disappointment, she found no cellular signal at all in the office. There wasn't even a window to let in natural light.

"Damn," she sighed.

She tried to angle her phone differently. Not a single bar appeared. She tossed her phone and reached for the one in her office. It was an older model with raised buttons to make calls. She picked it up and listened for a tone. For some reason she half-expected not to hear one. She half-expected for it to be a prop and not even a phone. The place felt false to her. It was the vast emptiness that made her question even the simplest of things. She stared down at the buttons and saw that the number '0' was red. Underneath it was the tiny script that said Master Mayfair.

Was this the way to contact him?

She pressed the button and immediately the call connected. Several rings passed before she gave up. He was around, but not answering. When she hung up the phone Goodiva heard something outside of her door. A grinding noise. It froze her breath with trepidation. The office door was closed, thankfully. The sound didn't come across as welcoming. She listened. The noise eventually drifted away. The hairs on her arms and the back of her neck began to stand on end. She listened with her breathing growing rapid and her eyes stretched wider and wider as anxiety crept in and took over her sense of control.

"What was that?" she asked herself.

Goodiva hung up the phone. She sat still. The sound faded. She plucked her cellphone up from the desk and put it back into her pouch. She put on her shoes. The noise had all but gone by the time she reached the door, but her anxiety was at an all-time high. Goodiva pressed her ear to the cool surface and listened.

She heard nothing.

"What the hell is that noise?" she said after a few minutes of silence. Her hand slid down the surface to the doorknob. She turned and winced when the squeak of the lock disengaging clanked louder than she wished. She jumped. Could it be Andella or one of the staff coming into the cellar? Maybe a delivery man was wheeling in something and passed her door? Slow and easy, she turned the knob and pulled the door open to absolute darkness. She was greeted by nothing. The lamp cones that were spaced a few feet apart across the walls had been extinguished. Someone had purposefully put her in darkness.

Goodiva stepped back.

Her throat went dry.

It was as if the darkness outside of her door began to seep inside her office. There were shadows everywhere. She closed her eyes and opened them to cast most away. Nothingness was all she found. It was just her stupid fears, she told herself. It was all in her mind. When she absconded from Los Angeles, she suffered from panic attacks. But if she were really honest about her attacks, she would have to admit that they started shortly after she moved to America as a kid. After she moved to Falcon Cove. After she met Mr. Collins.

She reached into her pouch and removed her cellphone. She turned on the light of her phone and aimed it at the darkness. The reveal was as she as had hoped. There were no boogiemen in the shadows. The hall was empty.

Six turns. Six turns and you're out of here. Fuck this spooky place. Get to the lift and go back upstairs. You're the boss. You don't have to be confined to a cellar. You can take any of the rooms upstairs to be your office. Are you dumb? Why are you even down here?

She silenced the voice in her head and started away with hurried steps. She was about to turn right to return the way she came, but she heard another noise. Immediately she aimed the light on her cellphone into the darkness approaching her. She squinted to see beyond its reach.

"Hello?" she called out.

Her voice emptied in the darkness and nothing spoke back to her. Her instincts had saved her many times in the past. Even as a child. And Delilah always told her and Queen to trust the feeling inside of them when they knew something bad was coming. *God put that feeling in little girls for a reason.* Her best friend would say.

"Hello?" she said again and again.

There was no sound, not even a whimper of an echo. Before she realized it, she had taken several steps back in retreat and with each step backwards the darkness advanced. Or did it? The fear settled into the pit of her stomach and her instinct to flee was all she had left. She'd find another way to the lift instead of the way she came. Without hesitation, she did just that. At first, she walked rapidly from one corridor to another. But the faster she went the more her panic increased. In each hall she was confronted by extreme darkness. The absence of light was intentional.

"Hello. Hello? Help!" Running in the dark was dangerous, especially when she didn't know where she was headed. She turned and fled down the next hall but was stopped by a wall. She hit it hard. She had to put both hands to the surface to keep from slipping to the ground. Her lungs were punched clean of air. All she wanted was to breathe again. Instead, she panted hard, feeling as if her anxiety would squeeze the passageway to her lungs shut. Fear did strange things to common sense—suddenly she didn't know left from right or up from down. Wheezing for breath, she backed away from the dark into the dark. She retraced her steps. There was a faint glow of light at the bend of another corner. She prayed it was the way out. But inside she knew it couldn't be. Careful to keep her phone light in front of her, she ventured toward the unknown. At the end of the next hall there was nothing to be found but a door. It was eight feet tall and four feet wide. It was made of darkest wood or painted black with intricate carvings. To the left of the door was a keypad. This hall was not like the others.

The hall was for the door.

Goodiva looked behind her. There was no one with her, though she sensed she was not alone. She approached the door fast. To the right, up in the corner of the ceiling, was a camera. She waved at it.

"Mr. Price? Hi. It's me, your new estate manager. I'm sorry, but I'm lost down here. Can you send someone to help me?"

The camera of course didn't answer. But the door with the keypad and the red light above it beeped. The red light flashed green. She could hear the locking system disengage.

"Is there a way out through here?" she asked the camera.

There was no answer. She took a step forward then paused.

"I was told that this room was off limits."

"No answer."

It felt strange. *Why was the door here, and locked? What was behind it?* "Mr. Price can you send someone to get me please?"

The door locked. The green light above the keypad flashed red.

"What the hell is going on?" she demanded.

The lamplight in the hall shut off. She screamed again. Panic swept through her so powerfully she stumbled, and her fingers fumbled to work her phone. Before she could capture it in her hand, it slipped away to the floor. Then, just as quickly, someone grabbed her as she knelt to pick it up. An arm around her waist and a hand to her mouth forced her back up against the tall frame of a man. Goodiva choked on her surprised scream and gagged. The hand pushed a cloth over her mouth and nose. The strong ammonia-like smell was all she could take in during her struggle. And soon the darkness in her mind competed with the darkness of the hall. Soon the darkness owned her.

JAXON REMOVED HIS POCKET watch. It was his father's. The only personal possession of the old man's that he kept. Since he despised most modern technology now, the watch kept time perfectly for him. He flipped open the golden hatch and checked the hour and the minute. The second hand ticked time away. She was more than twenty minutes late. He sent word down to her office for her to join him half an hour ago with his new budget. He didn't invite many to dine with him. In fact, dining alone was half-expected. The staff stood still and silent.

"Master Mayfair."

Andella approached in the obedient way she often did. "We've checked the office. Ms. Johnson isn't there."

"What do you mean she isn't there?" he asked from his wheelchair.

"She's not there, sir. I sent Hutch to check her cottage. She isn't there either. She hasn't been seen since she went into the cellar. Hutch and the men are searching for her. The cellars can be confusing."

"This is nonsense," he said. He forced his wheelchair to glide back and rolled away. "I'll locate her. Have her things packed and ready. Send for Ahmed, he is to drive her out of Mayfair immediately. She's fired."

"Yes, sir," Andella said obediently. "Francine will arrive tomorrow sir, if you wish."

LATER THAT EVENING, after the search for Ms. Johnson ended and half of Jaxon's staff was dismissed, he went to the cellars. Ahmed and Hutch both accompanied him.

"*Salam alaykum, Abu Fikrit (the son of Fikrit)*," Dr. Nine bowed his head.

Jaxon's eyes remained trained on Goodiva. She lay on the medical table, covered by a thin sheet, sedated.

"How is she?" he asked.

"Fine sir, we were just finishing."

"And?"

"She's healthy. Her vitals are strong. She has no tattoos, no piercings, no signs of surgery or augmentation. She does have a condition called hexa-dactyly." The doctor drew up the sheet at the corner to reveal Goodiva's foot. "A sixth toe. It's a birth defect. We could remove it if you like."

A sly smile tipped the corner of Jaxon's mouth. He was very aware of her perfect imperfection. "Is it in her genetics?"

"It is," the doctor said.

"Leave it," Jaxon replied.

"We will have completed our report after her blood work analysis is done." Dr. Nine glanced to the equipment they would use to do the tests.

"Make sure she is clothed and shown respect," he said after a glance to her folded clothes on the chair. He knew they were professionals, but he felt a burn of anger at the thought that they'd even dared touch her.

Dr. Ten stepped before him. "Sir, there is something else you should know."

Jaxon's right brow lifted.

"We had to perform an ultrasound and a vaginal probe," he said.

"Why?"

"Procedure. She had an implant. An IUD. Birth control."

"What does that mean for fertility?" Jaxon asked.

"We're not sure how long she's used it. It wasn't done here in the States, or we would have found it in her medical records. We've removed it."

He glanced to her. "Did it harm her? This removal?"

"No, she is fine sir. But as for fertility, I'll need to examine her in a few days to ensure we have no scarring or issues. It may take time before she is ready for the procedure."

"We're done with your examinations today. She's been through enough."

"But sir, we agreed to do—"

Jaxon gave the doctor a silencing look. The man bowed his head in reverence.

"Yes sir. Nothing more needed."

"Let's be clear," he said to both doctors. "I didn't approve of the removal of anything from her. In the future you make no medical decisions about her health or fertility without my consent."

"*Na'am, sayyidi*—Yes, sir," the doctors said in unison.

THE PAIN SPEARED HER skull so sharply she woke with a deep sob trapped in her throat. It was the worst headache she'd ever felt. She turned on the bed and tried to open her eyes, but to do so caused her more discomfort.

"Ow," she winced when she sat up. Goodiva touched her brow. She expected to feel blood or some terrible wound. She did not. She was fine. With extreme effort she opened her eyes wider to chase away the haze in her mind. Her vision was unable to lock on anything solid, so she closed her eyes again. She sat fully upright. That too sent a sharp pang of agony through her skull. Then her memory returned. She was in the hall. She was at a door and someone attacked her.

"Oh crap!"

She was clothed, she even had her shoes on, but she felt strange. Between her legs. Not a sexual ache, but still an ache that spread through her pelvis and throbbed like a beacon of torture.

"Geesh," she said. "What happened?"

Her vision swiveled left and right as she swept the room for an explanation. She was indeed in a room. There was a bed. There was a table and chairs. There was a gas fireplace and above it a television. The only eerie thing about her confined space was that the room was windowless.

Goodiva tried to discern where she was. There were three doors to the room. One to the front of her, one to the left and one to the right. All doors were closed. She felt afraid. This place was not familiar. Again, she tried to remember what exactly happened. She was in the hall. It was dark. She was scared. Someone had attacked her. A person, who was both tall and strong, had grabbed her. He covered her mouth and then there was something else. What? A doctor?

Goodiva put both hands up to her head and held her skull tight to try to understand her memory. None of it made sense. She couldn't stop the pain of recollection. She'd been drugged. She was certain of it. After what felt like an eternity the strength returned to her legs and she was able to walk without difficulty. She went to the large door to the room and found there was no doorknob. She stared at the intricate carvings. Her memory flashed to the other side of the door. The keypad that had blinked from red to green. She was now in the room. Locked inside.

It all made sense to her. Goodiva panicked. She hit the door with both open palms. She hit it repeatedly. "Hello? Hello! I'm trapped in here! Hel-llllllloooooooooooo! Can anybody hear me!" She beat her fist on the door until they were raw. "Please! Somebody! I'm locked up in here!"

Defeated, she wiped her tears away with the back of her hands. It took her several long deep breaths to calm the mounting panic she felt in her chest. She practiced and practiced breathing. How did air get in? Did air get in? She couldn't capture her breath.

"I can't...I can't...be here," she wheezed. She went to her knees and bent until her brow touched the cool floor. She'd rarely been able to control her panic by herself. Attacks could cripple her in the past. They had been increasingly worse since she was ten years old. But today she found an inner strength something buried deep inside of her.

Slow and calm, she lifted her head. She was alive. She was fine. She had to focus, and she did. She noticed the two other doors in the room she hadn't tried. A calm settled in over her racing heart and she mentally relaxed. The key was to practice her breathing through her fears and anxiety. Even if the fear she carried was justified. She approached the door, hopeful that it would be an exit. However, inside she found only a bathroom and a shower.

"Okay. Okay. Everything is okay," she said as her bottom lip began to quiver. A mixture of fear and dread shimmied through her in cool waves. Goodiva went to the other door. She threw it open to find another room, a smaller one than the one from before. There was a cot for a toddler or child and children's drawings on the wall. She flicked on the light to reveal more. There had to be at least fifty drawings. They wallpapered the room. There was a toddler size desk with a notepad and crayons. There were toy trucks and other little things for a child to play with.

Children's drawings were everywhere. Several were taped to the wall. The images went from odd to weird, as the child depicted a life of solitude and loneliness.

"This is awful."

When she was ten, her mother and father were still together. They took her to the doctors who made her sit with a box of crayons and draw her pain. She tried. She remembered the terror and the shame of putting in the pictures what Mr. Collins had made her do. She remembered how scared she felt when the adults questioned her to see if she was telling the truth. And she remembered the pact she made with her two friends to keep the secret of their revenge. That day she didn't draw the pictures from her mind.

And just like Delilah said, the evil left their lives and never returned. Some secrets are better left buried.

As she scanned one drawing to the next, she realized something that couldn't be explained away. Just like the child or children who drew these images, she was trapped.

"MISS GOODIVA JOHNSON has been removed from the property."

Andella stood at his side. The rest of the staff had been summoned, and they all gathered with keen interest over the news about the new hire who had been fired after only a day. They'd had many estate managers before. None of them were as young or beautiful as Goodiva. Jaxon spied on the staff. He had heard the whispers about how long she would last. He intended to explain her exit, to put the gossip on the correct course.

From his wheelchair he addressed his employees. "It is unfortunate that I have to share this news. Michelle Johnson has been terminated," Jaxon announced to his staff. "For dereliction of duties. Violation of her privacy contract. She was unable to perform to the expectations I set for all of you. Frances will resume her role as estate manager. Also, I've decided to cut short your tenure for the winter."

Several employees groaned. The job at Mayfair was the most lucrative one they could find during the winter months in the Cove. He continued, "All of you will be paid a full salary."

The staff clapped.

"Friday you will be dismissed. Transportation will be provided to take you out of the mountain. That will be all," he said to them. One by one they left. Hutch was the last to give him an obedient nod before walking out of the door. Jaxon Price sat still for a moment. When certain he would not be disturbed, he pushed the button on his wheelchair and rolled himself out of his suite into the room he had next to it. He stepped out of the chair and walked over to the cellphone Hutch had left for him on top of the desk.

Dee: *"Sorry I didn't text sooner. I have crazy news. Call me as soon as you can."*

Jaxon stared at the text message. Dee could stand for Delilah Montgomery. He decided to respond.

Response: "*Hi. My phone died.*"

The phone immediately rang in his hand. A FaceTime request came up on the screen. He declined and sent another text.

Response: "*Can't FaceTime right now. U okay?*"

Dee: "*No! I need to talk to you. Queen can't be reached. It's the fertility clinic. They are telling me they made a mistake with my insemination. Call me.*"

Response: "*What? I can't call. I can't be seen with the phone.*"

Dee: "*I need to talk to you now! I can't do this over the phone! I'm being watched! Charles' brothers. I need you Shelly.*"

Response: "*Things are weird here too. I'm leaving. Where are you? In New York?*"

Dee: "*I'm at the penthouse on the Upper East Side. Why are you leaving? What happened?*"

Response: "*I quit. It turns out that the man who hired me is Jaxon Price. He's here. I can't stay here. I'm leaving. I'll meet you in New York. I'll come to you.*"

The phone once again rang in his hand. At least this time she didn't bother to FaceTime. He sent the call to voicemail and texted.

Dee: "*Call Queen! Get her out there to pick you up from Mayfair. Call her now!*"

Response: "*No. I quit. He's not the same person. He has some kind of memory loss. I don't think he knows me. I'm leaving now. I will call you when I land. Stay where you are.*"

Dee: "*Okay. I'll tell Queen you are headed here. Just get here soon. I need you.*"

Response: "*Hold on. I'm on my way!*"

Jaxon powered off the phone. He opened the drawer to his desk and threw it inside. Delilah Montgomery's trap had been set and sprung. Queen Douglas' trap should snap on her any day. Both women should be out of his way and unable to stop his plans. He then went to his desk and punched in the access code. The rooms to his lower level residence were at his fingertips. He pulled up the one room in particular that he cared most about.

There he found his goddess. She paced a tight circle in the room with her face in her hands. The door to the bathroom was open. The wide-angle lens of the camera built into the television gave him a 180-degree view. Jaxon rested the side of his face in his hand. He waited. After a while she dropped back onto the bed and buried her face in the pillow.

He smiled.

"Tomorrow. Let's start tomorrow kitten," he said.

Chapter Eleven

*L*ittle Mermaid was her favorite lunch box. Her mother bought her every-thing new for her first day in her new school. The lunch box and matching book-bag were the most exciting part of what her mother promised would be a good adventure. She sat obedient and quiet. Goodiva was determined to make the best impression possible on the adults staring down at her. Though Goodiva was born in Denver, soon after her birth she was taken back to Germany to live with her enlisted parents. At the age of nine her mother decided to relocate back to Colorado again, this time to a mountain town called Falcon Cove. Her mother explained it all to the adults. Goodiva listened to her history as her mother spoke about her transitioning into the American education system that was markedly different than the school system in Germany. While she strug-gled not to focus on the loss of lifelong friends, she couldn't help but notice the defensive pitch in her mother's voice when questioned.

"Has she had all of her shots?" one adult asked.

"The shot record is in your hand, I've already told you my paperwork is complete," her mother said.

"Yes, ma'am, what about her transcripts? We haven't received—"

"I need the principal. This has already been done by that administrator Mr. Collins."

"Collins isn't an AVP, he's our school counselor ma'am," the woman of-fered.

"I don't care if he is the janitor. He was the only person here when I came last week and he said things were in order," her mother shot back.

"Excuse me ladies, can I be of assistance?" a tall man in dark brown trousers and a pressed white shirt asked. He had the nicest smile, with straight *white teeth and golden hair. Goodiva stared up at him understanding he was someone important.*

"Ah, there you are Mr. Collins. Yes, yes, maybe you can help us," the woman said.

A young girl was then dragged into the office by the arm. She protested quite loudly, with a thick ponytail of tangled hair that sat at the top of her head but flopped around. It didn't look like her hair was combed often.

"Let me go! Let go of me! Leeeeeet meeeeeeee goooooooooooooooooooo! Nooooooooow!"

The young girl made such a scene everyone in the office stopped to look at her.

"Let me go! Let me go! Let me go! Let me go!"

"That will be enough Queen," another adult said, and gave her a hard yank. "Enough. I am calling your mother and you will be sent home!"

"I don't care! I hate you and I hate this school!" Queen shouted.

The principal of the school walked out from his office. "What is all the fuss out here?" He was a short white man with a balding scalp and a round belly. He glared at everyone in the office. The young girl was released. She crossed her arms in defiance and pouted. Though Queen appeared tough and ready to fight, she silenced at the sight of the real authority.

"Principal Carter, I can handle this," Mr. Collins offered. All the adults looked on concerned. Mr. Collins smiled at Queen like a proud father would. "What seems to be the problem Ms. Davis?"

"Should I tell him or will you?" the teacher asked.

"Doug threw a pencil at me," Queen tried to explain.

"He tossed a pencil at the person seated next to you. It accidentally hit you. And what did you do?" the adult who brought her into the office asked.

The principal waited for a response, as did Mr. Collins.

Queen offered none.

"Principal Carter, she slapped the student. I can't have her in my classroom any longer. She's dangerous, disruptive and defiant"

"The three D's!" Queen laughed.

The adults were stunned. The teacher shook her heed in disgust. "I want her suspended."

"I disagree Mr. Carter," Mr. Collins said.

"Of course, you do," Ms. Daniels gave an exasperated sigh and crossed her arms.

"Calm down," Collins said. "I'm working with Queen. Let me deal with this incident."

The principal stared at Queen and her mocking grin. He then glanced to Mr. Collins. He shook his head. "Ms. Davis, please call Queen's mother. Have her see Mr. Collins. And place a call to the parents of Daniel Thomas to ask that one of them come to the school for a meeting."

"Yes, sir."

"Queen, go to my office and wait for me there," Mr. Collins said.

"Yes sir, Mr. Collins," Queen gave him a military salute. She rolled her eyes at her teacher and looked quite smug to have won the battle.

Queen had to pass Goodiva as she headed for the door. She cut a look at Goodiva. It must have been the first moment she noticed her. Goodiva smiled in an attempt at friendship. Queen was unimpressed. Queen stuck out her tongue at her and then left. Goodiva wasn't sure what she'd make of the new school. But she had to admit she did like the girls attending it.

Mayfair Estates, Day 1

Goodiva opened her eyes. She hadn't dreamed in a very long time. If she did, it was about a movie or book she had read. This time she dreamed of the past. She never enjoyed revisiting it. She sat up in the bed, suffering severe stomach pangs that often preceded anxiety.

Things had changed. In the corner of the room was her luggage. All of her things had been brought in while she slept. To her left was a tray of food, a pitcher of water and a small plate of peeled, sliced fruit. Feeling nauseous from the sight of it all, she leaped to her feet and ran into her bedroom. She reached the commode in time and emptied her stomach. When she was done, she flushed and fell flat to her back.

Goodiva stared up at the ceiling while she tried to calm her fears. *What was this? A kidnapping? Torture? And by who? And for what?* She asked herself a hundred questions and came back with twice as many in answers.

"My phone," she said.

Goodiva pushed up from the floor with her hands. She returned to the room, finding herself weakening with each step. Was she still drugged? She wasn't sure, but she didn't feel good. She searched the luggage and her things for her pouch. Even though she remembered she had the phone with her in the hall when she was attacked, she prayed it would have been brought in with her belongings. There was no phone. Enraged, she tore through her things trying to find it. She found her laptop instead.

The last of her strength had gone. She literally crawled back to bed. Once on top of the mattress, she opened her laptop. She remembered that there was no internet in Mayfair and her heart sank with grief. Delilah told her to get a hotspot, and she refused. She believed she could use the Wi-Fi on her phone. Defeated, she tossed the laptop to the bed. She screamed and screamed for release from her prison until her voice went hoarse.

She glanced to the food and her anger took complete control of her senses. She staggered from the bed and destroyed the offering. The food, bowl of fruit and pitcher crashed to the floor. In tears, she went to the corner of the room and waited. She sat there for several long hours. She drifted to sleep before she shot up awake again. No one had come. She had no real sense of time, but she found a knife and fork that came with the food. She kept it and she stayed in the corner. Minutes ticked by, time extended, then it disappeared, and her anger slipped away with it. Before long exhaustion began to settle in over her illness and her eyes fluttered shut. She couldn't resist sleep.

Hidden Park Elementary, 2002

"Give it back!" Goodiva pleaded.

"Or what? What will you do? Huh? Huh Gaaa-diiii-vavavaaa. What kind of girl is named after chocolate balls? The kind that comes to school with a lunch that smells like monkey balls!"

It was a stupid joke, but the kids laughed.

The bucktooth boy with chapped lips and pear-shaped head had been taunting her ever since she accidentally stepped on his shoes. He was relentless. She was on the verge of tears when he got in her face, mocking her. He looked like some creature out of her Goosebumps *books. She almost told him so when the kids began to laugh at her. Now she was surrounded. About ten of them waited to see what she would do. It was only her third day at the school and already she was a joke. And even worse, she hadn't made a single friend.*

"Give it back to me," she pleaded. "Please!"

He held up her lunch box and made a face as if it stinks. "Monkey balls! Monkey balls!"

This time Goodiva wept. She'd never encountered someone so mean. In her frustration, she began to yell at the bully in German, and all the kids laughed at her speaking foreign words.

Then, from out of nowhere, the bully took a hit to the back of his head and dropped to his knees. Her lunchbox fell and popped open. Her sandwich and chips spilled out. She looked up from her lunch to the girl behind the bully. Queen stood with her fists ready to take another swing. All of the children around them took a collective step back. Another girl, smaller in stature, touched Queen's arm and took a bold step forward.

"If you move one inch, Jamison, Queenie gonna stomp your little pea brain to dust! She part Jamaican and can do it too."

The kids began to back away. The young girl then looked at Goodiva and smiled. "It's okay. He talk big, but he only fight girls. Ain't that right Jamison? Bet you won't go over there to the basketball courts and tell Robbie he smell like monkey balls."

The one named Queen kicked him in the back. It couldn't have been hard, but Jamison howled as if she broke it. He held the back of his head and cried like a big baby. Three kids ran away shouting they would go get an adult. The others snickered and thirsted for a fight. The bell would ring soon for them to go into school. Goodiva had wandered to the side of the school and run into the mean kid. And now she was in awe of her saviors.

Jamison didn't move from the ground. He held his head and cried. The strange girl with pretty long-lashed eyes went to her lunch box and put her lunch back inside. She dusted it off and handed to her. "Hi, I'm Delilah. My friends call me Dee. What's your name?"

"Good...ah...Goodiva," she stammered.

"Really?" Delilah looked back at Queen who continued to stare down at Jamison, waiting for him to make a move. "What's your middle name?"

"Michelle," Goodiva said.

"I like it! We are going to call you Shelly. Okay? Shelly. No one will make fun of you with a name like Shelly."

Goodiva nodded in agreement. "I like the name Shelly."

"Let's go see Mr. Collins and tell him what Jamison did. He's the counselor and real nice. He'll take care of you. Besides being a goofball, Jamison is a tattle-tale. He'll make it out to be all our fault if we don't tell first."

"Thank you Dee," Goodiva said.

Delilah dropped her arm around Goodiva's shoulder and grinned. "That's what friends are for."

Mayfair Estates, Day 2

Goodiva opened her eyes. She lay on the floor in the cool room. Had she fallen asleep again? She must have, because she felt more rested than she did before. She couldn't tell if her stomach hurt from hunger or her distress. The room wasn't completely dark. The light in the bathroom was on. Goodiva frowned. Her last memory was of her fear and anger while she paced the room and screamed at her kidnapper to be freed. She destroyed the room. Her clothes were taken from the suitcases and thrown everywhere. The food was splattered on the floor. That is what she remembered.

However, it was not what she found.

The food she had spilled was gone. A new tray with the same meal and plastic pitcher of water was placed exactly where the old tray had been left. Instead of silverware, she was now given a plastic fork and knife. Goodiva slowly got to her feet. She glanced to her things. The clothes she had tossed about were all neatly folded and placed on the end of the bed. The suitcases were once again standing and neatly pushed to the corner of the room.

"Where the hell are you!" she shouted to no one. She searched the ceiling and walls for a camera. She went to the lamps by the bed and turned them on. She spun around, looking for her kidnapper, but she was light-headed from the lack of food and water. "Where are you!"

With no answer to the mystery or her pain, she glanced to the food again, thirsting for just a drop of it. Whoever it was, was definitely concerned about her eating and keeping healthy. The concern made her trust the food even less. She believed her refusal to eat had piqued some kind of extra attention from her kidnapper. He or she had to be watching her. How else would they know what she had done? How the hell did they get inside and she not wake up?

Then her eyes caught sight of something that didn't belong. A newspaper had been left on the bed. She walked over to find that it was the *Los*

Angeles Times, and it was dated June 24, 2016. The date wasn't something she remembered at first, but the horror of that day did immediately surface thanks to the picture and byline: JAXON PRICE IN NEAR-FATAL AC-CIDENT. With a shaky hand, she picked up the paper. The mangled remains of the burned car gave her heart palpitations. The accident that destroyed his life and hers flashed up from her memory. She sat on the bed and re-read the article. When music in the room began to play, Goodiva looked up to the television. A rainbow swirl spun around the television moving in harmony with the lyrics.

The songstress was Lisa Fischer and the song was "How Can I Ease the Pain". Over and over Lisa sang the question over betrayal and redemption.

"Stop," she said, as if swatting away a mosquito, and kept reading.

The music played on.

"...a fool for love is a fool for pain..."

"Stop it!" Goodiva threw the newspaper across the floor and fought back her tears. She staggered and sat on the bed. "Turn it off!"

The song stopped. Goodiva put her hands to her head to force the lyrics from overruling her distressed thoughts. But Lisa Fischer's song continued to play in her head. She was an idiot. Armand didn't hire her to help Jaxon. This was their revenge.

The song began to play again.

"How can I ease the pain..." Lisa Fischer wailed at the highest pitch of her voice.

It was all planned. Goodiva looked upon the television with a new awareness. He watched her. He was watching now.

The song ended. Her stare never wavered.

"It's you isn't it?" she said to the television. "Jaxon?"

Goodiva wiped her tears.

"I know you see me. Can you hear me?"

Of course he could. That was part of it. Her suffering while he listened and watched. There was no answer.

"I'm sorry. For everything I've done. I'm very sorry. You can call the police. Call them. I will confess everything. But a confession won't change anything will it? Twixt and his brother are dead. My only crime was leaving you behind with them. I didn't cause the accident. What you really need is answers. Right? If you come down here and meet with me, I will tell you the real reason why I ran away that night. And why when I found out you were here; I took the job. Let's talk. We should have talked long ago."

The television flashed and a video popped up on screen. It was an interview on the red carpet from Access Hollywood. Goodiva stood next to Twixt. They'd done it a few weeks before she met Jaxon Price and her world was changed.

Reporter: "*So when is the tour Twixt? Can we ask?*"

Twixt: "*You can ask, but I won't tell because you will hold me to it.*"

The reporter laughed. Goodiva grinned with adoration of her man.

Twixt: "*Seriously, the tour dates are going to be announced next month.*"

Reporter: "*Goodiva, are you here promoting your new movie Hollyswirl?*"

Goodiva: "*Yes! It releases on Netflix this summer. It's about the industry—music, that is. I play myself, a DJ slash musician girlfriend.*"

Goodiva walked over to the television and stared at the interview in disbelief.

Reporter: "*Who else is in it?*"

Goodiva: "*Jussie Smollett and Willow Smith are both my co-stars.*"

Reporter: "*Oh that sounds delicious!*"

They all agreed. Reed smiled proudly at her.

Reporter: "*Okay girl, tell me who you're wearing?*"

Goodiva: "*My dress is Roberto Cavalli. My diamonds are from Eve Battaglia's collection, and my shoes and purse are from House of Mirabella.*" She took a step back and turned. Reed helped her with the train of the dress to make sure she didn't step on it.

Reporter: "*Wow! Nice! Nice! I love Eve Battaglia's jewels. Anything Battaglia.*"

Goodiva: "*Me too. But this Cavalli is my dream dress.*"

Reporter: "*Of course. Twixt, what are you wearing?*"

Goodiva: "*Oh, he's wearing Versace. Isn't he handsome?!*"

Reporter: "*He sure is. How long have you two been together?*"

Goodiva: "*Two years,*" she beamed.

Twixt: "*Seems like longer.*"

They all shared a laugh. The television switched off. The screen returned to a swirl of rainbow colors. Again, he played an old-school tune. But this time the lyrics rolled up the screen. Goodiva frowned. Miki Howard's song "Baby Be Mine" came through the television.

"What is this?"

"*...I've been trying to tell myself I don't need you....*" Miki sang.

Goodiva shook her head in disbelief. "You coward! You play this sick game instead of facing me!" She wiped her runny nose with her sleeve. "What's your end game? You want to destroy me? Torture me with these pathetic songs?!"

Miki sang "Baby Be Mine", over and over again.

"You want to break me? You can't! You evil bastard!"

"Turn it off! Now!" she shouted at the television.

"STOP the damn music!" she shouted.

The music stopped playing.

Goodiva wept.

Silence answered.

"Please," she sobbed. "I was scared. I thought they were going to kill me. I couldn't do anything. I just couldn't. So I ran. I'm sorry. I'm very sorry. Please. I'm so sorry!"

The television blinked off. Gone was the rainbow swirl. She was left in silence. Goodiva wept so hard her body shook all over.

"I'm sorry," she cried to herself.

She continued to weep until all of her tears were spent. The television didn't come on. Nothing happened. The hunger pangs were so severe she felt a cramp in her side and back. She glanced over at the food. She realized that if she didn't eat she'd get sick. And maybe that was the best choice. Maybe being sick would force Jaxon Price to stop the torture and free her. Weak from her grief and anxiety, she got to her feet. She walked into the bathroom on shaky legs. She turned on the faucet in the sink and stuck her head under the running water. She drank as much as she could. And it helped. Tired, she wanted a shower but didn't bother. She went back to the bed. She kicked the folded clothes off the bed and pulled the covers over her head. She wept until sleep claimed her.

Hidden Park Elementary, 2002

"She needs to see Mr. Collins," Delilah said.

The assistant principal looked down at the three girls. Delilah held Goodiva's hand in a protective manner. Queen stood to her left, with her arms crossed as her guard.

"Go to class," the A.P. said.

"We need to see Mr. Collins. Matt Jamison pushed Shelly behind the school. We want to report it as assault."

"Assault?" the A.P. frowned.

Delilah gave him a defiant toss of her chin. "Assault means an attempt or act of physical violence against another person."

The A.P. stared at Delilah in shock then snapped out of it. He sighed. "She can go to the office and you two can go to class," the A.P. said as he directed kids to keep moving in the hall.

"She's new to the school. She'll get lost. Let Queen take her for protection, or I will tell the adults you didn't help us after she'd been hurt," Delilah said.

"Fine. Move it along ladies. Just go to the office."

Delilah smiled at Goodiva. "Don't worry, Queen has your back. You'll be okay with her."

Queen nodded and took Goodiva's hand and said, "Mr. Collins will take care of you."

Delilah then walked off with her book-bag flapping against her back.

"Mr. Collins. He's the principal? Right?" Goodiva asked.

"No, silly. He's our counselor. He's really cool. I go to his office all the time. You just have to be nice to him. He keeps me out of trouble," Queen bragged.

"Oh? You and Dee go to this school from the beginning? Since kindergarten?" Goodiva asked.

"Kindergarten? You have a funny accent."

"I do? In Germany we pronounce it kindergarten. It means garden for kids," Goodiva smiled.

"Is that what it means? Cool. Yes. Me and Queen have been best friends before that. We live not too far from each other. She's smart and bossy but she's the best. She likes you."

"She does?" Goodiva asked.

Queen smiled. "We saw you out there with Jamison acting all tough. Delilah asked me who you were and I told her I saw you in the office the other day. She said she liked your ponytail. And that's why we came over and kicked his butt. Because Dee liked you."

Queen opened the door to the office. Goodiva went inside.

"What are you doing in here Queen?" the school secretary said from behind the counter.

"I'm bringing her to Mr. Collins. She was bullied by Tyler Jamison today."

The secretary narrowed her eyes on Queen as if she didn't trust her. "She can go into the office. You go to class."

Queen ignored her and took Goodiva by the hand. She threw open her counselor door and pulled her inside. He was on the phone. He looked up, surprised.

"Hi Peter. This is Goodiva. She's in trouble," Queen announced.

Mr. Collins smiled at them both. He nodded for them to come in.

"He's cool. You'll see," Queen whispered.

Day 5

Goodiva's lids fluttered. She had heard a noise. The room was in total darkness, but her mind was sharp. It was her weakness that kept her very still. It was debilitating. She'd fasted before. Going without food shouldn't have affected her so badly as long as she stayed hydrated. It must have been her emotional state that drained her. She turned her head to the sound of movement in her room. She could not see anything. She tried to lift her head. She could not. She wasn't alone.

"Jaxon?" she said.

A soft kiss was placed upon her forehead.

"Respect," the person said in return.

She drifted back to sleep.

An eternity later she shot upright in bed. Music. She glanced to the television. Glenn Jones' song "We've Only Just Begun—The Romance Is Not Over" played. Her stomach hurt so bad she was aching. She drew back the covers and managed to stand. She went into the bathroom and used it, then turned on the tap. She drank from it so the dryness in her mouth and throat went away. Too weak to return to bed, she fell asleep right there on the bathroom floor. Glenn Jones continued to sing to her as she slipped away.

Hidden Park Elementary, 2002

"*What seems to be the problem?*" Mr. Collins asked.

Goodiva sat in the chair in front of his desk. Queen went around the desk to stand next to the counselor. She put her arm around the chair he sat in and looked genuinely happy. Since Goodiva met Queen she'd never seen her smile so bright. Her new friend brimmed with happiness.

"*Henry Jamison was being mean to her. He called her Monkey Balls and made fun of her name,*" Queen shared.

Mr. Collins looked concerned.

"*What's your name?*" Mr. Collins asked.

"*Goodiva Michelle Johnson,*" she replied.

"*We call her Shelly,*" Queen said.

Mr. Collins nodded. "*I like the name Shelly. It fits you.*"

Goodiva nodded. "*I think so too.*"

"*No one should ever bully you. Make you feel like you aren't special. Because little girls are very special. Do you know that?*"

Goodiva glanced to Queen, who nodded her head. So she nodded her head.

"*Stand up for yourself Goodiva. Deal?*"

"*Yes,*" she replied.

"*Good girl. I will have a talk with Jamison and his parents.*"

"*Okay,*" Goodiva said.

"*You're new to the school, right? I met you and your mother the other day?*"

"*Yes sir,*" Goodiva responded.

"*Well, it can be confusing here. I'm going to give you a hall pass. Come see me at two pm today. We'll take a look at your assignments and make sure you understand everything.*"

"*Can I have a pass too? Can I come see you today too?*" Queen asked.

Mr. Collins smiled. "*Not today Queen. I'll give you a pass for tomorrow. Okay?*"

"*Okay,*" Queen said.

Mr. Collins wrote passes for both of them. He then told them to hurry to class. When she and Queen were out of the office and in the hall, Queen stopped. "*You go on. I forgot to tell him something.*"

"*But you'll be late to class,*" Goodiva said with concern. "*The announcements are almost over.*"

Queen shrugged. "*I'll see you at recess.*"

Goodiva stood there unsure for a moment. She felt safest with Queen around. But Queen wasn't in her class. Neither was Delilah. She wouldn't see them until recess, and possibly lunch. She would have to stand up for herself just like Mr. Collins said. And for some reason she felt strong enough that day to do it.

Same day

"Drink," a man said, and lifted her head from the pillow with his hand cupping her nape. She blinked awake. Jaxon was at her bedside. He leaned in from his wheelchair. He wore that half-leather mask that covered the side of his face and made him scary. But she could see the fire of concern burning hot in his brown eyes.

"Drink," he insisted.

"Please let me go."

The glass was forced to her lips. The water spilled from the corners of her mouth and went down her neck. And she drank as he insisted. She gulped it down. She was too tired and too weak to do anything more than drink. He then forced two pills into her mouth. She gagged, surprised. He gave her more to drink. She swallowed it all. When it was over, she felt she could breathe freely. He set the glass down. Her lids were weighted by her weakness, so it was hard to see him clearly. His chair moved back away from the bed. The noise sounded familiar. It was the sound of something dragging and grinding gears. It was the noise she heard when she was in her office. The noise that drew her out of the office. She realized it was the motor of his chair.

"Jaxon, please, wait."

He didn't. He wheeled himself to the open door. He then wheeled himself out of the room and was gone.

"Wait!" she said and nearly fell out of the bed.

"Let me go!" she yelled.

Goodiva pulled herself upright. The lights to her room flickered on and off, then on. She was blinded by the brightness. She had no concept of time, but she knew days had to have passed. She glanced over to see food was brought in. If she had been awake and stronger, she could have easily taken him out and escaped. Her plan had backfired on her.

"No one should ever bully you. Make you feel like you aren't special. Because little girls are very special. Do you know that?"

Goodiva glanced to Queen who nodded her head. She nodded her head as her friend instructed.

"Stand up for yourself Goodiva. Deal?"

"Yes," she replied.

"Good girl," Mr. Collins said with a smile.

Goodiva forced herself to sit up. She got to the point of standing. She supported herself on the bed to walk around to the other side. With one hand on the mattress for aid she sat in front of the tray of food. It was different. He'd brought her soup with fruit and grilled cheese sandwiches. It all smelled divine. Goodiva ate in a famished state. She stuffed her mouth and swallowed, barely chewing. She drank from the pitcher as if she were trapped in the Sahara for weeks. She burned her tongue on the soup, but it tasted so good. When she was done, she burst into tears. She lay back on the bed and curled up in a ball and cried. The chills were the worst of it. She shook all over and feared her chattering teeth would bite through her tongue. She had a headache, and muscle pain too. Her throat was sore, her temperature so hot the sheets were warm. What did he do to her? And then there were the hallucinations. She kept envisioning Peter Collins and that time long ago when she and her best friends committed murder.

She was in hell.

Several days later

When she woke again the lights were off in her room. She found she had a cough that wouldn't stop. She sat up in bed and gripped her throat. She did feel a bit stronger and aware. She could smell herself after not bathing in a week. Her hair was a tangled mess. She scratched her scalp and other places. How long had it been this way for her?

On the nightstand near her bed were two pills and a glass of water. She stared at it. Then she glanced at the television that had to be monitoring her. She didn't care anymore, she couldn't suffer through the pain in her throat. She picked up the pills and took them and drank the water. She then opened her tongue to show her captor she'd swallowed. She could feel her fever all over her body. But her chills were gone, and that to her was the best news.

She saw her laptop on the floor. When she got up, she swayed a bit and then she steadied herself. She took the laptop to bed and opened it. The date surprised her. It had only been five short days since her kidnapping, so she thought, but in reality she had lost a total of eleven days. How was that possible? How could she sleep so long? Was she sleeping or were the strange dreams real? The doctors, the convulsing at night and seeing Peter Collins trapped in this room with her during the day. Nightmares, night sweats, body aches so severe she couldn't stand. All of that had happened. Or had it?

"Okay. Enough of this. It's time to get out of here. It's past time," she mumbled. She walked over to her suitcase and removed her summer dress and cosmetics bag. She went into the bathroom but took her time. She found she was breathless when she hurried. Breathing without exertion became a concentrated effort. She turned on the shower and willed herself to be stronger. She stripped of her soiled hospital gown and spent over thirty minutes in the shower washing her hair and every crevice of her body. She brushed her teeth twice. She put lotion on her skin and used her curl cream with some ECCO gel to bring the curls to life. When she left the bathroom, she was renewed.

The television blinked on, and music began to play. Johnny Gill's "My, My, My" sang throughout the room.

"...*you sure look good tonight...*"

Despite her fury she smiled, even laughed a little. The song spoke of how fine she was, and how he wished he could make love to her.

"Not going to happen," she said in response to the lyrics. "Trying to appear playful."

Johnny Gill continued to serenade her. The pills began to have an effect on her. She didn't feel feverish. But her weakness forced her to return to bed. She opened her laptop. She pretended at reading something on the screen, while the music played. And she knew he watched.

She waited.

Chapter Twelve

The elevator he took to the third floor was slow to climb. The doors opened and he wheeled himself down a long empty hall to a room he often avoided when he returned to Mayfair. Though most servants were dismissed, he did not dare be seen without his wheelchair on any floor. Not until he was certain that his plans were secure.

The third level of his new home was never occupied. He was alone. He entered his father's room and closed the door. He sat in his wheelchair and stared at the large bed the old man slept in. He used to fear the room. He could see his father there with his glasses perched on his nose as he read the Quran. He could remember the long hours he would have to stand in one spot before him, silent until his father was ready to deal with his behavior. The terror still lived in him all these years later. Now he was the terror. Just as his mother predicted.

Jaxon dropped the brake on his wheelchair and stood. He walked past the bed to a dresser with a mirror. The man before him was nothing like the man she knew. He didn't want her to meet him this way. And it was time they met. He reached behind his neck and unfastened the gold chain that held the family crest and on an oval onyx stone crested upon a golden locket. He put it into his father's jewelry box. He removed the ring that all Mayfair men for centuries wore. He fetched the pocket watch with the long golden link chain that he kept with him since he returned to his father's home. He put it away as well.

It wasn't enough.

Jaxon touched his beard. His hair was longer, he hadn't shaved in weeks. He walked into his father's bathroom and retrieved a long pair of sheers and clippers. He cut his hair and let it fall into the sink and on the floor. He cut his beard. Slowly the man he needed to become surfaced.

"WE NEED TO TALK," JAXON entered the room.

Dr. Nine and Dr. Ten stopped in the middle of conversation. He stood before them with his hands pushed down into his trouser pockets. And they couldn't mask the surprise on their faces of his transformation. The men had never seen him with a shaven face and hair trimmed short. He waited for their collective shock to pass before he spoke. "What is her condition?"

"We've been trying to understand it," Dr. Nine blurted.

Dr. Ten put up a hand to silent his colleague. "What he meant to say is that we're working on her diagnosis."

Jaxon narrowed his eyes on them. She was perfectly healthy when she arrived. It wasn't until two days later under their care that she fell ill. "I suggest you explain it," he said. Jaxon's men entered the room. He didn't summon them but whenever needed they were always there. Even in the cellars.

The doctors looked nervous. Dr. Ten was bold enough to speak. "We thought it was the flu. But it isn't. She's better. She seems better. There's one possibility..." the doctors voice faltered. He looked to Dr. Nine and then back to Jaxon. "A virus that seems to be surging in China. Has she travelled recently too?"

"Virus? Is that all you have?"

"We're still running tests," Dr. Nine said. "But she is better. She's recovering. It could have been a different strain of flu. We'll continue to monitor her recovery of course."

Jaxon stared at the men for a second. "Hutch?"

"Yes?" Hutch stepped forward. "Stay with the doctors. Make sure their motivated to keep her well."

"Will do," Hutch said.

Jaxon checked his watch. He was late. He turned and walked out of the lab he had much to prepare.

The next day

GOODIVA WOKE ON THE thirteenth day determined to try something different. Instead of the routine boredom of eating and sleeping, she decided to test her nightly visitor by staying awake for her next food delivery. She had failed in her all her previous attempts, so this time she changed the game. She went into the bathroom with her laptop and food. If she was right, he didn't have cameras in the bathroom. He wouldn't know if she were asleep or awake. His fascination with old-school R&B music was purposeful. He must have assumed it was a way to connect with her.

The bastard was really trying hard to get into her head.

However, nothing had changed for either of them. It was as if he intended to keep her trapped forever. She made it through the first eighteen hours of her trap with no sounds coming from her room. Eventually she lost her own battle and drifted to sleep on the floor. When she woke, it was to the sound of music, again. Goodiva immediately opened the door. Food had arrived.

"Damn it!" she cursed and slammed the door to her bathroom.

Day after day since she recovered from her illness she tried to shut him out by retreating to the bathroom and sleeping on the floor. At least there he couldn't reach her without opening the door and waking her. She woke on the fifteenth day of her captivity to a different kind of music. Her mother played the song when she was a kid whenever she cleaned the house. The memory of that time rocked her. He couldn't know that about her? How could he? She'd only told her friends, and maybe Twixt about those times and how much she loved the song. It was from *The Art of Noise*. It was called 'Moments in Love.' Goodiva walked out of the bathroom to the melodic tune almost as if pulled through a trance. She looked around and saw he'd come again and delivered food. He wanted to communicate with her. She was ready.

"Good morning," she said.

The screen began to do a rainbow swirl as 'Moments in Love' serenaded her.

"How bad is the weather now?" she asked. "I know they said this mountain will be inaccessible soon. It's been almost two weeks since I came here. Right? Or close to it. The winter storms should be here by now, but what about the blizzard?"

The television flashed to the weather report. The news reporter stood before a map of the township delivering the grave news. They anticipated the snow to reach 13 inches by the end of the week. If she wanted out, she had a small window to make it possible before the anticipated blizzard arrived.

"Thank you. Thank you for showing me that," she smiled at the television. The weather broadcast blinked off. The rainbow swirl returned and 'Moments in Love' began to play again.

"I missed Christmas," she said.

No response.

"It's my favorite time of year. I can't believe Dee and Queen haven't come looking for me," she said.

No response.

She sighed. She tried to humble herself to keep the anger from her voice. It was hard. "Don't you have questions for me? Or have you already tried and convicted me of my crimes? Is this my prison?"

The rainbow swirl continued.

"What about Twixt? He was the one that hurt you. I know he's dead, but you had to move past it. Right? Can't we move past this?"

"...moam...ments...in love..."

She summoned more patience.

"I'm hungry," she announced. She went to the tray of food.

"What do we have today?" she asked and faked interest.

There was the customary fruit, which she supposed was offered for some kind of fiber sustenance. There was a sandwich and a pickle with homemade chips. And there was a salad mixed with cranberries, pecans, spinach, and blue cheese crumbles.

"Nice. I like this," she said and tasted a chip. "But I have to have organic food. Non-GMO. And I don't do dairy. Especially cheese. I hate cheese. I really hate pizza. Oh, and macaroni and chess. It's just a glob of cheese on noodles. Yuck! Can you make sure to tell the chef? Or is the real reason I get sandwiches every day because you're making the meal for me yourself? That's it, isn't it? No one knows you have me down here, do they?"

She glanced to the television screen for an answer. There was none.

"I bet you're eating steak and some pasta dish. Fresh baked bread. A nice glass of pinot to bring it all down. Huh? I can't even get a glass of juice. I deserve a better meal than this," Goodiva said. "Can I at least get lemonade? Water is nice but really boring."

Goodiva paused.

She frowned. Each of those songs had a different meaning. They were too personal.

"...moam...ments...in love..."

"Jaxon?"

The music played on.

"How do you know that 'Moment's in Love' is one of my favorite songs? Are you listening to my playlist?"

The music stopped. The rainbow swirl stopped. The screen went black.

"Did you go through my things Jaxon? Did you read my journals?" She walked over to her suitcases, and found her journals in her bag packed away. She pulled them out and checked for them all. They were there. Then she glanced to her computer. She kept a lot of her journaling on her computer over the years. The stories of her family and even some of her secrets. She created a playlist for her painful breakup. For the times she was in love. She had oldie but goodies for her parents. Songs they would play, dance and make out to when they thought she was asleep. She even had a playlist for Mr. Collins. Jaxon had randomly chosen songs from her past.

"You hacked my computer?"

Goodiva checked her system bio and found that there was a program running on her computer. It was Arabic. And so was the script in the Bios. All of it was Arabic. "What is this?"

Her computer blinked off and the webcam turned on. She gasped and shoved it away. The violation had her shivering with anger. How long had he been hacking her? How long had he been in her life? Years, possibly. *Stay calm Goodiva. Stay calm and don't let him see you sweat.*

She picked up the bowl of fruit and sat down in the recliner chair in her room. She ate a piece of melon and stared up at the screen.

"I guess you're wondering how someone as young as me has a playlist of music that was out before I was born, huh?" she said. It took finesse to keep the anger from her voice. "I'm a disc jockey, DJ, master maestro, pancake turner, mixer on the ones and twos," she said, keeping her eyes leveled on the screen and thus him. "Because I am music. I have loved music since I was born. Trust me, I know all the latest hits. I can turn out some Ella Mai and Frank Ocean. I could mix up some good Jaquees and Trey Songs for you to seduce the ladies. But I like Luther and Joe even better. This music. It's a different kind of soulful melody I keep private. You are wrong to pry into my privacy. Especially considering how paranoid you are about protecting yours."

He didn't answer.

She plucked another piece of melon, sucking on the juices with a slow seductive lick. "Delilah hates all of my '80s and '90s classics. Queen says the music makes her sleepy. You like it though? Huh? Turns you on?"

He didn't respond.

"Fine. Forget music. I have another question. What sick things did you do to me?"

She waited. Nothing.

"Huh? Experiments? I know you did something when you trapped me in here, made me sick, hallucinate. Gave me those pills to keep me weak. Some nights I couldn't even breathe. And all you did was watch!" The television flashed on. The credits of a romantic comedy began to play. It was her movie, *Hollyswirl*. He was trying to provoke her. She felt her anger rising and her lips thinned to a pressed tightness. She set the bowl of fruit back on the tray and rocked back in her chair. She glared at the screen. He wanted to play games, she intended to master this one. She gave him no further emotion. She sat there and watched her starring role without complaint or comment. She wondered if he watched it too. Twice she had to go to the bathroom. Upon her return she found he had paused the movie so she wouldn't miss a scene. She had smoothed her hair up into a ponytail that put a crown of curls at the top of her head. When the movie was over, the television went dark. She waited. Nothing happened.

"Oh, so we done?" she asked.

No response.

"How'd I do? Think I can land a part in one of your boring films?" she asked.

No response.

"It's weird. This thing we got going. You sure are Mister Tough Guy with me locked up in here. Why not meet with me face to face? What are you afraid of? That wheelchair got you sitting too long on your balls?"

No response.

"I was so stupid. I was soooooo stupid! I thought it was fate. I mean, who could script how we met? You trying to rescue me, the accident. Sounds like a cheesy movie you'd produce, not my life," she sighed. "You started this. Sending those flowers, stalking me. Harassing me!"

And there was no answer.

"*Can I see you tonight?*" she mocked his tone "*Where are you, when can I see you?* We slept together once. Once! And you were harassing me! Look at how old you are. We got what, almost nine years between us. Can't you find a woman your own age?!"

No response.

"It was your fault you got hurt. That's the real truth. Yours! I said let me call the police! But you wanted me to come to you. You wanted to get involved. You should have minded your own damn business!"

No response.

"Okay, okay, I'm done arguing. Let's start over. You know who I am and what I did," she began. "I ran from the accident. That was the only crime I committed. I was being chased by an abusive..." she sighed and stopped herself from speaking ill of the dead. "I did. But I later came to my senses. When I did, you were in the hospital and alive. Twixt and Kumar were telling a different version of the story. They didn't kill you. They saved your life. I know it's wrong what happened. How it happened, but I just thought you would be okay. When I found out how serious it was, I wanted to confess. Tell the police what Twixt and his brother had done to cause the accident. Your friend Armand had to have told you that I came to visit." Goodiva frowned. "Wait a second. How long have you been planning this? Huh? I wasn't even in the country for two years? How did you know that I would return? Or even come back to Falcon Cove and apply for this job?"

After ten minutes of silence, Goodiva realized that her captor was probably not even listening to her. She began to pace. She paced and paced. And he never responded.

"MASTER MAYFAIR," ANDELLA said through the intercom.

Jaxon looked up from the laptop screen. He removed the earbuds in his ear. He was in his private office and the staff knew not to disturb him during the day unless it was of great importance. However, until he was able to dismiss his seasonal staff at the end of the week ahead of the worst of the incoming storms, he made himself accessible.

"What is it?"

"Visitors," Andella informed him.

It was the most unexpected news. For one, he didn't have visitors. For two, it was impossible for them to arrive via the roads with the storm. He would have to fly his staff out when the time came.

"They arrived by police helicopter," Andella informed him.

"Who are they?"

"One of them is a detective. The other is Mrs. Delilah Montgomery. They are here to speak with you about that young woman. The estate manager you fired. They are quite insistent."

"Where is Frances?"

"She is doing her routine checks."

"Have her join me after you escort the ladies into the solarium."

"You will meet with them?" Andella asked, a bit surprised.

"Isn't that the point of you bringing this news to me?"

"Ah, yes sir. No problem at all. I will bring them to the solarium and send for Francine."

"Andella?"

"Yes?"

"Delay them ten minutes."

"Yes sir," she said.

Within five minutes he was in the solarium. There he wheeled himself to his desk and opened the laptop. He missed the last part of Godiva's confession. When he accessed her room again, he found her pacing the floor and chewing on her nail. She'd changed her hair to an upward do that showed her dark roots and the blondish-yellow tips of spry curls. They cascaded from the top of the ponytail to her brow. He punched in the access codes on the keys of his laptop to turn the feed to the room where he was. And he made sure to give her audio. He thought it best she got a front and center viewpoint of the visit. Jaxon's gaze lifted from the laptop to the camera pointed at him and he smirked.

The television switched on. Goodiva felt her heart freeze. She became riveted by what would appear next on the screen. She at first thought it would play another movie. But she soon realized this was indeed reality. Jaxon Price had parked himself down in his solarium in his wheelchair. He often handled his business affairs by the orchids, Andella had once told her. A desk fit for a king was there for his use. He sat behind it and stared directly into the camera. He stared at her. She could hear sound.

"Hello?" she whispered. She cleared her throat. "Ah, hello—can you hear me?"

"Master Mayfair. Please meet Detective Douglas, and Ms. Delilah Montgomery," Andella said.

"Thank you for seeing us, Mr. Price," Delilah said. She marched straight to him. She extended her hand across his desk. Jaxon shook it. Delilah wore a long wool cashmere coat and dark slacks. She looked as polished as she always did whenever he saw her on the local stations or in the town's newspapers.

"We are sorry to intrude," Delilah said.

"No intrusion. Welcome. I hope you didn't have a hard time getting to the mountain?" Jaxon Price asked.

"The helicopter helped. The storm broke for us to make the trip. Thank you for the generous donation to the Charles Foundation. I knew it came from the Mayfair Trust, but I had no idea it...uhm...that you were the donor."

Jaxon gave her a polite nod of respect.

"When was the last time you saw or spoke to Michelle?" Queen cut in. She had on a dark business suit under a heavy wool trench coat. Her hand was placed at her hip and revealed her badge and her gun. To this, Jaxon feigned concern.

Goodiva smiled at the television screen. "I knew it! Yes! Kick his ass Queen! Yes! I knew they would figure out his crap and come for me! Get him Queen! Get him!"

Jaxon Price gave a look of concern behind the half-leather mask he wore. "I'm sorry. Is something wrong?"

"Yes, something is wrong," Delilah interjected. "She hasn't been seen or heard from in over two weeks."

"Mr. Price, we know she came here to work for you. The last time either of us spoke to her she informed us that she quit this job on her first day. Can I ask why?" Queen pressed.

"Yes, she broke the most important rule. No electronics. She brought a cellphone onto the property. Since my accident, my privacy is of the utmost importance to me. A photograph of me in this chair could be sold for seven figures. The staff informed me, and she and I agreed it was best she leave. Especially after...I learned who she was. She was driven off of the property that very day."

"That makes no sense. She never made it to New York!" Delilah said to Queen. "It's been over two weeks."

Queen didn't speak. She stared at Jaxon Price. Goodiva held her breath. She put both her hands to her mouth. Her friends had always been there for her. In the direst times of her life, they were front and center, offering rescue. They wouldn't buy the bullshit Jaxon Price was selling them. Not them. They'd seen and been through too much.

"So you knew who she was? Who she is?"

"Goodiva Johnson? The young woman that left me on the side of the road to die. Yes. I know her. I will admit I didn't at first. But she confessed who she was to me."

"How could you not remember her?" Delilah scoffed. "You're lying."

"I suffered brain trauma. It's affected my long-term memory. All because of her."

"That's a serious accusation," Queen said.

"It's the truth, isn't it?" Jaxon countered.

"Why did you lure her here? Hire her?" Queen demanded.

"Lure her? I posted a job. She showed up for the interview. I didn't even meet with her until after she was hired. I think we were both equally shocked as to who we were to each other."

Queen and Delilah exchanged a look. Goodiva could see the confusion and concern on their faces. "No! Please, guys, he's lying. See through him. He's a liar. Just like Peter Collins was a liar. Please! Don't fall for it!"

"Where was she staying?" Queen asked.

"In one of the cottages to the back of the estate," he replied. "She didn't have much time to unpack before we had our talk. It was after that she was discovered with her cell phone. I tried to fire her, but she informed me that she wanted to quit. I agreed it was best."

"And how did she leave?" Queen asked.

"My personal driver," Jaxon answered.

"Where did he take her?" Queen asked.

"I'm not sure. I never inquired."

"Can we speak to him?" Queen asked.

"I'm sorry, but he isn't here today. He comes in on Tuesday and Fridays—or at least, he does when the storm isn't wreaking havoc. Now that we are in the thick of it, he's furloughed," Jaxon answered.

"I'd like his name and number," Queen insisted.

"Of course," Jaxon Price reached into the drawer and pulled out a pad and pen. "Unfortunately, he has returned to the Middle East. He works for a company out of Dubai. This is the number for the driver service we use. They can track him down for you."

Delilah began to pace. Her purse swung back and forth from her hand at her side. She looked as if she were going to turn and throw it at him like a boomerang. Since they were children, they never went a full week without talking to each other. Never. And Christmas was a special holiday between them. She missed Christmas. Delilah knew something was wrong.

"I want to see the cottage. Maybe she left something behind," Delilah said to Queen.

"I'm happy to help in any way I can," Jaxon offered. "I will have you speak with the staff I have remaining and visit any room you wish at Mayfair. I barely met her before she left, but if she's in trouble I would like to be of assistance."

"That's nice of you, considering your accusations against her," Queen said.

Jaxon nodded. "That night she was in trouble. I tried to help her then. I know why my accident happened. I don't blame her or the young man who caused my condition. He's dead, isn't he?" Jaxon asked.

"Yes, he died in Dubai. A plane crash. Where your driver has now disappeared too."

"Strange coincidence," Jaxon said.

Queen glared at him.

He handed Queen the piece of paper with the number of his driver service.

"Don't believe him! He's a lying piece of shit! A fucking psycho! Queen! Delilah! I'm here! I'm here!" Goodiva shouted. To her horror, she saw her friends show gratitude to the conniving bastard. And then the witch who she replaced arrived.

"Master Mayfair, I was told you wanted to see me?" Francine asked.

"Yes, Frances. Please meet Delilah Montgomery and Detective...ugh..."

"Queen Douglas," Queen answered.

"Right. Detective Douglas. They are friends of the young woman I hired for the estate manager position," Jaxon Price said. "Frances has been with the family for many years. I terminated her role a few weeks before Michelle came to work here. She has since returned. She can help you conduct all interviews."

"We'd like to meet with the staff who saw her escorted from here. And anyone else who she met or spoke with before she left. We're trying to find out where she could have gone," Queen said.

"I understand ladies, of course," Frances replied. "Most of the staff has already left for their winter break due to the storms. But the last of the staff that remains leaves in a few days. I can summon them."

"Make sure they meet with Hutch too," Jaxon offered. "He was helping Ahmed with her luggage when she left. He might know something about Ahmed's final destination when he dropped her off."

"Thank you, Mr. Price," Queen said.

"I would escort you myself but my chair won't allow me to venture out into the snow," he said.

"Thank you," Delilah Montgomery repeated. Queen put her arm around Delilah's shoulder and walked her out.

"Noo! No! He's lying. He's frickin' lying!" Goodiva groaned.

She turned around and looked for something to throw. Something she could use to make a disturbance. But there really wasn't anything she could use. Jaxon Price watched them leave. His gaze then slowly went to the camera. The triumphant smile on his lips made her skin crawl. He then turned the dagger in her heart. He punched a few keys and the surveillance video feed tracked her friends. They walked out into another foyer where Andella waited with Hutch. She couldn't hear the question and answer session, but she knew that the servants all would lie to protect him. More servants were brought in. Queen asked many questions but the answers were typically a nod for 'yes,' a shake of the head for 'no,' a shrug of the shoulders for 'I'm not sure.' It was useless. And then Hutch led her friends on a tour that Goodiva sat through before they ventured out into the snow. The storm had covered everything in the past two weeks. Soon they would be trapped at the mountain during the harshest winter month of the season. What would happen then?

Queen and Delilah went into her cottage. The place was scrubbed clean. But the cameras had obviously been returned. How else could she see her friends and hear them so clearly?

"This makes no sense!" Delilah said, shaking her head. "Why the hell would he put her out here and not in the house, knowing that you need a damn snowplow to get to the front door?"

"Maybe he didn't think she'd last the winter?"

"Exactly!" Delilah huffed.

"I agree," Queen continued. "Putting her here does seem strange. That place is big enough for the both of them."

Queen walked around.

"He's too calm."

"Yep!" Delilah said. "He saw her and figured it out and then—"

"Don't go there, we don't know it went that far," Queen reasoned.

"What? You said he's too calm."

"He is, but it could be for many reasons. He's in a wheelchair and disfigured. He knows who she is and from the look he gave you, he knows you too."

"Me?" Delilah frowned.

"Who in this town doesn't know you Dee? Didn't you say you gave her a recommendation? That means he knows you lied for her. He's checking us out too. He doesn't strike me as a man who would take well to being a cripple."

"Okay. Then what? She's been gone for two weeks! You made me wait a whole week before you even considered it a problem. And now it's been two weeks!"

"Lower your voice," Queen sighed.

"Stop chastising me! I'm pissed. And scared!"

"Me too, me too," Queen reasoned. "We couldn't get out here sooner, Dee. The snow made it hard to reach, and we got no replies to our calls. What do you want me to do?"

"I want you to do your fucking job! Stop making excuses for that man. Did you see him? With that creepy mask on his face. I'm telling you, he's lying."

"About what exactly? His story matches yours. She quit. She found out who he was and called you and quit."

"She didn't call, she texted," Delilah shook her head. "She's in trouble Queen. I feel it. I know it. She's in trouble. None of this makes any damn sense!"

"What makes no sense is you setting this all up for her," Queen said.

"I didn't know he was the new Master Mayfair. How would I know?"

"From what you tell me, you should have known. He's the son of that weirdo son of a bitch Yaşar Fikrit. Your family does business with these Arabs."

"Fikrit isn't Arab. He's Turkish. And Jaxon Price changed his identity to conceal who his father was. I had no idea they were connected. Why would I send her here, Queen? Answer me that! After everything she's been through?"

"Calm down. Stop yelling," Queen sighed.

"No! You accused me! I had no idea that Jaxon Price was or is Asad Fikrit. I only found out when I couldn't get in contact with her and forced the estate to respond to me about what was going on up here. How the hell would I have known?" Delilah wept. "I protect her. I always protect you guys."

"Okay, hey, stop it. Stop crying. Okay?" Queen pulled Delilah into her arms and hugged her. "I believe you. We've just got to figure this out."

"Something is wrong, I can feel it!" Delilah sobbed. "Two weeks! She's been gone for two weeks!"

Queen cupped her friend's face. "Look at me. Take a breath. We're stronger than this. I know. I'm scared too. But we both know this isn't the first time she's disappeared on us. She's been depressed. Maybe seeing him again freaked her out. Maybe she has gone back to Ghana? To escape everything. It's possible she wants to escape us too. Remember? After she got out of that facility we put her in, she ran from us. She went to Europe. Didn't even warn us for days."

"Days, not weeks," Delilah sniffed. "But yea. Maybe."

"Check upstairs. I'll check down here. We don't have much time. We have to get out before the copter can't lift and take us back."

She let go of Delilah, who raced up the stairs to check the rooms. Queen was left to look around the living area, the kitchen and the downstairs bedroom. After ten minutes, they both returned to the living room, exasperated.

"There's nothing to prove she was here, Dee," Queen said, now on the verge of tears herself.

"You're a detective. You telling me that she up and left and disappeared on us? All in the matter of three weeks? Then nothing from her since?"

"You said she texted that she would meet you in New York?" Queen asked.

"Yes, but—"

"Then I will contact Luvie again. Have her put in a missing person's report on her. See if we can get her phone records. That will help us," Queen said. "Wherever her last text was would be a good start. We can then access her financial records. She may have left, but she had to leave a paper trail."

"Yes! Yes! Queen! Do it. Then you'll know what the sick bastard has done to me!" Goodiva said.

Delilah wiped the tears from her eyes and picked up her purse. She took another look around at the cottage. "If we don't find any proof that she left the country, or even the state, promise me we come back here. Jaxon

Price is not a good person." Delilah said. "If Yaşar Fikrit was his father, then he's the spawn of Satan."

"Why do you keep saying that?" Queen frowned.

Delilah shrugged. "Charles, he said things about that Fikrit. And after the past week I've had I'm beginning to believe it."

"Tell me what you know."

"I don't know any—" Delilah quickly backpedaled.

"Stop it! Don't lie to me. And don't protect your husband if it means the information can help us find Shelly."

Delilah paced. "All I can say is that Fikrit was sick. He had some kind of blood disease. And he was obsessed with finding a cure."

"So? That doesn't make him evil."

"There's a lawsuit, against the fertility clinic. The one Charles and I used to get pregnant."

Queen's brows lowered with concern.

"It wasn't just a fertility clinic. They performed abortions there."

Queen let go a deep sigh. "And?"

"That man, Yaşar Fikrit, he wanted it done. And Charles' brothers tried to bury the reason why. But I found it. He was using the fetuses and embryos for stem cell research. To experiment. To find himself a cure."

"What?"

"I can't talk about it, Queen. All I can tell you is that this family is dangerous. I don't know how Shelly got mixed up with that Jaxon Price, but he is not who he pretends to be."

"Why didn't you tell me this before?" Queen asked.

"I dunno," Delilah mumbled.

"Bullshit! You're hiding something from me."

Delilah looked away. "It has nothing to do with Shelly. It's just ugliness in my marriage. That's all. I swear it. On my son's life. I told you everything you need to know."

"Secrets Dee? Haven't we kept enough secrets?" Queen asked.

"I'm sorry," Delilah wept.

"I'll talk to the driver. Trust me, if that fucker has done something to Shelly I'll find out and throw him and his wheelchair off the side of this mountain."

"Yes!" Goodiva cheered. "Oh God, please help them. Help me. They won't give up. They will find me. You hear that! They will find me!"

And just as her hope soared the video feed cut off. Goodiva screamed in frustration. She clenched her fist and glared at the television. "You think you won? You think so? Well, you haven't. I'm done with these games. This is criminal. Do you hear me! My friends won't stop. You heard them. They are going to get the cellphone logs. They will find out that I never left this crypt. What will you do then? Huh? Huh! Mr. Psycho?"

Goodiva went into the bathroom and slammed the door. She let go a sob of defeat. If she didn't get out of that room soon, she'd do something crazy.

SITTING ON THE FLOOR with her back to the door, she rested her forehead against her knees. She was half asleep, half awake. She'd been that way behind the locked door for several hours and she had no desire to get up. What was the point?

Then she heard a noise inside of her room. She was certain of it. The same droning sound she heard before she was taken. Goodiva got up from the floor and yanked open the door. To her surprise Jaxon Price was in her room, waiting in his wheelchair. The door to freedom was ajar. Her eyes swiveled between him and the only escape from hell.

"We should talk," he said.

Goodiva stepped out of the bathroom and stood over him.

"Have a seat," he instructed.

She glanced to the bed where he pointed and then to him.

Run. Run. Run. Run. Run.

"I will only ask once—"

Run. Run. Run. Run. Run.

She ran for the door. He grabbed her arm; his grip was terrifying and strong. She nearly went to her knees to twist free. With courage pumping through her veins, she found strength she didn't know she had. When you needed the strength to fight for your life, it came in the most unexpected ways. So she did what she learned to do at ten. She fought back. Goodiva hit him in the face. The smack almost knocked his mask up. She went wild. She pulled and hit at him. She even kicked at his chair. Each blow brought the release of all the hatred and frustration she felt toward men like him that thought they could control and damage women just because of their Y chromosome. The sudden rousing of energy she felt gave her herculean strength and she was able to break free of his grip. Jaxon Price fell out of the chair to the floor. He reached for her ankle but she jumped from his hand and ran with lightning speed out of the room.

The hall was dark. That didn't matter. *She was free.* She raced against time and fear through the corridor of shadows in desperate search for freedom. "Help! Help! Help! Help!" Her destination remained blurred by the darkness, but still she kept running. No crime she had committed was deserving of what he had done to her. Trapping her the way he did unleashed buried trauma she had convinced herself, her doctors and her best friends she was long over.

"Help! Somebody! Please, help me!"

She zig-zagged from corridor to corridor, ran until she was out of breath through a blinding maze of darkness. She was suddenly in a lit hall. She paused. Her breathing was so rampant and fast she clutched her chest in stark panic. She looked back toward the darkness. No one chased her. Even if the creep managed to get into his chair, she was certain he'd never catch up with her. She panted like a marathon runner but kept going. Soon she entered the open area where the lift was. The sight of it sent another jolt of relief through her heart.

"Thank you God," she sighed. "Thank you sweet precious Lord."

She limped. The bottoms of her feet ached and her left ankle was sore from the barefoot sprint. Now winded and a bit disoriented, she pushed herself to go onward toward the lift. The front of the lift was a caged door blocking the elevator. The button to summon it was to the left. She pressed it and waited. The button didn't light up, and she heard no sound in response. She pressed it again, and again. Nothing happened.

"No! No, damn it!"

She beat at the button with her fist.

"No!" Goodiva yanked on the gate that would automatically open once the lift arrived. It didn't budge. "No, no, no, no, no, damnit! Help me please!" she pleaded. Nothing she did made the elevator move. It dawned on her that this could be the reason why she wasn't chased. Why did he take the risk of confronting her after showing her friends attempt to save her? This was again one of his sadistic games.

"Help!" she shouted upward. "Anybody? I'm down here! Goodiva Michelle Johnson is down here!"

She refused to cry. There was no time for tears. She looked around for a weapon. Something to beat the living hell out of him until she found the key or remote control to make the elevator work again. She found nothing. Goodiva started back through the hall. She went in the opposite direction, but it was nothing more than one dead end after another, so she backtracked. This wandering of hers went on for eternity and her ankle burned so hotly she felt the need to drop to her hands and knees and crawl.

Again she found herself in the hall with no lights. She hesitated.

Wouldn't it be safest to wait by the elevator? she wondered.

Eventually he'd have to return. Then she thought of ambushing him. The control had to be part of the electric chair he rode in. That would work. Her thoughts soon became darker. Maybe he had a gun? She knew he had to have help to get her into the room and on the bed as he did before. What if there were more people down below than she knew? A harem of women trapped and locked behind the doors in the hall.

A horror story played out in her mind. Before she arrived, she spent the night with Queen who told her horrible stories about the serial killer stalking Falcon Cove again. Could he be the serial killer? *No. No. No.* Nothing she worked through made sense. Her throat went dry. Her mind swam with conspiracies as she walked slowly and cautiously through the halls. It didn't take her long to return to the room she escaped from. The door was open, as she left it. The keypad outside of it was lit green.

Was he still inside?

Was he waiting for her?

Was this another trap?

Goodiva readied herself for the confrontation. He knew she'd fight. She'd shown him she'd defend herself. Whatever he had planned for her couldn't be any worse than the hell he'd thrown her into. With renewed courage she ventured inside. On the floor was the wheelchair turned to its side. Jaxon Price was not in it. She glanced to the bathroom. The door was half open. Had he dragged himself inside? If he did, why?

"Where are you?" she asked.

After a long pause she approached the door. She'd never seen him without his mask since his accident. She only saw him twice since her arrival. Other than trapping her here, he'd done nothing violent to her. Maybe he was hurt and had gone into the bathroom to get something to help him?

Goodiva pushed the door open. The bathroom was empty. Confused, she turned to leave, and then screamed.

Jaxon Price stood before her.

Her gaze slid down the length of his body and returned to his half-covered face. She didn't speak. How could she? She didn't move. Where would she go? She stared at him, thinking her fear had finally turned into madness.

Chapter Thirteen

"You...you...you can walk?" she pointed at his legs. When she returned to the room, he was inside the small room that had been his jail for the earliest years of his childhood. He heard her and considered his options. He could release her. He often prayed his mother would find the strength to release him from his father's tyranny.

"You let me...think...I thought I made you a cripple?"

"Disappointed?" he asked.

"What kind of sick game is this?" she demanded.

"Our game."

"Our what? I'm calling the cops. I'm going to report you, report this kidnapping and poisoning of me—" she began.

"You're willing to risk your best friend losing her job on the Falcon Police Force? You're going to have Delilah Montgomery arrested and separated from her son for helping you two cover up a crime? The scandal will destroy her life. Her mother in-law will have the power to kick her out of the family and keep her from her son permanently."

Goodiva blinked in disbelief.

"You think I don't know what you three did? How you pulled it off?" Jaxon Price asked. "Ten years old, and you committed the perfect crime."

"No. No, we didn't. We...we didn't do anything. And this isn't about them. This is about Twixt," Goodiva stammered.

"Yes Twixt. You want to play it that way? Okay. Let's talk about Twixt. You two destroyed my life. You forced me back here. To be trapped in Mayfair again. Locked away from the world. Just like he was."

"He who? What are you talking about?" she asked. She looked around as if expecting someone else to enter the room.

Jaxon smiled. "You're a good actress. Should have saved this performance for that little movie of yours. Would have gotten you further than your skills as a DJ."

"Go to hell! Kidnapping? Who kidnaps a woman and locks her down in a cellar? A deranged lunatic! That's who!"

"I delayed your leaving. Nothing more."

"Liar! Kidnapping asshole! And what about rape? I woke up sick. I could tell something happened to my body!"

"I did not rape you," he scoffed. "I would never. You came here sick. With some kind of virus. It's all over the news—"

"Don't deny you're crazy enough to do it. Because this is crazy!" she shouted. "And the music? The sick mind games by using my music. Crazy!"

"If I'm crazy, then what are you?"

"Huh? Confused," she shot back. "Confused as to why I'm standing here listening to this crap!" She turned to leave.

"I suggest you finish this conversation with me, beautiful."

"Or what? Huh? You can't keep me here forever!"

"I don't like to be yelled at," he warned her.

"I will yell all I want!" she shouted at the top of her voice.

He smiled at her show of defiance the way a cat toyed with a mouse.

Goodiva glared but that smile chilled her.

"Are you going to let me go or kill me?" she asked. "Because I need you to make a decision," she demanded.

Jaxon smiled.

"When you were ten you watched a man die. That's what you told me, right?"

"I never said that," she paced.

"I'm wrong?"

"You're wrong!"

"And when I needed your help you watched me die. I remember that clearly."

"You're not dead!"

"Is that what you thought when you turned and ran away? That I'd live? Is that why you didn't call the police?" he asked.

"What is your point?"

"Maybe it wasn't Twixt. Maybe you ran because of what you did to Peter Collins? Because of your secrets."

"You know nothing about Peter Collins."

"I said I'm sorry," she mumbled.

"Well fuck your apology," he said.

"At this point there's nothing to discuss. You're not saying anything to justify what you've done to me. And I don't have anything else to offer you."

"Delilah Montgomery and her dead husband were stealing from my family's trust for years before I returned to collect what was mine."

"Liar. Delilah's no thief. It's your daddy who's the real thief. I heard her. Stealing aborted fetuses for experiments? Sicko. Disgusting. Is he the devil you drew on those drawings? What kind of experiments did he do on you?"

"The kind that the Montgomeries still participates in."

"Not Delilah!"

"You don't know her, not like you think you do," he warned.

"Oh, please. I do know her!"

"The Montgomeries handled my father's estate. Who's to say they didn't use you to try to kill me by setting me up that night? I'm the only living and breathing heir to Yaşar Fikrit."

"You are crazy." She shook her head with disgust. "Your father has nothing to do with me or my friends. No one cared about him. None of this is about him."

"Did you know that if I died, the trust is liquidated by the trustee board and the Montgomeries get a very large share of the pie?"

"How would I know that?" she threw her arms up in defeat.

"I'm supposed to believe that my accident, your disappearance, changing of your identity, and then you coming here to work for me was all a coincidence?"

"It was. You sent me flowers. You made my boyfriend go crazy and attack me. You were my stalker up until that night. I never pursued you!"

"I made him crazy?" he scoffed.

"Whatever. You know what I mean. He went crazy. It was you who told me what roads to turn down when I called you that night. You drove your car in between us. How could I have planned any of that, psycho?"

He chuckled.

"So now it's funny? I'm some kind of joke?"

"You snuck into my hospital room. I have a confession upstairs signed by you. I have a taped conversation of your boyfriend bragging about trying to kill me. He said you were in on it."

Jaxon let his version of truth settle in between them.

"You've twisted this into something sick and evil, when it is all orchestrated by you," she said.

"I am the victim here," he said.

"You're an imposter playing the victim. How did you get a tape of Twixt confessing anything?"

"UPS," he answered.

"You're lying to me. Twixt died in a plane crash in the Middle East. Did you have something to do with that?"

"I'm no pilot," Jaxon said with a smirk.

She put her hand to her brow. "Wow. You did? Oh my God?"

"We need to talk about how you can save your friends," Jaxon said.

"From what?"

"From me," he replied.

"I'm leaving."

"Fine. Give Delilah my sympathies. I'll send it all through the press. They can join you in jail after they reopen the case on Peter Collins."

"You don't know anything about him!"

"True. I don't. Why do you write so much about being guilty then stand in front of me and play innocent?" he asked.

"You're lying, you're trying to trick me. It won't work. I'm going to expose you. Do you hear me? I'm going to expose you."

"Delilah Montgomery was the first person you called after you left me on the side of the road. Not the police. I have your phone records. She checked you into a mental hospital a few weeks later. More like a relaxation spa. To meditate and sip champagne. While I underwent skin grafts for my burns and had my spine snapped back into place. She handled your legal affairs with the studio for that little film you starred in. She buried your identity and gave you a new one with my money to relocate to New York, which you took and ran away to Europe and Africa."

"The Montgomeries have their own money."

"And then she forged your employee records to get you hired at the agency that put you here. Should I tell you the laws Detective Douglas has broken? Starting with sneaking you into my hospital room dressed as a cop? I had the hospital pull the video to get a good look at you both."

Goodiva shook her head in disbelief.

"I had three long years to get my facts right about you, Goddess."

"You won't listen to reason. What do you want from me?" she asked.

"I've lost everything. So should you. I want this." He opened his hands to her surroundings.

"To keep me here? You can't do that. For what? Sex?"

Jaxon laughed. "You think I waited three years and planned all of this for sex?"

"With that face? Yes," she said.

He laughed. "Good one. No, kitten. You're not here for sex. I'm a Fikrit. We aren't the best of men. But we're not rapists—at least I'm not. You stay here with me."

"Why! Why do you want me to stay?"

"My life is over, but you can give me a new one."

"That makes no sense."

"It will." He walked over to the wheelchair and turned it upright.

"I can't just stay here. For how long? To do what? My friends will continue to look for me."

"The world's a strange place right now. Getting stranger by the day. In a few days not even a helicopter ride will be able to bring the authorities back to the mountain. There will be no way in and out of the roads for two long months. After you agree to my terms, you will speak to your friends and solve the mystery for them. They will leave us alone."

"And then what? When the snow melts? What then?"

"Then it will be too late. Our terms will already be agreed on and our business almost finished."

"What business?"

"We'll discuss the contract at dinner. I suggest you dress for the occasion. Hutch will come for you in an hour. Don't keep me waiting."

"What is this place? That room with all those kids' drawings?" she asked, trying to prevent him for leaving. He was tall even by the standards of a tall man. And he was strong. She could see that strength in his biceps and chest. If he wanted to subdue her, he could. To defeat him she would have to use her brain.

"If you run from me I will expose your friends and you. If you alert my staff that you are here, I will expose you and your friends. The only people you will see or speak to will be me or Hutch."

"You're a crazy person."

"Maybe. Or maybe I'm the sanest man you've ever met."

He pushed the chair to the door.

"Wait a sec!" she said.

He paused. He looked back at her with the side of his face that was not covered by his leather mask. For a moment he looked like the man she remembered. And for a moment she had hope. But he turned and she saw the other side of him. The dark evil side that had laid in wait for years for this moment. He wanted something, and whatever it was would cost her dearly.

"I'll play your game. But not here; I won't stay locked in this room. Let me come upstairs with you. I can keep you company upstairs." She looked at the ceiling. "If I'm willing, there is no reason to keep me a secret. Right?"

He reached in his pocket. He removed a phone. *Her cellphone.* "You'll need to call your friends and tell them you are okay. If you agree to our arrangement at dinner, you can do so. If not, use the phone to call the police. See how far that gets you."

She pressed the button on the side of the phone with hope in her heart. But the phone was dead. She looked up at him for an explanation.

"I'll give you the charger at dinner," he said.

He pushed his chair out of the room and she heard the door lock and engage behind him. Goodiva sat on the bed too shocked to believe what had happened.

Chapter Fourteen

Goodiva chose one of the three dresses she brought with her. It was purple and slimming in the way it trimmed her figure with a very short hem. Her thighs, backside, and hips made the hemline inch up further. She'd have to pull on both sides when she sat. That was the point. The dress cinched like a corset at the waist, adding definition to her up-tilted breasts and curves. She had little time to fix her hair, so she washed it and let it air dry with curls that would eventually puff to a shoulder-length fro. Goodiva made sure to not wear too much makeup, which would detract from her sensuality and imply more sexuality. She stayed in the bathroom over her allotted time, adding lotion and perfuming her skin.

She had no desire to seduce Jaxon Price. She was disgusted by his threats. But she knew men like him. Hell, she'd been running and succumbing to powerful men's affections since she was ten. Beauty and the perceived fragility that they preyed on. When she left the bathroom, she found the man named Hutch waiting for her. He entered her room without ever saying her name. He did, however, peruse her body with his eyes for longer than she liked..

"Phone?" he said.

"Huh?"

"Your phone?" he asked. "Where is it?"

"There." She pointed to the bed.

He looked over at the phone and then to her. "Bring it with you."

She picked up her clutch bag and the cellphone from the bed. She put the cell in her purse. He nodded that she was ready and went out the door. The two of them walked through the winding halls of the cellar with Hutch leading the way. When she got upstairs she would play nice with Jaxon

Price—as nice as necessary. However, as soon as she saw an opening, any kind of opening, she would take it and escape.

The walk to the lift took longer than she believed necessary. Goodiva didn't think there was a hall she hadn't explored when she ran around looking for an escape before. There were many.

In the dark the man named Hutch led her to what she thought was another dead end. He pushed at the side of the wall and it opened to a sideways split. She and he had to go through the narrow passageway. There was another dark hall, but this time with a door similar to the one she was kept behind. She had to wonder if the other dead-ends she encountered below had secret entrances like the one before her. It was completely masked by the shadows. To the right was a keypad that only lit up by the touch of a hand. He pressed his palm to it and the door slid opened. Her guide then stepped aside. She looked at him for a moment. Could she reason with him? Could he be bought? Delilah had more money than God. According to Jaxon Price, that money was his. But Jaxon Price was playing mind games with her. She was certain of it. Maybe Hutch could be bought. The older man stared into her eyes with unwavering conviction. Maybe not.

"I didn't do the things he accused me of. It was all an accident. What he's doing to me is wrong. You know that, don't you? You see this? It's wrong."

There was no discernible change in his reaction.

"Can you help me?" she asked and looked down at the syringe in his hand. Her bravery folded inside of her chest when he smiled. "Is that for me?"

The cold hard look he gave her was answer enough. There was no walking away from this. She went inside. It was a well-furnished old room bright by candlelight. It had cathedral-high ceilings and a sunken spacious sitting room with a formal setting for them to dine next to a gas fireplace. The walls and surrounding furnishings were in grays, mauves, and blacks. It was indeed an elegant upgrade to the gothic bleakness of Mayfair above. And it appeared to be divided into two distinct areas. There had to be a bedroom, and possibly more of a living space, beyond the oval-topped entryways on either side. Maybe there was another door outside of the locked one she came in through?

"Please, join me," Jaxon said.

Stretched out and silently staring from beside his chair was a Rottweiler with a black shiny coat. She hadn't seen a dog in the place since she arrived. Never heard barking. The animal looked peaceful in its chosen spot, but was large and intimidating.

"What is this? You live down here?" she asked.

"We're neighbors," he answered. "Down here I don't have to pretend. And neither do you. Please join me."

"Or what? You'll have your hitman inject with me with poison again?" she crossed her arms. "You'll sic your dog on me? What happens if I refuse after that nice speech you gave me earlier about me having a choice?"

Jaxon looked over to Hutch. Goodiva's gaze went back over her shoulder at the older man with the syringe. Hutch whistled. The dog got up and casually strolled toward him. The animal appeared a bit sluggish as it heaved itself up the stairs. He approached Hutch and then sat on its hind legs. Goodiva's arms lowered from her defensive stance. She watched as the man gave the dog an injection under the collar.

"Henry is diabetic. He needed his insulin," Jaxon informed her.

"Diabetic? Dogs have diabetes?"

"Just like people," Jaxon Price informed her. "Just like me."

He nodded in response to the shock in her eyes. "Type 1. Was diagnosed as a kid. Made it quite difficult for me to survive on the streets when I left here. But I found a way. I always find a way."

"You have diabetes? That was never told to me when I was hired."

"It's not important to our conversation. Henry belonged to my father. Now he belongs to me."

"How sweet," she mumbled.

Jaxon stood to pull out her chair. It felt odd seeing him stand or walk. However, nothing was stranger than being cordial to the man who kidnapped you. From over the candlelight at the table she found him charming in a mind-bending way when he returned to his seat. The leather side of his face covered his scars and added to the mystery of the dinner he prepared for her. What could she possibly give him? She didn't have money, fame. He didn't want sex—or so he said. What was any of this really about?

"So? I'm here. Now what?"

"Yes, you are. At last."

"Yes, yes, before we start. I need you to clarify your statement."

"Which one?" he asked.

"Twixt. You said he confessed at a party before he died?"

"Did I?"

"That doesn't sound like him. He would never confess or brag about anything criminal."

"And?"

"You evidently have money and power. You spent some time in the Middle East. This plane crash...did you hurt him?"

"You mean did I kill him?"

She nodded, her heart beat so hard she clenched her hand into a tight fist.

"At the time of his death I walked with a cane and couldn't stand without it. How could I kill anyone? As for his verbal diarrhea, it was recorded while he snorted coke and entertained dangerous men in Dubai. I have the tape if you want to watch it. Do you?"

She shook her head no.

"Satisfied?" he asked.

"That's not an answer. When a person didn't do something, they simply say no. You had him killed. In that plane," she said.

"What if what you say is true, why would you care? Was he not abusive to you? Or was that a lie too?"

"Death is permanent. I never want to see anyone die."

"Tell that to your teacher," he countered.

She flinched. "Peter Collins wasn't a teacher, asshole. He was my guidance counselor. A school counselor for elementary kids. And this isn't about him."

"I think it is," Jaxon replied.

"What do you want from me?" she asked. "This deal you think I'm going to make with you."

"I'm almost positive you will accept my offer," he said.

He reached across the table and lifted the silver dome that kept her food warm. She was given a charred filet, with broccoli and risotto. It looked divine. The bread on the table was freshly baked. He poured her a glass of rosé. It was her favorite wine, if she were to tolerate alcohol. It was her favorite meal if she were to tolerate beef. Goosebumps pimpled her arms and she felt chilled that he knew more about her than she knew of him. How long had he been invading her life?

"I need an answer to my question please. What do you want?" she asked again.

"Eat," he instructed her.

She picked up the fork and knife. The meat was medium, how she preferred it to be cooked. She tasted it and the beef was so tender and sweet it melted on her tongue. She tried not to savor the loveliness. Living off of sandwiches and soup had made her cravings insatiable. She ate to appease him, and kept her eye on him the entire time.

"After I woke from my coma the doctors told me I'd never walk again. I didn't believe them," he said as he sliced through his steak. "I didn't feel like a cripple. I didn't feel different at all. But I was," his gaze lifted up to hers. "I was very different."

She listened.

"I think it was three months later. They moved me to a private recovery center in the Bay area. Only doctors and Armand visited."

"He's your friend?"

"A relative."

"You're related to Armand Al Jabar, the actor?"

"The first and only priority of mine was to walk. But even money didn't make that easy. It was six months after the accident that Armand and I became interested in justice for why I became a cripple. He had already told me about your visit. At the time, I was too focused on my self-pity to care."

"Because you didn't think you would walk again?"

"Something like that," he said and chewed his steak. "I left the country to work with a specialist that helped me take the steps I needed to, to be here. And then I got information. On you and your lover."

"Ex-boyfriend," she corrected him.

"Right," Jaxon said. "A little research and I was really surprised. You were connected to the Montgomeries. You are best friends with Charles Montgomery's wife. I don't believe in coincidence. Especially when coincidences are tied to my father and an accident that nearly killed me."

"That you caused—" she interjected.

"You knew. Just as you know the history of this place."

"You aren't a Mayfair? What is there to know?"

"My father is Yaşar Fikrit."

"So what? He isn't a Mayfair either. He isn't even an American."

"He's a Turkish businessman who bought this place from Hamilton Mayfair sixty years ago. When you move into Mayfair, you inherit its legacy. He became Master Mayfair just like any owner would."

"Who cares?" she shrugged.

"I suppose I'm spending too much time on the wrong conversation."

"Yes, you are."

"Okay, where should we start?"

"What is your real name? It's not Jaxon Price, right?"

"True. My real name is Fikrit."

"First and last?" she asked.

"Asad is my first name."

"What does this have to do with you kidnapping me?"

"Charles knew," he said and glanced up at her. "Charles Montgomery knew that I had an accident, and that you were responsible. He knew that his wife helped you get out of LA and set you up with money and a new identity in Ghana. He knew about my medical condition. And that my father was close to curing his own."

"Why would Charles know you?"

"Because like I said earlier, he sat on the board of trustees. Delilah was right: he and my father used that clinic as a cover for stem cell research."

"Okay?"

"Charles told me all about you. After I found out that you were connected to Falcon Cove."

"Stop! Right there."

His brows raised.

"How? When? When did you find out?"

"A year after my accident. Twixt..."

"Yes, I know he confessed about everything. But me? He told you I was from Falcon Cove? Why would he do that?"

"I didn't give him many options in our conversation," Jaxon said and took a drink.

"What did Charles tell you about me?"

"What you like, what you don't like, what you need, what scares you and his wife. The secrets you three keep. He didn't know the gritty details. Only that it had a lot to do with Peter Collins and what happened when you were ten—put the man in the grave."

"Charles was a good man—" she began. "But he talked too much."

"Ms. Montgomery knows differently now after her little trip to New York. And I know enough about them and their family to destroy that pristine image she works so hard to protect."

"There you go insulting my friends again," she said in a huff. "How did you even know that I would come here? How did you know I'd return to the Cove from New York?"

"Because you were searching. Peeking into my life, asking questions of people connected with me. Dr. Sean Talbot is how I know," he said.

"Dr. Talbot is my therapist. He is—"

"The one I hired for you."

"Okay, I'm done," she threw her fork down. "I can't take any more of this! What the hell do you want!"

"You caught me when I was vulnerable. My father had died the night we met. I inherited his debt. My *jin* had returned to collect my life."

"What's a *jin*?" she frowned.

"I couldn't hold on to the Jaxon Price façade forever. With my father's death, people would eventually connect me to him. No secret in this world of data and information can last. And my family would bring me back in. Like I said, I was vulnerable. If you only wanted to be friends that would have been fine. I sent you friendship roses."

"You were stalking me," she countered.

"That's a stretch. But I won't deny I was persistent. When you called me that night in trouble, I was desperate to help you. I actually did the most honorable thing—"

"Don't flatter yourself."

"Do you know what I remember most about that night?"

She shrugged.

"Your face. How you looked at me. It was Jaxon Price you were looking at. And Jaxon Price didn't matter to you. He was a token to be used, just like he was for every other woman he's encountered in LA. A ticket to fame. A quick fuck for celebrity. A tag for profit. A nothing."

"You think so lowly of yourself," she said.

"I'm a realist."

"Realist huh? If you really were you'd have seen in my eyes what it was. I was scared," she explained.

"Maybe. I wasn't. Not of dying. I've never had that fear. I was born to die. I have a different kind of fear, and that night when you looked at me dying then ran from me you helped me remove it."

"What in the hell are you talking about?" she asked.

"This is the man I am now. And this is what I want."

There was a black box with a black ribbon. It was next to the gravy dish. She saw it earlier but didn't bother to ask. She wasn't interested in gifts from him.

"Open it," he said and kept eating.

It wasn't a ring box, she was certain, or a bracelet box. It was square and it didn't look like much of anything except for its fancy wrapping. She picked it up and untied the bow. She let the ribbon drift and tore at the paper. She lifted the lid. Her brows drew together in confusion. On top of a black velvet cushion was a sterling silver baby rattle.

"Oh my God?"

"You like it," he asked.

"What is this?" she asked.

"My son," he said, staring at the rattle as if it were a picture of his future heir.

"Say that again?"

"I want a son. A child. And I want him with you," he replied.

She laughed. "What!"

He continued eating his steak as if she hadn't laughed in his face.

"Are you insane?"

"My terms are very simple. You will stay here, and we will use the May-fair Fertility Company to impregnate you."

"That abortion clinic Delilah talked about?"

"It's a women's health facility. It was where Delilah Montgomery conceived. She can attest to the success rate. You will give me a son, and I will release you from any obligation to me or the truth."

"I...I...I—can't. I won't. Why would I? No. No. You really have brain damage. Not going to happen. Ever."

"Don't worry. You will not have anything to do with the child. I will fully compensate you and protect your secrets."

"I won't do that. Give birth to a baby and walk away."

"Why?" he glanced up at her while chewing. "You said you didn't want kids."

"I never said that?" she frowned.

"The night we met. You said you didn't want kids. You said you would never change your mind. You said it," he looked her in the eye.

Her eyes stretched in shock.

"Problem?" he asked.

"I won't give you a kid. For you to do what with? Torture?"

"Nothing obscene, I assure you. My son will have everything I didn't. He'll inherit the Scorpion."

"Scorpion?"

"What is that?"

"A legacy of power. A future greater than anything my father or I have ever done. Like I said I assure you, everything will be fine."

"You assure me? Everything about you holding me hostage is obscene. And that room for a child? I will never participate in something as sick and twisted as the abuse of kids."

"Careful!" Jaxon slammed his fist on the table. "I'm not a pervert. I would never hurt my child. An child. Ever! I want a son. A family of my own. You don't like it, Ahmed will show you the door tonight. Walk your ass out of here in the snow back to your fake life and secrets!"

"I don't like it!" she snipped back at him.

He glared at her for a long pause. Then he withdrew his anger and his interest. Reaching inside of something she could not see, he put the charger to her phone on the table. He stared directly at her when he spoke. "Take it kitten, charge your phone. Be ready to leave the mountain in the next two hours. Hutch will assist."

She grabbed the charger as if it were the winning lottery ticket..

"I suggest you inform your friends that my people and the authorities will be in touch," he said.

"You're going to jail. Not them!" she said and left him.

He smiled.

"We'll see. Goodbye Goddess."

"Burn in hell crazy man," she said.

Goodiva walked out half expecting to be attacked or dragged back in. But when she reached the door and glanced back, Jaxon Price was finishing his meal.

"Creep," she muttered under her breath. "Have a baby? A baby? He's fucking insane."

She ventured out of the second door, and to her surprise and complete shock the entire hall was lit. Gone were the dark shadows that shrouded her vision and kept her trapped in a blind maze of confusion. If the light had been present before, she would have seen scribbled on the dark walls arrows to direct her toward the exit.

She couldn't believe her freedom. She checked the phone in her hand and confirmed the charger was indeed hers. Her things were in her room. She went there first. While she was inside packing up, she had her phone charging in the bathroom. Jaxon Price was not going to win. She would call Queen first and tell her to come with the cops. And when she shared her story of kidnapping and torture, nothing he had on her friends or her would stand. He would be arrested and she would enjoy it.

She walked out of the bathroom and found a folder on the bed. It had her name on it.

Don't look at it girl, just get your stuff and leave. Leave...

The television in the room blinked on. Her head slowly turned to the screen. Delilah's husband was there. This had to be before his diagnosis of stage 4 pancreatic cancer. She sat down and watched the two men converse. When Charles was confronted with the mis-handling of the trust and the money he'd stolen for the Montgomeries, he did not deny it. When Charles was told he could keep his illegal affairs from being exposed if he helped locate his wife's best friend, he didn't hesitate to accept the offer. He gave up more than was asked.

The betrayal she witnessed didn't hurt as bad as the realization of who her best friend was married to. Jaxon Price was right. Delilah cared more than anyone about her reputation, and the legacy of the Montgomeries for her son. Delilah had done everything in her power to protect Goodiva over the years. More than her own mother. But she done quadruple to protect Charles' family. The scandal would destroy her. Goodiva reached behind her and picked up the folder. Inside were the documents Charles sent on her life, down to her social security number. Everything was there. The documents included something strange. A contract for the IVF procedure Delilah had gone through. Why would Jaxon Price have it?

The video changed. It was a hidden camera. It had to be attached to someone's face or lapel. Twixt and his brother had naked women of all races swarming around them. There were several men who looked like Arab sheikhs in their traditional thobe's laughing and enjoying the entertainment. She listened as Kumar bragged of his power and influence. It didn't take long for Jaxon's name to come up, and both brothers exaggerated story of what happened that night to Jaxon. It made her stomach muscles twist into knots.

The television blinked off.

She got up from the bed and wiped her tears. She walked into the bathroom and unplugged her phone. She had two bars. She tried to make a call. An emergency call to the police. Of course, there was no reception below in the dungeon. She glanced to the folder on the bed and thought it best to retrieve it. With tears in her eyes she walked out of the prison he left her in and tried her best to trace her steps to where she left Jaxon Price. She got lost twice before she found the correct hall. And inside she found Jaxon Price seated by his fireplace waiting with a brandy glass in his hand. He stared at the fire but he knew she was back.

"I thought you were leaving Ms. Johnson?"

"You know damn well what this means to my friend."

"She could be prosecuted, along with her brothers-in-law. Yes."

"What do the fertility documents mean?" Goodiva asked.

Jaxon Price took a sip of his amber brandy and didn't respond.

"Answer me. Why did you give that document to me?"

"Poor Charles. His wife wanted a baby. He was incompetent in business as well as in being a man."

"You're an asshole," she said.

"Does the boy look like him?" Jaxon Price asked. "African American?"

Goodiva opened the folder. She looked at the document again. She scanned the medical statistics for the information. It was stated who the donor was. It wasn't Charles.

"Why would Charles do this to her?"

"He had a vasectomy years ago. Tried to reverse it. For Charles, it didn't go so well. He had a low sperm count. Didn't want his wife, who blamed her inability to conceive a child on herself, to know the truth. So, he took control of the situation with the help of my father. If I had known he needed a donor I would have spared us both the trouble of this agreement and offered him a sample myself," he said, and cut her an evil smirk.

"Not funny," she said.

"I don't tell jokes," he replied.

She struggled to keep the tears brimming her eyes from falling. She knew he enjoyed her struggle because this time he didn't look away. "Charles and my father shared many interests. Especially when it came to blood disorders and cancers. Cures can be made from stem cells. Dad agreed to find the perfect donor for his wife, and my father got the stems cells he wanted. Helluva bargain. Considering what my father really wanted was Delilah to conceive him a son. The best stem cells for his research would need to come from a son."

"Wait? Your father? He wanted to impregnate Delilah?"

"To ensure that Charles belonged to him, yes. The lab screwed up my father's plans. Gave your best friend the sperm of a man who was married and trying to use the clinic to conceive with his wife instead of his donation. It didn't matter. My father had inseminated several other women who gave birth to boys that were his, not their husbands. To continue his research."

"It was a mix-up, but the end goal was achieved. The baby was born and my father delivered the news to Charles that boy was not African American. You can never make deals with the devil and not pay with just your soul. The Montgomeries have a secret to protect. For his cooperation and loyalty, my father kept the true conception of his child from his wife. But my father is dead. Those secrets belong to me." He set the brandy glass down on the readers table next to his chair. "I know that the man who is the father of Delilah's baby is a widow. No family. Just a lot of pain over his wife dying in childbirth. He has no idea he has a son, but imagine what could happen if he did?"

Goodiva put her hand to her mouth to stifle her shock.

"I wonder what he would do if he found out that he had flesh and blood that was being raised without him?"

"This will kill her. It will destroy her, and everything in her life."

"Funny, Charles had the same reaction when my father told him the truth. See, Dad liked to videotape every visit to Mayfair, and every conversation. I could play that one for you."

"Stop."

"That's why Charles gave me all of the information on you when he and I met face to face. But he got sick shortly after our new bargain, convenient. Isn't it?" Jaxon Price chuckled. He then snapped his fingers. "And that was the end of Charles, the end of our game."

"You're enjoying this," she said.

"A little," he shrugged.

She stood there for a long moment digesting his version of the past. He watched her.

"Can I ask you a question Goddess?"

"What?" she sighed.

"How did three ten-year-old girls kill a man?"

"We never killed anyone," Goodiva said. "I can't give you a baby. I have an issue, I can't conceive children. That's why I don't want any..."

"Don't lie to me," he said.

"I can't do it."

"You're healthy, I've checked your medical records. You were examined shortly after you came here. You had that virus. But we saved your life, and you're healthy."

"Virus? What virus? Wha-whaaa—you—did what? When I was locked in that room? You drugged me? Examined me? Violated me?"

"It was necessary. You signed a release form upstairs with Armand for the procedure."

"Oh my God! I did not!"

"You should read every contract," he picked up his brandy glass again. He swirled the drink in the glass goblet. "You can and will give me a son."

"Did you...did you—"

"Consider this contract no different than being an egg donor, like the sperm donor for your friend's baby. As you can see, my son will have the best life. He will have me."

"Something is wrong with you!" she said.

"That's the offer. Do you accept or not?"

"And this!" She shook the folder at him. "What happens with this?"

"We can burn it in the fire. Together," he toasted her with his drink. "Oh, don't worry. Delilah already has that information. It was given to her in New York. My people said she destroyed it. The scandal would be too much for her to take on. Looks like she keeps secrets too. Haven't figured out the Detective Queen Douglas. She's a by the law kind of girl. Well almost, considering Peter Collins."

Goodiva couldn't think of a thing to say or do. She stood still, trapped. And he kept talking. "Don't you see? You will be helping her, just like she helped you."

"I can't believe I was so wrong about you. I can't believe I've spent three years of my life praying to see you again, to make things right between us," she said. "All this time I should have been running as far as I could from you."

"I'm not all evil."

"Are you kidding?" she asked. "You're the personification of evil."

"I thought about you a lot too, after my accident. Especially after I found out you were my destiny."

"I'm nothing to you!"

"How else do you explain it?"

"I can't explain anything about you!"

He chuckled. "How do you explain us both growing up here? In Falcon Cove? How do you explain us running away from our problems, our parents? You said you we met by accident. I believe you. A serendipitous accident. We are survivors. My son will be a fighter, a warrior. A survivor. Give me a son, and the past is forgiven all secrets stay buried, like Peter Collins."

"You don't know me. If you did, you would know I could never do this."

"I want this more than anything in the world Goodiva, and I have prepared for every action you think to take. I'll take our son if I can't have you both. But I will have a part of you, regardless."

She blinked away her tears. She refused to give him any further sign of weakness. Godiva bit on her bottom lip and wondered if she could reach the knife on the table fast enough to plunge into his black heart. She shook her head in disbelief.

"Prove to me that you are loyal to your friends. Prove it to yourself. Stay with me. Give me a son."

She put a hand to her brow. She closed her eyes and thought of everything. She thought of the worst moment in her life and the scared ten-year-old girls that saved her from it. How many times had they come to her rescue? What had she ever done, even close, to sacrifice for them? She had to think of something. It had to be as outrageous as his plan. Something to buy her time. Something to help her defeat him. And the only thing that kept coming to her mind was to give him what he wanted to gain leverage.

"I have a few conditions to this contract," she said.

"I'm listening."

"Six months. I will give you six months to try for a pregnancy. If we don't get pregnant in six months, you let me go and you keep this secret."

"A year," he countered.

She bit down on her bottom lip. "My friends won't last a year looking for me. It's too long."

"A year," he repeated.

"Fine. A year. But we don't do IVF."

He frowned.

"You want a baby. You have to make one. The old-fashioned way," she said. "You said Charles wasn't man enough to do it. What about you?"

Jaxon Price sat forward. He chuckled. He shook his head smiling. "This I didn't expect." He said through his laughter. He stared at her from behind the mask. "You want me to make a baby with you?"

"Yes. I won't have your doctors doing to me what was done to Delilah. I won't let you have that much control over my body, not again. It's my body. So, I, uhm, will do it."

"Do it?" he smiled. "All of it?"

"You like sex. I remember. I've already slept with you before. So, uh, sure, I'll do it. That's my terms."

Jaxon shook his head to the offer.

"Are you saying no?" she asked.

"No," he forced himself to stop laughing and regained control. "I need a son. I want you, and I hope to have your body again, soon, in time. But my chances are secured if we do the IVF."

"It's my body! You aren't God. You can't play God when creating a life. You want a son, you have to make one the same way any other man does."

He stared at her. A sly smile lifted the corner of his mouth. "IVF," he repeated.

"Three months. We try for, uhm, let's say three months. If it doesn't work then I'll consider the IVF," she said.

"Why are you stalling? What can you do in three months to change any of this?"

"Who says I'm trying to change—"

"IVF. It is my preference, it is the only offer," he insisted.

"I won't do IVF. No matter what you threaten me with. I won't."

He glared at her. He studied her. She was careful to not lower her gaze. He sat back and considered her move. She sensed he saw through her tactics to control or manipulate him. But did he really understand the lengths she would go through to escape their deranged agreement? If he really knew what she and her friends did to Peter Collins he wouldn't be so smug. "Fine Goddess, we can play house for three months. I think I'll enjoy it."

"Play house?" she frowned.

"The only deal to end this game is a son. You understand? That means you're mine, beauty, pussy, and soooooooouuuuuul," he crooned.

She turned to leave before she lost her nerve.

"That belongs to me," he said.

"What?" she paused.

"Cellphone. It belongs to me. You'll get it back when you're ready."

She looked down at the cell phone in her hand. She sighed. She walked over to the table with her half-eaten meal on top and set the phone and charger down.

"Thank you, Goddess."

She had one last hidden secret. He hadn't found out about her IUD. Something his research could not uncover, because she had it put in when she was in Europe.

"Goodiva," he said.

She glanced back at him as she headed for the door.

"I'll see you soon," he said.

Chapter Fifteen

Goodiva gripped her hair and tugged so hard the roots burned. Everything she knew about herself came into question. How could she even consider agreeing to such a horrible plan? How could she go through with it?

"Goddess? He had the nerve to call me Goddess!"

She turned to find he had followed her into her room. The mere thought of their agreement sent a cold shiver of dread through her already queasy stomach. She took a step back from him, thinking of a hundred excuses she could conjure to send him out of the room and keep him from her bed.

"You left before I showed you where you will be staying. Come with me and I will give you the tour."

"Down here?"

"Where we dined. Yes. There's much more to the place than you've seen."

"I don't want to stay underground like some science experiment. I agreed to your terms. I want to come upstairs."

"Not yet. The staff can't know that you are here. They'll be gone soon."

"Today? You said they will be leaving today."

"Did I?"

"I won't tell them. I'll go to your bedroom upstairs and stay there. I know the staff is forbidden from entering it without your permission."

"No. They will not connect my son to you, so you can't be seen."

"He will be of mixed race. DNA will forever bind me to this child. Have you thought of that?"

"I have. Trust me, I have it under control. After my son is born I'm returning to Saudi Arabia with him."

"Saudi... what? You're going back to the Middle East?"

"It's my first home."

"You're American?"

"I'm Muslim. I'm Arab. I'm American in that order."

"My friends will look for me," she insisted.

"I'm aware. I've made provisions."

"How? How do you stop people who love me from caring? How!"

"My father taught me how. Grab your things. I'll wait," he said.

Goodiva didn't know what to do or say. She refused to let him think he could order her around. She folded her arms in defiance. "If you're taking me to my new prison, then this should be my last night of freedom. Uhm, right? I want you out of here. I want to stay here tonight. Alone. I'll be ready to leave in the morning to honor our agreement. But right now, the sight of you... it makes me sick."

The smile on his face dimmed. He looked disappointed. Did he actually think she found him charming?

"As you wish," he said and walked out.

Goodiva went to the bed. She tossed the blanket to the floor and ripped off the sheet. She went to the television mounted on the wall and covered it with the sheet. No matter where the camera was, he wouldn't see her. Suddenly she felt safe. And suddenly she could breathe. She hadn't realized it, but she'd been close to hyperventilating since their talk. He wanted to play games. She intended to teach him the lesson of his life. And if she had to use her body to do it, so be it.

JAXON EXHALED DEEPLY before he pressed the speaker button on the phone.

"This is Price."

"Mr. Price, I've left several messages," Dr. Talbot said.

"I'm aware," Jaxon replied.

"Huh? That's it? You know why I'm calling? What are you going to do?"

"I'm afraid I don't. Do about what?"

"Hold on," the doctor sighed. "I had a visit from a Colorado detective. She is looking for Goodiva Johnson. Demanding to know if I knew where she'd gone. She told me a missing person's report has been filed. Where is Goodiva? Do you know? Is she okay? What am I supposed to tell the police? What?"

"I don't know where she is. She quit after she discovered the truth about me."

"What am I supposed to tell the police?"

"Where are you now?"

"New York. My office."

"What have you said?"

"Nothing. Are you crazy? I'm not saying anything without a lawyer. I accepted money from you. If the detective pushes too hard, I'm lawyering up."

"My money was a donation to your foundation, not for services."

"Are you serious? You paid me—"

"The detective is looking for her friend. Nothing to worry about," said Jaxon. "There was no crime. Goodiva Johnson left my estate weeks ago, they'll find her."

"But I am worried. Worried that you did something to her."

"Why would I harm her?"

"I thought—"

"I'm sure they will find her soon."

"Thank you Mr. Price. I was so worried that—"

Jaxon hung up the phone. He drummed his fingers on the surface of this desk. Ahmed looked up from his computer screen. He informed him that the call was indeed being monitored and traced. It was to be expected. Detective Douglas was doing what any officer would. She was trying to smoke him out. It wouldn't take long before she understood the depths of his deception. When Hutch walked into the room, Jaxon got up and plucked his bottle of water from the desk. He drank from it as he paced, working through his next move. His diabetes made him prone to thirst. His staff left glass water bottles for him in every room.

"What is it Hutch?"

Hutch glanced to Ahmed. He was one of the few Scorpions that Jaxon kept at Mayfair, and the supposed driver that the detective was trying to track down in Dubai.

"She hasn't gotten the phone records. She must be working rogue on this. My contacts in the NYPD assure me there is no active investigation. My contacts at the FCPD here in Falcon say she has taken a leave of absence. She's investigating you."

"Homeland Security?" Jaxon asked as he took another swallow. "She has friends with the FBI, correct?"

"I'm working on it. That one isn't as easy to solve," Hutch confessed.

"The storm? Is it too late for me to move Goodiva? Take her out of the country?"

Hutch nodded his head.

Jaxon drank the water and glanced to Ahmed. He exhaled. "Hutch?"

"Sir?"

"Am I...am I him?" he asked.

Ahmed looked up at Hutch in anticipation of his response. Jaxon didn't bother to ask Ahmed. He already knew what the Scorpions wanted. What they believed in.

"No, sir, you are not your father. Your father was a traitor. You have proven your loyalties."

"I don't have much time left. I don't want it to end like this. I'm doing what I can to fix things. I'm doing what I have to."

"Eventually she will understand sir. When the child is born, I will protect them both," Hutch said. Henry, his doggy companion, lifted his head and stared at his master as well.

"I want this problem to go away. But don't hurt her friends. Do you understand Hutch?"

"We need a body. Something to throw them off your scent," Ahmed suggestion.

"No. I don't want them to think she's dead. Just toss the bait in a different direction."

"Understood sir, I can handle a problem like this. Make it simpler for you," said Hutch, before he turned on his heel and walked away. Jaxon toyed with his empty bottle of water. Ahmed continued to work on his laptop, building the business that Jaxon could someday inherit.

Once upon a time he had escaped Mayfair. He had run from the devil himself. He did it all to ensure he'd never be the man his father was. But when he tried to be the hero, he was almost crippled because of it. Armand was right. He was mother's son, not his father's.

Cedars-Sinai Medical Center, July 12, 2016

Jaxon opened his right eye. When he swallowed he felt alive. This time it didn't taste like razorblades. This time he tasted his own saliva. His entire body from the neck down had numbed.

"You're awake?"

Jaxon's right eye went as far left as it could. He couldn't see the man who spoke to him, but he sensed his presence.

The House of Saud in Saudi Arabia is composed of descendants from Muhammed bin Saud and his brothers. Prince Khaled bin Abdallah was one of those descendants. He stepped to the front of Jaxon's bed and faced him. He was older, a man in his mid-80s. He had fathered twenty-two sons and six daughters. One of those daughters was the tie that bound Jaxon to the prince forever.

"Armand called me. Told me everything."

Jaxon was surprised his grandfather chose to speak in English. It wasn't a language the old man respected.

"The American press think the men who almost ended your life are heroes. Scorpions tell me a different story."

Jaxon blinked once for his answer.

"They still don't know who you are. I understand that choice. I've allowed you to be your own man. This Jaxon Price person you admire so much. I did so because I understood what your father did to my daughter and to you is my wrongdoing as well."

Jaxon looked to the left to see if Armand was in the room. The only men accompanying the Prince were those who had no names. He turned his gaze back to his grandfather.

"Who is she? This woman? Armand said he doesn't know who she is to you."

"She's no one..." Jaxon voice croaked.

"We'll find her," the prince assured him. "And these heroic men? When the media looks away we'll find them too."

"Wait," Jaxon croaked.

The prince stared at him.

"Let me. Find her...them."

"And?"

Jaxon took a deep breath. He had to summon the will to speak. If he didn't speak, Goodiva and her boyfriend were dead. There was no way he could save her life. Her only crime was knowing him. He didn't blame her for running. He wanted to warn her when the men started beating on him to run fast and to keep running. But now it had gone too far. She was in real danger.

"And?" the prince said again.

"No more hiding," Jaxon replied. "I am not Jaxon Price. I am your grandson."

"You always were," the prince waved off the comment as meaningless.

"I go back. Family. Everything. I go back. As my mother's son."

"And?" the prince asked.

"Through Allah all things are great. As is the Scorpion."

"All of my sons are Scorpions," the prince said. "You are saying nothing Asad."

"I will be your Scorpion," Jaxon corrected himself. "I denounce my father."

"For this woman?"

"No. For you. Jin," Jaxon said.

The prince stared at him for a long time. He didn't blame the old man for not trusting him. Jaxon had bargained with him twice before. But not once had he ever agreed to accept the family. He and Armand had been taught to always refuse.

"We will take you out of here. Get you the medical care you need. Don't listen to these American doctors. They don't know about the blood in your veins, the cure for your sickness. I do."

Jaxon blinked. Sickness? What did he mean, sickness and cure? The prince walked over to him and took his hand. "I love your mother. She is my desert rose. I failed her. Twice. And I failed you. Once. That is why I let you go. That is why I let you be this man. But you're my grandson again. You belong to the family. Understood?"

Jaxon answered in Arabic that he did.

The prince kissed his brow.

"Kill them both," the prince whispered in his ear. "Then come home to me son, where you belong."

"Yes jin. As soon as I am able, it will be done."

The tiny beep of Jaxon's monitor attached to his hip reminded him of the need to take his medicine. With a burdened sigh, Jaxon pushed up from his chair and walked into the bathroom.

Cedars-Sinai Medical Center, July 12, 2016

*"What are you thinking! Telling (jin) that you will be **the** Scorpion?"*

"Why did you call him?" Jaxon asked.

"I didn't!" Armand said. "It's all over the news! Are you insane?"

"He's going to kill them if I don't," Jaxon said in a hoarse whisper from his hospital bed.

"Who? That bitch who put you in this bed? Those freaks that beat you on the side of the road?"

"It's not her fault, or theirs. I caused the accident," Jaxon reasoned.

"Bullshit. Jin had his people speak to the witness and pay them off. They said those hip-hop frauds were about to throw you over the side of the road when they drove up."

Jaxon didn't remember. He was unconscious shortly after the beating started.

"You're doing this for a woman you barely know."

"I'm a dead man regardless. You and I both know that. Jin confirmed it. My blood work is back. I have the disease, don't I?"

"We are going to get you help."

Jaxon sighed. He knew all too well what that kind of help would mean. The madness that consumed his father would soon consume him. "Doesn't matter. She's innocent. Fuck the rest of them. I won't let jin hurt her."

"You think this little deal is going to stop jin? She's already dead. And so is her boyfriend," Armand said with disgust. "You are throwing what's left of your life away on a woman you don't know. It makes no sense. And her of all people. She's beneath you."

"Shut up," Jaxon warned his cousin. "She stays safe. When I'm out of this bed I'll deal with the boyfriend. But no one touches them. If I'm the Scorpion, I say who lives and dies."

"And if you're sick? Or go insane from that blood disease? When you're dead? What then? What protects her from  (Jin's) wrath then? Huh? We both know he never forgives or forgets an enemy."

It was a valid question. His grandfather would possibly outlive them all. Goodiva was marked. Whether it happened today or ten years from that moment, another Scorpion would see to his grandfather's wishes.

"I'll think of something," he said.

JAXON LOCATED HIS INSULIN that had been part of his life since he was a boy. He took his dosage. He closed his eyes when he was done and tried to settle on one emotion instead of the hundreds of questioning feelings tormenting him since he made his proposal.

After a moment of reflection Jaxon returned to his chair and picked up his remote. He turned on his obsession. Her starring role in her only movie. She wasn't a good actress. She was a far better DJ. However, he could see potential, and with a bit more training she could definitely be better than some of his chosen leading ladies. And the movie wasn't well crafted. There wasn't much to the plot or her character development. Still, he'd watched it over a hundred times to see her smile, to hear her voice, to burn her beauty into his brain. Jaxon picked up his laptop. He had the sub-level suite wired and could connect to any video feed on the estate. Once again, he preferred her room, to watch her sleep.

He could see nothing.

She found a way to shut him out. And he admired her bravery for doing so. He loved their differences, but in learning about her he discovered they had similarities too, such as music. All of the soulful rhythm and blues songs he got from her playlist he replayed over and over. He turned off the television and put the music on instead.

August 26, 2016

Jaxon took another step, and then another. His arms shook but he was able to drag each foot and feel every muscle strain in his legs. His grip on the iron bars that were on either side of him was unyielding in strength and purpose. His upper body had gained even more muscular strength due to his rigorous physical therapy. He was in control.

"Good, you're doing good," said his nurse in Arabic.

He nodded his thanks to her. Two of his men helped him to his chair.

"You done for the day?" Armand asked.

"Almost, he has his bath next," blushed the nurse.

Armand's brows arched. Jaxon shook his head that her blush meant nothing to him. The women knew who he was. And for them that made him appealing. An arranged marriage was already pending thanks to his jin's fast work. He wouldn't get a say.

"I got a surprise for you," Armand said with his hand behind his back.

"I don't like surprises."

"You're going to like this," Armand chanted, and danced around, concealing his gift.

"What is it?" Jaxon frowned.

"A new face!" Armand laughed. He revealed a mask of some kind. It was made from a very fine, thinly cut, black leather. Jaxon accepted it. It looked like half a mask to wear. He then glanced up to Armand with a question in his eyes.

"Try it on," Armand said.

"I'm not wearing this! I'll look like a freak."

"Have you checked a mirror lately?" Armand chuckled. "Here, let me help. He put the mask on him and then pushed his wheelchair over to the mirror. "You look bad ass. Like a deadly Scorpion. A man soon to be married."

"Very funny." Jaxon stared at himself in the mirror. He had to admit it did give him a dose of confidence to have the terror on the left side of his face covered.

"Is that a smile or gas I see on your face?" Armand chuckled.

"Can you be serious for a moment?" Jaxon asked.

Armand put his hands up and backed away.

"I have a plan," Jaxon said.

"What kind of plan?" Armand asked without genuine interest.

"How I can make sure she is safe."

"She who?" Armand asked.

"My kitten."

"What? You're barely out of this chair. They're pumping your body with all kinds of chemicals and you're still thinking about her?"

"I want you to find her," he said.

"It's been months. Why?"

"Because 进 (jin) has not forgotten. He won't forget. He's just waiting to see what I intend to do when I can stand as a man before him. Why do you think he is arranging my marriages?"

"What do you intend to do? What could you do that would save her life? Because no matter how long it takes, those three have one ending." Armand gestured his finger like a gun and pointed it to his temple. "I'm surprised they are alive now."

"They're alive because I have not taken the oath. When I do, it all changes."

"Like I said, there is nothing you can do to stop it," Armand reminded him.

"I'll kill the boyfriend and the brother," Jaxon said.

"Wait? Kill? Are you fucking mad? Are you?" Armand walked over to the door to the rehabilitation room and closed it. "You really do think that wheelchair is giving you superpowers. Kill them? We aren't killers. We aren't these men. We chose a different path."

"I am a different man now."

"No the hell you aren't! You make movies, and fuck blondes on top of stacks of money. Have you ever shot a firearm? Held one?"

"Doesn't matter," Jaxon reasoned.

"The hell it doesn't. Look. I know you accepted jin's offer to come home and join the clan. I know what our family is. But killing someone is different. I'm not going to be a part of that."

"Fine. I'll do it without you," Jaxon said.

Armand took a deep breath, and made a long sigh. He closed his eyes and paced with his hands to his head.

"Will you help me?" Jaxon asked.

"Shut up, I'm thinking of a way to get you out of this."

"There is no way out," Jaxon said.

"But kill them? Ourselves? Say you do take the Scorpion, and kill the boyfriend and brother. How does that save her?"

Jaxon smiled.

"Am I missing something? What will you do?" Armand smirked.

"I'll give her a son."

Armand's smirk faded from his mouth.

"You know what that means. No one would touch the mother of my son. And جـ (jin) will not want this son to be a Scorpion. Will he?"

"You're going to impregnate a black American woman? Give her your heir to piss off your grandfather? That's your plan?"

"It's a good plan."

"The son is yours, whether he is mixed race or not. Jin will take him."

"Maybe not. But even if he does, he won't harm her or him. Will he?" Jaxon said.

"It's a stupid plan."

"Are you going to help me or not?"

"Well let's see. From what I know, she's gone. Where the fuck she went, who knows? And since she never came forward to tell the truth about what happened that night, my guess is she doesn't give a fuck about you. Let alone carrying your seed. As for the fake rap-star, he's out living his life in the UK. A very public life. He gets a pimple and it's on CNN. He has paparazzi as part of his entourage. How do you kill a man like that and not get caught?"

"There's a way. Like I said, I have a plan. I'm getting out of this chair first, then returning to Mayfair."

Armand's eyes looked as if they would pop from his skull. Jaxon ignored it. He had more important things to do. For one, he was talking about giving his soul back to the devil, turning his back against the light he ran toward when he escaped his father and his past.

"What do you need me for? Sounds to me like you have it all worked out," Armand asked.

"Everything. I need you to stay close to jin. To make sure he doesn't do anything before I can handle him myself."

"Are you sure? You got a second chance. A chance to be better than this. I for one would not throw that away on a woman I barely know."

"What life do I really have left with this bad blood in my veins? I want a son. But not the son that the family will take and destroy. My son. And I want her. I don't know why, yes, I do. When I was in the hospital you told me, she came. I remember it. I remember her, being there. How it felt. I can't explain it, but I want her. I'll have my son with her."

"Then I was wrong. You're just like your father," Armand said with disgust.

Jaxon sat forward. He felt like shit. The medicine wasn't working like it used to, and his diabetes didn't help. He left the chair and tried to sleep in his room. But he kept missing her. It had been over three hours since they last spoke. It was late enough for her to sleep, but what he really craved was the sound of her voice. Something from her. Anything. He went back to his laptop and accessed her room. The camera installed on the television provided perfect clarity in the darkness. Yet, nothing could be seen beyond a gauzed distortion that he soon determined was a sheet or pillowcase. She had intentionally shut him out.

He refused to accept the loneliness.

Chapter Sixteen

Goodiva knew what was happening between them was wrong. Yet, under the weight of him, with the feel of his bare skin pressed against hers and the swirl of movement of his pelvis to her hips, he was a blur and so were her emotions. The temperature in the room climbed a thousand degrees. His damp lips fit perfectly to hers and his urgent. Intensity increased in their kiss and she had no choice but to match it with her own. Three years of longing for him collided with the stark reality of his betrayal and murderous intentions. Still she gave him no resistance. Goodiva's thighs cinched his waist. She locked her feet just under the crease beneath his buttocks. The full force of his desire and surging penetration compressed her breathing. It restricted the airways in her lungs. Desire for the man he clearly had pulled her even deeper into the tidal wave of lust rolling over and over her loins. Her lids fluttered. They threatened to shut, but she didn't dare do so. *Why should she surrender? Why her? Why now?* Trapped in his embrace she moved as he did. He thrust his hips, lifted his pelvis from hers, and then sank into her deep and deeper. Goodiva clawed at his biceps while heaving her pelvis upward in timing to meet his bone crushing downward strokes. There was so much raw emotion and energy between the lips of her vagina she mistook his invasion for love. She groaned and pleaded for more as he pounded thickness in and out of her. Her vagina convulsed and a heat wave seared her skin, boiling the blood in her veins. Tears turned to steam upon her cheeks her body was so hot.

He was her tormentor, her kidnapper, her monster. She owed him her soul.

"Stop! Get off!" she shouted over his shoulder. She wasn't prepared. Not for this, not for him, not for the consequences of his sick bargain. She didn't want it no matter what her body gave consent to.

"Stop!" she cried out and pushed her way forcefully out of her night-mare. Goodiva sat up in the darkness drenched in her own sweat. She choked on her own breath. She looked around, half expecting him to pounce on her again wearing his mask and nothing else. But she was alone. She ripped the sheet from her body. She could still feel the sticky heat of sexual pangs deep within her pussy. Terrified, she kicked off the covers and got down on her knees as she often did when her nightmares were too vivid to be unbelieved.

She clasped her hands together and prayed. She prayed for her escape and salvation. She prayed for Delilah and Queen to not be harmed. She prayed for Twixt's soul, because she feared he burned in hell. She prayed that the evil man tormenting her would find forgiveness in his cold heart to release her. She prayed for him hardest of all. And praying helped. He wasn't in the room with her. She was safe. For now. But the nightmares were back, and they taunted her with thoughts and desires she suppressed when awake. It was sick. It was pathetic. She hated the weakness in her. And she would not mistake that weakness for actual feelings. He was to be defeated, destroyed. He was her enemy. She had to remember that always.

Slowly she climbed back in bed. She held her pillow to herself in fear. She felt real terror. He wasn't there. But his presence felt so real. Her lust for him felt so dangerously real. Was she losing her mind? Then she glanced to the television. The sheet she had used to cover the television had been removed. She stared directly at the TV and deep down inside she knew he stared back.

JAXON LIFTED HIS FACE from his palm and sat forward. What had happened? He'd watched her sleep every night since she arrived. Not since she suffered feverish dreams when he first kidnapped her had he seen her react so wildly. No matter how late or for how long her nightmares lasted, he enjoyed watching her. It was how he knew when exhaustion claimed her enough for him to sneak into her room and leave her food. Tonight had been different. She tried to shut him out. He went into her room expecting confrontation but found her asleep. She hadn't used her sheet to cover her beautiful body. Instead the sheet was draped over the television. He stared at her ingenuity with a pride-filled smile. She was smart, strong, resilient, and even if he had to put her through the worst of him, she'd be a good mother to their child. A protective one. The one he never had. Jaxon took down the sheet and turned to leave but her light snoring tempted him. He stopped at the foot of her bed. She was a deep sleeper. Several times he'd thought she'd catch him creeping about to leave her fruit and water or folding her clothes she had thrown around the room. She never woke.

She wore a colorful silk scarf that had slipped back on her hair and her perfect lips were parted as she gave a slight snore. Jaxon wanted to join her. He would confess in any court of law how badly he wanted to wake her after slipping inside of her without permission. Deep in his loins he burned to do so. But he did not. He'd crossed so many lines, first as an admirer, then as a stalker, and now her kidnapper. There was no denying how much he had wronged her. No matter his intentions.

Instead he indulged himself enough time to touch the tiny sixth pinky toe on her foot. She'd painted it pink along with the other five. And with the tip of his fingernail he touched it. She thought it was a birth defect. He considered it as beautiful as her eyes, lips, breasts and hips. Imperfection was not hers to assume. Imperfection was his to admire.

He left her as he found her.

Now she was on her knees praying. He remained riveted. She ended her prayer and got in the bed. It was then she saw the television. The accusation in her eyes was clear. Whether he'd been there or not, she was accusing him of violating her.

"Don't you ever touch me without my permission!" Goodiva shrieked at him. "Do you hear me! Ever!"

He glanced down to the keypad and the button he could press to give himself a voice in the conversation. But he decided against it. Whatever nightmare she had, he was a part of it. He was most certainly the cause of it. She tried again to sleep, but couldn't. It got so bad for her she got up from the bed, picked up the pillow and blanket, then went into the bathroom to close the door and shut him out.

Armand had warned him on more than one occasion his family home felt creepy, haunted, and too dark for anyone to live in for a long time.

There was madness in the cellars, and if he kept her locked away in that room, she'd slip into it. That room was no place for the future mother of his child.

WITH A HAND THAT TREMBLED, she turned off the tap. She dried her face. The dream felt so real she was certain that he'd done something to her. He might have drugged the food. He might have drugged the water. How could she be sure? What had left her so enraged? The fact that he locked her away and returned in the night to spy on her? Or was it the fact that even a dreamy touch from him sent a lustful surge through her that perverted her emotions?

"Come out. We should talk," he said.

She stood straight from her forward lean over the sink.

He was in the room. He was there.

"Leave!" she answered from behind the door.

"I can stay here for as long as it takes. We will talk."

Goodiva opened the door to the bathroom. Jaxon waited for her. She stepped out, but not far. She crossed her arms and faced him.

"What do you want?"

"To talk," he replied.

"You said what you had to say. You made it clear what you expected. *IVF! IVF! IVF!* Now what do you want from me? Our bargain isn't sealed until tomorrow."

"I need to explain—"

"I don't want to hear it. Leave me the hell alone."

"I don't expect you to understand, but I feel…it doesn't matter what I feel. I should, explain."

"Fine, it's your game. Do whatever you want. But I don't have to listen," she turned to go back into the bathroom and shut the door.

"Do you know what this room is?"

"A place you kidnap and hide women in to torture them?" she asked from under the door threshold. It was his last chance to reach her. If she closed the door on the conversation his pride would overrule his need to appease her and he'd again retreat to his secrets.

He pointed to the floor. "I was born in this room. Conceived in this house, but born here." He walked over to the other door in the room and opened it. "I was broken as a boy and abandoned by my mother in this room."

Jaxon looked back to see if she was still with him. She stared at him and listened. "I lived here until I was nine or seven. I'm not sure what my real age is. But I lived her until I was at least seven. Then I was allowed to live upstairs. But upstairs was different. It was his place. His rules. And if I broke them. Well, it was never smart to break his rules. This place was mine. So even after I was freed to be his son in front of everyone, I would come down here and sleep on that kids' bed until I was too big for it. Then I slept on the floor until I was strong enough to run away from Mayfair."

Jaxon pulled the door shut.

"You're right. This is not the place for you. I'll take you to where you can be more comfortable."

"Upstairs? With you?" she asked in a voice that was almost childlike. He saw hope light up in her eyes. And he felt like a bastard all over again for doing what was necessary to extinguish it.

"No."

"Upstairs!" she demanded.

"My answer is the same."

"Then my answer's no too. I'll stay right here thank you very much."

"Nightmares? You're having them? When you were sick, shortly after I locked you in here, you had them for days. Hallucinations. One time you sat up in bed and was talking to Peter Collins. You don't remember, do you?"

She frowned. "No."

He nodded. "She had them. My mother. I had them. It's almost like this room is the cause of them."

"No. It's not this room or any ghosts, or a fever. It's you. You give me nightmares. Being a prisoner is giving me nightmares," she sighed. "I don't want to hear your pathetic lies anymore."

"I'm not lying. But you're right. What I'm telling you is pathetic, because even if part of me wants to let you go upstairs just so you won't hate me as much, I'll never do it."

She blinked at him in surprise by the conviction in his tone. She knew he was serious. That was a good thing. Because he was.

"Come with me. I won't touch you. I won't hurt you. I won't even stay with you. But it's time to leave this room."

Goodiva stared at him during a long, angry pause. She grabbed her robe and put it on then tightened her scarf on her head. She put on her shoes last. Jaxon watched her gather her things, and helped with her luggage. Neither of them spoke as they walked out through the halls and returned to his private residence beneath Mayfair. She'd seen the place where he dined and entertained, but hadn't been invited to go further.

"You'll have your own room."

She stared after him and refused to show gratitude.

He turned and started into the darkness.

She could run from him again. She could try for the elevator again, and even make it upstairs. And then what? He had enough evidence to destroy her friends. What else could she do? Instead of flight, she followed him past the darkness to a room open to her by the absence of a door. Inside she found everything.

A bed fit for Cleopatra was to the center of the room. It was raised on a platform two feet off the ground. To the left was a sofa and chair with a television above a stone fireplace. To the right was another lounger next to bookshelves that had to reach twelve feet upward. And the bottom shelves were the most interesting. There were rows, and rows, and rows of albums. Goodiva stared at the record player and speaker system that looked as if it came out of the 70's.

Jaxon went to the walk-in closet and left her luggage. She walked over to the bathroom and turned on the light. A steel-gray clawfoot tub with copper lining was on a dark marble swirled tiled flooring. The shower was separate and the lighting fixtures inside weren't very bright, like the lighting fixtures throughout his subterranean home.

"Goddess?"

She whirled on him.

"Sorry. Didn't mean to startle you."

"Uh, uhm, I'm okay."

He stared at her for a moment. She felt completely undressed in front of him with how long he stared. He then managed a smile. "You're settled. There's a kitchen here, and everything works. My room is to the left of this one. I'll let you sleep and we'll talk in the morning."

"It's night time? Again?"

"Time seems to pass very fast in this place," he said. "But it's still the same night, the sun hasn't risen yet."

"Aren't you leaving? You said you would."

"If you want me too, then yes," he said, hopeful she would change her mind.

"I want you too. And no peeking at me either. I want you to leave me alone."

He stared as if he would object. He then nodded that he understood.

"Why do you have all of this? Below ground. Are you into some sadistic rituals? Kidnapping women and—"

"It's a long story. But the short answer is no. You're my first abduction," he tried to smile.

She didn't dare laugh.

"I know it all seems nefarious. And maybe it is. But I am serious. We stick to the deal and then you are free to go, once I have my son."

"Adopt a son, hire a surrogate, fall in love and make a child. You're rich. You can have a child any way you choose."

"I know. And this is the way I choose," he told her.

Stunned, she couldn't answer. He then left. Godiva crossed her arms. She walked around the 800 square foot bathroom thinking and rethinking her plight. And nothing made sense. She missed Delilah. All her life Delilah was there, no matter what the circumstance. She missed Queen. There was no stronger defense in her life than Queen. How could she go a year without seeing or speaking to them? It was impossible to conceive. She had to find a way to reach the madman. By any means necessary, to escape him. She'd find a way. She returned to the bedroom and slipped under the covers. They were so silky soft she felt like she slept on clouds. When her lids slid closed, she prayed silently that he didn't visit her in her sleep.

Chapter Seventeen

As far as she could tell it had been three days since he released her from her prison into more livable quarters. The first day she spent in bed depressed. She cried until all of her emotion over the circumstances bled out of her. The second day she felt stronger. It was the day she stopped menstruating. She got up from bed and expected to find him waiting. She even mentally prepared herself for sex if he demanded it. She refused to believe that he had any power greater than what she granted.

He was not there.

However, Jaxon had provided well for her. The television only had Netflix, Hulu, and iTunes Movie apps to watch instead of live broadcasts. It meant the internet was available in the cellars—somehow. There was no phone. The food storage was filled with organic veggies, and no dairy. She had her choice of red and white wines. And she had company. Henry the dog stayed close to her snuggling her feet as she ate popcorn and watched old films. Hutch arrived to give him his injections. She waited for Jaxon. He didn't come, so boredom drew her over to the album collection.

There was everything. So many bands she didn't know existed. Jaxon had pulled out a few crates of '80s and '90's R&B classics. It must have been from his own personal collection to be added to the ones on the wall, because some of the artists shouldn't have been on vinyl. She was immediately calmed with her music. It healed her every single time she played a song. For two hours straight she did her own battle between Michael Jackson and Prince. She spun around in a chair next to the album player and cranked up the volume. Poor Henry was so unnerved he left her and went into the kitchen to hide under the kitchen table. She then let the wine subdue her as she turned her tastes to classics her mother loved. She played everything from Regina Belle, Toni Braxton to Deborah Cox. There was plenty of Anita Baker to play throughout the night. Suddenly she didn't feel so alone. And her blues had a voice.

On the third day he returned.

"Hi?" he said after an unexpected appearance in the kitchen. Goodiva snapped her head around and found him staring at her with a strange yet sheepish grin on his face.

"What are you doing?" he asked.

She held an oven mitt in her hand. Her intentions should be evident. She reached inside the stove and removed the salmon she had cooked to a medium-well baked perfection. Garnished with just slices of lemon and basil leaves, it sizzled a bit in its own natural juices on the cedar block she used. She closed the oven door and removed her mitt, taking her time in her manner. He watched. They locked gazes in a wordless conversation, or at least to her, it felt like they did. This was his check-in. Three days later? When he didn't speak, she forced herself to do so. It was time to set the pretense aside. He owed her an explanation.

"Where have you been Mr. Price?"

He glanced from her to the table where she had set the bowl of tossed lettuce, tomatoes and cucumbers. There was a bottle of vinaigrette dressing and glass of wine was chilled for herself. Also, the inside of an album cover was present, one she had read during her prep of dinner. She'd found a few new artists that sang R&B in the 80's that she didn't know. Without the internet to provide her research, the album jackets gave the biographical information she craved. This was the music her friends frowned upon. Jaxon stared at the setting for a moment as if he was uncertain of her comfort. Did he expect her to cry her entire time he kept her there?

The way he dressed hadn't changed. He wore dark slacks and a black cashmere crewneck sweater. She could see the sculpted fitness of his chest and biceps pressed against the sweater. The half-mask he wore was the only barrier between them. In black he looked more like a sadist to her than a long-lost lover returning for dinner. Maybe it was the circumstances, or the bargain.

"Can I join you?" he asked with politeness she didn't expect.

"It's been three days. Why haven't you joined me sooner? I thought we had a deal? Until...you know?"

"We have a deal, nothing's changed." He walked over to the table without an official invitation. He sat and made himself comfortable. She wanted answers, but he didn't seem to be in the mood for questions. So she plated the salmon by splitting it in half for them both to share. She poured from the bottle of rosé she'd selected for the meal. He got up abruptly from his chair to pull out hers when she set out the food for them, and waited until she sat.

"I'm sorry for my absence. It's very rude," he began.

"No apology needed. I kind of enjoy not having your company," she smiled.

Jaxon chuckled. "What's this?" he asked.

"My favorite. Atlantic salmon baked in lemon and garnished with spinach cream. And right there is a crouton salad with asparagus. You have everything I enjoy cooking in here. I guess your prying into my life really paid off for me this time."

"I think our tastes are similar. I'm not all-seeing and all-knowing."

"Really? Sure as heck feels like it to me," she said.

She reminded herself that a touch of honey in her disposition and tone could get her further than hostility. So she smiled for him whenever he looked up into her eyes and pretended to be open to his conversation.

"It looks good," he said and picked up his fork. He drew the salmon to his mouth when his gaze lifted and his hand froze mid-motion.

"Something wrong?" he asked.

"Hands please," she said and extended hers.

Confused, he set the fork down. He put his palms on top of hers and she gripped his hand tightly. Goodiva shared a blessing of the food she'd learned from her father and often repeated before his hand was released to eat.

She smiled. "Are you a Christian?"

"Muslim," he said.

"Oh, yes, okay. Do Muslims bless their meal?"

He smiled.

"Yes or no?" she asked.

"Of course we do."

"Fine. I don't want to be rude. Bless the food," she said and offered him her hand again.

He took her hand and closed his eyes. He said: "Allah, bless the food you have provided for us and the hands of the preparer. *Bismillahi wa 'ala baraka-tillah.*"

"What did that mean?"

"In the name of God and with God's blessing," he said.

"Oh, okay, thanks." She let go of his hand and nodded for him to enjoy what she had prepared. Jaxon tasted the asparagus first after slicing off the tip and swabbing the lemon sauce. He nodded that the sample was delicious. She knew it would be. The lack of conversation throughout dinner wasn't uncomfortable. It was clear that he was a man of few words and used to solitude. However, it only deepened her curiosity. Where had he been the past few days? Why disappear at all when he called the shots? She ate, but found herself peeking up at him from time to time trying to gauge the right moment to ask her questions.

"You must have been hungry?" she asked.

"Haven't had a solid meal in days—" he said and swallowed another mouthful.

"Huh?"

"Staff gone. Well, uh, most of them. The food I'm served isn't as good," he corrected himself, but never looked her in the eye.

"Why don't you cook it yourself?" she sipped her wine.

"Maybe I can cook for you?" he asked.

"Maybe," she said.

"You know, once you are pregnant you won't be able to drink wine," he said with a frown of concern. "I forgot how plentiful it is down here. In fact, it may be best that while we are trying to conceive you cut back on your consumption."

"Says who?" she asked.

"Says the doctor I've consulted. The one who will be handling our case."

"About that," she said. "Exactly how do we do this without a doctor to examine me? You said it's impossible to get anyone to the mountain during these storms. Has the winter blizzard moved in?"

He nodded.

"And?"

"I will make a way," he assured her.

She tapped her fork on her plate to demand he look up at her and in her eyes when she spoke. "I have another question."

"I'm listening," he said.

"How do we do this?"

"Do what?"

"Sex!" she said a bit too sharply. "We have to have sex. You haven't been here. When do we start? How do we start?"

"I was giving you time to get used to the idea. Last time I saw you, the thought of having sex with me gave you nightmares," he said.

"I'll never get used to the idea because it's blackmail. It's something I can't even name."

"I agree. So the offer still stands," he said.

"What offer?"

"Insemination. IVF. We can make this clinical and we can do it clean and quick," he said.

"Wait, wait, what are you talking abou—"

"In vitro fertilization. The doctor can harvest your eggs here and then we use my fertility clinic in New York to do the proper work before you have them implanted. We won't have any mistakes and risks to your health if you are constantly monitored the correct way, and it guarantees that I have a son. They told me there will be injections you will need to take. That may be painful. I'll get all the details for you—."

"No...I...don't want to do that!" she insisted.

He blinked. "I thought you understood."

"I—we had a deal. Natural conception if possible, or no baby at all."

"There is no deal that means no baby, Goddess. You aren't paying attention. You will give me a son," he insisted.

She gripped her fork tight, her lips sealed with the restraint. She stared at him. He stared at her. The silence between them felt unappeasable. Then he wiped his mouth with his napkin and scooted his chair back.

"Maybe we should finish the conversation tomorrow. I'll clean up in here. You can go have your wine near the fire and listen to music if you want."

"You're comfortable with me having wine now?"

He gave another defeated sigh. "I don't wish to argue, do what makes you happy."

"Like leave? Like go upstairs and see the sun for a few days? Like bash your face in with this bottle?"

"Except that," he chuckled. He picked up the plates and carried them to the sink.

"You are uncomfortable with idea of having sex with me. Aren't you?"

"Why would I be?" he asked. His broad-shouldered back faced her as he ran water over the plates.

"Because it's rape," she said.

He didn't turn to look at her. He just stood still.

"Any use or force or blackmail to get sex without consent is considered rape. Google the definition."

"I've offered a solution," he said with measured calmness.

"An easy way out. Make me a surrogate. Still rape. You are using my body against my will."

"I have my reasons," he mumbled.

"RAPE!" she shouted.

"I wish I could explain all of this to you."

"Yea, I bet you do," she said and drank more wine. Her anger was surfacing again. The wine didn't help.

"I've upset you. After I finish the dishes I'll return upstairs."

"If you aren't uncomfortable, then why do you always find reasons for us to separate?" she demanded.

"I'm only suggesting—"

"That we part ways. I tell you that I want to conceive the traditional way and you don't even try to touch me. In fact, you don't want to touch me. Huh?"

"I do want to touch you," he said and looked back at her. "But you're right. If I do, under these circumstances, it changes things," he said. Then he turned back to the dishes. "I understand what I'm asking of you seems like the most barbaric thing a man could ask of a woman. But if you give me a child the way that we agree, I will not only compensate you but none of yours or your friends' secrets will leave Mayfair. You will be free of the past and me."

The way he spoke to her. The way he behaved. It was almost as if he felt as if he was doing her favor in their bargain. That too pissed her off.

Goodiva watched him clean the kitchen. He went about each task ignoring her presence. She sipped her rosé. Slow and steady, her anger melted inside with a warmth of understanding. Whatever troubled him probably started when he was as young as she was, when she suffered her own trauma. Maybe the key to gaining her freedom and defeating his plan was actually trying to understand him.

"When will this doctor come? To 'harvest my eggs,' if I agree?" she asked with air quotes.

"I wanted to talk to you about that. In order for us to start, we will have to begin what is called COS. It's a controlled ovarian stimulation process. We start on the first day of your period."

"You're out of luck. My period just went off," she said.

He nodded, but she could tell he was a bit disappointed.

"After the stimulation of your ovaries and when the doctor says your follicles have grown to a mature size, you will receive a trigger shot that—"

"That's okay, I don't want to hear anymore," she said and tossed down the last of her wine.

"It's pretty simple. The shot is probably the worst part of it," he offered.

"How the hell would you know? Have you had your ovaries triggered by a shot?"

"No but—"

She rolled her eyes. "Well?"

"Well what?" he answered.

"Answer this question: have you attempted this before?"

"I studied up on this process and I prepared," he said before he turned off the water.

"This IVF could take months, right? I mean all these things we have to do don't guarantee a pregnancy. It takes time."

"It's a process, yes, but most of it, like I said, can be done here. The embryo implant will have to take place in New York."

"So you will take me to New York?"

"If necessary."

"Do they have dungeons in New York?" she asked.

He smiled. "I'm not sure, I'm looking."

He leaned against the sink and folded his arms across his broad chest. Even in his half-mask, he had an undeniable sex appeal that messed with her head.

"Andella told me that you kept medical staff at Mayfair. You said that you never kidnapped a woman before. So why do you have doctors here? The ones violated me when I first came. Aha! You think I forgot? You conveniently avoid talking about them. Are they still here? Huh? They can't be for me, and only me. Right? You're faking your paralysis, so it can't be to help you walk."

Jaxon didn't respond.

"So? The doctor is here? He stays on staff for you too?"

"It's not uncommon. I told you, I am a diabetic. After the accident my health has had some complications."

"Right. Right."

"I assure you this doctor will be helpful. But we will work with other doctors too, who specialize in the procedure."

"You prefer those doctors take care of me? Instead of you?"

"I'll be there..."

"For what? Will he be taking care of me after the procedure? Or will you be performing your own medical checkups? Vaginal exams, those are definitely necessary."

"If you want me to examine your pussy, we can do that right now," he said in exasperation.

She was making him uncomfortable.

She poured herself another glass of wine and sipped. "Maybe I should meet this doctor? To tell him my medical history. He could answer some of my questions about the procedure."

"When it's time you will."

"You're lying. I don't know why, but you're lying to me about all of this. You probably want to harvest all of my eggs to do some stem cell research like your father. Who's to say you haven't already?"

"You can't get stem cells that way," he mumbled.

"Prove it. Let's log into the internet and Google it."

He appeared to consider his answer carefully. He stared at her from across the kitchen.

"You're keeping secrets. Lots of them," she said. "Want to know what I think? I think there is no doctor. No IVF. No secret baby. I think Delilah is right. You and your farther are both wierdos who were into weird experimental bullshit. I think you attacked me in the dark by yourself. That you put me in that room. You probably did your own little examination of my body to get yourself off. This is all a lie and a charade, and, and, and—" she burst into tears. He didn't react. She cried for a few minutes before she was able to speak. "I'm scared. I'm scared of you."

Jaxon gaze drifted from her to the bottle of wine she'd finished. He then looked at her as if to suggest that the wine had diluted her judgement. But before saying so, he walked out. Goodiva sat alone, crying. She tried to understand what she'd done and said. Her mind stumbled over the events in the past weeks since she found him again. As nefarious as his actions were, there was something needful and almost apologetic to his manner now. She got up from the table and returned to the front of her prison to find Jaxon wasn't there. Curious, she went into her bedroom. He was there, seated on a sofa next to all the albums she had spread across the floor to listen to. The mask to his face shielded his forgotten handsomeness from her. He stared into the fireplace he lit for them and didn't speak. She walked over to sofa and sat close to him. He looked at her and then back to the fire.

"Sorry. It's the wine. I didn't mean to accuse you of...you know. And I'm not scared. Well, not really. Being here with you like this is beginning to affect me. You know?"

He didn't answer.

"You've been watching me. Before I came here you were stalking me. Right?"

Again he didn't answer.

"The first time I saw you, I mean when I came to the interview, I...I...I was shocked. I didn't believe I'd ever see you again. I think I'm still in shock that this is the man you became. I remember a different man. A nicer man. You may have been Romeo, but you weren't—"

"Romeo the Asshole. I told you that night you were wrong about me," he said. "Maybe you were right."

"Was I?" she asked.

"I don't want to scare you. I never want you to be afraid of me," he said. "But if it will give me what I want I will be the monster you keep me accusing me of becoming."

"Okay," she said. "I'll stop."

She rubbed her hands across her thighs and searched for the words to explain her feelings as the silence between them became awkward. "You know what I don't understand? If you can walk, if you can be whoever you wish, why be this? Why trap yourself here and be miserable? I mean, we all got our share of problems, right? But this? I can tell this place makes you so...sad?"

"Who says I can be whomever I want to be?"

"Your money, your connections, your power—"

"I leave here and the media takes a different kind of interest in me. Somebody, somehow, somewhere, they uncover who I really am. They eventually find the trail that leads to my family. My real family." He looked at her. "And you're not safe. None of your friends are."

"How haven't they figured it out by now? Nothing is really secret anymore."

"My life is. I don't have medical records or even a birth certificate that is genuine. My life began its paper trail when I ran from this place and became someone else."

"Why?"

"Doesn't matter. I can't be Jaxon Price anymore. I can't go backward. I can only go forward if you go with me."

"Where?"

He didn't answer.

"What are you now?"

"No one. Not until I'm a father. Then I'm someone. I assure you I'll teach my son all the things my father never taught me."

"That's just weird. But I think it fits this Master Mayfair person you are," she said. The shadows cast by the flames of the fire danced across his face. That face was what kept him prisoner, she assumed. It had to be horrible to live behind a mask. Considering how handsome he once was. She reached over and touched his hand. Whatever trance he fell into by staring into the fire broke. He glanced at her with the good side of his face. And she felt compelled to touch him.

"Why did your father live here, instead of in Falcon Cove?"

"Because he had powerful enemies. America, this place, Mayfair, it was his sanctuary and his banishment," Jaxon said.

Again they settled next to each other in silent retreat from the questions they wanted to ask of each other. There was, however, one secret she couldn't resist trying to learn. One she had to uncover. Jaxon shifted his position and slouched a bit against the sofa cushion. It made her draw closer. And then her hand lifted and she summoned the courage to touch his face. He caught her by the wrist with a tight grip right before her fingers reached his mask.

"Don't," he warned.

"Why? I know what you've been through. I was there."

"You only think you do," he replied.

"Well, how about this? You've watched me. Seen me at my worst moments. I don't think it's too much to ask that I see you. You want my trust. You want me to not fear you? This...this makes you real to me. Not the monster I hope you aren't. Does that make sense?"

His head turned and he looked into her eyes. This was the closest they'd ever been since her captivity. It dawned on her how beautiful his brown eyes were. Like polished amber stones.

"How bad did *we* hurt you?" she touched his jaw.

"We?" he repeated.

"Me and Twixt," she said. "We caused this. Right?"

He tried to sit forward. She pressed her hand to his chest and forced him to sit back, so he looked into her eyes and answered her question. "You didn't hurt me. I was there. You are right. It was an accident."

"I did. I made you like this. I'm sorry."

"I don't need your pity." He seemed to squirm.

"You sure? You want me to care, right? What if pity is the only way you can have me? Sexually? Would you still want me while I pitied you?"

She never lowered her gaze.

"You would, wouldn't you?" she smirked. He looked back to the fire.

"How bad is it? This thing you have for me?" she asked.

"Who said I have a thing?" he mumbled.

"You do, don't you? I see the way you look at me. How bad is it?" she asked.

"Bad," he admitted. "It's an obsession."

She felt a surge of power to hear him reveal himself to her. It made her even bolder.

"When can I see your face? Today, tomorrow, when I give you a son? When?"

"If I take it off, it'll be the first time since I put this mask on that I let anyone see my face," he said. "Not even my doctors."

"Why? They can help."

"There's no fixing me. The truth is I am what I am. Trust me. You prefer me covered this way."

"Let me be the judge and the jury. I'll trust you," she pleaded. "Because that's what you really want? Right? My trust and my pussy?"

He didn't deny any of her charges. He didn't deny her touch. She ran her fingers over his mask and then down to the bottom of his chin. She pulled up on the leather that had fit so securely over the left side. He closed his eyes as the mask peeled upward and off. The handsome charisma she'd met years ago at that party had melted away in the fire. Leaving one side of his face to tell the true story of what he'd become. His left eye was a bit sunken with a slouched lid that was tugged down to his misshapen cheek-bone and jaw. He'd obviously grown his hair longer to cover the worst of it before. But he'd cut his hair and shaved since their fated meeting over a month ago when she entered Mayfair. The disfigurement reached the cor-ner of his mouth and drew it down in a permanent frown. The skin, which was lumpy, had a wrinkled pinkish-orange discoloration from the burns. There were also a few deep gashes that spread across his cheek, and reached back to his ear.

She could feel the suffering beneath the pads of her fingers as they gen-tly brushed over each scar. He allowed it. The trauma looked extreme. There had to have been something his doctors could have done for him. Why go through life living with so much disfigurement and pain?

"I'm sorry," she said, and kissed his jaw like a pretend lover. "I'm so sorry for everything that happened that night."

He turned his face to hers and their noses nearly brushed. His expression had lost some of the tension she saw before. And his eyes smoldered with the same deception she'd seen in them before. She intended to use his nature against him. She made a move to scoot back from him to control their passion, but his arm slipped around her waist and pulled her in closer. She braced herself from completely giving in to him, with her hands to his chest.

"Show me what pity tastes like," he said. His lips met hers and he kissed her first. "Pity me."

Since her kidnapping she'd been cautious. A kiss wasn't supposed to happen so fast and feel so natural. In a single deft move, she was in his arms. She was lifted from the sofa seat and brought to his lap with her thighs parted so that her sex and his groin were pressed nice and firm against each other. Her hands gripped the back of the sofa for balance that was not needed. He had her. Jaxon slid a bit lower in his position so he was face to face with her breast. But his head titled back and the kiss he initiated intensified in passion.

He was so virile. How could she forget that? As his tongue moved lazily over hers and deeper into her mouth, she breathed in slow breaths through her nose and exhaled into his mouth. Breathing together stilled the quivers that trembled throughout her torso. He wasn't a monster, she told herself. But each time she opened her eyes, she couldn't help but see how physically he looked like one. He wasn't the devil, she told herself. But she'd never feared any man in her life the way she feared him. He was just a man. Flesh and blood. And she could defeat flesh and blood. Her heartbeat went wild when he slid his hand up her back. All ten of her fingers let go of the grip to the sofa and spread wide. His kiss, his lips were both soft and warm. She almost lost herself in how it all felt. She would have lost herself if she didn't see his face. She pulled away before she permitted herself to go too far.

"I think we need to slow down," she blushed and looked away from him.

"It's my face, isn't it?" Jaxon asked.

She didn't know how to respond. She kept her gaze averted.

Jaxon cupped her breasts in both his hands and she relaxed as he mas-saged them. "It's okay. I understand. Most women can only go so far even with my mask on."

"I'm not most women," she sighed. Because with her eyes closed he was all man to her again.

"I know, trust me I know," he said and kissed her neck. "Put my mask back on," he whispered. She felt awful about her inability to not see past his disfigurement.

"Put it back on," he ordered her.

She fumbled a bit while reaching for it. She held on to his shoulder to lean left to grab it. Just as she did, he bit at her nipple through her blouse. She tensed only for a second and then released another slow even breath as the sting dissolved when his mouth closed on her areola. He now had her ass in both hands and he lifted her to reposition her sex on his groin.

"Will you keep your promise?" he asked.

He looked up at her as if dazed. She had to blink to clear her head as well. She forgot how much he turned her on that night in the bathroom of the guest house. The wine was doing something to her. She fit the half-mask on his face and pulled the very thin elastic strap behind his head to secure it.

"It's on," before she was ready to escape him.

"Answer my question." He flipped her over on the sofa. His long hard body pressed upon her. Goodiva closed her eyes and felt him grind his groin hard on her lady parts. Really felt him. "Answer me, kitten," he plead-ed before his head bowed and he sucked her nipple through her bra and shirt. "Answer me." Eventually his mouth found hers. Goodiva tried to speak under the hypnotizing pull of persuasion his mouth had over her en-tire areola, and when his hand went between her thighs to discover that underneath her shorts she wore no panties, she felt her arousal pitch the highest it had been in years. Jaxon yanked down her shorts and she kicked free of them as well. He touched her between her thighs as he unzipped. In those fleeting seconds she forgot everything about the plans she had made for him. Without warning, he took over. She felt her lower body seizure with pleasure as inches of him thrust in fast.

Goodiva wrapped her legs around his waist and licked his neck. She tried to desperately hold back her own climax distressing her clitoris. Quivering lust consumed every nerve sensory in her vagina. Her nails cut into his skin she dragged them so hard over his shirt. Jaxon's hard fucks caused tension throughout her body to soar until she released by saying his name. The pressure combusted within her with shocking force. It zipped from her toes to the top of her head. He kept thrusting no matter how hard she trembled. After a few grunts his balls were emptied and his cock went flaccid. He was moving even then. Together they lay wrapped with their arms around each other on the sofa, half dressed and dripping in sweat.

It was done.

What was done?

Goodiva opened her eyes. His head lifted and the mask on his face shielded her from her indecision. All she could think at that moment was how much more she wanted. He brushed his lips over hers.

She was done.

She caught her breath in time to sit upright. He lifted her into his arms and brought her to the bed.

Chapter Eighteen

Goodiva Michelle Johnson was no virgin. Sex had been something she experimented with and then mastered since the age of eighteen. Though she remembered their first encounter as being an ardent, blazing, hot-blooded, torrid affair, nothing in her memory prepared her for the supercharged way he worshipped and loved her body. She could count on one hand how often she climaxed during sex without clitoral stimulation. It had to be the wine to push her so far so fast.

Jaxon stepped off the platform and began to undress. To see him better, Goodiva turned to her side and rested on her pillow. Clothed, he'd been mysterious, and starkly handsome. Naked, he was something to behold. The muscles in his thighs and arms, the sculpted beauty of his gladiator ass made her ache with desire between her legs. Skin discoloration from burns were all over his shoulder and left arm and torso like some macabre tribal tattoo. It was when he turned his back to her that she saw the most remarkable battle scar. Burned like some horrific stamp to his flesh between his shoulder blades was a large scorpion. It wasn't old or a tattoo. It had to be something he recently endured. She searched her memory of his body when they first met. He had no tattoos or brands that she saw or recalled.

"What is that? When did you do that?" she asked.

Jaxon glanced back at her.

"It looks painful. Was it?" she sat up with genuine concern.

"I don't remember the pain," he smiled.

Margahm, United Arab Emirates, November 2016

The largest oil fields in Saudi Arabia were located in Magahm, which was the home of his jin Prince Khaled bin Abdullah. Asad hadn't ventured far into the Saudi desert in all of his life. He knew his mother remarried and had been rumored to live in Sharjah. That was all he knew of her or the region. The

Dubai Supply Authority had the desert under lock and key by mercenaries un-heard of in the Western world. Asad closed his eyes to his discomfort. The Rolls Royce truck took to the sand dunes with reckless maneuvers and he suffered be-cause of it. The continuous bumpy ride off the main roads across the sand made his back ache and heat up with pain. He walked with the aid of a cane. He had healed himself as fast as he could. But he was no fool. He wasn't well.

The truck stopped. His jin's men, sons of the Scorpion, were all cousins to him. They greeted him in their thobes and turban scarves that wrapped from their heads, then around their lower faces only revealing their eyes. He didn't know one from the other. But they all knew him. It was in their eyes.

Armand was not granted the privilege of attending the meeting. The tem-perature boiled at 51 degrees Celsius, or 125 degrees Fahrenheit, but when he left the vehicle he could swear it was twice that. It hurt to breathe in the hot air. The men escorted him to the large black and red tent secured in an enclave of the desert with the flags of his clan's emblem waving. He did his best to walk the path with his cane.

Inside, the royals waited. The king had only been dead a year, and already everyone feared the new crown prince most of all. Asad's jin was seated next to the prince. Asad listened as a brother to his mother spoke of who he was and his allegiance to the family. He listened as he was reminded of his jin's abili-ty to protect the royals for decades under the House of the Scorpion. He said nothing when the charges against his father for his crimes were recounted. He would have to account for that transgression. But his jin had named him his successor, to the direct envy and hatred of those of his cousins and uncles who felt they should inherit the title.

The crown prince stared at him with an unwavering glare and seem unim-pressed during the ceremony. It was to be expected. Asad was not from them, no matter what his bloodline said. Asad knew not to speak unless spoken to. He saw his jin lean over and whisper something secretive and private to the prince. Several members of the royal family had already been arrested and beheaded for crimes far less serious than the ones he and his father were accused of. In a blink of the prince's eye Asad's life could end right there by the swing of a sword. He glanced to the executioner who held a twelve-inch blade. He then glanced to the prince.

It was decided.

Asad was forced to the floor. He was brought up by both arms and stripped of his robe. He wore his pants and shirt only. His left wrist was tied to a post. His right was tied by a cord to an opposite post. His arms were outstretched as he bowed his head. He closed his eyes and waited.

The prince stood and said a few words that he'd never repeat in or out of his nightmares. Asad had heard that, when beheaded, a man lived for several seconds before the life slipped away.

Death was not to be his fate.

The shirt he wore was cut from him. A poker was pulled from coals outside of the tent. It smoked and burned hotter than the sun. He could feel the heat approaching before the rod of the Scorpion scorched his flesh. He was given something to bite down on for the pain; it wasn't enough. Asad remembered the worst of his childhood. He remembered the worst of his suffering. But nothing prepared him for the death of Jaxon Price. Soon after the burning heat of the iron rod pierced his skin, he blacked out.

Asad woke breathless. The pain seared and slashed through his black. It throbbed all the way to his buttocks. He was forced to lay on his chest. Covered in sweat, he tried to catch his breath. But it remained too hard of a struggle. Weak and suffering, he opened his eyes. A woman wiped the sweat from his brow. She wore a niqāb that covered all of her face except her eyes. And it was her soft clear gray eyes that he knew.

"Mama?" he said.

She wiped his face.

"You shouldn't have come back Asad. Why?"

"Mom? It's you?"

A woman above him laid a cloth soaked in solvent to his back. Asad groaned in agony as its healing liquids soaked into his wounds. His mother leaned in and kissed his brow. She touched his face.

"Rest. Rest my boy. And pray you survive the night."

"Did it hurt? When they did that to you?" Goodiva asked.

He let the question dissolve in the irony of her concern. She abandoned the concern and settled back on her pillow. He faced her again; her gaze drifted lower. Tight ridges formed a six-pack that spread down to his trim waist and flat taut pelvic bone. It was his cock that she refused to look away from. Deeply tanned skin stretched over every inch of him, even his groin.

His penis, normal in length and uncircumcised when flaccid, sprung out with the righteous thickness of a rhinoceros horn when erect. Her thoughts darkened and glazed over with visions of remembrance of what a night under him, on top of him, to the side of him would bring. She buried her face in the pillow with embarrassment of his flirtatious seduction when he stroked himself. He did not. The long hand stroke wasn't a tease, it was a warning. She'd felt him, but had she ever really felt all of him?

There weren't enough words in his vocabulary to explain how lonely he had been for this woman's affection over the years. When she moved, her breasts and sex were both exposed. Jaxon's mouth filled with saliva when she turned over to her back as he approached the bed and parted her knees. She cupped her breasts and massaged the small globes, stroking her thumbs over her nipples, turning them into tight peaks. His brain shut off. The world narrowed down to the physical and nothing more. Her erect nipples beckoned his mouth. He wanted to suck, bite and nibble but all he could do was stare.

Before he reached her, the descent of her hand was all he could focus on. He watched as her palm slid down her flat stomach to her sex. She parted the lips with two fingers and stroked the hot-pink center with the middle. Her head tilted back in a pleasured move that his touch had yet to provoke. He watched her tease her clit with one hand and massage her breast with the other. He was caught in a haze of indecision—should he taste her or fuck her, or both? The decision was made for him when she released the sexiest moan he'd ever heard from her and rolled to her stomach. She lifted a bit on her knees and her ass cheeks shuddered as she fingered her pussy and she rolled her hips. Jaxon joined her on the bed. He peppered her ass with kisses and slipped down into position. She remained on her knees. He was half on the bed behind her face to face with her sexing herself. He pulled her hand away and gained all the access he needed.

The sweet sight of her slicked inner walls gripped his manhood and squeezed until his testicles begged for release. But he would not detour the course. Her pleasure, her wanting him to please her, her acceptance, was all he needed. He reached behind his head and pulled off his mask and threw it to the side. It would be him and her only. No barriers.

He kissed on her labia before burying his face between her buttocks to sweep his tongue from her anus to her pussy. The first touch of his tongue caused her thighs to quiver and she gripped the sheets with both hands, bit down on her pillow, raised her feet higher and crossed her toes. Her sweet tangy scent, edged with spice, intoxicated him. He lapped her pussy with soft strokes of his tongue.

"You like that?" he asked. All he heard was a muffled groan in response. He teased her again by flicking at her clitoris with the tip of his tongue, tracing the entrance of her opening before plunging into the tight wet channel. Her inner muscles contracted and relaxed.

"Oh yes!" she gasped, her head lifting up from the pillow as she inhaled deeply. And then said his name and she sank back into position. She turned over her will. His name became a chant that praised him further and further to do acrobatics with his tongue and send her pussy into complete distress. Reluctant and winded, he pulled away from such a lovely snack, causing her to let out a small cry of frustration. All she did was complain. He found that cute.

He came up behind her with his cock aimed at her opening. He gripped her hair with his fist and pulled back to cause her to dip the arch in her back. She raised her ass perfectly for him. The throbbing in his dick became unbearable. Not wasting any more time, he positioned at her entrance and fed her pussy inch by inch his cock. Desire rushed over his skin in a tsunami as every muscle in his belly tightened. He sank ball deep into such velvety soft tightness he grunted and his head lolled back as his lips parted with a deep sigh.

Goodiva was his.

Her sex took all of him without restraint. Jaxon pulled out and thrust forward, rocking against her cheeks as he tried desperately to hold back the climax that was building within him. He was on an overload of pressure.

"Faster! Faster!" she pleaded.

He let go of her hair and gripped her hips. He thrust into her harder with repeated strikes until her pussy fluttered and clenched in spasms. This time she cried out and arched her back as she shuddered through her untimely climax. The rush of sexual pleasure felt so extreme it was almost painful for him. He kept thrusting until his balls were empty and his cock deflated. He hadn't realized her complete surrender, as he was the only one holding her position to take it all over and over again.

He went in. She went limp. He released. They both collapsed.

He closed his eyes and focused on the feel of her, the smell of their sex perfuming the room, the hard shudder of his defenses. He focused on pleasure like he hadn't done in years.

Three days earlier

Jaxon slipped into a boiling hot fever. He woke through a seizure that had him flipping like a fish out of water on the bed and then off to the floor. He could do nothing but curl his hands and toes as his body was ravished by the surging tremors. The bucking and jerking along with the painful spasms took an eternity to cease. And even when they did, he had no hope that it wouldn't return.

She can't find me like this, *was all he thought.*

Paralyzed at first, he stared up at the ceiling and willed his body to return to his control. He willed it with all his might. The spasms ceased but fatigue had liquified his bones. He couldn't move, let alone sit.

Don't let her find you like this, *he thought.*

He had just brought her out of his mother's room to the one he built for her and him. The one he intended to remain in with her until they conceived. But his father's curse was winning. He wouldn't last as long if this became a regular battle for him. He closed his eyes and focused on his breathing, trying to move his hands and toes first. Slow and steady, he felt himself stabilize. The seizures didn't come often. What had caused such a violent attack so suddenly, *he wondered? He couldn't dwell on the answer. Instead, he sat up and forced himself to heal. The seizure wasn't the real problem. It was the fever. If he didn't get it under control he could black out.*

Jaxon pushed himself up from the floor and used the bed to bring himself to his feet. He staggered to the bathroom. He grabbed his silk robe from the hook and pulled it on. He went to the cabinet, looking for his pills. They weren't there. Only vials of his insulin.

"Damn it Hutch, I told you to make sure my meds were here," he grumbled.

Before he brought her into the room he had been staying in there himself. He decided to go inside to see if he left his pills there, but stopped at the sound of her crying in bed. He put his head against the wall. The room had no door. Still, he could imagine one. She lay under the covers wounded by his actions and miserable because of his deception. He shivered from the guilt and illness wracking him as well. He'd gone too far to call it off. But he couldn't punish her or himself this way. It would be best if she didn't see him. Instead of going for his medicine, he staggered back out to the front of his underground home and then to the door. He used the keypad to get the door to open, and then went through it to the next door and opened it. He kept a hand to the wall to keep himself steady.

The plan was simple. He'd go upstairs and wake his doctors. He'd get a shot to calm the effects of his diseased blood. He'd get it under control and then rest. He'd give her space. A day or so before he returned. He had it all planned out until he felt a dizziness that had him missing a step.

"Shit. Shit," he said, foreseeing the future. He turned and made sure to lock the panel again to keep her inside before darkness descended and he collapsed on the floor.

A day later

Jaxon opened his eyes. He was in bed. Doctor Nine was present and Andella was at his side.

"He's awake doctor," she said.

The doctor turned and looked at him. Jaxon glanced between them both. He frowned. He wasn't downstairs with Goodiva. He was upstairs in his master bedroom. How did he make it so far?

"So he is," the doctor said. "How are we feeling today?"

"What happened?" Jaxon asked.

"Yesterday, Hutch found you unconscious. He brought you upstairs to bed. We've finally gotten your fever to break. How are you feeling? Breathing okay? Any dizziness?"

"No," he tried to sit up.

"No sir," the doctor pushed him back down. "You stay still or I'll have Andella here strap you to the bed."

"I said I'm fine."

"Master Mayfair, I'm worried. You haven't had an attack this bad in months," Andella said.

"She has good cause to be worried. Your white blood cell count is low. Your pressure is low. Add to it the shock you went into, I'm deeply concerned. We get in trouble, we can't get you off this mountain for a few days. I suggest when the storm lets up we move you into a hospital for the next phase of your care. As soon as possible. Dr. Ten has already made some calls."

"To who? I told you, I'm not leaving this winter for another stretch in the hospital."

"Sir, your cousin Armand was called. We informed him that you were ill. He's been asking for daily updates on your recovery," Andella chimed in.

It was information overload. His servant and doctor were both speaking at once. He put his hand to his head and tried to focus. The doctor's voice rose over Andella. "I suggest you trust us to make these decisions for you going forward," he countered. "The Mayo Clinic can be discreet. Dr. Ten has suggested—"

"I don't give a fuck what either of you suggest! I said I'm fine!" he shouted at the doctor. The man froze. He cut his gaze to Andella. "Find Hutch. Now! And get that other doctor in here."

She nodded obedience and left. Dr. Nine stood silent. Jaxon pushed himself up against his pillows to get to a sitting position. He was weak, but he didn't feel as bad as he had before. He glanced to the phone.

"Call my cousin. Get him on the phone," he told Dr. Nine.

The doctor did as he instructed. After a few minutes, the phone was given to him. Jaxon had a sinking feeling that his cousin's warning was manifesting into reality.

"Hello?" Jaxon said.

"Is that you?" Armand asked.

"It's me."

"What the hell Jax! Man, I was worried. They had me thinking you were on your death bed. I've been trying to reach you for two days. They said you were in some kind of coma?"

"I'm better now," Jaxon said. "What is it? What's changed?"

"Everything. Some crazy virus is spreading. Have you been watching the news?"

"Virus? Yea, I saw that. What does that have to do with anything?" Jaxon asked.

"Doctors, that's what. The few we were using are being pulled in to do some studies on virus in China. And that has set us back. It's not the only bad news. Those fucking bastards in that crypt betrayed you. Jin knows what you've planned. He knows the truth Jax."

"Why does he care?"

"He's going to have the semen you put in the clinic used on one of those wives he chose for you. He's furious."

"You have to stop him," Jaxon groaned.

"How? What the hell can I do? You're the damn Scorpion now," Armand said.

"Destroy my samples. All of it. Every drop," Jaxon sighed.

"If you do that you won't be able to get her pregnant. You won't have a son," Armand said. "I thought that was the plan."

"Doesn't matter. I'm getting worse. Besides, I can still pull this off. Make sure she is safe." He glanced to the doctor who watched and listened. "Send me another doctor. One that can continue my treatments and handle my plans. The two I have here are dead."

"I just told you there is a virus in China that they think might turn into a pandemic. We can't get these doctors—"

"Do it!" Jaxon snapped.

"I'll do my best. But they will come for you."

Jaxon ended the call.

"Sir," Dr. Nine started.

The door opened. Dr. Ten walked in with Hutch, who held a gun to his hand. Ahmed was the last to join them. The doctors looked at each other shocked by the turn of events. All of Jaxon's suspicions were confirmed.

"Which one of you is working with my grandfather?"

Neither doctor spoke.

Jaxon glanced to Hutch. He pulled the trigger and blew a hole through the face of Dr. Nine. The man's brain and blood splatter sprayed the wall behind him. Dr. Ten hollered in shock and jumped back as if he'd dodge the next bullet. He raised both hands and shook with shock.

"That leaves you doctor. Let's hope you have some answers."

"It was the both of us. We...ah...he...he informed him, not me. That the woman was here. After we examined her."

"*Does my grandfather have a sample of my sperm?*"

"*It's under the control of the Dr. Eleven. The procedure would take place in New York. They should be arriving in New York any time. I've arranged...ah...Dr. Nine arranged it. They are bringing two of your wives.*"

Jaxon groaned and sat up further. He forced the covers off him and his legs off the bed to plant his feet to the floor. He glanced at Hutch. One look at his trusted employee and his wishes were clear. Hutch nodded and left the room with the smoking gun in his hand. He then turned his gaze to Ahmed. "*Armand will be sending in another doctor to care for me. Handle this,*" *Jaxon said to the dead man crumbled on the floor. He eased to a standing position and grabbed his robe. He felt better standing.*

"*Sir! Please. I can assure you that we still have this under control. I can place a call tonight to make sure that nothing changes. But you need me. I'm close to finding a cure. Very close.*"

Jaxon's gaze slipped over. "*You're lying. Take him.*"

"*Wait!*" *Dr. Ten yelled. He grabbed a syringe and held it up like a weapon.* "*You need me. Even if they can bring in another doctor, it won't be for a few days at the earliest. I can help you.*"

Jaxon considered his state. He made sure to stand erect in front of the men but he felt like dropping to his knees. Ahmed gave him a questioning look. Jaxon nodded. "*Keep watch on the doctor. Lock him in one of my guest rooms.*"

Ahmed nodded and forced the doctor to leave. Jaxon looked to Dr. Nine and then away. He sat on the bed and waited for the room to stop spinning. The wait felt like an eternity.

Hutch returned. "*I spoke to the clinic. They have begun with the women. No insemination at this point the pre-procedures will take weeks. I've given the order to not proceed. To make the women believe that they will undergo the procedure. I'm not sure if it will be obeyed. I'm not sure any of them can be trusted, with your jin involved.*"

"*Be sure! Do you understand?*" *Jaxon said weakly. If either of my wives become pregnant Goodiva is dead.*

Hutch nodded he would try.

Jaxon relaxed and released a deep sigh. His hopes of fatherhood were over. In his weakened state, with his disease, it would be a miracle if he could provide healthy sperm again for an insemination. "*How is my kitten?*"

"I checked on her an hour ago. She is playing the records you left for her, sir. Still very hostile to my presence. Last time I saw her she had a knife in her hand and threatened me."

Jaxon smiled. "She's hostile to me too."

"Should I make sure the doctor understands what is expected?"

"No. Ahmed has him. I don't need him scared, just focused on keeping me breathing until I can come up with another plan. We can't keep killing doctors who betray me. Now go."

"Yes sir," Hutch said and walked over to Dr. Nine. He lifted the dead man in his arms, put him over his shoulder and carried him out.

Jaxon closed his eyes. He reclined back in bed. The diabetes was something he could live with. The blood disorder he inherited from his father was not. The best he could do was save her. But how? He didn't know the answer. He didn't know anything anymore.

Present

She slept. Shortly after giving her body to him she cuddled up and rested on his chest. He held her like a lover should. He wanted to say so much to her. Thank her for even allowing him the privilege. However, he was afraid to speak. What if she woke and hated herself for being his? Blamed him for taking advantage of her? Called him a rapist again and erased all tenderness between them? What if she realized that this was just a physical thing for her, and he was still the monster that forced her to live below with him? What could he say to convince her otherwise?

Nothing.

After allowing her to relax and sleep, he eased out from beside her. If she woke she would question him, as she often did. The first night he brought her to her new prison he suffered an attack that kept him away from her for three days. He had to be careful. He had to stay the course. He was both physically and mentally exhausted. He couldn't take her rejection. Not after discovering the obsession he had for three years over finding her had turned into something more. He'd fallen in love with her.

Jaxon found his pants and pulled them on. He picked up his sweater and pulled it on. As he walked over to his shoes, he noticed the album jackets all spread out over the floor. He couldn't decide on what song he wanted to play more. From Al Jarreau to James Ingraham she had selected the very best of his collection. And then he noticed the R&B boy band from the 90's that he knew was in her playlist. He stooped and picked up Jodeci from her selection. Jaxon removed the album and took it over to the record player to select a song for her. He dropped the needle on the spinning disc.

"Forever My Lady" began to play as he left her to sleep. He set the switch so it would restart once finished, to ensure she'd wake to it.

Chapter Nineteen

The sound of the ocean lulled her awake. Slowly Goodiva's eyes opened. A soft melody played like chimes in the wind before the soulful voice crooned. She turned over now aware of her surroundings.

"...so you're having my baby..."

Her brain tried sluggishly and unsuccessfully to connect the aches of her sexual adventure to her burning embers of decisions she made earlier to make love. The music helped. She turned her head and found herself alone in bed. She sat up.

"Jaxon?" she looked around for him. He was gone. Goodiva scooted off the bed and dragged the sheet with her. She walked out of the room to the front of the place to find it empty. Henry slept near the door that he left out of. The dog lifted his head and looked at her curiously.

"He left again. Didn't he?"

The dog settled back to his resting position. She turned and went inside the room.

"Forever my lady..."

Goodiva went to the record player and lifted the needle form the spinning disc. She then went back to the bed. She lay there thinking about her choices. The afterglow faded. At that moment she didn't feel beautiful, desired or even empowered. She felt stupid. There was a strong chance her IUD was removed when she arrived. He hadn't said so, but she suspected. So, any sexual contact with him was a gamble.

The next day

Goodiva showered. After fixing her breakfast and feeding Henry, she had a visitor. She hurried out of her room to greet him. Instead of Jaxon, she found Hutch calling Henry over.

"Where is he?!" she demanded.

Hutch ignored her. He gave Henry his shot. He rubbed the pooch under the ear playfully and then stood to leave.

"Hey asshole! You hear me talking to you?!" she shouted.

Hutch paused. He glowered at her.

"That's right. You're an asshole!" she said.

Hutch shook his head and again started for the door.

"You tell that master of yours that I want to see him! Do you hear me! Tell him what I said!"

Hutch left.

TWO HOURS LATER SHE was on the sofa sleeping when she felt something. She opened her eyes to find him standing by the sofa. His hand had grazed her ankle. The fingertips only touched her. She sat upright.

"Hi," he said.

"Where did you go?" she asked.

"I thought you might want to sleep alone."

"After making love to me you play that album and leave me alone? For a day? Or was it just sex? The kind of sex that you prefer. Screw them and leave them! Right?"

He gave her a patient smile. "I'm sorry."

"I hate you and your apologies. Neither are sincere."

"I know," he said and sat on the sofa. She tried to leave but he grabbed her feet and made her legs stretch across his lap.

"How was your morning?"

"Morning? Is that what it was? I can't tell the time down here." She sighed. "Boring." Goodiva kept her eyes closed as he massaged her foot. "This can't work."

"No?" he asked.

"I'm not here to be your sex slave."

"Of course not," he said. He used his thumb to massage the center of her foot. Doing so relaxed all the tension in her belly. "Don't start thinking I will be. Don't."

She opened her eyes when he didn't speak. He gave her a mysterious smile and her heart melted. "Why are you being nice?"

"I am nice. You just seem to forget that," he said.

"Be nice and let me go home. Please," she said.

"I can't do that Goddess."

"This is wrong. Keeping me here against my will. Forcing me to make kids—"

"Not kids, a son."

"It can't work!"

"It has to work," he said.

"Dear God, why me?"

"Will we do this every day for the next year? Every time you begin to accept the way things are, you want to fight with me to remind yourself to not trust me."

She didn't know how to respond. He caressed her foot. He stared at her toes. The polish needed a retouch. He didn't seem to mind. When he touched her sixth toe she flinched.

"Does it hurt?" he asked.

"No," she said. "What is your name?" she asked. "Your real name?"

"I told you. Have you forgotten already?"

"Yes. Tell me again," she said.

"Asad Fikrit Mayfair," he answered.

"Why did you leave here? When did you leave here?"

"I was young. I ran away. You know the story."

"How young?"

"Fourteen or fifteen," he confessed. "I'm not sure."

"That's young."

"It is," he replied.

"And?"

He looked up at her.

"Why did you run away? Tell me the real story. The true story," she asked.

"Will we be friends afterwards?" he asked.

"Maybe," she smiled.

"Then give me a little time. I'm working up to it," he said.

"I understand," she said.

He glanced at her with surprise in his eyes.

"What? I have my own secrets too. It's not easy to tell another person everything about yourself. Even when you kidnap them," she admitted.

He smiled. He had to nod and agree. "I don't know where to start."

"Start anywhere," she said.

Part of him knew this has to be more manipulation than genuine concern. But he wanted her understanding. He'd do anything to have it.

ANY OTHER KID RAISED in privilege and then thrown out onto the streets would have broken and turned to drugs. But the tough rearing from his father and the silent consent from a mother who mistreated him just as badly made street life paradise. There was of course another option when he was on the run as a child. To reach out to his *jin*, and beg for rescue. But that too would mean a life as foreign to him as the hard streets he ran off to. As a young boy he'd only met his jin once. His mother told him the most heroic stories about him. He didn't trust him, even when that young. Jaxon took a chance on freedom his way. After touching and being near Goodiva, his defenses fell one by one. The moment she crawled over and went into his arms he sang like a parakeet. He told Goodiva how two days after he was on the run he broke into a Walgreens pharmacy and stole the insulin he needed. Of course it was the wrong dosage and he nearly killed himself. He woke up in a hospital thanks to a Samaritan who found him unconscious on a sidewalk. The authorities tried to determine who he was. Where he belonged. He would tell them nothing. It took a doctor who happened to be from the world his parents came from to understand the need for secrecy. The doctor recognized a tiny brand on his hip. Something so distinct it could be missed as just a birth mark.

"You have a scorpion on your hip?" Goodiva asked.

He paused mid-sentence.

"I never noticed that," she said.

"It's faded, tiny, a bit larger when I was an infant."

"Is it like the scorpion on your back?" she asked.

"Similar, yes," he said.

"Why would your father mark you that way?"

"My father didn't do it. My mother did," he said. "It's her father's house. The one we belong to. She did it to protect me. To connect me to my grandfather."

"Isn't it against your faith to have tattoos or marks?" she asked.

His brow lifted in surprise. She was smarter than he assumed. "Sunni Islam says that it is an impurity and against the natural creation of God. I am Shia Islam, my family is. And it is not forbidden. The Quran does not mention tattoos or tattooing at all."

"What did this doctor do when he saw the tattoo? After he learned who you were?" she asked.

"Protected me by keeping my identity and ethnicity a secret. It was shortly after 9/11. Arab Americans were not in good standing here."

"He let you go?"

"It was easy to do. There was no birth record of me. No record at all. And my parents never celebrated a birthday."

"Wait? That's right. You don't have a birthday."

"I've picked a date but that is another story. Besides, the doctor really had no choice. He knew who my father was. Who my mother's father is. He gave me information on where to go. Where I could be safe with people who rejected my family and found asylum like my mother and father did in America," he said.

"So, your father and mother rebelled?"

"Not exactly. I ran away from the hospital and police custody," he said. He told her that the doctor gave him enough time to escape his bed with medication to hold him over for a journey he'd take on foot and by hitch hiking. The doctor also gave him money. He went as far as he could. He slept in old train cars, under highways, even drainage pipes to keep from the storms and child predators. Sometimes in places so dark he could see nothing but the memories of his mother's warnings about what would happen to them both if his father was displeased.

How could he explain that history without revealing too much of his father's betrayal and madness?

"Is that all?" she asked.

"I told you everything."

"How did you become Jaxon Price?"

"That's a different story."

"Price isn't your father's last name. Right?"

"My father is Turkish. My mother is Saudi. She was his fourth wife." He paused to remember his mother and father from his child's point of view. He never saw his mother upset or angry. He never saw any emotion from her. But his father was a different story.

"How did they meet?" she asked.

"My father was once a mercenary under Prince Khaled bin Abdullah, who is my grandfather. The man I call *jin*. There were two betrayals by my father. The one that cursed him to exile isn't the crime against my mother."

"What did he do to your mother?"

"I don't know. I don't know if the story I was told is the truth. My mother had come to visit him and his wives in Yemen. Soon after she arrived, he brought my mother and two of his wives here to Colorado. She was kept in that room."

"So your grandfather didn't approve?"

"At first he did. Well, it's complicated. My mother was with my father in Yemen because he was to be her guardian to arrange a marriage. He was supposed to bring her to America to meet her new husband. Another story I was told was that he was supposed to be her guardian in America so she could be educated. But she never enrolled. He kept her prisoner and sent false information to my grandfather as if she was well. Then she became pregnant with me. My jin was told. A marriage agreement was arranged. My father already had three wives, and two of them lived here in America. In Mayfair. My mother became the fourth."

"Four wives?"

"I believe so. Like I said, I only knew of the two who lived above us."

"And children?"

He shook his head.

"No kids? You're the only one?"

"Oh, sorry. Yes, he had children. Daughters. He had seven daughters between his three wives. None of his wives could give him a son. And that fertility clinic he had sons as well, not sure what happened to them."

"Where are they? Your sisters," she asked.

"They are all older and married off. A few of them live in Yemen. I never knew any of them," he said.

"And your mother?"

"She lived upstairs for a while during her pregnancy and then down here when I was born."

"No. I mean where is she now?"

"Saudi Arabia."

"When was the last time you saw her?"

"I don't remember."

"And his other wives?" she asked.

"His first wife who lived here died shortly after I was born—I don't know how or from what. I was never told. The second wife accused my mother of poisoning her. My father sent her back to Yemen. So my mother became his only wife in Mayfair. But again, my father was displeased, so she left or was sent away. I'm not sure why."

"Have you ever tried to understand her story?" she asked.

"No," he said.

"Why?" she asked.

"It's not how it's done. And she has a new husband and kids. A different family. She wouldn't want to know me. I'm my father's son."

"A mother never forgets her child. You said she gave you that scorpion to connect you to her father."

"Some mothers do."

"But are you sure?" she asked.

"From what I remember of her, she didn't care for my father or me. So leaving was a matter of survival for her, I suppose. Any kindness she shows me now is because he is dead and I'm reborn."

"I still think that must have been hard for her. For you."

"I lived in that room with my mother for years. I think I knew her well enough. The only hard thing for her was waiting on freedom."

"School?"

"She schooled me by teaching me the Quran. Never taught me English. I learned it from television. *Sesame Street* is a good teacher. I read books after she left. And music," he rubbed her ass. He smiled. "Music, American music, it taught me a couple of lessons. Healed me."

"Friends?"

"None. No one but doctors."

"Why?"

He stopped his caress of her backside. She lay on his chest listening to his story and his heartbeat. "At first my father thought a son could help them find a cure for his illness. Especially if I was born healthy. He considered me damaged goods when I was diagnosed with diabetes. I ran away when I realized my life wouldn't be any better than what it was. My father didn't care."

"The night we met. The night we...were together in that pool house, you said your father died. You were upset."

"I was relieved," he sighed.

"I understand. You were abandoned by your family. You grew up as a runaway. Became your own man. But why kidnap me and drag me into this? And a child? If I get pregnant down here, then how am I different from your mother and father?"

"It's different."

"How?"

He didn't explain.

"If you won't let me go, you have to let me out of here. I can't stay here. Your mother suffered down here. You suffered down here. I'm suffering."

He considered what she said. He nodded that he understood, but he also knew that the defiance in her would remain a problem. How could he win her trust again if he treated her like a prisoner?

"I can't stay down here," she pleaded.

"Let me see how it can be arranged," he said.

"Who's upstairs?"

"A few members of my staff and...my doctor."

"Okay, I'll need one when I become pregnant, right? Right?"

He didn't answer. A ray of hope shone in her eyes.

She wouldn't become pregnant. After all his planning and plotting, that opportunity was gone. If he ended the entire affair, she'd run from him and straight into his grandfather's trap. She loved to travel. Africa, Spain, Europe, she'd been all over. That too would make her vulnerable.

"I need to leave for a moment," he said as he sat forward.

"No. Don't go. I'm sorry. I won't ask any more questions. Just stay here with me."

"I'll come back. I need to a make a phone call and check on a few things."

"Then bring your phone down here. I'll see where there are connec-tions."

He smiled at her. "Nice try."

He leaned in to kiss her, but she pushed away from his chest. She glared at him. "You leave, don't come back to my bed. Sleep on the floor with Henry."

He ran his hand up her leg. She moved her legs and crossed her arms.

"Twenty minutes. And then I'll be back. We can listen to music? Any kind of music."

She didn't answer.

"You can tell me about you. The secrets you keep. I told you some of mine."

She stood. She wore a jean skirt that was high up her thighs. She pulled it down and walked past him, leaving her floral scent behind. It was his soap that cleaned her lovely body, but she had a fragrance of her own. It was probably from those creams she used after showering. She didn't glance back at him. Didn't say goodbye. She left him sitting there staring.

Jaxon gave in to his defeat. He pushed up from the sofa and left her. When he returned upstairs, he found emptiness and silence. It was closer to night. He didn't expect to see staff. Both Andella and Frances were in their quarters. And Doctor Ten was certainly in his room as well. Jaxon went to the ballroom where he knew his men waited for him.

Hutch sat at the long table. It was big enough for thirty people to dine together. Ahmed chose to stand. He looked up once Jaxon walked in. His loyal employees nodded that all he requested was handled.

"Dr. Eleven arrived a few hours ago," Hutch informed him.

"How?" Jaxon asked.

"Helicopter. An emergency one was used, saying you needed medical attention. The weather is improving. Sooner than we expected," Hutch said. "We should be clear of it early this year."

"I figured that," Jaxon glanced to Ahmed. "I want you to deal with Dr. Ten. The men should not meet or conspire. Be sure of it."

Ahmed nodded and walked out.

"Do you think you can trust him?" Hutch asked after Ahmed left. "He's a Scorpion."

"If you're asking if his allegiance is to my grandfather then the answer is yes. However, I can trust him because he sees me as authority. Until my jin decides otherwise."

Hutch nodded.

"Have you spoken with Armand?" Jaxon asked.

"Yes, he thinks he's been successful with destroying all of your samples in New York. And your grandfather believes the women have undergone the procedure, but it failed. Armand told him that you now have a pregnant bride."

"Jin believes Goodiva's pregnant?" Jaxon frowned.

"Armand had to think of something quick to stall him. He sounded confident that your grandfather accepted the story. Is she pregnant?"

"No. I've barely touched her."

"It only takes one time," Hutch said.

"With me it takes several."

"Then what will you do?" Hutch asked.

"Continue the lie. If Jin thinks she's pregnant, then at some point I have to convince her that she is and without the IVF I'm not sure I can," Jaxon said. "It might be best that we bring Ms. Johnson up here among the living. I don't like keeping her trapped below, it makes things harder between us."

"Sir, I must advise against it. She's still a security risk. There are many ways she could communicate with her friends and the authorities. I wouldn't trust her just yet."

"What other news do you have?"

"Dr. Talbot is no longer a problem for us."

"And the bad news?"

"The Feds are officially involved. That detective friend of hers had the doctor record the call he made to you. It was enough for her to convince them that you are a threat. She's also connected you to your father. The intelligence agencies are looking our way."

"How did this move so fast?" Jaxon asked.

"The Feds had an ongoing investigation into your father and his clinic practices before he died. They have the phone records to prove your lady friend made her call to Ms. Montgomery from here on the mountain. Mayfair is the last place the call was traced to."

"They're coming?" Jaxon asked.

"They're coming. But not only the blizzard will slow them down. Have you seen the news on this virus?" Hutch asked.

"The COVID19 virus?" Jaxon asked.

"Corona. Yes. We got a few cases in the States. My guess is they are going to be all over this in the upcoming weeks to make sure it doesn't spread. Might buy us some more time." Hutch said.

"You know, this virus is strange. Dr. Ten thought she had it when she came here," Jaxon said.

"If she has this virus you have to stay away from her."

Jaxon chuckled. "Too late. Plus it's weeks. She's fine. Healthy."

"You aren't," Hutch said.

Jaxon sighed.

"I believe they picked up the scent of the Scorpion on you long before your accident. They've been waiting, just like the family, to see which side you will choose. And your return to the Middle East made that choice very clear."

"I agree."

"You will have to make a choice just as your father did. I know you don't believe this sir, but your father loved you. He feared this for you. It's why he let you run."

"Let me?"

"He let you go. You decided to come back. All for her," Hutch said.

"Can I get her out of here? Take her somewhere else?"

"If they storm the mountain, and I believe they will, the safest place is in the cellars. We can lock it down and they won't find you or her," Hutch said.

He nodded.

"Then let them come. I'll stay below with her. For the next few months. Until she's pregnant."

"The labs? They'll find the labs," Hutch warned.

"Destroy everything in the labs. Have Ahmed help you. We have Dr. Eleven. He'll help me through the worst of it. Prepare your wife and Francine for whatever interviews there are to come. Take down the security cameras so they can't demand footage. Sweep the place clean."

"The CIA?"

"I am not ready. Not yet. Buy me more time. I will have to make to save her life, and Armand's if it goes that far. Eventually I'll make it. When the time is right."

"We'll take care of it all."

Jaxon paused. "I want to see the doctor. Tomorrow."

"Okay," Hutch said.

Jaxon pushed up from the table and left.

Chapter Twenty

After a deep yawn Goodiva shifted to her back under her blanket. She felt a bump to her elbow. Opening her eyes, she expected to find her friendly canine companion in bed with her. It wasn't. Jaxon had returned in the night. He stripped down to his boxers and got under the blankets with her. And he didn't have on his mask. He lay still, no snoring, no anything. She pushed out from under the burial of covers to see him clearly, and her sudden movement must have woken him.

"Morning," he said.

"How do you know it's morning?" she asked.

He gave her a sheepish grin.

"Are you cold?" she asked. It was a senseless question. The place felt as if it were built on a glacier. The cold settled deep in the cellar by design. The night before after their lovemaking she had collapsed in exhaustion without igniting the fireplace. She had stripped the linens from the bed. She tossed the covers over him and then scooted in close.

"Warmer?" she asked.

"Not yet," Jaxon replied. He moved over on top of her. His mouth found hers and she tried to turn her face from the morning breath kiss, but he wouldn't allow it. To her delight, it was both gentle and sweet. She imagined her own breath was the offensive one. Goodiva always slept without underwear underneath her camisole. Once he was inside of her she enjoyed every moment of his lovemaking. It was about the physical. And she wanted every inch of the physical.

There was certainly no doubt in her mind who was in control. In the middle of making love to her so gloriously, he withdrew and slipped under the covers. She gripped the bare mattress as his tongue made her delirious. Her hand went under the covers. She should be protesting or playing hard to get, instead of combing her fingers through his silky hair as she bucked her hips and fed her pussy to him.

She came for him, hitting notes higher than an opera singer. And then he was on her again. Thrusting her hips and grunting, he shook down every wall of defense she had constructed the night before like a wrecking ball. Her emotions and abandonment issues battled for attention. She had to focus on the physical not the mental. She tilted her head back and her mouth parted to a shockingly real proclamation. "I love you."

Jaxon found her body soft everywhere. Her vagina, her skin, her thighs and chest were softer than satin. He wanted every inch of her. Need clawed at his insides and threatened to explode from his testicles. The climax she had for him earlier was intense. Then he heard her speak. Buried under the covers and trapped between her thighs, he thought he heard her say she loved him. He had to let go of sucking her clit to lift his head to be sure. But only soft moans followed. He dragged his tongue up over her pelvis past her navel to her nipple and drew it in his mouth. Was it real? Did she say it? And then he was power drilling the wettest pussy he'd ever had. Soon he was sobbing, as he let go all of his love and desire into her.

It took several long minutes before they both stopped shuddering.

He kissed each nipple and pulled out of her.

She groaned with satisfaction and the sexist purr. But she didn't open her eyes. Was he too monstrous-looking for her to enjoy him? He was certain he was. Still his lust was not done. He needed only a small reprieve and then he wanted more.

"Let's shower," he said, and tossed aside the heavy blanket covering them

"Huh? Now?" she frowned. "I'm cold. I just want to lay here."

He didn't wait. He scooted off the bed and then swept her up in his arms and carried her to the shower with little protest.

In front of the shower Jaxon let her go, yanked open the shower door, and gestured for her to enter. It was large enough for six adults. She stepped in looking back at him to see if he was going to join her. He did. Both the shower and bathroom were well lit—a difference from the dark chamber rooms of her hidden home. The shower was tiled with pretty pearl and peach accents trimmed in gold. There was also a stone seat on the wall opposite of the shower, which could serve as a spa retreat. Jaxon got the water warm for her as she sat and observed him. Her body again ached in that familiar way, but she felt revived as the heated steam swirled all around her skin. And with him she felt safe, protected. He must have felt the same, since he now didn't bother to cover half his face from her, and she barely notice his scars.

Jaxon extended his hand to her. She accepted. With quiet love, she was guided through the steam to the warmth of the shower. He ran his fingertips down her body, marveling at her curves. He placed a soft kiss to her forehead as he lathered up a sponge with jasmine scented soap. He rubbed the suds all over her, from her neck to her feet. He stopped to kiss her body every now and then. It felt so nice. Never had a man been that attentive to her. Twixt certainly never cared for her in such a way. No man had.

This is just sex Goodiva. You aren't falling for him. It was good last night, but today you're in control. Forget what you said in the moment of passion. You didn't mean it. You're the one in control. You're seducing him. Remember, he kidnapped you. He blackmailed you. He's demented, and a bit crazy.

He pushed her gently under the water and it cleansed away the morning evidence of their union. It felt wrong to rinse away all of the good feelings he had brought out of her. She opened her eyes despite the water streaming down her face and reached for the scarred side of his face. She drew him in to kiss him. His arm circled her waist and he kissed her in return as water pelted them from above. Together they stepped out of the spray of water and she lathered his body. He was hairy around his thighs and legs. He even had hair on the knuckles of his toes. All of it lay silky smooth as she knelt and cleaned him. She circled him and washed his back and admired his ass. She loved exploring every inch of him.

When she returned to face him they were as bare and as uncovered as Adam and Eve. Nothing beyond the world of steam and glass existed. She stared up at him and saw the beauty in his face. Even though he had suffered horribly physically, there was strength and resilience in his face. Her hand naturally went to his cock. She kissed his chest as she ran her hand up and down it. She could hear a deep moan rumble in his throat. And then she went lower...

Jaxon's eyes opened. He looked down just as her lips parted and his dick slipped over her tongue into her mouth. His hand went to the back of her head as she swallowed nearly half of his cock without gagging.

"Slow," he murmured. "Oh yes, it's good."

Oh yes she was so fucking good at it.

His lids slipped lowered. The soft sucking sounds graduated to loud, sloppy noise and he bucked his hips. She licked and swallowed with her head bobbing back and forth with increasing frequency. He'd go boneless if she kept it up. The velocity rolled like a boulder down a hill, picking up speed.

"Mmm," he breathed.

And she kept going. When she squeezed his testicles he nearly let go. He had to pull out of her mouth with a big slurp just to gain his bearings. Her laughter tickled him. He smiled. He reached down and swept her up against him. Her thighs and legs fastened around his hips. He turned her to the shower glass wall now sweaty with heat from the steam trapped within. She kissed him. Her arms went around his neck. He cupped her ass and brought her down on his upturned cock for re-entry. She choked on a murmur as her sex tensed under the intrusion. He established an unrelenting tempo by driving his body deep inside of her over and over. And she celebrated each successful passionate thrust with equal eagerness in her loving of him, all of him. Soon he too lost control. His face buried deep into the curve of her neck, he squeezed her ass brutally tight as he released all of himself.

She held on to him and let him take her.

Was he done? Because she wanted more. Goodiva exhaled deep. She tilted her head back against the shower glass. It had to be 90 degrees inside the shower. She sweated everywhere. He withdrew and her legs slowly went down. Standing, she felt her knees buckle. He did his best to keep her up. But he seemed weak himself.

She gave him a weak smile and felt a pang of guilt over even considering he had violated her by removing her IUD. He was the monster she thought she was. She was deceiving him.

Jaxon stepped under the shower and washed himself. She joined him. They soon began to wrestle with each other over the soap and he hugged her from behind until she laughed, squealed and dropped the soap. She bent to retrieve it and he slapped his cock against her ass.

"Don't try it!" she teased.

"Give me a few hours. I'll definitely give it my best shot."

She nodded that she would. They left the shower and dried each other, then brushed their teeth at a his and her sink. She kept peeking over at him. He kept peeking over at her.

"What was your favorite breakfast as a kid?" he asked her.

"It was what everyone likes. Pancakes," she said and spit her toothpaste and sudsy water from her mouth.

"Not me," he said after he gurgled.

"Really? What was yours? Cereal? Oatmeal?"

"Beans and eggs, and most times with rice. Mixed together."

She gagged. "What?!"

"Yes!" he grinned. "Have you ever tried it?"

"No, yuck!"

"You cook the rice. Then drop it into a frying pan of butter and crack an egg. Scramble it together and put the beans on the side. Add some sausage links and it's the perfect breakfast. And when you mix it—"

"Stop! Stop!"

"Listen, I can make it," he reached for her.

"Never! I'll never eat it!" she laughed and put her arms up around his neck.

"One try. Please."

"Eew."

"Goddess..."

"Eeeeeeewwww!"

"Goodiva!" he squeezed her and lifted her off the floor.

"No freaking way. I'll never let you feed it to Henry."

He laughed so hard he nearly dropped her. She shoved him playfully and laughed too. When the laughter stopped, he stared at her smiling. His smile changed his face. All of the youth and vitality returned when he smiled. She wished he smiled more often.

"I'll make you pancakes. And put beans on the side. How's that?" she asked.

"Deal. But let me cook for you," he offered.

"No sir, you're too weird on this beans thing."

"I can handle pancakes," he said. She nodded and gave her his hand. He kissed it and then went down on one knee. "Goodie. Can I call you Goodie?"

She shrugged. "Some people do. It's better than Kitten."

"Aww, I likè Kitten," he pouted.

"I don't. Makes me sound like your pet."

"Oh? I didn't think of it that way," he frowned.

She winked. "Sure you didn't."

He kissed her ring finger and stayed in his proposal kneel. "Thank you. Thank you for agreeing to make the baby with me. I know I haven't been the best at explaining why, but you have made me very happy. I swear it will all make sense in the end."

Was he serious? Instead of questioning his sanity again, she smiled. "Can we practice again later?" she asked. "The making the baby part?"

"No practice," he said. "Every time we make love, we get closer to conceiving my son."

"Whatever you say Jaxon."

He kissed her hand again and walked her out of the bathroom to the kitchen. Goodiva sat at the table watching him with her chin propped by the palms of her hand. Henry walked lazily into the kitchen. Goodiva glanced over at him as he meandered over and under the table. He snuggled close to her feet, keeping her warm.

Jaxon pulled out the all-purpose flour, milk and eggs. He had a lemon and butter stick. He whipped up his homemade batter and squeezed lemon juice to give it some zest. His pancakes were the perfect brown saucers flipped over and over. While tending to her request, he opened a can of beans and put on some rice to boil.

Goodiva shook her head. "You ran away as a teen?" she asked.

"Yep," he said as he whisked eggs in a mixing bowl.

"And you were a diabetic?" she asked.

"Yep," he said.

"How did you survive? For the long haul after the medicine from that doctor ran out. I mean, I understand initially he helped. But you needed constant care. You couldn't get a job."

"I was tall for my age. I was able to do some odd jobs."

"Really?"

He nodded. "The doctor who helped me gave me the name of another doctor when I told him where I was headed. I met the person. This man was different. He knew my *jin* personally."

"And he took a child in, without wanting something in return?"

He glanced back at her. "It wasn't like that. He was a doctor. He listened to my story and told me stuff I didn't know. What my father's illness was. How my mother became trapped with him. Why my father fled to America, and why he wanted..." he paused. He looked back to the food he cooked. "Why he wanted a son. At first I only showed up to see him when I was feeling bad. Eventually I was working out of his clinic. Eventually we gained enough trust in each other for me to stay at his clinic and then move in with him."

"What was his name?"

"Jaxon Price," he said.

"Wait? The Jaxon Price?"

"When he died my *jin* gave the name to me. I didn't have any real identification before. Now I had a name and a birthdate. A rebirth."

"I'm confused. How did your *jin* give...so your *jin* found you and him?"

"Yes."

"How old were you?"

"Again with the age questions. Let's say sixteen."

"And he wanted to take you back to the family of Scorpions?" she asked.

Jaxon laughed. "Sort of. He would need permission from the king. My father's crimes had made us both targets. I asked for another life. One I could have here in America. And I told him what my father had done to both me and my mother. I guess my *jin* saw how I survived without any of them and felt some pride in my perseverance."

"But what about your father? You were a minor. He had a say in what you could and couldn't do."

"My *jin* doesn't answer to my father," he said. "My father couldn't provide any legal proof of me being his son. It wasn't that hard."

"You said that your *jin* gave you Jaxon Price's name. How? How did the real Jaxon Price die?"

"Plane crash," he mumbled.

Goodiva felt a cold wave of dread in the way he said it. Plane crash was now a confirmed way that Jaxon and his family dealt with a problem.

"Don't feel sorry for him. He wasn't a good man, trust me. But he died after being a friend to me. I owed him my life. So I took on his name. I planned to be a doctor myself. Things went in a different direction."

She was riveted by his story and his openness. She didn't want him to stop talking. "So your *jin* left you at sixteen with a new identity, but where did you stay, how did you live?"

"There were conditions on my freedom. With my *jin* there often are," he sighed. "Armand, who you met, I went to stay with him and his father. We are family. The press believes I'm an orphan adopted by Armand's parents. But they are my blood. And my cousin was *very* American. We became friends. He was already an actor. Doing a series for a kid's show. It's how I got introduced into the movie business. And the rest is history."

"Not quite. I mean—"

"Taste your food," he said.

She had so many more questions. Instead of asking, she ate. The pancakes were divine. She nodded that she loved the taste.

"How about some beans with it?" he asked and picked up the bowl.

"Oh God!" she said with a mouthful. She put up her hand. "No!"

He went back to the stove and she watched him stack his plate up with beans, and scrambled eggs and rice. He even made a bowl of it for her to taste. When he came to the table, she tried to avoid looking at his plate as she ate her food. To this, he chuckled.

"I was seventeen when I got my first legitimate job with Paramount studios. I was a stagehand. Just on set doing technical fix it jobs. But one time a producer took a look at me and said I was perfect for a stand in role."

"Really? What movie?"

"*The Long Rider*, it was a spaghetti western. Something outdated that you will never see. The movie flopped. But I got an agent out of the deal and a few commercial slots," he said, forking the beans and rice in his mouth.

"So, you were an actor?"

"For a short time, yes."

"And?"

"Armand's father died. I was the oldest. It was just him and his mother in my life. I stepped up and took on the role as Armand's manager. I took on a few more clients and started to make money from inside of the business. From there I started to buy scripts."

"Buy them?"

"Writers often try to sell their scripts and pitches to get them in front of production studios. They hire a guy like me to take a percentage. I did, and got a few low-budget movie deals. Then I bought a few scripts outright. Put my name on them and sold them myself to get movies made. After the producing credits, I got into directing and so forth and so forth."

"Interesting. I always wondered how men like you gain so much power. You really did it all on your own. Your *jin* must have been impressed."

"He was. And for that reason no one ever exposed me for who I really was. I've been protected by the Scorpion all my life."

"Did your father ever find you?"

"When I was twenty-six he reached out to me, yes," Jaxon said.

"What happened?" she asked.

Jaxon ate. He didn't finish the story for a long time. He just ate. She ate with him, hoping to give him enough patience that he would share. When he didn't, she tried again. "What happened when he found you?"

"He told me that his new wife had died in childbirth. He had a daughter, but she was sent to Yemen to live with a sister of mine. He could not, and had not conceived a son. He then told me about a fertility clinic he planned to purchase and some other pharmaceutical investments for his research. He said he wanted me tested. He was diagnosed at twenty-six with a rare blood disorder. He wanted me to enter his trial program to see if I would at some stage inherit the same condition," Jaxon said. "It was then that I was introduced to the doctors. Doctors One through Twelve were the leading scientists in cures for diseases most people believe are incurable."

"Like AIDS?"

"Yes. AIDS was cured decades ago."

"How? Stem cells?" she asked.

"Possibly. I don't understand that research, how it all works. But there is a cure. The goal however was to profit from the global crisis. So the cure is actually mutated into medicine that makes it a disease you can live with. Like what AIDS is now."

"Wow!" Goodiva eyes stretched.

"It's quite fascinating. Working with stem cells, scientists are able to understand different diseases and origins to determine a cure. Before this kind of research many scientists experimented on animals, and even people."

"Like the Tuskegee experiment?" she asked.

"Exactly," he nodded.

"So, your father wanted to find a cure? To diabetes?"

"No," he chuckled. "You can live with diabetes, even Type 1, to some extent. What he had was not something easily treated. In fact, his father and brothers all died from the same disease. He lived much longer thanks to his clinics and the CIA."

She looked up. "CIA? Are you for real?"

"When I was twenty-six he told me he may have identified the key to the genetic link to the illness. It was in the blood. He would need bone marrow from his son."

"Was he telling the truth?" she asked.

"I dunno. I didn't care. I didn't have the disease. So why care?" he answered.

"But you are his son?"

"Only by genetics," Jaxon replied. "When I refused to allow him to take my bone marrow to do tests with, he said he understood. What he really needed was the stem cells from my first-born son. He gave me my trust. Told me to make sure that I never use the Mayfair name until after his death. And we parted ways."

"You never saw him again?" she asked.

"I saw him plenty. In my nightmares," he mumbled.

"The devil?" she asked.

He looked up at her.

"The pictures, and drawings. They were of the devil. All in that room you stayed in as a boy."

"That's right. The devil." Jaxon stopped chewing. "I saw the devil a lot after my accident. When I was in my coma I saw him every passing moment. Had several talks with him."

"About?"

"Life, death, me. When I woke up, I knew. I needed to come home. So, I came here."

"Oh, so you still consider this place home?"

"Try the beans. Please," he insisted.

"Oh good grief! Alright. I'll try them!" she dragged the bowl over to her and picked up the spoon. She pinched her nose as she brought the spoon to her mouth. He watched her. She expected to gag the moment it touched her tongue. To her surprise, she didn't. He'd added some kind of spice to it. A flavor she couldn't name. And it was quite good.

"You like it. Don't you?" he grinned.

"It's not bad."

"Our son will like it too. Wait and see," he winked.

Her smile faded.

"Jaxon, about me getting pregnant—"

"What happened to you when you were ten years old?" he asked.

The question was like a hard slap across the face. She sat back. "You made charges against your teacher, and they were later dropped. What happened?"

"What makes you think we killed him?"

"Are you serious?" Jaxon chuckled.

"Yes! I am."

"Well, let's see. You told me you saw a man die at the age of ten to start with."

"I never said I killed—"

"Yes. You did, Kitten."

"Don't call me that!"

"Oh, I forgot. I'm sorry."

She looked away as if she could escape the conversation.

"You have an entire playlist on your computer dedicated to this man with some of the angriest music. That killer rap music. And my final clue is he died shortly after the charges were dropped. Am I close?"

"I don't want to discuss him," she said.

"Why?"

"It's none of your business that's why!" she snapped.

He continued to eat. In a flash her anger revealed her vulnerability. Whatever he suspected of her past was confirmed by her overreaction.

"It's insulting to have you prying into my life. Doing research on me. It's kind of invasive and very disrespectful."

"Once I took a peek I couldn't look away," he chuckled.

"Got to hell."

She got up from the table. She walked out of the kitchen. She went to the bedroom where her clothes were kept. After she dressed and tended to her tangled hair, she felt less angry. In fact, she was smiling as she thought of his bean dish. She left the room hoping to find him in front of the television waiting for her. He wasn't. She checked the kitchen and the bathroom. She checked the other rooms as well. Jaxon was gone. Henry walked in and looked up at her curiously.

"Where does he go? Huh? When he leaves me?"

Henry gave her a wide mouth yawn and turned and walked out. Goodiva left the room with him. Mentally, she was exhausted. But emotionally she was fulfilled. Maybe she could tell him her secret?

Jaxon returned an hour later. He found her watching a movie. He sat on the sofa with her and pulled the blanket over to share her comfort.

"Miss me?" he asked.

She nodded yes, because it was true.

"I don't like being left alone."

"I wasn't far. Just on another hall. Had to take care of something for you."

She looked back to the television but dropped her head on his shoulder. She spent a lifetime protecting one big secret. She didn't even know if she could share it.

"Knowing you is a privilege, not a right," he lifted his arm and dropped it on the top of the sofa. "I crossed so many lines with you Goddess. I want that to change. You don't have to explain anything to me. Do you understand?"

"Yes. I do. I kind of want to. I never talk to anyone. Except for Dee and Queen. And neither of them want to discuss the past. It's all trapped inside of us."

He kissed the top of her head.

"I'm...confused. Are we dating or am I your prisoner?" she asked.

"A little of both," he smiled.

She ran her hand over his chest. "I'm sorry for the other day. When you took off your mask. The way I reacted to your face."

"I'm not the man you knew."

"It's not that bad. I just, I don't know. It's everything. I don't want you to think I find you repulsive."

He chuckled.

"You kind of proven to me you don't."

She smiled. "Yeah, I guess I have."

She let her hand ease down his chest to his groin. She squeezed his cock to awaken the real man in him. "One to know a secret?"

"Mmm?"

"I made a pact."

"With who?" he asked and she could feel his erection form in her hand. She let go of his dick and ran down his zipper under the blanket. She eased her hand inside to access his dick. It felt hot and strong. She kissed his chest.

"I made a pact that I would never discuss the past. Ever."

"Ah," he sighed. His head dropped back. She looked up to see his chin lifted and the Adams-apple in his throat bob with a deep swallow. He was hers.

"Well pacts are important," he breathed.

"I came to Falcon Cove when I was ten," she said and eased over on his lap. He opened her eyes. She pulled her summer dress up to her waist. She wore no undergarments.

"Okay?" He stared at her breast, half revealed when the slender strap to her sundress slipped off her left shoulder. "Mmhmm," she said as she lifted a bit on her knees to sit on his dick. "I started school. Made friends," she gasped. "Mr. Collins was my counselor. He was the school counselor for all the fourth graders. Because I was new to the school, he took an interest in me," she said as she moved up and down on him. She needed to feel something other than terror and grief. It may have been obscene, but she couldn't share her story any other way. "Oh Jaxon," she said as the rhythm got better and better. He sucked on her nipple and pulled its tightness between his teeth. "Yes, Jaxon, mmm, you feel so good."

She bounced on his dick.

"At first I liked Mr. Collins. He gave me gifts. He let me talk about my parents fighting constantly. And about my missing Germany. He was the only adult who seemed to speak the same language I did."

"Yes! Yes! Yes!" she was near climax.

Jaxon stopped her. He grabbed her by her waist. "Don't do this Goodiva."

"Do what?" she looked down at him a bit dazed.

"Don't tell me the secret this way." He pushed her up off of him. Horrified over what she had done, her mouth gaped in shock. He reached for her. She ran from the sofa to the bathroom and slammed the door. What was happening to her? She didn't comprehend.

"Goodiva?" he knocked on the door.

"Go away," she said on the verge of tears.

"I'm sorry. Okay? Let me in. To talk. Please."

"Go away!" She held the sink. She cried hard. Of course, she remembered it all. She felt queasy. The tears did not stop. But with each one she shed she felt a safety she hadn't known with any other human being. Jaxon Price finished her story.

"You weren't the only one. Were you? Your friends? That's why you have a pact. He was doing this to them too?"

She nodded. Jaxon of course didn't see her, but she nodded.

"You told adults, eventually. Your father believed you. He tried to kill Collins. But the school and authorities pressured your family and the charges were dropped?" Jaxon said.

"He made me do things," she said. "I knew it was wrong. Delilah was the first person I told. Then we told Queen. And Queen tried to explain to us why he did the things he shouldn't have with me, because he had been doing it to her, for a long time." She wiped the snot and tears from her face with the back of her hand. "Delilah was only ten, but she was smarter than the both of us. Much smarter. It was probably why he never tried anything with her. She wanted to punish him at first. She forced us to tell the adults. That went wrong. My dad went to jail. I was afraid because the kids in school blamed us. Counselors came and talked to all the girls. He hadn't done it to any of them. Just us. They said we were liars."

"But you weren't," Jaxon said from the other side of the door.

"My father went crazy. He nearly killed Mr. Collins," she confirmed his version of the story. "And he was in a lot of trouble for it. The adults had a meeting. People came to talk to us. Made us draw more pictures. Like how you drew pictures when you were a kid. All I know is that my father was out of jail and Mr. Collins got an apology from my family in exchange for the charges to be dropped against my dad. It changed my father. I don't have a relationship with him today."

"It broke him? He should have defended you to the end," Jaxon said.

The door opened. Goodiva stood before him. He pulled her into his arms and hugged her as tight as he could without hurting her. And she hugged him.

"Maybe he tried to protect me and couldn't. Maybe he couldn't face me because he failed. It ended my parents' marriage. It tore my family apart."

"And then...what happened?" he asked her. Goodiva spoke with her face buried against his chest. He had to strain to hear her clearly. But he didn't stop her.

"Mr. Collins kept his job. It made us all sad, scared, especially Queen. She cried constantly. Mr. Collins wouldn't see her any longer. And the parents were demanding he be let go. They just didn't know what to believe. So he quit." Goodiva lifted her face and looked up at him. "That wasn't enough for Delilah. People at school said we were liars. That we caused it all. Remember, he was the favorite to the fourth graders."

"I read the police report," Jaxon said. "He had an accident. He'd been drinking. Fell into a well and drowned?"

She shook her head no. "It was no accident. He went into that well because of us. We watched him drown. We watched him die."

"He's lucky he didn't die in a plane crash," Jaxon said.

Goodiva couldn't help but smile. She hugged him again. She rested the side of her tear-streaked face against his chest. "Do you understand why I can't have a kid with you Jaxon? Children, they're fragile. They need real adult supervision and constant care. I'm nobody's mother. I'm barely a good friend."

"You're the strongest woman I've ever met. You would protect your child from all the Mr. Collins, Fikrits, or *jins* of the world. It's why I know you would be a good mother. I'm in love with you too, Goddess."

Goodiva stepped back.

"I'm not in love with you."

"You said—"

"I don't care what I said. I'm not. And you're aren't in love with me!"

"I had three long years to learn all the things a man should know about a woman he wants to love. I fell in love with you from the start."

His confession didn't have the desired results. She didn't know what to say, but her eyes did reveal her belief in him. And that was a start. She shared her secret. He shared his. Nothing could ever take her from him. God help anyone who ever tried.

"Will you play some music for me?" he asked.

She smiled.

"No."

"Please," he asked.

"What do you want to hear?"

"Surprise me," he said, and zipped his pants. She smiled and walked past him to the records. He followed.

Chapter Twenty-One

Five weeks later

"See? I told you. I feel fine doc. Healthy as a horse." Jaxon picked up his shirt, which he had thrown over the chair, and pulled on. The doctor took the labeled vials of blood he'd drawn and put them each in the slotted medical container. Hutch and Ahmed had broken down the lab Dr. Nine and Ten worked from. His new doctor had quarters hidden behind walls in the cellar that could not easily be discovered. Jaxon ensured that what medical equipment he needed was available to him. This convenience meant he never had to be away from Goodiva for more than an hour at a time. It had to be this way. The Feds or something worse would arrive soon.

The doctor's silent brooding over the test results from his past examination were a bit concerning. Dr. Eleven was one of twelve physicians who saw to his father toward the end of his life. Big Pharma in the United States kept doctors like him under lock and key. They were the scientists who didn't work to find cures. Instead they sought treatments that would enslave Americans to a life dependency on medication for profit. Autoimmune diseases of all kinds and blood disorders were rumored to have cures that even the wealthy couldn't buy. But the crown prince and his brethren were beyond average wealth.

"The change in my medicine so far is working. No issues," he said. "Are we done?"

"Your hyperglycemia is still abnormal," the doctor mumbled.

"Here we go again."

"Pardon?" the doctor asked.

"I'm a diabetic. It will always be abnormal in your fucking tests!" Jaxon said.

"Diabetes is irreversible. Type 1 is irreversible. Yes. But we aren't worried about your diabetes, are we? Instead of this cold mountain, you should have let me admit you into the Mayo Clinic," the doctor said. "You threaten my team each time I give you advice. My advice is only given as truth."

"Mayo Clinic? Again with this bullshit? There is no cure. I'm only looking to survive. For as long as I can."

The doctor peered over the top of his glasses. "Is that why you destroyed the sample we took from you months ago? After all the tests and hormonal treatments. You just flushed it away."

"It was my decision."

"Of course, but the work. We were so close. We'd have to start all over."

"We won't," he said.

"Hear me out. We've advanced since your father's case. A son or daughter could save your life. It doesn't matter what gender. All we need is the umbilical blood to extract the stem cells and—"

"It's done. I'm not going through hormone therapy, medications, and that holistic fertility bullshit again."

"I'm told she's still here?" Dr. Eleven asked.

"She's none of your business."

"Maybe not. But I must advise you that, with the diabetes, extreme physical stress will only make your condition worsen. Are you two having sex?"

"Well, that is none of your business either doctor," Jaxon said.

"I advise against it. There is no need for you to be physical with her if you don't want children."

"You haven't met her," Jaxon said.

"I'm serious. You're living on borrowed time. You refuse all medical advice."

The doctor shook his head in defeat.

"Since you have been sexually active, there is something I need for you to do?"

"What?"

The doctor turned and retrieved an EPT box. He opened it and pulled out one of the wands for the test, which was individually wrapped. He handed it over to him.

"A pregnancy test?"

"We should know," the doctor asked.

"She's not pregnant. We both know that's not an option."

The doctor stared at him for a moment.

"Dr. Ten said her IUD was removed? Isn't that right?"

"Yes, but it doesn't change my problem."

The doctor set his clipboard down. He pinched the bridge of his nose, causing his spectacles to lift. "I've explained to you the possibility. These games you are playing..."

"Slow down Doc. I admit, she had become an obsession. You and I know that a pregnancy could and would save her life and mine. My *jin* has lost patience, and this virus out there shutting down the world keeps him off my ass. I know I'm on borrowed time."

"All the more reason for you to take my advice."

Jaxon gave a bitter chuckle. "The sample we have here is what you can use. She's not ready for IVF. I'm working on convincing her."

"You are out of time sir," the doctor reminded him. "No son of your father's has ever lived past a year old. Did you know that. Not even the ones he created through that fertility clinic. There is no male heir, except for you, of course."

"I didn't know that."

The doctor nodded. "We know so much more about this disease, about six other cancers linked to this disease thanks to your father's research. If she is here and you two are sexually active, there is a chance—small, yes—but a chance she could conceive even with your low sperm count. Overall your problem is a chromosomal disorder, so don't rule it out—."

"Back off doctor," Jaxon warned and handed him back the EPT wand. The doctor refused to accept it.

"Listen damnit! Sometimes it could be impotence, but that's obviously not the case with you. Other times infertility in men with your condition could be caused by retrograde ejaculation. What you might call a dry orgasm. In your case specifically, it's genetics. None of your father's daughters have this disease, and they have all been able to have children. Their sons don't have the disease. But you and your father, you're different. My research will explain why and possibly unlock the key to other diseases. We can change medicine."

"I'm not your science experiment, and neither is she."

"I'm begging. We're so close. Not just for a cure for you, but cancer. Think of what a cure means to the world? Your grandfather has high hopes for you. He wants to give everything to you. This can work."

Jaxon shoved the pregnancy stick in his pocket and went for the doctor. He seized him by the throat and pinned him down on the lab table. The man was forced to bend back so hard and far it could snap his spine. "You are living on borrowed time just like me. Do you understand me?"

"Calm down son."

"I'm not your son. Another symptom of my illness is madness. And since I've become the Scorpion I've tasted it. You keep after her, I can show you where I buried your colleagues."

"I understand. I understand," the doctor said with both hands up. "Please! Please! Release me."

Jaxon let the man go. He resisted the urge to pound his fist into the man's face until all of his rage was gone.

"Mr. Price." The doctor stood with his hand to his throat.

"Asad. Asad Fikrit. That's who I am. Jaxon Price is dead. You of all people should know that."

"I understand why you are protective of her. The lab in New York is closed. The quarantine has frozen the entire state. Even if you convince her to do IVF, I'm not sure I can harvest eggs and do the procedure here. Natural conception, no matter how small of a chance will work, it is the only option. I just want you to know."

"I was wrong," Jaxon said. "Having a son does not save her, it damns her to the same experimentation that my father started. I'm dying. That will be the end of it. There is no fucking cure."

Two weeks later

Jaxon lay on the floor on his side. Album covers were strewn about. It was his turn to play music that he liked. And his little DJ was very into it. She was up dancing around in a loose fitted mini-dress that swirled around her thighs. From his lowered position he glimpsed her cheeks more than once. She also wore a white lace choker fastened around her neck and her hair was thick as a sponge. It bounced lively on her shoulders with bangs in her eyes. His bohemian goddess snaked her hips and raised her arms as she hit the dance moves to his favorite band Vertical Horizon. The instrumentals to the song 'Everything You Want' were almost hypnotic when coupled with her swaying hips.

He smiled. She was happy. The past two days had been transforming for them both. And today they finally finished their game of chess. The student had beaten the teacher. The song ended. Goodiva picked up another album and walked over and put on the record for him. It was Faith Hill's 'Breathe.' She turned and smiled.

"I won," she said.

"Yes you did," he said.

"What's my prize?"

His gaze lowered and then scaled up. They'd found another way to communicate. One that didn't cause him to lie or her to pretend. A wordless exchange that spoke to the deepest spark of desire that fueled their passion. Goodiva rolled her panty down and let it to drop to her ankles. She stepped out of it.

"Lunch?"

He nodded.

She got down on the floor. He smiled as she crawled toward him. Just as he thought she would come within reach, she turned left to the bookshelf where the crates of albums were stacked. In doing so, her mini-dress draped over her hips revealed her apple shaped bottom, shapely thighs and the dark lips of her sex. She pretended at searching for something. He knew her game. Jaxon reached for her. His hand closed on her ankle.

Goodiva looked back at him with a startled cry of surprise. Her hair was so long over her brow, he could barely see her eyes.

"Come here," he pulled her foot.

She laughed.

He lay flat on his back. Goodiva crawled over and then on top of him. She drew up his shirt with her teeth while looking down at him. She revealed everything below her navel. His hands went to her thighs and he drew her closer and closer. On her knees she slowly lowered her sex to his face. His tongue slipped in and she exhaled. The dress hem fell from her lips and covered his face. But his mouth kept working. Both of his hands caressed her cheeks.

She rocked back and forth in timing with the music. His mouth and tongue gently worked her over without restraint. It got so good to her she fell forward on her hands. Soon her body worked a rhythm all its own. Her hips swirling and thighs shaking. She released and released and released. She was so addicted to him now it was hopeless.

"Come here girl," he said and pulled her down into his arms. He turned her and he was able to look her in the face as he showed her his passion. Her legs parted. Her pussy was drenched in her arousal. He dove deep with a single thrust followed by another and another. She could take it. When it got so good to him he thought he'd be reduced to whimpers, he collapsed on her. Jaxon kissed and licked the sweat from her shoulder and kept thrusting into her. In full distress, he ejaculated. It would be unimaginable luck that he got her pregnant. But he knew the odds of that happening.

"You're heavy buddy," she wheezed.

"Oh, sorry," he said and moved off of her. She turned over and let go a deep belly laugh. Laughter with her was always contagious. Jaxon laughed too. He felt heat rush to his face and neck.

"Whew, this is becoming a habit. Let's keep to the bed. The floor is too hard for sex, she said and rubbed her tender nipples.

"Yeah, ah, sure," he said.

She looked over at him, catching the apology in his tone. "Oh, don't go getting serious on me. I'm fine. Want me to show you?"

"No. No. I'm good too." He tried to sit up on his elbows but his body went weak. He gave a nervous chuckle and tried again, but collapsed. She sat upright, alarmed. "Is it the diabetes?"

"Can you get my medicine bag out of the bathroom," he asked. She scrambled to her feet and rushed to the bathroom. He lay there praying his body gave him the strength to stay relaxed and alert. If he seizure on her, or worse than that, blacked out, he was in trouble. Not since their love affair began had she ever seen him weakened by his illness. He'd pushed himself too far. Sex three times in a day with her was beyond his limit.

"What do I do?" she asked, sitting on the floor, naked, by his side.

He glanced at the bag. It wasn't his inulin. He knew that. He needed the doctor's remedy. "The black pills."

She nodded and went digging in the bag past the insulin vials, syringe and pill bottles. "Shoot, wait a second," she said and left in a hurry. He heard her in the kitchen and fridge. She returned soon with a glass of orange juice. Jaxon sat up and put his back to the sofa. His hands were shaking so bad he couldn't hold the glass. She gave him three pills and then held his chin as he drank. He could only look at her with gratitude. The pain was moving into his joints. He felt as if someone was hammering nails into his legs. Though he bit down on his agony, his legs began to shake beyond his control.

"Jax?" she said.

"It's fine. A muscle spasm." He tried to laugh, but the words came out strained as he clenched his teeth. She pulled him over to her chest and held him. She put his face to her breast and rubbed her hand down his back. He hugged her waist and suffered in a different kind of way. Never had he been comforted through anything in his life with so much tenderness.

"Hold on to me. I have you," she said and kissed the top of his head. "It's okay Jaxon. It's okay," she said.

She'd paid attention. Every time he left her, she paid attention. Goodiva sat on the floor staring down at her unconscious lover. He was covered now by a blanket. She'd brought in a pillow for his head. Goodiva knew that this would be possibly her one and only chance for escape. To leave him this way was as criminal to her as his crimes against her. But time had come to a stop in the cellar. She'd been below with him for at least two months. There seem to be no end to it. She leaned in and pressed her ear to his chest. She heard his heart beat and it sounded strong. He was alive.

"Jaxon?" she said. "Jaxon!" She shook him.

He didn't move. She reached into his pocket and removed the tiny remote she knew he used for the lift. Goodiva \ rushed to her room and put on her clothes. She pulled on pants, a sweater and boots. If she made it out of the place, the weather could stop her in her tracks.

When she returned, he lay as she had left him. A strange emotion gripped her. It must have been the Stockholm syndrome she heard most kidnapped victims suffered. Whatever it was, it pulled on her heart and pleaded with her to stay. She fled before she changed her mind. She punched in the code he'd used in front of her day after day. She went out of two doors. But didn't make it into the hall before she heard voices.

She froze. The men were speaking in another language and they weren't far. *If they found her first, then what would happen?* Goodiva waited until the voices faded. It was a risk she'd have to take. The halls were dark, just as they were before. The lights were off. She kept her hand to the wall in darkness and remained thankful for it. She was protected from being seen. She was also vulnerable to a surprise attack or getting lost. She kept going. Escaping wasn't really a possibility if she didn't seize the moment. The best she could hope for was to get upstairs to a phone to call the police. It was her only plan.

A man spoke. He barked orders to another man in a different language. The voices were from the other hall. She peeked around the corner. The man whose name she remembered as Ahmed was speaking. He was with a man she hadn't seen before. He was short, balding and wore glasses.

Was he Jaxon's doctor? Should she get him for help? Something in the way the men argued in the dark stilled her. Whatever it was they discussed, she feared it wasn't good for her or Jaxon. Both of them were in the hall that led to the way out.

If they found her, she would be taken back to Jaxon. If he woke and found her gone, all the progress she'd made with him would be destroyed.

Think, Goodiva, think...

JAXON OPENED HIS EYES. He lay flat to his back. Under his head was a pillow and across him a heavy blanket. The floor was coolest on that side of the room. He stared up at the vaulted ceiling trying to remember what happened.

"Goodiva?" he groaned.

Feeling stronger but still weak from exhaustion, he pushed up to find himself alone. No music played. The albums they had all over the floor were now neatly put back in their crates in alphabetical order. She was gone.

It was then he glanced to the door. A few days ago the Feds arrived with her friend Detective Douglas. Everyone in protective masks and gloves searching while half the country was under quarantine. It only meant they were serious in their investigation of her disappearance. They searched the premises for nearly seven hours before Andella convinced them that he had left and there was nothing to find. He kept her company below. Even if they were in the hall outside of their chamber, the soundproof walls made it impossible for her to know.

"Shit!" he winced.

Somehow she'd figured it out. Somehow she'd gotten the door open. Had she watched him use the code during his frequent coming and goings? How did she do it?

He scrambled to stand.

"Goodiva!" he said and went for the door. He had to stop to pull his pants up over his bare ass. If she made it upstairs, she couldn't escape. Still, she could call her friends and send for help. What if the Feds had returned and were upstairs when she arrived? He feared this moment most of all. He often slept next to her with one eye open, afraid she would sneak from the bed and leave him. She found the remote to the lift once when he was cooking and threatened to use it. She threatened to escape him often. Still, whenever he touched her she responded with the kind of passion that had to be rooted in feelings. She had to feel something for him, he reasoned.

He made it to the door but had to keep his hand to the wall to keep standing. His legs were the worst of it. They were always the last of him to recover after one of his episodes.

"You leaving?" she asked.

His head whipped around. She stood there in her bare feet and his button-up shirt eating a bowl of cereal. Her hair was in her eyes and framed her face. He'd never been happier to see her. And the relief that washed over him cured his fear.

"I...ah, no," he said.

"Then sit down. I don't know what happened, but it's probably not over. I'll fix you something to eat," she said, before she scooped more cereal into her mouth. He touched his pants pocket to discover the slim and thin remote was tucked inside. He nodded that he would obey and stiffly walked over to the sofa. She turned and went back to the kitchen.

Jaxon's heart beat fast. Instead of showing weakness, he straightened his spine and sat on the sofa. He was grateful for the relief when he took a seat. He slumped forward and put his face in his hands. The past three days he'd spent down below with her. They'd done everything from movies and music to sex. Always sex. And she rarely mentioned escaping to him any longer. But their free time had expired. Physically, he had deteriorated. It was happening faster with the physical exertion he put upon himself. After several deep breaths, he sat upright able to breathe without staining. He glanced to the bag near the fireplace. He brought it down with him several days ago.

"Tonight. I'll do it tonight," he said to himself.

"PAINT MY TOES!" SHE said and grinned at him from across the table.

"What?"

"You heard me," she said. She put her foot on the table.

He frowned.

"I don't know how."

"Oh please, you telling me you never painted a woman's toes?"

"Not a woman with six toes," he countered.

"Actually I have eleven, smart ass."

He shook his head smiling. She laughed to the point of tipping over. She loved to argue with him. She loved to insult him. And she loved to debate him. He loved her.

Jaxon continued to eat. She had learned how to make jollof rice in Africa. She promised to make it for him someday. Today she made him rice and peas with baked chicken and spiced it up nicely. He was famished. His appetite was never satisfied.

"Here's the thing. I won and you said whatever I want I get. I want you to paint my toes," she continued.

"We don't have nail polish," he reasoned.

"I have it. We can begin after dinner." She got up to go for a bottle of wine. He glanced at her and wanted to tell her not to drink it. But to do so would only make her defiant. So he held his tongue. She came back and poured her glass humming to herself.

"You know, it's time to move upstairs," she said.

"No, it's not," he replied.

"I'm ready to move."

"Do we have to do this every week?" he asked.

"Is it every week? I don't see days," she said and took a sip of her wine, staring at him.

"We discussed this. You won't—"

"I will, and soon. I'm sorry Jaxon, but I've had time to think about it. To really know you. I don't believe you will destroy my friends. You won't do it."

"Goodiva..."

"You're in love with me. Would you hurt the woman you love?" she smirked.

He stared at her. The confidence and boldness she gave him was his own doing. And soon it all began to make sense. The way she cared for him. The many times she snuggled him. The magnificence of her lovemaking. And why when he was out cold she didn't even bother to escape. She had turned the tables on him. Made sure he felt for her in the deepest way. She'd done it all for this moment. He couldn't just let her walk out of the door. Not now. He had to come up with another plan to deal with his jin. She wasn't safe until he destroyed his grandfather. The only thing he had for her was the planned pregnancy, and he intended to make her believe he still wanted to perform the IVF.

"When the storm breaks, I'm leaving," she announced.

"We had a deal Goodiva."

"And I'm breaking it. Well, not really. My agreement was for us to try for a baby naturally. That's what we've been doing, haven't we? Did I ever stop you? Did I ever say no?" she grinned. "If I take this test and we aren't pregnant, then we won't be. End of story. Let God decide. And you aren't God!"

She revealed the pregnancy wand the doctor gave him. His eyes stretched. "What are you doing with that?"

"What are you doing with it?"

"Give it to me," he demanded.

She shook her head no. His little viper had it all figured out. She believed she had her IUD in place and she had successfully outsmarted him. "Worried?"

"Give it to me Goodiva."

"No."

Jaxon put his face in his hands. "Do you care for me?"

"I care," she smiled.

"Do you love me?"

"No," she said.

He lifted his face from his hands. "Well I love you. And I'm going to tell you the truth. There is no storm. The one we thought would come last barely two weeks."

She frowned.

"So, I can leave."

"You can't. There's something worse out there than the snow."

"What are you saying?"

"A virus. It started in China. It spread the last few months. Now we have a global pandemic."

Goodiva laughed.

"I'm serious. We are quarantined. The whole state is on lock down. You can't leave. Falcon Cove is shut down. There is nowhere to go."

"You will say anything to keep me here."

"It's the truth love."

"You're afraid. I take this test and I'm not pregnant this game ends. You're afraid because I'm calling your bluff. You're in love with me. You won't hurt me or my friends. You're scared."

"You should be scared," he warned. He glanced at the test in her hand. Maybe the doctor was right. Maybe there were miracles, and Allah had performed one. Maybe she was pregnant and belonged to him. "Are you sure you don't love me?" he asked.

She nodded.

"Are you sure I won't expose you and your friends. That I'm so in love with you I'd let you walk out of here? After everything we've been through this past three months?"

"Yes, I understand now, who your father was, and what your mother did. I know you suffered and don't trust people. You helped me too. You listened to my secrets and didn't judge me. You're a good man pretending to be a bad man. I'm not pregnant Jaxon. I going to prove it to you. I can't give you children."

"A son. All I asked of you Goodiva was to have a son."

She rolled her eyes and sighed. "This game has to end between us. Okay? No more lies. There is no virus. There is no baby. There is no us."

"Take the test, let's let God decide then," he agreed.

"And when I prove I'm not?" she asked. "I need your word that we are done."

"*Insha'Allah*. I have faith."

"*Allah*? I forget you are Muslim," she mumbled and stared at the box.

"*Allah* means God. When I say *Insha'Allah* I am only saying 'God willing.' Allah is actually the literal translation of God."

"Oh, I didn't mean to offend you," she quickly corrected herself.

"Non-Muslim Arab's say *Allah* all the time. It is offensive when a person dismisses your faith. Have I ever done that to you?"

"No," she said softly. "Sorry."

He shook his head. "There is so much you don't understand. That's my fault."

"Well we agree there. It's all your fault."

There was nothing to fear. She at first worried that he had experimented on her and taken out her IUD. But she'd spent a lot of time knowing him. Though his mission to impregnate her seemed strange and sadistic, he was genuine in everything else. Besides, her body felt no different. She was not pregnant. Her period was due any day, and already she was feeling pre-menstrual cramps.

"Be right back," she smiled.

Not much had changed about him. He was a liar. First it was the threats to her friends, now some fake virus story to make her think it was dangerous to leave. He'd do anything to keep her locked down in prison with him. She would not bring a child into this world under these circumstances or any circumstances that could lead to abuse. She walked over to the toilet and lifted the lid. Goodiva pulled down her panty and sat on the commode. She opened the box. She removed the wand from the plastic. The EPT would simply tell her 'pregnant' or 'not pregnant.'

And then she intended to end this crazy affair. She pulled out the wand and removed the blue cap on the end. She stuck it between her legs and peed on it. After a few seconds she was done. She put the cap on it and wiped the urine from the wand. Goodiva set it on the sink as she finished tidying up. When she flushed the toilet, she happened to glance at the stick. Her breath caught.

"No. That's not...possible."

PREGNANT – 3 weeks.

Chapter Twenty-Two

Jaxon paced outside of the bathroom door. He heard nothing. He tried to be patient, but ever since the toilet flushed his stomach muscles kept him on the verge of throwing up his dinner. He didn't believe she was pregnant, but what if there was a chance?

After five minutes of no noise he knocked on the door. She didn't answer. It was then his worry morphed into fear. Jaxon knocked twice before he opened the door. Goodiva sat on the toilet seat. She held the wand in her hand. She stared at it.

"What's wrong?"

She looked up at him with extreme distress and tears in her eyes. "You lied to me."

"Lie? What lie did I tell?"

She held up the wand. "I'm pregnant."

He blinked at the stick and then her.

"You had them take out my IUD. You lied to me this entire time."

"I never lied. We never discussed your IUD."

She threw the wand at him. It hit his chest and dropped to the ground. He picked it up and read it.

"I'll never forgive you for this Jaxon. Never," she said.

"Godiva?" Jaxon said.

She ignored him. He sat next to her.

"You've destroyed my life!" she wept.

He reached for her.

"Don't touch me! Don't you ever touch me!" she shouted. She got up from the sofa and stumbled back crying. "What is wrong with you? Why are you like this? Why!"

"I had no idea it would work," he said.

"What? What?" she demanded.

"I can't have kids the natural way because of my impotence," he began.

"You aren't impotent!"

"It's complicated. I never believed we could conceive this way. IVF was the only sure thing," he said.

"That's a lie!" she pointed her finger at him. "You knew. You took out my IUD! You lying bastard."

"That was always the plan. How else could you conceive with it?"

"Bastard!"

"Goddess, you have to believe me. None of this is my choice."

"We always have a choice. And you took my choices away from me!"

"I have no choice in who I am. I have no choice in what I am. I have no choice in loving and wanting to protect you. None of this is a choice for me. All I can do is make sure that you and my child live...with better choices, without me."

She didn't hear him. She didn't want to hear him. She left the bedroom. If she had a gun, she might use it.

"Wait!"

"I said stay away from me! Stay away from me!" she shouted.

"Okay, I was wrong. To do it this way. I was wrong." He approached her. "But I do love you. And I did all of this for your future."

"Ugh!!" she shouted through her tears.

"Listen to me. The other day, when we were playing chess, do you remember how the lights kept flickering on and off? Remember? I told you we were losing electricity because of the storm."

She frowned.

"I lied. It was a signal. Your detective friend found out the truth. She brought the police and the FBI here. They searched for you. They were outside of this chamber looking for you. There is no blizzard, but the quarantine is real. And your detective friend isn't giving up. You were right. Your friends aren't going to abandon you. Now I believe this lockdown the state is in and the investigation by the feds can protect you better than I can. Go to them. Alert the FBI. And I know you'll be safe. Our baby will keep you safe if you tell the public about me and what I've done. About my father. Force Delilah to expose the clinic. Then you are all free."

"Shut up!"

"It doesn't matter what I want anymore. If you want to leave, I can't stop you."

"You're lying. It's another trick."

"It's the truth."

"No. You don't tell the truth. You tell versions of the truth. There's a reason why you want me out. Especially now that I'm pregnant. You're up to something. Tell me! Tell me!"

"I've told you everything."

She wiped her tears and looked around. He wasn't sure if she even understood him. However, her hesitation gave him hope.

"I'll let you go, tonight. As soon as you're packed and ready." He put up both his hands.

"Those men are in the hall waiting on me."

"What men?" he frowned.

"Don't play dumb with me!" she shouted. "This is a setup. You're setting me up!"

"I'm not lying anymore. Ahmed can get you off the mountain in my snowcap."

"But you said there was no snow!"

"I didn't. I said there was no blizzard. There's always snow this time of year."

"Liar! Liar!"

"Goodiva calmed down."

"Liar!"

"Ahmed will drive you directly into Falcon Cove police department. Tonight. You'll have to wear a mask, gloves and protect yourself from the virus," he explained.

"Liar!" she screamed.

He walked over to the coffee table, and picked up his mask and put it on. He tried one last time to reason with her. She kept screaming and crying that he was a liar. And he was. "If you stay. If you decide to stay and forgive me for all of this. I promise I'll tell you the rest of it—"

"I hate you!"

"Hutch and—"

"Shut up!" she demanded and walked past him. She went back into the room and started to drag out her suitcases. She found what she wanted to wear. A pair of jeans, a thick cable knit sweater and some snow boots. Goodiva dressed fast. She pulled the luggage out of the room into the front area. To her surprise, he was gone. The door had been left open for her. She stared at it, not trusting her own eyes.

She took a deep breath. It was a trap. She knew it. But she'd rather risk it at this point. She passed through the next door to the lit hallway. Goodiva followed the exit signs until she arrived at the lift. This was the test. Not since her last escape attempt had she tried to access the ancient thing. Would it work for her this time?

Goodiva let go of the handle of her suitcase and went to the gate of the lift. She pulled it and it slid right easily. Too easily. She glanced back behind her, expecting the worst. However, there was no one. She was all alone. She grabbed the handle on her suitcases and dragged them both inside. The lift took her upstairs without incident. She exited to a dark and empty house. The draft blowing through the halls chilled her. It was amazing how cold it was above instead of below. She could actually see her breath.

"Hello!" she called out. The echo from her cry out responded in the distance. "Jaxon?"

She pulled her suitcases and headed to where she remembered the front of the estate. There was sparse lighting. Enough to be seen and to see.

"Hello?"

"Ms. Johnson," a voice said behind her. She stopped. Andella and Francine both approached. She glared at the women, who didn't seem in the least surprised to see her. "We were told that you were leaving tonight," Andella said.

"Were you told that for the past three months and a half I was trapped down in the cellar?"

The women exchanged a look of concern. Neither of them answered.

"When I go to the police I will make sure to name both of you witches as co-conspirators!"

"Ma'am, Ahmed is waiting. This way," Andella said.

Goodiva was reluctant at first, but the women walked away and the place was too big for her to find her way alone. She followed them. They led her to the side of the estate. Hutch came through the door covered in snow. His hood dropped over his head and he wore goggles over his eyes and several scarves wrapped around his nose and mouth. He looked at her and then to the table. She glanced to the table and frowned.

"Ma'am. You will need to wear the mask and googles. Keep your gloves on as well. Do not remove them even when inside until you are in a quarantine safe place. Once you are there make sure to wash your hands and change your clothes. Put them and your shoes somewhere else. Quarantine is 14 days, but I'm told you should be fine," Andella said.

"Quaren-what? What the hell is this?" she scoffed.

"Master Mayfair told us you knew all about the Coronavirus. It's precaution. Everyone is practicing social distancing. You have to be careful," Frances said.

"He has you playing his game too."

"Listen to them We don't leave unless you do as they told you." Ahmed informed her.

"Hutch will take her," Andella insisted.

Goodiva didn't care who took her but she saw the serious admonishment Andella gave Ahmed with a distrustful scowl. Ahmed was the man whispering in the dark to another. Goodiva's instinct warned against being alone with him. She looked down at the gloves and mask and felt her heart race. Could he be telling the truth? Her freedom still felt like an illusion, but her heart surged with hope that she could escape even if there was some killer virus waiting for her out the door. It had to be better than being his hostage. Especially now that she knew she was pregnant.

"She can't go down the mountain in that. Get her a proper coat and scarf," Hutch said.

Francine nodded obediently and left. Andella helped her put on the mask and cover up. Francine returned with a very heavy hooded snow jacket, scarves and gloves. Hutch took her luggage out into the winter mix of snow and wind and then came back for her. She glanced around. She expected Jaxon to make an appearance. To demand she stay with him. To levy threats. To possibly restrain her. But he never appeared.

"We're ready," Hutch announced.

"Where is he?" she demanded. "Tell him to come down and face me."

Hutch frowned.

"We need to leave. The weather gets worse in the evening. I have to make two trips."

"I want to see him. He should face me. Face what he did to me. What you all did to me!" her voice broke with emotion.

"He doesn't have to do anything," Hutch said. "You have him vulnerable now. If you push this too far it won't end well. Now, do we leave or not?"

Goodiva glanced back over her shoulder to the women. She walked out with Hutch. The moment they hit the snow she was overwhelmed by the cold darkness. Suddenly the cellar reminded her of warmth and light. She wondered if others kept in captivity had such a disassociation with reality. She struggled to walk in a straight line. Hutch was at her side. He helped her into the snowmobile and secured her in the seat before shutting the door and going over to the driver's side. She was grateful for the warmth, but even with the heat blasting from the vents and the layers of clothes she wore, she felt bone shivering cold. The mask to her mouth and nose was partially covered by the scarf around her neck and she struggled to breathe under the claustrophobia.

There was no visibility. The darkness made her plight even worse.

"Is this safe?" she asked, and her voice was muffled.

"Not for many. But I can handle it," said Hutch. "He wouldn't put you at risk."

"Hmpf! You mean the man who kidnapped me is concerned for my life? The man who lied and got me..." she couldn't even say the words.

"The man who is the father of your child," he finished for her. "Yes. That man."

"Then it's all bullshit," she said as the snowmobile wobbled a bit going over the dunes of snow with the wind slamming at it from both sides.

"What is bullshit?" Hutch asked.

"That he wanted a son. A family. The moment he knocks me up he opens the doors for me to leave. Especially if there is some killer virus out here. He's a fraud. I don't even know if I am going to keep it—"

Hutch slammed his foot on the break. The abrupt stop made her lurch forward. She looked at him and the cold fury in his eyes dissolved her courage. Her mouth was worse than Queen's when angry.

"I have never betrayed Asad, or his father. For forty years I have kept my silence. Even when Fikrit beat the boy and chased him from his only home. I have seen many things, young lady. However, I've never seen a more clueless, spoiled bitch like you."

"Bitch!" she snatched down her scarf and mask. "Who the hell are you calling a bitch? You old motherfucker!"

Hutch sneered at her. "He has lied to you. I think it's time you know the truth."

"Your version of it," she tossed back.

"That baby you carry is the only way he could save your life. And the only reason he is letting you go is because it's done. Now he can die in peace."

"What?"

"Life is over for him. And he knows that too. I suggest you stop blaming him for the sacrifice and show some God-damn gratitude."

"You are crazy as him. Save my life? Save my life from who? Him?"

Hutch started the snowmobile. "Let me get you off this mountain. Good riddance to you."

She crossed her arms in front of her and bit back her tears.

"MASTER MAYFAIR?"

Andella stepped into the room. Dr. Eleven came in behind her. "Sir. The doctor wanted to see you."

"I told you. I don't need the shot today."

"Can we speak?" the doctor asked.

Andella left, closing the door behind him.

"Am I hearing right? Did you send her out of here? Back to Falcon Cove at night during the quarantine?"

Jaxon gave a snort. "She's safer in the quarantine than with me."

"What precipitated this freedom?"

Jaxon smiled. "It's too late Doc. She'll go into that police station and tell them all about me. And then you and jin can't touch her."

"She's pregnant, isn't she?"

Jaxon smirked.

Dr. Eleven stared at him.

"Answer me!"

"Yes," Jaxon reached for his bottle of gin and drank more than a swallow.

"This child is what we all hoped for. The child could save your life. Are you on a death wish?"

"You don't work for my jin, do you?" Jaxon looked up from the floor. "The treatments you've been giving me, aren't working. None of it was to cure me. It was to make sure I got her pregnant. Wasn't it?"

"The doctor didn't flinch."

"You think I didn't know. The moment she walked out that bathroom pregnant I knew what you were planning."

"You're not protecting her by sending her out there from me. It's bigger than me. This is bigger than you," the doctor warned.

Jaxon smiled. He raised his bottle. "That's right. The cure to save the world."

"The CIA has been patient with my work, and your father's cooperation has changed medical science. We needed you. We've tested all of his offspring. Nothing is in their blood. We failed. And then we learned that he hid you from us. All these years, we had no idea you—the famous director Jaxon Price—were his son. But that accident. We finally got access to you. You didn't inherit the disease magically after that accident. While you were undergoing surgery and blood transfusions, we introduced the mutation into your bloodstream. We gave you the illness."

The door opened. Ahmed entered. It was clear that Ahmed wasn't working for the Scorpion but connected to Dr. Eleven for a different purpose.

Jaxon stood with the bottle.

The doctor looked back at Ahmed. "We've tried to impregnate several surrogates with your semen. To make the perfect specimen. The perfect child. Immunity from the herd. That's the key. Even now the world's greatest minds are working on a cure for a single virus, when a hundred more wait behind it. But my work has never changed. It's in the blood. Your blood. That child she carries could change the world."

"I get it now. You stopped trying to cure me and tried to fix my impotency?" Jaxon asked as his hand tightened on the neck of the vodka bottle in his hand.

"We watched, and we waited. We saw you stalk her, we saw you prepare for her. We understand why you chose her. My doctors said she's perfect in every way we need her to be. So we helped you."

"The other doctors? The men I killed?" Jaxon asked.

"Collateral damage," Dr. Eleven said. "When your *jin* brought you back into the family we all knew how far you'd have to go to be respected by your clan."

"It's not just my child they want. Is it? Not just the cure you plan to manufacture."

The doctor gave him a single nod. "No American has gotten as close to the Scorpion as you. When your *jin* dies, you will be his heir. You will be second in command under the crown prince. And we need you alive for that."

"I'm dying you fucking idiot. You killed me." Jaxon took another swig from the bottle of jin.

"I save you with this child. And then you help us protect our interests by bringing us into the royal family. We control the wealth of the world, we control the health of the world, we control the world."

He could swing the bottle and smash the doctor's face in. It wouldn't be wise. Ahmed was probably armed. He'd lose all control. And worst of all, she'd be alone to face doctors like him. If his plan worked. If she passed this final test. Possibly he had a chance. Hutch told him of the conspiring between Ahmed and the doctor weeks ago. He knew of the fake treatments to boost his virility and fertility. Now he needed someone he could trust. And he gave his heart to the only person he did. What would she decide?

"I will alert my people that she is headed to the police. The FBI will secure her," the doctor smiled. "And if you cooperate, we can make sure she is yours. Our secret."

Jaxon chuckled. He went to the bar to see what else there was for his thirst. It would be a long night.

The doctor gave Ahmed a nod and then turned and left.

"JAXON?"

His eyes opened. He stared at the ceiling for a moment.

"Why are you on the floor?" Goodiva asked.

Was he dreaming? He must have been dreaming. He turned his head an inch. She stood over him. Was he dreaming? He had suffered dreams during his seizures before. He blinked at her until she came into focus. Goodiva put a hand to his chest.

"Get up," she said, and pulled on his arm until he did. He needed her help to do so. His throat burned from the vodka. He felt rigid all over.

"Can you stand?" she asked.

He nodded that he could. He slipped back to his rump twice when he tried.

"Don't bother. It's okay," she said and sat next to him. He wasn't convinced that it was her. He must have suffered another fever that brought on the seizure that took him down. Or maybe he was just drunk.

"Jaxon?" she said and touched his face. "Look at me."

He managed to do so.

"You don't look well, sweetheart."

"I'm fine," he told her.

"No, you're not. And I finally understand why." She left him for a moment. Jaxon used the separation as a chance to gather his thoughts. She had returned. His plan worked. She didn't believe she loved him until he forced her to face the decision. It was a risk. He'd risked her life and his child life on the possibility that she loved him. And she did.

She parked the wheelchair by him.

"I don't need that thing," he mumbled and waved it away.

She came back over to help him heave him up on shaky legs. He had no choice but to plop him down in the wheelchair. She put his feet on the pedals, and then looked up at him.

"Better? Is this better for you?"

He nodded.

"Good, because you know better than drinking!" She picked up the bottle of vodka on the floor. She walked over to the can and dropped it inside. "You're a diabetic. You can't do this."

"Why did you come back?"

"I don't know," she mumbled.

"I thought you were done talking to me?" he asked.

"I am. I mean I was," she said.

He frowned.

"I made Hutch bring me back. Trust me, he didn't want to," she said. "He called me a bitch."

"He did what?"

She walked over to the chair in the room and brought it to him. She sat in it across from him. "No more lies Jaxon. Tell me why you would put me through this. All of this? And yourself?"

"Because I love you," he said with a lopsided grin.

"Are you dying?"

His drunkenness had put a smile on his face. The question sobered him. "Yes."

Her eyes began to tear. "From diabetes?"

He smiled again. "No."

"Jaxon. I'm pregnant. And you know I would never abort my child. You spent three years knowing me. You knew I would leave as soon as I got a chance, as soon as you gave me a strong enough reason to hate you. That was the plan. Right? Me hating you?"

"You're confused."

She nodded and wiped her tears. He wished he could touch her. But it took all his strength to remain seated upright.

"The plan was for me to protect you. It was flawed from the start. The plan was for me to have you. The plan was for you to love me."

"Huh?"

He grinned. "You love me."

"I don't love you."

Jaxon nodded drunkenly that she did. "You love me."

"Hutch told me you're sick. He said the word 'dying.' That's all he said. I came back because I'm confused and you're hurting. I know diabetics. This isn't diabetes. It's something more. What is the real truth?" she asked.

"I'm a liar. That's the truth."

"Then tell me something I can believe. Try."

"My story wasn't all true. The one I told you about my parents. My father didn't kidnap my mother, or hold her captive. She was gifted to him as a reward for his services as a fourth wife after his royal appointment."

"What kind of services?"

"Mercenary work," he sighed and put his face in his hand. "That's what they consider the secret police in Saudi. Mercenaries. My father was one of the most ruthless. Dealing with enemies of the royal family in ways that could give you nightmares. But my father wasn't Saudi. And he wasn't loyal. He worked with the British and American secret agencies, MI6 and CIA. He sold information on the king and my grandfather. When it was discovered that he had betrayed the king, he had already fled to Yemen, then the CIA relocated him here to Mayfair. He already had my mother and my jin went crazy trying to find her."

"That was the real betrayal?" she asked.

"Yes. Sons of the Prince are called Scorpions. My mother branded me so I could be one too. When my father became ill with a sickness that has killed his brothers and father, he had hope that he would find a cure. But he knew a cure would only be used by the Americans or Britons to secure their power over other countries. Dad outlived every prediction and helped agencies here in America learn more about the disease. His death caused them to look my way."

"What does that have to do with me?"

"Nothing at first. At least with the American government. My jin wanted me to be his Western pride. He loved the fact that I had made something of nothing. Born into the privilege of the royal family, we can be pampered with success. Few men stand on our own. Armand and I are different. When you and Twixt were involved in my accident, you drew his attention. A contract was put on both of your lives. My father was protected by the American government. So they could never get revenge on him. But you are nothing to any of them. They would have killed you. I had to decide who to save. I made sure I saved you."

"By doing this?"

"If you mean the baby, yes. My baby will protect you from *jin* when I'm gone. At least that was my only concern at first. But after you were brought here, I learned of another danger. The government had been watching me, so they had been watching you. They saw my obsession with finding and saving you and changed plans. What I didn't know at first when I locked you in that room is that my child's life and yours are not safe anywhere. The CIA gave me my father's sickness. Experimented on me after my accident. I'm the first test case that worked. My diabetes is only part of it. My illness isn't like his, it's something else. And they can use it as a means to trap me by taking our son."

"To experiment?"

"The doctor said there will be antibodies in our child's blood to harvest a cure for cancers like mine. Like the hundreds that go undiagnosed."

"Our baby can save people?" she asked.

He shook his head. "Are they saving people with what they learned about AIDS? Or are they just making a way for you to live with it? It'll be a weapon Goddess. Nothing more."

"The American government wouldn't do this."

Jaxon laughed. "It's worse than you can imagine. If I don't let them use our child, I die, because whatever they gave me they can reverse. It's why I'm strong some days and weak on others. They're torturing me. If let them give me a cure and live, they will send me back to the Scorpions and I will be the man my father was. But worse."

"It's too much information. I need a moment."

"They have tried before. Other surrogates, using my wives—"

Goodiva sat back. "Did you say..."

"—none of them could get a viable sample of my semen for insemination. So they gave me hormonal treatments to make me fertile. I thought they were treating my illness. I didn't know. I never thought I could conceive with you without IVF. I never thought it would happen. Now you are the only one carrying my child."

"Did you say wives?"

He looked her in the eye. He nodded.

"You have wives?"

"I have three wives."

"You're married?"

He nodded.

"I had to marry. The mark of the Scorpion is on my back. It's part of it."

"You want me to be part of a harem?" she asked.

"No, no Goodiva. I just wanted you. I'd marry a hundred of *jin*'s brides to get next to you. They mean nothing to me."

Goodiva stood. She paced the floor. "I don't think I want to hear any more of this story."

"I'm dying," he said.

She glanced back to him. "You said they have a cure."

"They have something, yes, but I'm not going to take it."

"Stop taking for a minute," she put her hand to her chest. "Let me think."

"Hutch is right. My father lived because the disease was all he had to treat. I have diabetes. This blood cancer of mine with my diabetes is a death sentence. A genetic cocktail that made me infertile before it worsened. I didn't tell the doctors to remove your IUD. I didn't suggest we sleep together. And even when we did, I didn't believe you'd become pregnant. I did manipulate you, trap you, force my way into your heart."

"I told you I don't love you—"

"I don't care what they do. I want you. Only you. That's what this is really about."

"They? Who are they? The CIA? The NSA? The FBI? Who!"

"People need me to live. Do you want me to live? Do you love me Goddess."

She stood silent for a moment. "You should have told me this."

"There is nothing you can do to protect yourself from my family. Nothing. Telling you only puts fear in you for the rest of your life. But our baby will be what is left of me. And if I'm dead our child will be even more important."

She put her face in her hands. He could see the distress had her on the verge of a full breakdown.

"Do you love me Goddess?" he asked and leaned forward in the wheel-chair.

"How is it done? What happens to my baby? How do they get his blood?"

"When you give birth, the umbilical blood has stem cells that could cure my disease. Depending on who gets it first. Those cells could give the royal family a cure for blood cancer. Make them even more powerful than they are with oil. Whoever gets our child gets the power. I promised my *jin* this cure and to become a Scorpion for the crown prince. That is the legacy he wants to leave behind. But you aren't from our world, our culture. He wouldn't present our mixed child as his supreme leader. I would have revenge for myself and my mother against the family."

Jaxon had a hard time keeping his head up. He dropped back in the chair and stretched his eyes to remain conscious.

"You made me care for you, made me a mother to a child who may die just like you, and then you will leave me with this? You should have let your jin kill me."

Jaxon shook his head. "Never. You're mine."

"You're worse than Mr. Collins. You're worse than my father. You've hurt me more than any of them ever could."

"But do you love me? That's what I want to know. I love you. I lost control of all of this because I couldn't stop obsessing over my love for you," he said in a hoarse whisper as he felt himself fading. "The doctors tell me that it's part of my illness, my mental state deteriorates. I can fix this. If I got you pregnant, then I can give them another sample. Give them a child to experiment with and let ours live in peace. I think." He pushed himself forward and focused on her. "Now answer my question. Do you love me?"

She shrugged her shoulders. "I guess."

Jaxon smiled. "I knew it. No more running. Promise me."

"I'm not running anymore. I'm going to stay, I'm going to learn everything I need to know about what could happen to my child. And you're going to teach me everything I need to know to protect him or her. Everything. Because I'm going to protect us, from you, your demented grandfather and from the stupid government."

"I love you so much," he said.

"You don't know what love is Jaxon. No one has ever taught you," she said.

He knew she was right. "But it felt good saying it."

Chapter Twenty-Three

Six Days Later

"I don't understand any of this," Delilah said. The women sat side by side on the police helicopter as they flew toward the mountain through dense gray snow clouds. "She's living there? With him?"

"That's what she said. She called me yesterday out of the blue. Told me that she was sorry for making us worry. And to come back to Mayfair so she can explain. That's all I know, Dee. We've gone over this ten times."

"Making us worry? Is that what she thinks? We were worried? We were fucking out of our minds, and terrified. We thought she was dead. You got the FBI involved. Plus we got this damn quarantine, we shouldn't even be doing this. Now we find out she's living with him. Goodiva has done some really stupid things over the years. We've always bailed her out. But this—Queen, this is too much."

"Let's hear what she has to say. Okay?"

"Why didn't she call me?" Delilah asked.

"What?" Queen asked.

"Why did she call you? She normally calls me. I'll tell you why. Because you are always going with this 'live and let live' bullshit. In your professional life you dig for answers. But with us, you always want to pretend the problems don't exist. She knew you'd let it slide. I won't."

"That's not fair," Queen said.

"Goodiva is hiding something. Watch and see," Delilah said. "Wait and see."

GOODIVA TOOK ANOTHER step over to the floor mirror to check her appearance. She turned sideways and sucked in her belly. She did a deep exhale to poke her stomach out. And nothing had changed. Her stomach was flat, and tight. There was no indication of her pregnancy.

"How are we doing today baby?" she said and touched her stomach. "You weren't good to mommy last night."

She'd spent half the night running to the toilet to puke. All this time she thought morning sickness only happened in the morning. It was the reverse for her. Most times it came at night. Dr. Eleven had given her prenatal pills, but could do very little to help end her suffering. She wasn't too keen on his medical help either way. The man gave her the creeps with how he constantly stared at her like she was some kind of lab rat.

It had been six days since she learned the truth. And the truth was harder to believe than the lie. When Jaxon fell ill a day later it no longer mattered to her why he did what he did to her. All she could think of was losing him and being left to raise their child with his enemies hunting her.

She had access to the world again. What she discovered was far scarier than her existence in the cellars. A global pandemic was spreading. Leaders from different countries were all at odds on how to address it. African American's were dying at a faster rate. The virus was something to fear. She's pregnant. Jaxon is a diabetic. They were both high-risk. No one was allowed to see him but her. And she kept her distance from the few people left in Mayfair.

It was a strange time.

She looked up in the mirror at his reflection. He was confined to bed. She spent all of her time in the room with him. Hutch, Andella and Francine didn't trust her. Ahmed and the evil doctor seemed to be in control of the house, and they didn't trust her either. If she were honest, she would admit her change in attitude wasn't trustworthy. One phone call and she could bring in the authorities and have them all arrested.

"Ma'am?"

Goodiva glanced back over her shoulder. She was folding laundry. "What is it Hutch? Is he awake?"

"No, he's resting, the doctor and Andella are with him."

She rolled her eyes. "Then why are you in my room?"

"We need to talk," he said.

"I prefer we don't," she said.

Hutch ignored her and came into her room. Exasperated, she turned and crossed her arms, ready to cuss and raise hell if necessary to send him away.

"I think you should reach out to your friends. The detective and the Montgomery woman," Hutch said. He tossed a newspaper to her bed. Goodiva picked it up. If they were in a pandemic on a mountain of snow and ice, how did Hutch constantly get newspapers? She'd gotten used to not being on her social media accounts. She had access to cable television, but the press conferences and fatalities reports gave her extreme anxiety, so she stopped watching. Still Hutch would arrive and throw the world news in her face. She preferred to spend her days either playing music in the parlor or reading books to Jaxon as he rested in a semi-comatose state. The article he'd shared with her was a picture of Queen. The byline read: DETECTIVE SEARCHES FOR MISSING FRIEND AT MAYFAIR ESTATES.

"Tonight they intend to do another interview with the local media. My suggestion is that you call them and invite them to Mayfair," Hutch said.

"Huh? No. We're under lockdown. I don't want them venturing out into this pandemic to play any games. Besides I bring them here and you are all going to jail. I'm not opposed to seeing you pay for what you did to me, but Jaxon needs my help. I told you I'm going to help him. I don't trust that doctor."

"You shouldn't trust the doctor. But you can trust me. I only work for him. I intend to deal with Ahmed and this doctor when I can. You and I want the same things."

"I don't believe you. He's tortured, and possibly insane now from all these cocktails of medicine you're pumping into him. He's this way because of all of you."

"They would have never had access to him if he didn't try to save you that night on that road. If I'm guilty, so are you."

It was true. She had her role to play.

"I want to help him," she said.

"Because you love him?" Hutch taunted.

She glared at him.

"He thinks you do. I know different. You're here because you're scared, and you want him to protect your child. So don't play concern with me. No one loves him. That's been his curse since he was born. He's a lone wolf. A lost wolf."

"You love him," she countered.

"He's like a son to me," Hutch said.

Goodiva sighed. "You're wrong about me. I do love him. And I will protect him. I plan to help him escape all of you."

"This helps him. Any attention right now to who he is puts us all in danger. I suggest you contact your friends and give them an explanation. They will not stop looking for you."

Hutch walked out, leaving her with the article. Queen gave all the details of how she went missing and the raid at Mayfair. She smiled at the love she could see in her friends words in the article her friends had for her. And she felt like a witch for not contacting them. What could she say to explain the unexplainable?

A small part of Goodiva hated him. Hated how he inserted himself into her life. Hated how he forced her to live his lie. But most of all she hated how easy it was for her to fall in love with a man who could control her life in the way he had. Hate was not what ruled her today. He needed her. She was going to be there, no matter what the cost.

She walked over and tucked in his bedcovers. She'd given him a sponge bath yesterday and changed his clothes with no help. Often he was lucid enough to sit up or move when she needed him to do so. Those were the times she helped him to the bathroom. His fever broke yesterday, but he was too weak to eat solids.

There was a knock at the door.

"Yes?" she replied.

"Ma'am? Your friends have arrived."

"Take them into the reading room. I'm coming," she said. Francine nodded and closed the door. Goodiva had chosen a pair of jeans and an off-white cashmere sweater with brown boots. She picked up her blue blazer she had left in Jaxon's room and pulled it on. It made her look professional. She fluffed out her hair captured in her collar.

"Showtime," she said to herself. She glanced over to the nightstand and saw his laptop. Goodiva picked it up.

"They're here?" he croaked.

Jaxon was looking up at her.

"How do you feel today?" she asked him.

"Like a million dollars," he smiled. "Maybe I should get in my wheelchair and come with you. Help explain?" His voice was deep and scratchy as if he'd been shouting for speaking for days.

She smiled. "Nice try. But no sir, doctor's orders are that you stay in bed."

"I don't want you hurt," he said. "They should blame me."

"Don't worry. They will," she said.

"Come closer," he said.

She came to the side of the bed. He lifted his hand weakly and pressed it to her belly. "How do you feel?"

"Like a pregnant lady," she said.

He chuckled.

"I think it's a girl."

"I'm sure it's the boy you all want."

His smile dimmed and his hand dropped weakly away. "I want a girl. I want her to look just like you. I changed my mind."

"You up to watch the show? I know how much you enjoy spying on me," she put the laptop on the bed.

"I might sit this one out," he said.

"Liar," she chuckled.

Before she turned to leave, he grabbed her hand. "I love you my Goddess," he said. "One day I'm going to prove it to you and our child. You'll see."

"I'll be back so we can eat lunch together. Relax. I can handle this visit. They'll believe what I tell them. I've learned how to lie from the best."

He brought her hand to his mouth and kissed it. She managed to hold her smile throughout the gentle gesture. And then he let her go. At the door, she glanced back at him once more. She kept her promise to him when he first fell ill. He wore his mask every day, except in her presence. Only she knew the man underneath. No matter how hard it was for her to admit to herself that she loved him, she never denied that her staying with him had less to do with his threats or the danger he said awaited her and had everything to do with the safety she felt in his space. She winked before she closed the door.

Goodiva exhaled a deep breath and took the long walk down the hall and then stairs to her friends. She could hear Delilah before she saw either of them. All of a sudden she didn't feel strong, or in control. Her hands tingled with numbness and her heart raced. Her stomach tightened to the point of spasms forcing bile to her throat. It was hard enough to control her nausea with the pregnancy, but even harder when she was stressed. She put on the N95 mask Hutch had given her. They were still under quarantine and she couldn't risk catching anything from them.

It's okay girl. Just do as you planned. Make them leave and make them stay gone. You can do it. If not for them, then for your baby. They can't help you now.

If she threw up in front of her friends, they would never believe the story she was about to sell them. For their sake and her own she had better put down the performance of a lifetime. Delilah turned and spotted her the moment she walked into the room. Queen stared at her with stretched eyes. Both of them wore masks. But she knew underneath they smiled.

And then it happened. All the barriers of anger, hurt, and guilt between them dropped. The three women ran to each other and embraced. Delilah was the one to cry in a loud wail. Goodiva too cried like a baby. Her tears mixed with Delilah's forced Queen to join them. She hugged her friends. She felt so blessed to have sisters to share her heart with.

"You're okay," Delilah said and looked her over for any signs she'd been hurt.

"Are you?" Queen asked.

"Yes. Yes. I'm fine. I'm so sorry for making you worry. I'm really sorry about that."

"Sorry!" Delilah took a step back. Queen continued to hug her. "Where the hell have you been? What happened? Two months! It's been two months!"

"I know," Goodiva sniffed. Queen wiped Goodiva's tears with her hand. "I'm going to explain it all to you."

She forced Queen to let her go. She needed space. Being this close to their nurturing made her weaker. And she feared she'd confess it all. What if she did? They'd haul him out of his bed to jail, along with everyone else in this place. It would awaken the media giant that had been sleeping on the real identity of Jaxon Price. And then what? The fertility clinic? The Montgomery scandal? The government finding a reason to charge her so they could steal her child away from her. The accident she ran from. All of it would crush her and destroy any hope for security and safety for her child. She stepped back and pointed to the sofa chairs in the room. "Let's sit down."

Her friends took off their masks. A show of solidarity would mean she'd remove hers. She could not take the risk. And they noticed.

"Tell me what happened," Delilah said.

"I came here and found out it was Jaxon, who had bought Mayfair. I should have told you both. But you know how stubborn I can be. I was in shock too. I mean, I had been obsessing over him for three years, and here he was."

"Did you text Dee? And tell her you wanted to leave?"

Goodiva nodded for her answer.

"Did you leave? Did he force you to stay? What?!" Delilah demanded.

Goodiva was losing footing with both of them shouting at her. Seated, Goodiva felt less queasy. She regained her focus. First, she would start with Delilah. Out of the three, Delilah had the most sensitive bullshit detector that could always sniff out deception and a lie. It was why Goodiva struggled with Charles deceiving her friend. How did he pull it off? How much did Delilah know about Jaxon, and who he was connected too?

"Well?" Delilah asked.

"Give her a chance, Dee. Let's hear her out," Queen said.

Goodiva smiled.

"Have I ever lied to either one of you? Ever?"

"No," they both said with certainty.

"Okay. Then trust me when I say to you that there is no crime. Except for this one time when I lied to you both. And I'm sorry. I didn't leave for New York. I was here the entire time. I was here when you two came to speak with Jaxon. I told him to lie to you. I watched when you went into my cabin searching for me. And when you questioned the staff. I was here

Queen when you came last week with the warrant and searched the place. I was here."

The friends stared at her in shock.

"I guess you're wondering why I would put you both through this? It was never my plan to hurt you or to worry you. But I knew if I told you what I wanted, what I really wanted, you would try to talk out of it. Because of what happened with Jaxon and the past. With you two I always am the broken one. The one you've got to put together, hold together, keep together. I needed to be free of my mistakes."

"You let us think you were missing or worse because you wanted to be free from us?" Delilah said.

She didn't know how to respond.

Delilah shook her head.

"This is bullshit. Do you believe this Queen? She's lying to our face! What the hell is wrong with you Shelly? What did he do to you?"

"I'm telling you the truth. We're in love. I'm here because I want to be."

"You're a gat damn liar Shelly!" Delilah shouted. She stood. "I know you. I know the real you. This is all a scam to cover up something. Something bigger than the secret we share. What happened here?"

"Stop Dee," Queen sighed.

"No! She's lying!"

"I said enough!" Queen shouted.

Goodiva held her breath.

Queen stood. "Friendship doesn't come with conditions or expectations. It does come with respect. To let us believe you were in danger is the most disrespectful thing you've ever done Shelly."

"I'm sorry," Goodiva said.

"The hell you are," Delilah mumbled.

"I said enough Dee. I don't need your apology Shelly. I need to understand. My love for you isn't conditional. So if this is what you want, what you need. You can have it. Just know there are consequences for what you did. There's a virus out there killing people. Do you even know if your mother and father are okay? They thought you were dead. I feel sorry for you Shelly. That this is what you want, over the friendship we gave you. I'm done."

"What? Queen! Are you going to let her—" Delilah gasped. Queen walked out. Delilah stood. She then turned her gaze to Goodiva and shook her head in disbelief. "We're sisters. I thought you believed that? I know you're hiding something. I taught you how to keep secrets, remember?"

"It's the truth. I did it because I wanted to be with him. And I wanted you two to leave me alone."

Delilah eyes welled with tears. The mask in her hand fell to the floor. She stood there broken hearted. "My life is falling apart Shelly. And you chose this man over me?"

"Dee, I'm sorry," Goodiva said.

"I have my son to protect. Why am I even here?"

"Don't come back," Goodiva said. She meant it in earnest but the look on her friends' face was as if she shoved a dagger into her heart.

"Fuck you," Delilah said and stormed out.

It was done. They were gone. And it felt like they would stay gone. Forever. Goodiva sat alone. She'd spent weeks crying. She no longer had the mental strength to shed tears. She slumped back and closed her eyes to force all of her emotions down.

Jaxon closed the lid of his laptop. He lay in bed caught between regret and relief. He'd won. She was all his. No matter what he decided for their lives he'd moved every piece on the board to make her his. And for that selfishness, he'd ultimately have to pay a price. For him, no matter the cost, it was worth it.

He looked around the room he'd been confined to for days. He should be stronger. He willed it. But the best he could do was sit up and breathe at the same time. That wasn't good enough. He drew back the covers and forced himself to move. At some point he was actually standing. But then he lost control and everything slipped away.

Chapter Twenty-Four

J axon opened his eyes.

"You awake?" the doctor asked.

He glanced down to see the IV in his arm. He frowned.

"You were severely dehydrated. Is she taking care of you?" the doctor asked.

"She's taking care of me. But I am always thirsty," he groaned. He felt stronger. He found that surprising. "Why are you here?"

The doctor seem to ignore his question.

"Where is she?"

"I don't know. People can disappear in this mausoleum. Francine found you on the floor and came for me. I had Hutch and Ahmed put you back in bed."

"What? When?"

"An hour ago," the doctor replied.

"Did she leave?" Jaxon asked alarmed.

"Leave? No. I don't think she knows how, now that she knows the truth about the pandemic. She's quite paranoid. Walking around the house spraying Lysol on everything and keeping her masks on."

"Am I getting worse or better?" Jaxon asked.

"My concern was the flu like symptoms you had. I tested you for Corona and you were negative. I tried to keep her away but she refuses to listen to me. As for your other conditions, you know the answer to that question. We've started you on the treatments again. The real treatments. We won't need chemo. You should be feeling stronger soon."

"I don't," he lied.

"A few more days and you'll be out of this bed able to make love to your woman." The doctor walked away. "Have you given any thought to my proposal. That we take you back to the Mayo Clinic? To treat you properly."

"No. How is she? Have you examined her? The baby?"

"She's okay, she's a healthy woman. But to answer your question, she's not really interested in my examinations. She will only answer a few questions at a time before she walks out of any room I'm in. That must change."

Jaxon chuckled.

"Goddess."

"What is the delay to your cooperation? What are we doing? Waiting for her to give birth? Waiting for you to die? What are we doing?" the doctor asked.

"Who are you asking for?"

"We are invested in your life and wellbeing Mr. Price. That is to your benefit. But at some point you will have to give a return on the investment."

"The delays are because of the pandemic. Plus, I got sick. Nothing happens until I'm on my feet. You want to see movement make that happen. Now, where is she? I need to talk to her," he said.

The doctor nodded. "I'll find Andella and have her sent for you. If you need me let me know."

Jaxon waited for her. Twenty minutes turned into two hours before he gave up and finally succumbed to fatigue.

Goodiva entered the room to find Jaxon asleep. She often found him in this state, but today he looked as vulnerable as she felt. Goodiva walked over to the chair next to his bed. She sat in it and reclined her head. She needed time alone. A few hours and he was asking for her to return. She didn't mind. His love, obsessive or not, felt comforting. She sat at his bedside and waited.

Jaxon woke. He sensed her before he saw her. A look to his left and he saw her seated in the chair next to his bed, asleep. Feeling stronger than he had before the IV was added, he sat up. His movement woke her. That was definitely a surprise. She used to be a deep sleeper.

"Hi?" he said.

"Hi," she said.

"I saw the meeting between you and your friends."

"They're gone. They won't be coming back." She got up from the chair and came over to his bed. "How do you feel? They said you got out of bed and blacked out?"

"Better. I think?" he looked down at himself. "But you weren't here. Where were you?"

"I was here. And what's this?" she tapped the IV.

"Doctor's orders," he said.

"Oh? Do you know what it is?"

"No. They think you're poisoning me," he smiled.

"I'm terrible at it," she smiled.

"Let's leave," he said. "Just you and me. Go somewhere."

She frowned.

"Let's leave. We'll go to New York, Chicago, leave the state or the country, if you want. The moment I feel better. We go."

"Have you forgotten? The quarantine?"

He frowned.

"We can't go anywhere. New York is still under quarantine and Chicago too. Why do you want to leave?" she asked.

"You keep disappearing," he mumbled. "I think it will help us be closer," he said.

"You're sick. I'm pregnant—"

"Then let's go back down below," he turned his gaze back to her. A dark serious look settled over his face. "Where it's just you and me."

Goodiva stood there staring at him. He expected her to use her sharp tongue to give him a verbal lashing. Instead, she looked worried. She looked as if he were speaking gibberish. Why? She reached and touched his cheek. She leaned in and kissed him between his brows. He grabbed her arm to keep her from pulling away. She stared at him a moment before she kissed his lips, and just the touch of them made him crazy for her. He kissed her for as long as she would allow, desperate, feverish with need.

"Will you lay with me?"

"No. Stop acting like a baby. Why don't you just rest a while and I'll sit over here?"

He tightened his grip on her arm.

"Jaxon, let me go," she said.

"Lay with me."

"Do you know what time it is? I should go back downstairs and see to your dinner. We missed lunch."

"Lay next to me," he insisted. "The both of you."

"Relax Jaxon, you're hurting my arm."

He frowned. He hadn't realized his own strength. He looked at his hand and released her and then her.

"It's okay, you're confused sometimes. It's the medicine."

"No. Something is wrong;" He lifted his hand and looked at it. He opened and closed it into a fist. He felt a jealous anger surfacing in him. It made him want to clench his fist. "I feel strange," he said and sat up.

"It's okay." She pushed down on his chest to force him to lay still. "See? I'm staying." She removed her jacket. She unzipped her boots.

"Take off your jeans. Your shirt," he said. "I want to be able to feel you."

"Are you still sick?"

"The doctor says no."

"But you're willing to risk my health?" she asked.

"You've already kissed me," he smiled. "What bigger risk is there than a kiss? Especially from me."

She shook her head smiling. "True."

She went to the door and locked it. She undressed in front of him. She knew he liked that part. She eased on the bed with Jaxon, making sure to lay opposite of his IV. He could feel her naked body heat warm and nice against his skin. Her soft curves were something to savor as well. The anger building inside of him over their brief separation began to yield. He pulled her in with his right arm and kissed the top of her head.

"You know what I've missed these past few days?" he asked.

"No. Tell me?" she answered.

"Music," he said.

"Aaah, of course," she chuckled.

"Yea," he said. "Your playlist."

"Me too. But after these past few months I think I need a new playlist. One for just us."

"And the baby," he said.

"Yes, sweetheart, and the baby."

"I think music heals me," he said.

"It can. There have been studies that playing music reduces anxiety, and pain." She lifted her head and looked up at him. "Are you in pain?"

"Not anymore. Not if you stay," he said.

"But sometimes you feel different?"

"What do you mean? Different?"

"Agitated?" she asked.

"Sometimes," he confessed.

"I heard you a few days ago yelling at Frances. Do you remember?"

"No. I don't yell."

"You were yelling then. You were yelling for me. Demanding to know where I was. Did you forget that you had asked me to make you some soup?"

He didn't answer.

"When I came in you threw something at her. Hutch and Ahmed had to hold you down. You kept screaming my name. They sedated you."

He didn't answer.

"You need to stay calm Jaxon. Don't let this disease control you."

He didn't reply.

"I'll play some music for you. What do you want to hear?"

"Something newer," he yawned as if she hadn't said a word before on his temper. "Not too new that I don't know the song. Something that will remind me of you," he said.

She eased her arm over his chest and rested her face there. She closed her eyes. He closed his. There was pain with his illness, he'd learned how to endure it. But there was greater pain when she was gone. He couldn't deal with losing her. He wouldn't lose her. With her in his arms he found he was truly strong enough to live with anything.

"I WANT TO TALK TO YOU," Goodiva said.

Dr. Eleven ate his meal in a television room alone on a tv tray. He looked up at her surprised. The food nearly dropped out of his mouth. She rarely initiated a conversation with him. "Ms. Johnson, yes, yes, please join me."

"Don't get up," she insisted. She walked over to the chair furthest away from him. The doctor sat back down. He wiped his mouth He moved the food tray aside.

"Is everything okay? Your morning sickness. Is it getting better? Any changes I should with the pregnancy. Are you okay?"

"I'm fine. This isn't about me," she waved off his concern. "It's about Jax on."

The doctor's brows lifted. "Okay?"

"Something's wrong with him."

"Wrong?" the doctor repeated.

"He's acting different. Paranoid. Obsessive. Controlling. Angry."

"Ah, he's had fevers," the doctor replied.

"No. He's changing."

"It's my understanding that he kidnapped you, hid you in a cellar and forced you into a pregnancy. Doesn't sound like he's changed much."

She glared at him. "I want to know about his disease. What happened to his father? Jaxon said that towards the end his father became a recluse in here. Really paranoid. That he experimented on people. He lost his mind."

"Cancer can make a person depressed, withdrawn, and yes even paranoid about dying."

"This is different. He's focused on me."

"Hasn't he always been?" Dr. Eleven smirked.

"It's different!"

"How?" the doctor asked.

"If he's awake and he sees me he wants me to... be there for him, only him. If he wakes and I'm not there he thinks I've betrayed him. It's got to the point where I have to spend most days in the room with him to keep him calm."

"Don't worry about that. He's adjusting," the doctor said.

"I want you to stop giving him that poison. I don't trust you. I know you're keeping things from him about his treatment." She struggled to hide her emotions. "I want him to see other doctors. I want him too—."

"This is not about what you want. In fact, what you want is the least of my concerns Ms. Johnson. If he lives, how he lives, all of it is up to me with the help of that child you carry. You want to keep him safe, then keep his secrets. Be the dutiful girlfriend, or whatever you are to him and keep him calm. Let me worry about the changes in him."

She recognized the evil in his eyes. There was no negotiation with him. She'd have to take another approach to protect him.

"Going forward I'm in charge of Jaxon's health. I love him. I'm going to help him. I'm moving into his room. Do you understand. I see through you. You haven't fooled me."

The smirk on the doctor's face didn't move. Goodiva sighed and stood.

"Strange isn't it?" the doctor asked.

"What?" she answered.

"Loving a man, if what you say is true and you do, that you should fear. How does that feel? Being his baby mama, especially to that super kid you're carrying. Living here and pretending to like you want to be here instead of with those friends of yours who blame you now. You haven't run away because there is nowhere to run too. I see through you too Ms. Johnson, I find you quite remarkable."

Goodiva started for the door.

"Ms. Johnson! I'm still waiting for that examination. I need to see how the baby's doing."

"Go to hell," she said.

Three Days Later

Jaxon felt strong enough to walk and care for himself. The doctor kept his cocktails of medication in his veins and his woman took good care of any other needs he had. He, however, knew that his recovery was far from over.

He heard the shower running. She had now moved into his room. She slept with him every night. She was his. Jaxon got out of the bed and walked stiffly to the shower door. She had her clothes laid across the other bed in the room. The one he didn't let her sleep in because it was too far from his reach. And next to her clothes was her laptop. She left it up and open. He looked down at an email she'd been composing. It was addressed to her friends. It started with an apology. He didn't dare read further, and that took some control on his part. Instead he went to the bathroom door. The shower turned off. He opened the door as she stepped out of it. Goodiva looked up at him surprised.

"Jax?" She grabbed her towel to cover herself. "What are you doing out of bed?"

"I feel better. Stronger. See."

"Go back to bed now!" she ordered him.

"Where are you going?" he asked.

"What?"

"Why are you showering and changing clothes. Why?"

She sighed. "I shower every day. You should too, if you feel better enough to interrogate me."

He smiled. "Sorry. I was worried."

"Jaxon—"

"How about we go for a walk? Today is the first day of sun," he said.

"How do you know that?" she frowned.

"I saw it yesterday on the news." He glimpsed her breasts before she hurried to wrap the towel around herself. He reached for her, but she sidestepped him.

"Fine, you saw it on the news. We're still in quarantine so."

"No we're not. There is no virus here. It's just us."

"You're weak, your immune system is compromised."

"I'm fine. I'm a man, aren't I?"

She sighed. "Let me dress and we'll go downstairs," she said. "We can see the sun in your solarium."

"Goodiva?"

"What?" she replied in an exasperated voice.

"Something wrong? Did I do something?"

She stood at the mirror by the sink wiping her face clean. She stared at him. "No. Why?"

"You seem tense."

He stepped behind her. He stared into her eyes by maintaining focus on her reflection in the mirror. She lowered her gaze first. "Do you feel better? Really?" she asked.

"I swear it. I want to get out of here. I know, you've been through a lot. Your friends."

"So you saw it, did you read it?"

"Your letter? No. I wouldn't invade your privacy."

She glanced up at him and frowned.

"I'm not going to break your trust anymore," he promised. She looked as if she didn't believe him. He touched her shoulder. His touch broke down the wall of tension between them. She turned into his arms. She hugged his waist as she buried her tears into his chest. Jaxon stroked her hair and held her.

"I need to get out of here Jaxon. I'm feeling, I don't know, I feel trapped. Maybe we can take a walk? Just us," she sniffed.

"I'll do something better for you," he said.

She looked up at him. He lifted her by the waist and sat her on the edge of the sink. Her arms went from around his waist to his neck. Her hand slipped up his nape to the back of his head and she drew his mouth to hers. Her thighs parted and welcomed him in. Her nearness overwhelmed and then calmed him. Their eyes locked as their breathing joined in unison. The first time their lips met, his kiss was slow and thoughtful. The moment he inhaled her freshness from her lavender scrub he was freed from his doubt.

It was Goodiva who abruptly ended their passion. Her hand to his chest, she pushed him back and turned her face. "I don't feel like we should risk it. You need your strength."

Jaxon nodded but felt the crush of his ego and pride. He tried not to force the issue so he stepped away.

"I'll shower and get dressed. Meet me in the reading room in about three hours."

"Why three hours?" she frowned.

"Some things I need to take care of first."

She fixed her towel to make sure it didn't slip, but her parted thighs almost revealed her treasure to him. He avoided looking down.

"I love you," he mumbled and walked out.

GOODIVA COULDN'T BELIEVE the beauty before her. It had been a long time since she rode a horse in the winter. And even longer since she enjoyed the Cove with a man. The trees leaned in over them with frozen branches and barely any leaves. Every inch of the forest was blanketed in pure white. Jaxon rode his horse with expertise. She glanced at his perfect posture. He wore a dark trench coat and leather gloves. His boots clicked at the horse's side to speed the trot. When he glanced back at her with his half-mask, the handsome memory of him gave her a smile. At first, the best she could hope for was the scenic route. That was until she saw a cabin with a chimney billowing smoke.

"Reminds me of Hansel and Gretel," she said to Jaxon.

"It's not made of gingerbread," he smiled. "But there might be some cocoa inside."

"Okay," she nodded.

They arrived at the front of the cabin. Jaxon got off his horse and secured his lash to a post. Goodiva looked around at the isolation of the cabin while she waited.

"Why is this here? Away from all the other cottages?"

"Used to belong to a private citizen who owned this patch of land. Forget his name. The owner before my father kicked him off of it years ago. I found it soon after I returned to Mayfair. Never even knew it was here as a kid."

He reached up to her, and she leaned in to let him pull her off the horse. Jaxon kissed her forehead and let her go before she could expect an embrace. Goodiva stroked Darla's rump and smiled. "She's such a good girl. Do you race her?"

"Yes," he said.

"Is it legal? I thought it was unsanctioned in this region."

"I can't say," he smirked. He took her hand and pulled her away. She smiled at Darla, who nodded her pristine chiseled head at her as if to say goodbye. They both stomped off the clumps of dirt and snow from their boots on the porch before going inside.

"Wow, this is nice," she said.

Jaxon removed his coat and helped her from hers. They took off their gloves, knit caps, and scarves, then removed their boots. All the while she admired the inside of the cabin. It was so cozy yet spacious. The cabin had oak hardwood floors, and real log beams and walls created a homey environment. The top level was open like a loft and held above them by thick tree trunk logs. She climbed the stairs and found a bed made of the same logs with a plush mattress and a large window that gave a beautiful view of Mayfair and the mountains surrounding her.

"Wow," she mumbled. "This the first time in months that I've been anywhere outside of Mayfair. This place feels almost magical too me."

"You like it?" he asked.

"You should have brought me here sooner," she said and walked to the picture window. "It's so pretty here, I love it."

"I thought it would be nice for us, away from...you know, where we were," he said.

She glanced to Jaxon, who had taken off his mask. That was a sign he too was relaxed. He walked over and leaned against the window facing her. "I wanted to take you someplace different. This would have to do."

"You sure you feel okay? That horse ride in the snow was kind of rough."

"Will you stop acting like my nurse every time I want to talk about us?"

"I don't act like a nurse."

"You're avoiding us, me," he said.

"No. I'm not. I've been supporting you. I'm with you every single moment of the day. I sleep in your hospital bed instead of the big one in the room to make sure you're comfortable. I—"

"Before you found out I was sick you didn't pity me as much as you do now. You treat me like I'm your burden. I'm not. I'm still the man who is in love with you Goddess."

"Really? You have the nerve to say that to me?" she walked away. She put both hands to her hips and closed her eyes. "You're a married man with three wives. I'm not pitying you when you want to be intimate with me. I'm pissed with you!"

"I've explained it."

"You destroyed my life Jaxon."

"I just replaced it. I gave you a new life."

"Do you hear yourself?" she snapped.

"I can't change my mistakes. I'm not sorry for them. Not any of them. I would do it again."

"That's horrible to say. You killed Twixt! You trapped me here!"

"So what!" he shouted. "What about me? What about my sacrifice? Do you care how I feel? I'm dying!"

She stared at him disbelief. The last thing she wanted to do was cause him more pain. She had never had someone so fixated on her. Was it healthy? She didn't know. He was all she and her baby had. And he was changing. His logic was warped, and his obsession was gaining with his paranoia.

"Say something," he said.

"I wish this was normal Jaxon."

"Me too. Me too. Fuck. I'll relax. It will all be normal soon," he said.

"And your marriages? Will that be normal soon?"

"I don't want any of them."

"That doesn't matter. You're married."

"I'll make sure you're my only wife."

"I never said I would marry you," she frowned.

He eased his arms around her waist. She pushed him off at first, but he just brought her back into his arms.

"I have cocoa," he said.

"With marshmallows?" she asked and relaxed.

"And Hershey bars," he teased.

"You should have led with Hershey bars," she smiled. She looked up at him. He didn't kiss her. She wouldn't have allowed it if he had. They weren't in that place any longer. Together they went downstairs. She plopped down on the leather sofa. Jaxon fixed her mug and brought it over with a tray of goodies for her that included fruit and chocolate.

She sipped and watched him stoke the fire to make sure it was warm enough for her, and then he returned to sit next to her. Goodiva put her mug on the tray, and then laid her head on his lap. He stroked her hair. "Why do you refuse to believe anything I say, sincerely?"

"I feel like trusting you is like sticking my hand into a lion's cage and feeding him by hand,"

He chuckled.

"What do you miss since you came to live with me?" he asked.

"I miss the ocean," she confessed.

"Really?"

"In Africa the ocean was amazing. I really loved my time there," she said.

"What else do you miss?" he said as he combed her hair with his fingers. "I miss my friends most of all."

"Yes," he said and understand.

She closed her eyes. The sensation of his fingers repeatedly grazing her scalp was so soothing. "I miss massages, pedicures, strawberries and my music."

"You have your music," he said. "And strawberries too."

"Mmmhmm, I mean my music, my way, deejaying for people. Entertaining the crowds. And I really love chocolate covered strawberries. I miss those."

"What about your writing?" he asked.

She flipped over to her back and looked up at him. "You know about that?"

He nodded. "Remember? 'Screenwriter looking for a place to escape'?"

She chuckled. "That's right. You were spying."

"I'm a spy," he agreed.

"My writing is more like journaling. I did sell a few screenplays. But the latest won't sell. I'll probably be sued for all the copyright infringement after all the music lyrics I used."

He laughed.

"I have good attorneys."

She smiled.

"I knew you missed performing," he said.

"No you didn't," she said and turned over to her side. She closed her eyes. Before long his touch, the fire, and the warmth of the cocoa she sipped lulled her to sleep. Goodiva woke on the sofa with an afghan blanket thrown over her. She looked directly into the fireplace and for a second she thought she was in the cellar. Trapped with her records and Henry the dog. Goodiva sat up. She was in the cabin and alone. She removed the blanket.

The cocoa was gone, and so was the snack plate. He'd taken the time to tidy up everything.

"How late is it?" she asked and checked her watch. The nap she took couldn't have been more than an hour.

"Okay," she mumbled. "Not too late. Where did you go?"

Goodiva started toward the stairs. The log cabin wasn't that big, but she could see he wasn't in the open kitchen. Then there was a blast. So loud it sounded like a cannon had fired. Her heart leaped to her throat and lodged there.

"Oh my God, no, no," she said and ran for the front door. "Jaxon! Jaxon!"

Chapter Twenty-Five

J axon aimed the shotgun and fired again. The shell popped out and he cocked the gun again. "Jaxon no!" Goodiva said and grabbed his arm. He misfired when he pulled up and shot through the porch roof.

"What are you shooting at!" she said horrified. Goodiva looked to the forest. She saw nothing.

"Jaxon?! What's wrong?" she turned to her lover. He stared as if almost in a trance. "Jaxon?" she touched his face.

"They're out there," he said.

"Who?"

"They're coming to take you away from me. I saw them." She glanced to the forest again. A doe and her fawn stepped out of the forest and froze in shock to stare at them.

"There's nobody there, Jaxon," she said calm and softly. She gently took the shotgun from his hand. "See? It's just a deer and her baby."

He blinked at the animals then he looked down at her. "You won't leave me? Ever."

"I'm not going anywhere Jaxon. Where did you get this gun?"

He turned and walked back inside. Goodiva let go the breath she'd been holding since she heard the first shotgun blast. She felt so weak with worry and concern she nearly dropped to her knees. The doe turned and led her baby fawn back to safety. "What's is happening? What is happening?" she said over and over. Something was wrong. He wasn't getting better. She swallowed her fear and went back inside. Jaxon was pacing the floor.

"It's okay, I checked. There's nobody out there," she said and emptied the gun of its shells.

"But they are coming. I know my jin. He's coming. We need to leave. Tonight. We'll head West. No. No. California isn't safe. They'll know me. Even with this face, they'll know me. I need another plan. I can't think.'"

"It's okay," she set the gun down by the door. "I'm locking the door. No one's coming in."

He stared at her. "Why did you scream? Are you afraid of me?"

"No," she smiled. "I heard the shotgun and thought someone would hurt you." She couldn't stop shaking. She walked to him and tried to remain calm. When she reached him, she tried to remember that the man she knew was inside there. What was happening to him wasn't his fault. She had to remember that. She reached up and removed the mask that covered half of his face. His deep-set brown eyes glistened with what she knew were tears he suppressed. The tragedy of his life was all in his face and his scars. "I'm so glad you're here to protect me," she smiled.

He nodded.

"I'll kill them all to protect you," he promised. All of her emotions crashed in on her at once. She dropped her head on his chest with her hands to his face and she cried. "We're going to fix this Jaxon. Whatever it is. I won't them turn you into a monster."

His arms went around her. "Don't cry."

She dropped her hands and hugged his waist. She calmed herself and forced herself to sound normal when she spoke. "Tell me what happened?" she said and let him go. "Can you do that?"

He looked down at her and nodded. "I took the horse to the barn in the back. I was leaving and I saw something in the forest. Scorpions. They were hiding. I went back into the barn and got the gun I kept there. When I came out I didn't' see them. But I had to get to you. They were coming for you. I got to the cabin and I heard them charging. I stood my ground and I shot at them."

She smiled and he wiped her tears with his thumb. "You're my hero," she said.

"I'm not so fragile that you have to be so afraid for me. But they should be afraid of me. My jin, the doctors all of them. I won't anyone hurt you." He cupped her face. "It's just us. And our baby. I'll protect you both. No one can take you from me."

Jaxon kissed her. She felt her heart respond. He kissed her in the ways he'd missed for so long. She needed his faith in her again, so she'd feed any delusion he had. The truth was she was the protector now. She'd have to find a way to keep him safe, and alive.

"Let's go upstairs," she said when her mouth left his. She took his hand and pulled him to the stairs.

The loft with just the bed for them was a perfect escape. She let go his hand. He pulled her turtleneck over her head and she let him. She wore a bra that clasped to the front. He couldn't believe how beautiful her breasts were in it.

Jaxon yanked down her pants first before he freed his. The moment he went to his knees and pulled her jeans off her ankles and helped her out of the pants, she sat on the edge of the bed. He pulled her forward and she rested the heels of each barefoot on his perspective shoulder to butterfly spread her thighs before him. Her steamy sex was pushed into his nose. His tongue swiped up in between the lips of her sex. When his tongue grazed her bean she let go the sexiest moan. He too shuddered with lust. Her hips were soft to hold, her pussy slick and wet, fragrantly aroused. The attention he lavished her with his mouth had her whole body quaking with shivers, especially her thighs. Goodiva's hands were behind her and her fingers were gripping the top sheet. Her head dropped back so far that her hair nearly touched the mattress. Her cries of passion grew stronger.

When he sucked her love button she came apart. Her hips bucked. He latched his lips around the nub and forced her to live with the pleasure ripping through her. He sucked harder and harder until she shouted her love for him and her back arched off the door. The orgasm she released shook them both. Her pussy spasmed for a long moment while he continued to torture her. She dropped back on the bed, heaving short and raspy breaths from her air deprived lungs.

He kissed her velvety soft, wet pussy and released her. She lowered her feet, but both her legs were too shaky for her to move. So he moved her up an inch on the bed that she lay across horizontally. His erection was released, and his intentions were clear.

"Catch your breath," he told her.

"I can't," she gasped.

"That's too bad, because I'm not going to stop."

He dropped on her. She grabbed his neck. "You talk too much," she said and swept her tongue over his lips, tasting herself on his mouth. She kissed him and moved her pelvis to entice him to make good on his promise.

Jaxon drove himself deep inside her an inch or two and then rocked his hips from side to side to dive deeper. Jaxon dragged his kisses from her mouth to her throat. He'd wanted her so bad, missed her even more, and suddenly she was his. If he climaxed, he'd lose the pleasure too soon.

He stopped moving.

He panted and breathed against her neck. She rubbed his back, mistaking his hesitation for weakness.

"It's okay," she said.

He slipped out of her. He flipped on his back and tried again to breathe.

"It's okay, calm down," she said and rubbed his chest. "You're okay."

He nodded and closed his eyes. His dick was hard. His heart raced. He wanted to continue with everything in him, but the rest of his body suffered.

A narrow strip of sunlight crested between the mountains and the sky was a deep swirl of magenta and purple. The darkness descending only tempted him to heal himself and go further. He had no trouble before. Why now? Was he really going to die half a man? Immediately she sat up and pressed her lips to his to devour him in a kiss. She didn't make him feel like a dying man. She made him feel alive. She moved over him and he ran his hands down her back to squeeze her ass cheeks. And her mound pressed down on his erection. His sweet kitten would not be patient for him. At the very least, he had her on the very bed where he'd dreamt of her over the years: in the cabin he escaped to when the staff was gone and his wheelchair wasn't a burden. He felt so free with her now.

His mouth found hers as he palmed her with one hand and pushed his middle finger deep into her anus as she eased her slick tightness down on his dick. They groaned together.

The kiss went from hot to blazing, but it was her body that he craved to explore. "You are the love of my life. The only love of my life."

"I love you Jaxon," she said, and tears slipped from the corner of her eyes. "Don't die, please don't die."

"I won't. I have someone to live for," he said and kissed her.

She pulled away and sat upright. Once again he was inside of her. But this time all of it felt different, felt real. His balls were so tight they cramped, his cock so engorged he knew he knew he wouldn't last long. She moved with her eyes connected to his, never blinking or looking away. And the pace was far more soothing than before. He could breathe, he could feel and what he felt was pure joy. And then the last of his strength snapped like an overwound rubber band. He released into her.

She lay back down on his chest.

"I was so scared. When I saw you with that gun, you looked afraid, and that scared me. Whatever it is Jaxon, talk to me. Okay. I'm going to help you. I don't care how. I don't care what I have to do I'm going to help you."

They lay still for a long time. Then she was forced to separate. He asked her to turn to her side and brought the covers up over them both. Confused for a moment, her wide eyes glistened with fear that he was going to have another crazy episode, but he was normal again. She turned to her side so her back was to him. He spooned her. His long body curved around her slender one. He dropped his arm over her and pulled her closer to his chest and looked to the window.

"The sun is gone, but wait, watch," he said.

Goodiva lay in his arms and waited with him as darkness completely descended. From the bedroom view she saw the sky. The stars were in the trillions, and each could be seen. The moon had to be somewhere close. He didn't speak. He just kissed the back of her head and protected her.

"Do you like it?"

"I remember it," she said.

"You do?"

"Yea, from when I was a kid."

"Tell me about you as a kid?" he said and kissed her shoulder.

"When I was a ten back in Falcon Cove I made two friends," she smiled. "Before Peter Collins stole my childhood, they were my sisters and the happiness I always wanted. I would slip out of my back door on a night like this and ride my bike a mile over to Delilah's house. Her house was the only one without the drama of fighting parents like mine, or the sad empty loneliness you could feel when Queen's mother had passed out on her. Me and Queen would hide our bikes in the bushes and then climb the tree that reached the second-story flat roof. Delilah would come out of her window and bring us snacks and Capri suns. We'd watch the stars to see if we could see one fall from the sky. Every night there was at least one that did. We'd tell stories of space adventures and aliens. I felt so calm then." She turned her head and looked at him. "That's how I feel now with you. Calm. Do you feel it?"

He smiled.

"I want our baby to have nothing but my love."

"I do too," she smiled.

"My surprise tomorrow is going to be even better."

She chuckled.

He closed his eyes and she turned her head and stared at the stars. After the baby was born she'd go to her best friends and explain it all. They would cry and fuss, but they'd forgive her. They always forgave and loved each other. She had faith.

GOODIVA FELT HIS HAND to her backside. She opened her eyes to brightness so blinding she put her face in her pillow at first.

"Time for breakfast."

Jaxon sat on the side of the bed. He wore a dark thick turtleneck and heavy leather jacket with lamb wool lining. On his face was his mask, and on his head a wide-brim fedora like that of a cowboy.

She frowned at his attire.

"I have to tend to the horse to get it ready. Breakfast is below. Beans, rice and eggs."

She laughed.

He winked with his good eye and turned to leave, but picked up the shotgun they had left at the door.

"Jaxon?" she said. "What are you doing with that?"

"I'm going to check the forest. Make sure they aren't looking for you."

"Oh?" she smiled. "That's nice, but maybe you should take your medicine first. Let us eat breakfast together."

"You eat. I won't be long."

"Jax—"

He left and called up to her as he went down the stairs. "I'm fine. Get dressed. I made a fresh pot of coffee too. It's snowing, so it won't be pleasant heading back to Mayfair."

She scrambled out of bed and went to the top overlook from her loft view of him. She watched him go to the door with the long nose shotgun tucked under his arm. "He'll be fine. You just need to get dressed and get out of here. Now."

She did just that thinking of their magical night together. Dawn had brushed away all the stars. Last night in bed they made love twice and she slept against his chest listening to his light snores, dreaming of the day when they were both healed. It felt so special. With all the windows, she felt as if they were making love in space. She'd thought she'd been in love with Twixt, and before him a few boyfriends. But none of them made her heart race with excitement and fear the way Jaxon Price did. Goodiva finished a quick shower. She dried herself and dressed in her clothes she wore yesterday that he had neatly folded and left for her. Using her fingers, she combed through her tangled hair and then separated her hair into a crooked part to give herself two braids.

When she went downstairs Jaxon hadn't returned. She hadn't heard him fire his shotgun, so that had to be a good sign. She drank the coffee, ate the cold eggs and left his beans and rice on the stove. To her surprise a phone rang. She jerked at the sound of it. For some reason she didn't think there was a phone. Goodiva got up from her seat and listened. It rang by the sofa. She walked over to it and stared. After another ring it stopped.

Jaxon returned. He was dropping clumps of snow.

"Hey," she said.

"You ready?" he asked.

She glanced to the phone and then him. She shrugged. "Yes. Take me to my surprise."

"Your horse awaits," he smiled. The shotgun was gone. She didn't mention it. Neither did he. She hugged him, and then left with him, never mentioning the phone call.

"EVERYONE TAKE A SEAT," Goodiva announced.

Jaxon entered the parlor. Hutch and Andella were already seated. Ahmed stood off to the side, refusing to obey. Jaxon shot him a commanding look. Ahmed nodded his obedience and took a seat. Jaxon went to the chair designated for him. Ahmed had brought in turntables for her and all the equipment he thought a DJ would want. She'd spent the first part of the day in the parlor setting up her equipment and getting her music together after they returned from the cabin. In a digital age she'd only need her laptop and a playlist for her jam session. However, Goodiva was a true artist. And not since he lured her into Mayfair had he seen her so happy.

Francine and Dr. Eleven were the last to join them. The only other staff was kitchen help and they rarely made an appearance. She started her set with 'Soul Capsule' by Lady Science. The low melodic tempo would pitch higher with a thumping beat that allowed her maestro skills to mix in Lauren Hill's voice: "You're just too good to be true..."

The music blasted them from speakers and everyone felt the vibrations. He tried to guess the instrumental swap. At first it was funk with neo-soul, then electric dance with hip-hop, and before her show ended with all of them listening she mixed in some classics with old-school R&B. Those in attendance didn't move or acknowledge her talent, but he smiled through the show. With one headphone on her ear and her head bobbing side to side as she performed, she looked masterful in her element. The show went on for a straight hour, and his favorite was her playlist. All the songs he serenaded her with when he stole her from the world were now being played for him in remixes that made him smile and laugh. He was the only one. His team stared at her unmoved. When she finished, he gave her a standing ovation. His people looked up at him confused, and then did what he expected. They all stood and clapped for her.

Goodiva grinned. She came from around her DJ stand and took a bow.

"Get out everyone," he said.

They left the room. Ahmed closed the door.

"You liked it?" she teased.

"I want more," he said.

She came over to him. He embraced her as soon as she was within reach and cupped her face to kiss her brow, her eyelids, her nose and mouth. She laughed.

"Was all of that for me?" he asked.

"I made you a new playlist," she said. "It's the remix."

He laughed.

She rubbed his back and stared up at him.

"How do you feel today?"

"I told you, I'm fine Goddess. The doctor has cleared me for fun. I'm all good now," he said.

"But for how long?"

"Nothing is going to take me from you."

"That's not my question."

"I'm fine."

"Hey?" she said in her most cheery voice. "I want to go back to the cottage. Why don't we just stay out there?" she asked, and let him go. "I'll go pack us some things."

"No," he said.

"Why?"

"It's snowing pretty bad out there. I don't want to risk it."

He looked down at her belly, and she did too. She touched her stomach. "Okay. Then let's go down to the cellar. I just want us to be alone."

He wasn't sure why she preferred isolation, but he didn't mind it. "I have a nice dinner being prepared for us. We can..."

"Have it down in the cellar. I'll tell the staff," she said and walked out. She passed Hutch who had come back into the room.

"Sir?"

"Have you searched the grounds?"

"Yes, there was no one in the forest. I don't know what you thought you seen but it wasn't Scorpions."

"Then it's the feds. Coming to take her away from me."

"No sir. No one is here."

"I know what I saw!" he shouted.

Hutch gave him an obedient nod.

"What is it Hutch? You have something else to say?"

"It's your cousin. He wants to speak with you. We tried calling you in the cabin earlier to tell you—"

"Tell him I will call him back," Jaxon said as he walked over to her turntables. He would have them brought downstairs to their chamber. A private show just for him tonight. He smiled at the thought of it.

"Fuck calling me back. I'm here!" Armand huffed and walked into the room. He glared at Hutch, who gave him a nod of an apology and made a hasty exit.

"What are you doing here? When did you get here?" Jaxon asked.

"I've been calling you for over a week. You haven't called me back. I just got here, no thanks to you. During this damn pandemic. The fucking driver didn't pick me up from the airport. I had to rent a car and drive out here myself. Risking my fucking life! The damn virus is everywhere!"

Jaxon opened his mouth to speak but Armand continued.

"You think I wanted to come back to this fucking glacier?" Armand asked through clenched teeth. He frowned and looked around the room. "What the hell is all of this? I thought you were sick?"

"I'm better. How long are you staying?" Jaxon asked.

"Long enough to talk some sense into you. Seriously, what is all of this?"

"I'm dealing with a lot. She's pregnant. She needs me to focus on her. I know jin has sent messages that we need to speak, and we will soon. But not now."

"Jin's dying," Armand said.

Jaxon froze at the news.

"That's right. If you had called me back you would know the evil bastard is on his death bed. He has cancer. Not the blood cancer you have, but the kind that's just as incurable. Doctors give him no more than three months."

"But what about our doctors? I mean, look what they are doing for me."

"That's the problem," Armand said as he paced. "Nobody knows what they are doing for you because you're isolated here being experimented on."

"I'm being cured."

"You think so?"

"Look at me. I'm standing, aren't I?"

Armand looked him over. He didn't appear impressed. He paced away. "Well, Jin wants to die."

"Now I'm confused," Jaxon said.

"He wants you to be his successor. Since he knows she's pregnant, he's doing everything to make it happen. That kid is more valuable than you realize."

"Let it happen. I have another plan."

"I know what you're thinking," Armand said. "You're thinking if you work with the CIA, you can save her. That's what that doctor is telling you. Jin being dead gives you power within the family. A win-win. Wrong." Armand sat down in the chair. He crossed his leg over his left and gripped the arms of the chair. "Have you forgotten what happened in Margahm? Or the three wives you left back home? Have you forgotten why any of this is possible? Why you can play house with her and not honor your duty? They duty I told you not to take on, before you became the Scorpion."

"I haven't forgotten a thing," Jaxon replied.

"Hood. Because the death of the old man has sparked the interests of many. You go to Dubai, pass the crown to one of our cousins, and you can come back to the world of the living. No CIA, no Scorpion, all of it is out of our lives. If you give them the child. We can be normal again."

Jaxon narrowed his eyes on is cousin. "What did you say?"

"Fuck her. Man, fuck that bitch!"

"Say it again?"

Armand stood. "I said fuck that bit—"

Jaxon went on the attack. Armand hit the floor and blood sprayed from his mouth and nose. Jaxon dropped on him and put both hands to his throat and squeezed with all his might. Before he knew his own strength he was crushing the life out of his cousin and he enjoyed it. Armand thrashed with bulging eyes. He shouted repeated threats of death and pain in Arabic at his cousin as he watched him die. Armand's face flushed purple just as

Hutch and Ahmed rushed in. It took both men to get him off his cousin. The violent eruption from him stunned them all. Because Jaxon wasn't done. He went after his cousin again and again until they had to pin him down to the ground to keep him from him. Everyone knew how much Jaxon loved Armand. They were brothers.

Hutch went to Armand and tried to help him. Jaxon stilled so Ahmed released him from the pinned down position. Jaxon feared that he'd crushed his cousin's larynx. Armand sat up with Hutch's help. He looked at Jaxon, shocked.

"What is wrong with you man?" Armand rasped. "You could have killed me. For what? For her?"

"Get him out of here," Jaxon wheezed.

"Don't fucking touch me!" Armand screamed hoarsely. He managed to stand on his own. Jaxon was still seated on the floor. "I don't know who you are anymore."

"That makes two of us," Jaxon panted. He looked up at his cousin with regret. "If you ever try to take her from me I will kill you with my bare fucking hands."

"You're an idiot. Pack your things," Armand said and straightened his suit.

"What?"

"You're headed to Dubai tomorrow."

"Tomorrow?" Jaxon asked.

Armand started for the door. Before he left, he turned to deliver one last statement. "One-way trip. *Jin* wants to the meet the mother of his grandchild. I'm done protecting you. She's his now. Go choke him."

Armand left.

Hutch extended his hand to help Jaxon from the floor. He was pulled to his feet. "It's true sir"

"Tomorrow?"

"We have no choice, sir. The Scorpions arrive tonight to ensure you're ready to leave."

"The government will intervene. The virus has restricted air travel and countries have bans. It's not safe."

"Not if they think sending you in is to their advantage."

Chapter Twenty-Six

Rhianna's song 'Love on the Brain' played into the hall. Jaxon smoothed his hand back over his hair. He then used the keycode to open the door to his hidden chamber of love. That's what he called it in his head. That's what he believed. Inside, Rhianna's soulful voice and strong guitar instrumentals greeted him. Dinner had been prepared for them and delivered before his arrival. He was greeted by a table set with candles and a meal fit for a king. Immediately he recalled the first dinner he arranged for her. It felt ridiculously void of his intention after seeing how she expressed her love.

"Voila!" she said with her hands in the air. "You like?"

His gaze swept from the meals to her lovely face and then down over her curves. She'd chosen the mini-dress that he asked her to wear before she was carrying his child.

"Nice," he smiled. "Especially you in this dress."

"I had said I would never wear it when you saw me unpack down here and told me it would be your favorite."

"That has changed?" he asked.

"A lot has changed. Come, greet me properly."

He did. He pulled her closer.

"Wait, say hello to the baby first," she said.

"What?"

"The baby. Say hello," she said

He looked down at her stomach. The baby was just an idea for him, a means to an end, not a real living person between them. Not in his head. But in that moment he realized he had changed everything between them. They would be parents. Whether he lived to see the child grow up to an adult didn't matter. Today he was a father.

"Well?"

He smiled. He put his hand to her belly. She closed her eyes and waited for him to do it: to pay homage. He leaned in and kissed her stomach. "Hello baby. I'm your father." He peeked up at her. "Did the baby move?"

"No, silly. It's too soon for that. Now, say hello to the mommy."

He pulled her into his arms and kissed her. Everything changed at the cabin. She was his again. She had his trust. The dress was a man's dream for her. It revealed her beautiful legs and defined her tiny waist. Snug to the front, it lifted her breasts seductively. She had blown her hair straight and wore no makeup except the copper gloss to her lips he had all but kissed away.

"I'm hungry," she grinned.

"Me too," she confessed.

Jaxon pulled out her chair for her. She sat and immediately reached for the food. He shook his head silently. His cousin's visit still burned deeply in his chest. Armand was upstairs in one of the rooms sulking. He was glad he arrived after her performance, because he feared his reaction earlier. Could he have killed the man he considered his brother?

"Who is that singing?" he asked as he scooped up the gravy to pour over his meal.

"His name is Khalid, the song is called 'Talk.'"

"Oh?" he said.

"Be right back," she said. She hurried to the kitchen. She found candles. He helped her place them and lit several of them.

"Now, your hand please," she said.

She extended her hand to him and bowed her head. She thanked the Lord for the food and his health. And they enjoyed the meal together.

"Sooooo," she began. "Things are weird."

"Weird how?" he asked.

"I don't know. Ever since you've been sick and I've been dealing with morning sickness, things have felt different between us, until last night."

"Things definitely changed last night," he agreed.

She moved her rice around on her plate with her fork. It took her a minute to decide where to begin. "When did you decide to kidnap me? Was it right after the accident? Or was it...before?"

"Before what?"

"You sent flowers before the accident. You had been trying to find me. And that night you wanted to see me. I remember the call," she looked up into his eyes. "Was it...really just for a date or did you want to use me? Like this? The baby? Was this always something you planned?"

"I wanted to date you. Have sex with you. That's what men want when they pursue a woman."

"Not all men."

"Most men," he said.

"And the baby? That night you asked me if I wanted children."

"It was a simple question."

"But you—"

"I didn't plan to lose have my face and sanity to have you. I was perfectly fine in my life the way it was. Who would plan all of this just to have a baby?"

She lowered her gaze to her rice and thought over her next question. "The actress, Leigh Anne? Remember her?"

"Yes," he replied. "I remember her."

"She was in your room," Goodiva said.

"What room?"

"Jaxon?"

"I'm sorry, but I don't know what you're talking about. What room?"

"Your hospital room. You knew I came to see you. She was there. She was really upset. Freaking out about me being close to you."

"Yeah, Leigh Anne tends to overreact."

"I don't think so—"

"When the doctors told her I would have to live with this face, she lost interest. Poof, like smoke, she was gone."

"So, she isn't one of your wives?" Goodiva asked.

Jaxon nearly choked. She handed him his glass of water as he coughed hard into his fist until he was able to swallow. He shook his head smiling. "No. Hell no. Is this what these questions are about? My wives?"

"Yes, stupid. I don't want to be in love with a married man. Let alone having his baby. It makes me...a tramp. The other woman are—"

"You are the only woman."

"Okay, so back to my first question," she said. "Dating. Would you have wanted to have a normal relationship with me? You know, dinner and yellow flowers, then red flowers. A movie, and maybe trip to Santa Monica pier. Camping? Uhm, ski-diving? Wine tours?"

"No," he said.

His answer was too direct. Her smile disappeared from her lips.

"Let me explain, Goddess," he said.

"I think you better," she replied.

"The man I was before didn't value the things I value now. He wouldn't have pursued you in that way. He would have wanted you, yes. Sex, yes. And maybe he would have toyed with the idea of something like keeping you around longer. But he would have lost interest, eventually."

"Thanks for being honest," she mumbled.

"That's Jaxon Price. Romeo the Asshole. Remember that guy?"

She gave him a half-smile.

"No problem."

"So, you're no longer faking it?" she asked.

"I fake it every day. Every day. Except when I take off my mask and I'm with you. When you said no one taught me how to love, you were right. For three years I had to learn to be by myself. Teach myself to care about the things I took for granted, like walking, talking without pain, living with this disease knowing my blood is poisoned. You became my focus. I didn't have the pleasure of dating you, take you to the movies, or camping, or wine tours. But I got to know you. My way. And I fell in love. Deeply. Obsessively. Completely."

"Oh, my goodness," she sighed with a short laugh and put her face in her hands.

"What?"

"That's not how love works Jaxon," she said.

"Says who? Who is the authority? I want to file an appeal." He slammed his hand on the table.

She laughed.

"It's an exchange of trust and understanding. That feeling that comes when you say something and I finish your sentence. Or when I leave the room and you can't wait for me to return. Where we discover each other mutually and find more things in common. It's natural."

"That's fantasy."

"And what is a masked man kidnapping you into some ancient mansion on a mountain to have some miracle baby that the government wants?" she smiled.

"Okay, that's fantasy too..."

"Aha!"

"Let me finish," he said.

"Go on, finish. I'm listening."

"Let me ask you this," Jaxon began. "The first night. Forget the alcohol, forget the party, forget your boyfriend and your revenge. That first night when you went into that bathroom and I came in behind you. When you looked at me in the mirror and knew what I wanted. What did you feel?"

"What did I think?"

"Nope, what did you feel," he said.

"Lust, attraction, kind of sexy," she said. "But I had been drinking."

"That's why I didn't ask you what you thought. I needed to know what you felt."

She nodded.

"It was natural right? That feeling came over you. I believe in lust at first sight, because I think lust and love are like two petals on a rose. Not the same, but closely related."

"Poetry, that's what I remember about you that night," she smiled. "The way you speak. It made me feel like I can trust you."

"Then trust me," he said.

"You have wives."

"I inherited my wives. Never met any of them before the day I married them, and only spent a short time with them before I left."

"So?" she asked.

"So what?"

"You consummated the marriages?"

He looked up at her. He looked away. That was all the answer she needed.

"Then why marry any of them?"

"As a Sunni, I can take up to four wives."

"You practice this faith? You want to make me the fourth?"

"No. Yes. I guess I do now."

"I could never do that," she said.

"Couldn't or wouldn't?" he asked.

"Don't play with me!"

"You asked me what I want. I want you to be one of my wives."

"Never."

"I can't have what I want," he pouted.

"Do you love these women?" she asked.

"I said I don't know them, and they don't know me. Not really," he said. "Love isn't even close to what we share. I provide for them."

"Will you see them again?" she asked.

"That marriage isn't recognized in Western society. Only in Saudi Arabia will it be. I want you. Only you. For as long as I have left."

"A harem, a kidnapping, a secret baby, all because me and Twixt had a fight and I met you at a pool party?" she shook her head.

He smiled. "Don't forget Twixt's plane crash."

"Not funny."

"It is to me," he mumbled under his breath.

"I told you I was afraid. This is what I'm afraid of."

"Dinner?"

"There you go with the jokes again," she said.

"What are you afraid of?" he asked.

"That the moment I trust in how I feel for us, you'll die, or become some kind of monster, like the one that put me in that room for weeks. And I'll be alone."

"Will I die?" he asked.

She waited.

He put his hand on the table and extended it to her. She eased her hand over his and laid it flat over his palm. Their fingers intertwined, locked in solidarity. He wasted no time in standing and pulling her from her chair. There was something she couldn't deny. She was happy, and she was in love, true love. She knew it would be the most risky and dangerous love of her life.

The music had long ago stopped, but he swayed with her in his arms. It felt so good to accept being his. Even knowing all of the ugly truths about his past and his present. It felt so good to be loved. They ate and joked through their meal until they both were sated. It was her idea to watch a movie. And with Henry back below with them, she snuggled him on the sofa and chose an independent film.

"Who is Luvie?" he asked her halfway through the show. "I've heard her name mentioned by you before."

"It's what my mother prefers I call her. She never let me call her mommy as a kid."

"I like it," he said.

"I don't," she sat back and tossed her fork to the plate. "But if we were normal, you'd meet her in person and understand why."

"Have you spoken to her?"

"I called her. She's upset with me like my friends. Very upset."

"I'm sorry."

"No you aren't. Not really."

"I think it would be great to be normal. So let's practice. What is your issue with your mother?"

"My issue is that since I was ten and her marriage fell apart, she became more like my sister than my mother. She yanked me from one place to the next, always searching to make my dad jealous and make herself feel something. She wasn't there as a mother. She never comforted me or protected me. She's just Luvie."

"Oh," he nodded. "Things will change."

"How?" she asked.

"You have to come with me to Saudi Arabia," he said.

"What?" she sat upright.

"I can protect you, I can comfort you, but I can't do any of that here. Not much longer."

"I disagree."

"We have to leave."

"The virus. It's still out there. People aren't flying. Countries are on lock down. I will not leave the country with you."

"I agreed to let my jin back into my life again," he reminded her.

"So?"

"I agreed to the arranged marriages and to being part of his clan."

"So?" she repeated.

"Now I have to tell him I want none of it. I only want you."

"But you said he was dangerous? Telling him that is dangerous. That's why you kept my pregnancy a secret since you found out."

"It is no longer a secret," he said.

"What aren't you telling me?"

"He's dying," Jaxon said.

"Even better. He dies and you're free. Right?"

"He knows that you are pregnant. He knows what I've done, and what has been done to me. If we go back together, I can end this for you and our child. You won't be in danger anymore."

"What about the CIA? The things they want from you?"

"This is one of the things they want from me," he said.

"Really?"

"You don't need to know more than that," he said. "Trust me."

"I can't do that. I don't want to go to Saudi Arabia. The thought of going there gives me anxiety. It's too much too fast."

"Dubai, it's beautiful," he said and reached for her, but she shrugged off his touch and left the sofa.

"No. You aren't listening to me. I don't want to go. No."

"You have to trust me, Goddess."

Goodiva turned to leave but realized how useless fleeing him would be. She sat back down. "Can this end?" she asked. "Or are you just playing one game after the next?"

"As long as you carry my son or daughter, no one will harm you. Your friends are angry now. Love will send them back here, for you. They will not sit back and let you disappear into my life. I don't want to take anything else from you. We go back and we settle things with my family, and then you and I start over."

"What about the baby?" she asked.

He looked away from her.

"What about my baby."

"Trust me," he mumbled.

She wasn't sure what that meant. He was completely obsessed with her and their love, but he barely mentioned the miracle child she carried. That scared her.

"What if I want to stay here with you. We haven't broken any laws…"

"That can't happen. Do you understand?"

"You want me to leave everything I know and follow you to the other side of the world. I don't have a choice, do I Jaxon? I'm beginning to understand."

THE MOVIE ENDED AND they went to bed. While Jaxon held her, she drifted to sleep. Goodiva woke a few hours later. She slept with his face pressed to her stomach. She touched his hair. She smiled. How she wished she could talk to Delilah and Queen to explain herself. She ached to share her news with her closest friends. But nothing she would say would ever explain the love she had for the man who no one trusted.

"What time is it?" he groaned.

"I don't know. I never know down here. I think it's late."

He smiled and then kissed her belly. "Do you feel any different?"

"Different than what?"

"Then you felt before we went to sleep?" he asked. It was a silly question, but she knew he meant it to be sincere.

"Besides the morning sickness, and my pure disgust for the smell of anything fried, I'm the same," she said. She felt relieved. He was paying attention to her pregnancy. He eased back up on the bed and faced her on the pillow.

"Have you thought of what I asked? About leaving with me. If you don't want to go, I understand."

"I thought you were taking me either way?"

"Well—"

"What?" she asked.

"What? What?" he answered.

"There's something else, isn't there?"

"Something else you should know?" he asked.

"Yes. What is it?"

"Armand is here. He arrived earlier."

"Is he?"

"I need you to come with me, but if you refuse and he sees it then it will make things difficult. You have to show me respect in front of them. A different kind of respect. We can't get out of this country unless you do. And I won't force you. I couldn't do that to you again."

"I still feel like you're playing games with me. One minute I leave your side and you are raising hell, now you say you'd leave me behind. You're just saying things Jaxon. Whatever you're planning I don't have a choice. Be honest. For once just be honest?" she asked.

He kissed her nose. "My Goddess. You are always so suspicious."

IN THE MORNING HE LEFT. She stayed in bed for a while, and once she decided on her answer she got up, ready to face him and her day. She showered, dressed and returned upstairs to the living room. Mayfair was normally quiet as a tomb, but today she heard voices, many of them. She followed the sound of his voice to find him in the cigar room talking to several men she'd never seen before. When she entered, they looked up at her as if surprised. One in particular she did know. It was Armand, and he didn't look pleased.

Jaxon saw her last.

"What time do we leave?" she asked.

He turned to her question. She could see the surprise in his eyes beyond his mask. A sly smile went up his lips, because he knew then she had accepted his terms. The problem was he never really told her what they truly were.

"We leave in three hours," he announced.

"I'll be ready," she replied. She nodded to his visitors, turned and left. In her room she struggled with what she could pack and what she should leave. Twenty minutes into folding and packing her things, Jaxon arrived. She smiled, but didn't stop her tasks. He looked at her selection of things and gave a few comments on what was appropriate for the weather and culture. And then he went into her closet and selected what she'd wear on the plane. More curious, she noticed what he made her leave behind. It said a lot about what the next few months of her life in Saudi Arabia would be like.

Goodiva did as he asked. She put on a long-sleeved shirt and sweater over it. She chose loose fitted slacks that went to her feet. A checkered white and black scarf around her hair and neck finished off the look. She snuck in a few personal items he tossed aside for her own comfort. Ahmed came for her luggage and suspected nothing.

Jaxon met them downstairs. She'd never seen him dressed in traditional garments. He looked like an Arabian prince to her. He wore a white thobe and a white turban. His mask was on and covering the side of his face, but his eyes revealed the compassion and love she knew he held inside of him. She decided to focus on his eyes.

The escape from the mountain was via a helicopter ride to the private airport of Falcon Cove. She was the only one on the helicopter in a N95 mask. Once she arrived, she was presented with her passport and then questioned by some of the airport staff who too wore masks and gloves. For Goodiva she figured this was something they all did now in the world. She boarded a private airplane much larger than a jet. Armand and the rest of the men she saw that came to visit were already onboard. These men were dressed as Jaxon was. At the sight of them, she felt herself slip further away from what she considered her normal reality. Dr. Eleven was the only one among them that looked as out of place as she felt. When Jaxon spoke to the men, he did so in Arabic. There was something imposing and serious about his demeanor. It reminded her of the look he had at the cabin when he shot at the forest for thinking they were in danger. It made her shy away from seeking his attention when he commanded others. She really wished she had Delilah to talk too.

"You need to read this," Jaxon said, speaking to her for the first time.

She glanced to the phone in his hand. She accepted it and read the byline of the article. "Jaxon Price: The Saudi Prince Hidden in Plain Sight."

"What? How?"

"Your friends gave me up to the press," he said. "I suspected they would sooner or later."

"Queen and Dee? They did?" she repeated.

It was difficult to read the entire interview, with the tears welling in her eyes. All she could think was how much she loved and missed them. Queen gave details about her disappearance, and Delilah jumped in to talk about how strange her behavior was before and after they found her with Jaxon Price. The two made accusations of his ties to the royal family in Saudi and then the interview took a dark turn. It spoke of a legal battle Delilah fought with a man who claimed to be the father of her son.

"I've seen enough."

"Keep reading," he said.

Delilah said that Jaxon's family tricked her husband through business deals and swapped his sperm with another man's to impregnate and blackmail her.

"Is this true about Delilah and Noah?" she demanded.

"Some of it. I told you the story of Charles Montgomery. He was complicit in the dealings with my father. She and her son are just a casualty."

"I need to tell her. She thinks you have me brainwashed," she said.

"Soon. Right now, I need you to understand how important it is you don't speak to press. No matter who approaches you," he said.

Goodiva looked over to Jaxon and then back to the phone. She couldn't stomach reading anymore. Her friends hadn't given up on her. In fact, they were just as worried about her as they were before. She couldn't help but smile at their persistence. It was the purest form of love.

"I won't be able to return to America for a long time after this," he said. "The government has cleared our leaving but there are conditions."

"How are you able to leave now? With the pandemic, and these men?" she nodded to the Arab men laughing and talking.

"Your president and his son-in-law have a very convenient relationship with the prince. It is working to our advantage, for now."

"My president? Last I checked you were American."

He smiled and said nothing.

Goodiva handed him the phone. She wanted to escape the window-seat and put distance between her and reality. But she couldn't. Why should she now? What difference would it make? Jaxon left his seat next to her to join the men. She cried.

Chapter Twenty-Seven

Somewhere between the second and third hour of the flight Jaxon woke her. "Come with me," he whispered in her hear.

The invite drew her to the back of the plane. Behind a door was a private bedroom secured away from the rest of the passengers. She couldn't believe the extravagance that awaited her. From the mink comforter to the gold and black marble fixtures, everything seem regal and lush. A television, a drink bar, and bathroom were all exposed to her.

"I should have brought you back here sooner and made you comfortable. But I wanted you with me. You can rest better and in private," he said.

"Thank you Jax—"

"Asad."

"What?"

"You'll have to call me Asad from here on out. Okay?" he reminded her.

"Even in private?"

"Especially in private," he said.

"Okay, thank you Asad."

"كنت موضع ترحيب جميلة "

"What does that mean?" she asked.

"It's my way of saying thank you to my beautiful lady," he replied before he kissed her forehead and left her alone in the room. Goodiva was too exhausted to care. Air travel often made her sleepy. Or maybe it was her hormones? The one thing she noticed that was absent from the room was a phone. She sat on the bed and removed her scarf and shoes. She undressed to keep from wrinkling her clothes and slid under the mink blanket to cozy warmth. The moment she dropped her head on the pillow, she drifted to sleep. The flight would take sixteen hours. It would be a dream if she managed to sleep the entire time.

AFTER DREAMS AND RESTLESSNESS Goodiva rolled over in her sleep and bumped into his chest. The moment she felt him, he embraced her. He was under the covers with her. His bare chest was more comforting than the blanket.

"Hi," she said with a squinted peek up at him. "How long have I been asleep?"

She tried to turn away but failed. He pulled her in closer.

"A few hours. We still have a few more to go."

"Mmm, okay. What happens when we land? Where will we land?"

"Dubai," he said. "We'll take a car to one of my family's homes in Al Barari."

"I'll meet your grandfather?" she asked.

"No. You won't meet anyone for a few days. Eventually you'll meet my wives."

"Huh?" she shot up.

"It doesn't mean anything serious."

"I don't want to meet them. I can't."

"Goodiva," he reached for her.

"Don't do that!" she pushed him away.

"Listen," he pleaded. "I have to gain my *jin's* acceptance and trust. And I have to show him that I accept things I've rejected all my life. I'm bringing you to be my bride to gain his blessing. To free you."

"I'm not marrying you."

"You need to work with me. "

"Why?! Why do I need to do any of this?!"

"It's too late to have that argument," he reasoned.

"It's never too late to change the future. I don't want to be your fourth wife, part of some harem. I don't want that for me or my child. I just want the man I love to love me."

Jaxon sat up in the bed. "You don't have to ask me to love and protect you. Trust me. It's what I want to do."

"You have some kind of cancer. I don't know. I don't know about any of this."

He smiled.

"Yes, you do," he said.

He eased back down under the covers and pulled her over to him. She turned and rested on his chest, thinking it over. "I am going to make you my wife. My only wife. In time. That will always be the plan."

"After we are married and you have both the crown prince and the CIA trusting you, do we leave and go back home?" she asked. He didn't answer for a long pause. He rubbed her back and stared up at the ceiling of the plane.

"The world knows about us now. Your friends made sure of that. We have to convince the world that you are with me by choice." His face dropped over to look at her. "You will have to convince them. Eventually. And then, in five years, you can leave with our child, if you want. In a few years after that I can join you."

"Five years? Five years! I'm going to live with you in this country for five years?"

"Give me five years. You'll have a new American president and new laws to protect you. And our child will be safe enough to not be a target."

"Five years," she repeated in shock.

"Maybe six?" he asked.

Goodiva chuckled. "Why not shoot for ten?"

"I may," he said and kissed her jaw. She turned to her back and he turned to his side. He ran his hand over her stomach. She stared at nothing and thought of everything.

"Asad?"

"Yes?" he answered.

"Have you ever heard of the story of Henrietta Lacks?"

"Who?" he asked and kissed her neck.

"A young black woman, a mother, she had cervical cancer," Goodiva said. Her voice slipped into emotion when his large hand eased into her panty. "She was treated at Johns Hopkins in the wing for black people. They stole her cancer cells and used them to experiment. They still use them to cure things like leukemia and study things like herpes and other cancers."

He dragged down her panty. "And?"

"It's what they are hunting for with you and our child. Those magic cells. Right? Something that could change the world of medicine."

"I guess," he said and kissed her lips as he moved over and situated between her thighs. She knew what would come next, so she put her hand to his chest to stop him. He looked at her with pure lust in his eyes.

"It didn't end well for Henrietta or her family. They used her. They are going to use you, and when they are done, they won't care about protecting any of us. We have to remember that. Okay? Always."

"Always," he said and kissed her with his tongue diving in and out of her mouth as his erection rubbed enough heat between them she was sure she'd combust. Goodiva his muscle thick buttocks as she tilted her pelvis up in response to the pending pleasure. This time penetration came nice and slow. Her vaginal walls clenched and loosened as he went up and down on her and she enjoyed his quick yet targeted thrusts. It was the way his broad chest rubbed over her stiffening nipples. And his mouth, the kisses that went from her lips to her cheek, to her neck to her close lids. The way he loved all over while driving her to the peak of bliss, which burned through her soul and sealed her fate.

The sex sounds they made in the back of the plane behind a thinly closed door were lush, raw—so wet and naughty she feared the men in the plane would hear them if she cried out any louder. But he was not a silent lover. He turned her and slipped into her from behind. The slapping, smacking sounds of him pumping his erection in and out of her. Goodiva bit down on her pillow because it felt so good.

Goodiva inched her knees apart, raised her ass upward and rejoiced when his balls bounced against her clitoris, adding one too many sensations to the mix. She clenched her teeth and cried out in pure ecstasy as her entire being went stiff and her pussy gushed. She climaxed in sheer pleasure.

He didn't stop loving her. But she was done, weak, barely moving beneath him. Eventually his body suffered the catastrophic bliss, and they lay there breathing hard together.

Asad withdrew and flipped over to his back. Goodiva was so satisfied with their lovemaking she didn't bother to speak. She closed her eyes and smiled. He leaned over, kissed her and smacked her ass before he left the bed.

Goodiva woke from her brief nap. The strong smell of his showered body and cologne woke her. When she turned, she didn't recognize the man dressing before her. She stared at him trying to understand the vision. He stood before the mirror in a long black thobe, the kind of garment a sheikh would wear. On his head was the keffiyeh headdress that too was black cloth crowned by a black triangular band.

"What is happening?" she asked.

He glanced back at her, half of his face concealed behind the mask. He gave her a small smile. "Get dressed, stay back here until I come for you."

Before she could respond he left. The door locked and engaged. Goodiva looked at her watch. It would take sixteen hours to reach Dubai, and that meant she had under an hour left of the flight. She fell back to the pillow and sighed. The fantasy was over. What she didn't know was what she should expect next.

THE PLANE LANDED. GOODIVA had dressed and made herself as presentable as she deemed necessary. She put on her N-95 mask and made sure she had her bottle of sanitizer. The wait behind the closed door during the landing left her feeling claustrophobic and forgotten. She found herself standing for no reason then sitting and chewing her nails. Another worry was her miraculous recovery. Lately she had to remind herself that she was pregnant. Was that normal?

After a long, drawn out forty-five minutes the door opened. Asad peered in at her and then opened wider. "You're beautiful."

"What's going on? We landed almost an hour ago?" she said from under her mask.

"Everything is fine. You ready?"

"For?" she asked.

"For whatever comes next."

She nodded. He took her by the hand and walked her off a plane that was now empty. As the last person to debark in a country she never visited, she expected to be greeted by some form of customs. On the private airstrip there were three large black SUVs waiting instead. She and Asad eased into the back seat of the middle truck. He kept holding her hand, and she kept holding her breath. The man driving didn't speak, and her lover was unusually quiet, so she minded her business and questioned nothing.

Dubai was surreal. She glanced out her window at the nighttime skyline of buildings so tall they could reach space. Each sparkled with trillions of lights. Zipping along the sleek curving highways were all kinds of exotic cars. She couldn't keep count of them all.

"You will stay at the Al Maha," he said.

"I thought we were going to your home you have here?" she asked.

"Change in plans. The Al Maha is better for you. A resort spa in the desert. Perfect for you and the baby."

"What about—"

"It's like waking up in the middle of an oasis, seeing camels walk across the desert. The stars are everywhere. You can almost see them in the daylight. You'll be rested and comfortable," he said and kissed her hand.

"What about us? You? Are you staying there?"

"Yes, but not right away. I have somewhere else to be."

"We agreed. We stay together. Always," she said.

"It's not the way things are. You can't come where I go. I can come where you are. And I will. Let me see my grandfather first. Let me connect with my family first. It's important you trust me now more than you ever have. Okay?"

She sucked in a deep breath and exhaled slowly. Her gut said she should demand more of him. But reality held her back. It might have been the keen look of interest the man driving them gave her from his rearview mirror. All she could see of him was his eyes. It was enough for her to trust Asad.

"I'm not sleepy. I feel like I should be starting the day, not finishing it. What time is it?"

"It's nine pm here. Back home it's around one in the afternoon," he said.

"Wow," she mumbled.

The SUVs passed the hotels she would imagine she'd prefer to stay in and went out toward the desert. It was so dark outside of her window she saw nothing but the fading lights. He wasn't exaggerating about the place he took her to. The villas were located in a conservation desert reserve. They were shaped like tents but much larger. And they were private. She and Jaxon arrived to find six men dressed in the same black thobes he wore, waiting.

"Who are they?"

"My men. They're here to welcome us," he said.

"Your men?"

He didn't answer further. The door was opened for him first. He left the car and she sat inside and waited. She tried to see his exchange with the men but the tented windows and the night mixed in with their dark attire and made it hard to see much of anything. He then came for her. He helped her out of the SUV as if she were his queen. He kissed her hand. The men who waited kept their faces covered. They wore turbans and scarves that only revealed their eyes. And they all stared.

"Come see, you'll love this."

She let him pull her along. They walked through the doors into her private home. The inside retreat was filled with opulence. He seemed proud of his selection and gave her a tour. There were three large bedrooms with custom-made king-sized beds. The place had an oval shape and from any of the rooms you could walk out of doors to an infinity pool that faced the desert. She looked up and saw so many stars it took her breath away. More than she ever seen in Falcon Cove. She looked back and saw the roof of her vista was made of large white tent sheets that pitched up like an Arabian fantasy. Inside her new home the walls were turquoise with golden fixtures and the floors were made of a cool teak brown wood that mirrored the color of desert sand. The sofa consisted of large pillows that went in a half circle. In the center was a tall golden teapot and cups as if set for them. There was so much more to the place, but she barely noticed.

"What do you think?" he asked.

"When are you leaving?" she replied.

"Do you like it?"

"Do you? This? All of this? Is this you? Or just something they give all your guests that stay here?" she asked.

"My guests?"

"You seem to be mighty comfortable. Since we landed," she said. "Is this your place?"

He took her hand and kissed it. "I own it. Two years ago I designed it."

"Hmpf. That's what I thought."

"I will come back for you. As soon as I can."

"Where will you sleep?" She sidestepped him to block his leaving.

"At my grandfather's," he replied with a look of concern. "Why are you angry with me?"

She crossed her arms defiantly.

"What is it?"

"So, I'm not welcome?" she asked.

"I don't want you to meet him. You are safest here. Come with me," he said. He walked through the mini palace. He went to the bedroom closet. He threw the doors open. Inside was some of the most beautiful layered robes and scarves she'd ever seen. An assortment of colors all trimmed in golden embroidery.

"This is yours," he said.

"How?"

"How what?"

"How is it mine? Are they all in my size?" she asked.

"Yes, see for yourself," he said.

"You were planning this?" she asked. She walked inside and touched the silk fabric and assortment of dresses, all of them were in her size.

"Sort of," he confessed.

"Or did these belong to your other wives?"

"No, these are yours," he said again, as if proud.

"Will you see them?" she asked.

"See who?"

She frowned.

"Yes. I will see them. I won't lie to you. I have to see them. But nothing will happen. I'm coming back here to be with you."

"Right? Because it's all about me," she sighed.

"You said you trust me," he reminded her. "Have you forgotten?"

"No. It's hard to forget anything I say or do. Everything with you has consequences," she said and rubbed her hand down her stomach. "You're leaving."

He nodded.

"All of this is going to be so hard if I have no one to talk too."

"It won't be. And none of this is forever. I won't be far." He took her into his arms. He kissed her. "The men are not allowed inside. They won't disturb you. They are only here to protect you. The staff will come in the morning to see to any and everything you need. And this is how you reach me." He put a phone in her hand. "The code is your birthday."

She looked at the phone and then him.

"You know my birthday?" she smiled.

"There's nothing about you that I don't know, Goddess. You call me, I come, no matter what I'm doing, no matter what time. So, promise me you will only call if you need me."

"I promise," she said. "I'll text though. All day and night until you come back."

He chuckled and nodded. He took her face into his hand and kissed her brow. She hugged him, afraid to let go. He kissed her mouth and that led to more kissing. He had to stop their passion too soon. She felt like protesting. She wanted to. She only nodded and smiled bravely. And then he was gone.

Alone, she walked through the villa, not sure what to do. She felt like running a marathon but the dark hour made her dizzy with confusion. She found herself drawn to the pool lit patio. She sat in a reclined chair and removed the phone from her pocket. The moon was full that night. She could see the sand dunes all around the horizon. It was picture perfect.

Godiva sent her first text.

G: *Hi?*

A: *Hi.*

G: *Is it too early to ask you to come back?*

A: *No.*

G: *Will you come back tonight?*

A: *No.*

G: *Tomorrow?*

A: *I will try.*

G: *Are you safe?*

A: *I hope so.*

G: *Am I safe?*

A: *On my life you will be.*

G: *I love you.*
A: *I live for you.*
G: *Goodnight.*
A: *Sweet dreams.*

Goodiva rubbed her thumb over the phone and found she had access not only to him but full connection to the internet and the world. She sat upright. She stared at the Google app uncertain. She thought of googling herself to see what the press was reporting on her second disappearance. She knew there was a lot in the world she had missed with the pandemic. However, any negativity would only resurface her doubt. And what would doubt bring in the strange land she was forced into? Goodiva's hand went down her belly. She sat back.

"Strange world I've thrown us into, isn't it baby?" she asked.

She heard a noise behind her and was immediately startled. A young woman appeared. She nodded respectfully. She looked to be Asian, possibly Filipino.

"Dinner?" the woman asked.

Goodiva sighed in relief. The woman spoke English. "Uh, yes."

"Tea?" the woman said and pointed back inside to the golden pot.

"No, just a salad maybe, and some water?"

The woman nodded and left. Goodiva sat back in the chair. She expected the desert to be hot, even at night. Her first night in Saudi Arabia the weather was absolutely perfect. She could see the moon. It was full and bright in the sky. She had gone far away from the trauma of Mr. Collins. She'd recovered after the pain of her failed relationships with Twixt, and her time trapped in Mayfair seemed like a distant memory. If only she could share her growth with her friends. She looked down at the phone in her hand and nearly dialed Delilah. Instead, she called her friend Queen, who answered on the third ring.

"It's me," Goodiva said.

"I know," Queen replied.

"How?" Goodiva asked.

"The number. You're not here anymore, are you? Did you leave with him?"

"Yes. I—."

"Are you okay?" Queen interrupted.

"Yes. Yes Queen, I swear."

"He's a dangerous man. There are things you don't know about him," Queen said.

"You went to the press. Why?" Goodiva asked.

"What do you mean why? You think we're stupid. We know something happened to you in Mayfair. Something crazy enough to make you push us out of your life."

Goodiva couldn't respond. She couldn't summon another lie for him or herself.

"Delilah is in trouble. Do you even know what's been going on with her?"

"No. I haven't seen the press... I don't know."

"Well that's strange, Shelly. Because the way I remember it you were never off of the media, never not in the know. And this thing with Dee is all over the news."

"Tell me?" Goodiva asked.

"Noah isn't Charles' son. The Montgomeries are trying to contest the will and kick him out of whatever inheritance the poor kid has. And to make it worse, the scandal has drawn the attention of some asshole ex-cop in New York. He demanded a test at first. He won. Then he demanded custody rights. He won those too. Now he's quarantined with her and Noah."

"Oh my God!"

"She needs you. You know she is always there for you. For us. Come back home," Queen pleaded.

Goodiva bit down on her bottom lip. "I can't. It's too late."

"Why? What's happened?"

"A lot. So much. I'm sorry. Tell her I love her and as soon as I can get out of this mess I will call her."

"I can help!" Queen said.

"I know you can. I know you both can. But this time it's on me Queen. I have to fix this thing myself."

"That's not good enough!" Queen said. "Listen, I was never the one to boss you around or judge you. I let things be with us. But this is too much. That man is dangerous. You've left the country with him."

"I know what I'm doing."

"Do you?" Queen shouted. "I can't believe we're here."

"I love you so much Queen."

"That won't change. I'm always going to love you Shelly. Be safe. Call me. Anytime. For anything. I have this number. Call me."

"I promise. I promise I'm okay," she said.

"Bye Shelly."

"Bye Queen."

The call ended. She sat alone on the deck until all of her guilt was released. But only more guilt surfaced in its place. There was nothing more she could do for her friends, and for the first time since they made the pact in fourth grade to be there for each other, she lost faith.

Chapter Twenty-Eight

The next few days passed like a dream. She'd wake in the morning to breakfast served in her room. She'd shower and be greeted by servants to give her the most relaxing massages. Her new home accommodated all her wants. Everything was run by technology. She could key in the temperature of her shower and the water would be perfect. She could cool the place from a remote control and play any kind of music she wanted. Television was satellite. She'd sit on the large pillows on the floor and press a button to have it rise from the floor and watch the American news conferences by governors and the president all at a loss on how best to defeat the virus that had plagued the world. Or she'd play movies on an eighty-inch screen.

She learned more about Jaxon Price in those few days than she'd ever imagined. The world knew his secret identity now. Every news station broadcasted her life history with past friends and lovers. She saw Hutch interviewed at Mayfair, speaking of his former boss fondly and denying the rumors that Goodiva was once a prisoner there or kidnapped.

In the evening she lounged at the side of the open pool in a pillow chair staring out across the desert. The only trees present were the ones that created an oasis around her private villa, fanning away the sun rays. The rest of her view was orange colored sand dunes. A few times she saw men on camels in white thobes and turbans. But mostly she saw nothing but sand and peace.

In isolation her visitors were mostly women. The Filipino women were all domestics. They cooked and cleaned for her. One who spoke English put her on a schedule for meals and provided her the prenatal pills she'd thought she left behind. She had an esthetician who gave her very relaxing facials and waxing's that made her skin glow like a pearl. The men who were there to protect her never made an appearance. But twice she saw shadows pass windows. Her male visitor was Dr. Twelve. A new doctor. She hated each time he came, but for the sake of the baby, she had no choice but to tolerate him.

Asad kept only part of his promise. He texted her daily. He sent her little poems of love. And each night he promised to return, he didn't. She started to question her sanity. Until the fifth day, when a visitor arrived to confirm her madness.

"Miss Goodiva," Jasmine said.

Goodiva sat up in the massage chair she relaxed in listening to her music. She picked up the remote and turned it off. "Yes?"

Jasmine gave her polite bow. "You have guests. They wait for you."

"Thank you Jasmine." Goodiva stood and looked at her appearance. She wore a halter top and shorts. The small bulge of the baby could be seen, so she grabbed her long sweater and pulled it on for modesty. She walked out of her bedroom toward the sunken living room. There were at least eight women waiting for her. All of them were in black burkas. Only one wore a hijab where she could see her face. She gave Goodiva a polite nod.

"*As-Salaam-Alaikum*," the woman said. "I'm Fatimah."

"Hello," she said to the women. Each of them nodded their heads. Fatimah was stunningly beautiful with large brown eyes, deep olive skin and dark hair.

"You are invited to visit mother today. I'm here to bring you."

"Mother?" Goodiva frowned.

"I'm Asad's sister. Our mother would like to meet you."

Goodiva's eyes swept over the women and then back to Fatimah. He said he had many sisters, but she couldn't conceive a family so big.

"I'll need to get dressed," Goodiva said.

"Can I be of assistance?" Fatimah offered.

"I think that might help," Goodiva said.

Fatimah smiled. Goodiva returned to her room with only Fatimah following. She wasn't sure what she could find in her suitcase that was suitable. Fatimah went straight to the closet. The clothes hanging inside were never fully inspected by Goodiva. She didn't care for them.

"This will be acceptable," Fatimah returned with several garments. She held up first a floor-length long black dress that looked very fitted. It had long sleeves and a covered neck with a hood for her that reminded Goodiva of what scuba divers would wear. To wear over it, Fatimah suggested a sheer black flowing gown with webbed sleeves trimmed in beautiful golden embroidery. And there was a black and gold scarf she'd probably add to the attire to wrap around her hair and face.

"Oh, okay, it's beautiful," Goodiva agreed.

"You'll look beautiful in this," Fatimah said.

"Will Asad be there?"

"No. But don't worry, you'll see him soon," Fatimah replied.

"How do you know I haven't seen him?" Goodiva asked.

Fatimah ignored the question. Goodiva collected the clothes and went into the bathroom. She did another quick shower but had forgotten her undergarments. When she returned to the room in a towel, she caught Fatimah looking through her things.

"What are you doing?" Goodiva demanded.

"Forgive me, I apologize. I was just curious."

"Don't touch my things!" Goodiva said.

Fatimah nodded respectfully and put the dress in her hand down. Goodiva walked over and picked it up. The dress was one of many that she had, and it was quite revealing.

"I'm sorry, I didn't mean to upset you."

"Do you mind waiting for me outside please? I'll call you if I need help."

"Of course. Again, I apologize."

Fatimah left and Goodiva found her phone. She sent a text to Asad. It simply said: "I need you."

He responded immediately.

A: *"Now?"*

G: *"Yes. You promised. I need you now. Right now. It's an emergency. Come!"*

A: *"I will."*

Goodiva refused to dress. She sat in the massage chair and waited. Over an hour later, the door to her room opened. Asad walked in. She was no longer surprised by his attire. She was just happy to see him. He seemed normal. Happy to see her too. Goodiva went to him immediately. He held her as she buried her face against his chest and cried. "Why didn't you come sooner? Why?"

"I wanted too."

She lifted her head. "Then why did you come?"

"Because if you and the baby need me, nothing is more important."

"Who are these women?" she asked.

"A few of them are relatives, wives of cousins. Fatimah is my sister. She told me she went through your things. Is that why you are upset?"

"No!" she pushed him away. She walked over to the bed and glared at him. "I'm upset because I've been here over a week. A week! You haven't come to me once."

"I'm here now," he said, and took off his robe and tossed it to the bed.

"For how long? Send them away. Stay with me all night." She crossed her arms in defiance.

He smiled.

"What are you smiling for? I'm serious."

"I missed you too."

She smiled.

"Are you okay? I mean, have you had an episode? Are you sick?"

"I'm fine."

"How? At Mayfair you were sick all the time. Bedridden. Why are you suddenly so much better?"

He didn't answer.

She narrowed her eyes on him. "And your *jin*? Has he forgiven you? For me? For what you've done?" she asked.

"We're working on forgiveness. It takes time in my family," Asad said.

Goodiva paced. "Your wives? Are you with them?"

"I've seen them."

"Are they with you?!" she demanded. "Staying with them. Sleeping with them in the same bed?"

He didn't answer. Goodiva felt her heart break into tiny crumbles in her chest. She'd never felt more vulnerable or humiliated. Her feet refused to work. Her mouth was locked shut. She looked away so he couldn't see the power he had over her.

Asad sat on the bed. He removed the keffiyeh and placed it next to him. He then took off the mask that covered the burned side of his face. "Things are complicated, my Goddess."

"With you they always are."

"You're a strong woman. I've always known that about you."

"Really? Because strong women where I come from couldn't do this! An insane woman could."

"Don't give up on me now. We are so close."

The soft sound of his chastisement turned her annoyance into an explosion of feelings like that of a grenade. She lunged at him, slapping, hitting, shouting in both anger and hurt. He threw her off him and she landed on the bed. She kicked at him but he caught her foot and dragged her toward him. Queen had taught her how to defend herself. Now naked, the towel having slipped off, she did a back kick that landed dead center to his face and knocked him back. She scrambled across her bed to reach the lamp, but he was on her again. She screamed at the top of her lungs. It didn't matter. No one came. He pinned her down to the bed and put his weight on her to keep her there.

"Calm down. For the baby," he demanded.

She screamed as loud as she possibly could to release all of her fury. If she didn't, she'd never stop fighting him.

He kissed her face, then her lips. She turned her face away from his.

"For me. Calm down. Please," he whispered. "Don't let them hear you upset."

She nodded she would try and then she wept. He lay with her and held her as she cried into his chest. She was scared, she didn't know how to even control so much fear. She was even more clueless as to where to put it. He kissed her and held her. He spoke to her about how the meeting with his mother was an honor. He told her that there would be a ceremony. She would be his wife. After they were married, he would never leave her side again, he promised. He'd received the permission from his first wife. It was custom. He had to follow the customs to the letter if they had any hope of making it through his plan. And his plan was always her. He said he didn't return because he was weak. If he came back to her he wouldn't leave and they'd pounce on that weakness. He told her she was in danger, because

of the baby. They wanted the baby. Everyone wanted the baby. He pleaded in a whispered voice to listen to him and believe. That they were being
watched. No place was safe. She hugged him and held so tight to him all of
it felt comforting and nice. And then he made love to her. He did so with
such tenderness and sweetness she felt as if she was making love to him on
clouds. Later he took her to the shower and pampered her. She wasn't sure
how long it all took, but he didn't seem to care about the time or the delay.
She was his, and he made sure she felt that way. He dressed her. The gown
was so different from any she'd ever worn.

"You look beautiful, and you are," he assured her.

"Married? Me and you?" she asked now dazed and submissive.

He kissed her cheek.

"If you will have me."

"I love you Jax...Asad."

"I love you too, be strong for me, for the baby. We need you to be
strong."

He put on his clothes and mask. He was the Scorpion again. He left
without another word. Fatimah joined her. "My brother asked that I do
your makeup."

"Oh? No thank you. I can do it," Goodiva said in her voice weakened
by defeat.

"He prefers that I do it, if that's okay?" Fatimah insisted.

She didn't know how to respond. Jaxon never made comments about
her makeup. He never ever commented on it. She smiled graciously and
pointed to her bag. Fatimah collected what she needed and spent more
time on Goodiva's eyes, lashes and shadow than any other part of her face.
It was as if it were the most important part of her face. Then she helped her
with her niqāb.

"I thought Asad grew up and spent all of his life in America?"

"No. That's not true. When he was sixteen he came here for almost a
year to live. And over the years he has visited the family."

Stunned, she wasn't sure what to say. She distinctly remembered him
saying that he ran away and when he was found he was given a new identity.
There had to have been time in between those years that he didn't share.

"Are you close?"

"Close?" Fatimah frowned as she finished Godiva's makeup. She picked up the niqāb and then helped her put it on and covered the lower part of her face.

"Brother and sister, you know, friends."

Fatimah smiled. "No. He isn't my friend. He's my brother. There, we are all done."

Goodiva faced herself in the mirror. She looked regal and her eyes were stunning. She didn't even know her natural lashes had such length. "Thank you."

Fatimah nodded and smiled. "Mother will love you."

"Thank you," Godiva said again.

"Shall we?"

Goodiva picked up her purse and walked out. The women all stood at once. They stared at her. She could not tell if any of them smiled. One by one they walked out to a limousine SUV. She'd never seen a Bentley as a limousine before. It was beautiful. They got in together and were driven across the desert.

"They do not speak English," Fatimah whispered. "Only I do. So, ask any question and I will interpret for you."

"Are you married?"

"Yes, I have a son who is two and a daughter who is six months."

Goodiva was surprised. She looked to be no older than twenty-one or twenty-two.

One of the women asked a question in Arabic. A few of the ladies giggled, and they all stared with mocking delight in their eyes. Goodiva looked to Fatimah for a translation, but instead the young woman said something to the woman who had dared to speak and the ladies looked away.

"Something wrong?"

"No. We're all excited to have you here."

The rest of the trip went in silence. When the SUV came to a stop there wasn't much to see. The ladies were not allowed to leave. Goodiva removed her cellphone. She texted 'I love you' to Jaxon. He didn't respond at first. Then he texted back an emoji smiling face. She smiled.

"Sorry for the wait. It will be over soon," Fatimah whispered.

"Anything wrong?"

"No. But we need permission and we'll have it soon. Don't worry."

"Permission?" She found that word an odd choice. And before she could ask, the limo was flagged in and they were driven through the gates. She hadn't been nervous since the trip started, but the moment she saw the palace and all of the extravagance, her stomach began to do flips. She prayed nausea wouldn't surface. The door opened and they were escorted out. When she emerged, the heat was unbearable. She glanced around, surprised by it. She wondered how it got so hot so quickly.

"This way," Fatimah said.

She followed her and the others to the palace steps. Fatimah reached over and took her hand. It was a nice gesture. It comforted her. They walked inside to the friendly sounds of children. Several kids ran around playing. She saw no adults. She found it strange. They then went through the palace to the back doors and then back outside. She discovered there were private quarters behind the grand place. At least seven different homes. Some were larger than others. The women all went in the direction of one.

"Is this where his mother lives?" she asked herself.

"Yes. And her husband's family. They all live here."

"Do you?"

"No. I'm not that lucky," Fatimah smiled. "I have another family that I belong too. Come, you are the guest. Don't worry. Asad has made sure that everyone understands how important you are to him."

She didn't know what to expect, but she knew Jaxon had made it so that Fatimah would be at her side. When she entered the house she felt a big relief to see the women removing their religious apparel. Fatimah removed her headdress and then helped Goodiva remove hers. All of a sudden she felt assurance. The ladies were friendly with their smiles except for two. They asked her questions at once. So many questions, and none of them in a language she could understand.

Fatimah waved them off and gestured for Goodiva to sit. Food was served. A small boy no more than two walked over and climbed on Goodiva's knees. She helped the child. The hug she received eased her anxiety. He was the sweetest and most beautiful little boy.

"That's my baby boy, his name is Arham."

"He's so adorable. I think I'm in love."

"He's my everything," Fatimah said. There was a commotion and Goodiva looked up. It was only the hurried voices of other women collecting their children. A very beautiful woman appeared. She looked to be no older than her mid-forties, and the moment she entered the room she stared directly at Goodiva. She wore a cream pant suit. Her hair was dark brown, shoulder-length with blonde highlights. She was so polished her eyes sparkled as bright as the diamonds in her ears and the strand of diamonds around her neck.

"Is this her?" the woman asked.

"Goodiva, please meet Princess Al Jawhara bint Saud Al Saud, my mother and the mother to Asad."

Goodiva gave a respectful nod.

The woman smiled. "Fatimah, leave us."

"Yes mother." Fatimah picked up her son from Goodiva's knee and then left. The beautiful woman before her couldn't be the mother Jaxon told him about. The one that never loved him and abandoned him. If she was, she wanted to know why. Was Jaxon's story of his life all a lie?

"Are you okay?" the princess asked her.

"I'm not sure. I...everything is beautiful, but it's been strange since I arrived. I don't know what is really going on."

"You're pregnant?" The princess looked at her belly.

"Huh? Oh? Yes I am."

"That's a huge blessing. When my son told me, I had to meet you. Welcome you into my home."

"Thank you."

"Are you Muslim?" the princess asked.

"No."

The princess' brow arched.

"Christian."

"Your son or daughter will be Muslim," she said.

Goodiva gave a smile and nod. The princess took Goodiva's hand. "I know what Asad has been through since he was a small boy. And I think I know what he has said about me. Most of it is probably true from his point of view. You're going to be a mother soon. And you will learn very quickly of the sacrifices we make for our children. I love my son. And I will love you and welcome you and my grandchild."

That was all too easy. Goodiva was stunned. She expected an interrogation. Something felt off to her about the congenial way the woman who everyone around her feared seem to be with her.

"Thank you," Goodiva replied.

"Now. We have a wedding to plan."

"Wedding?" Goodiva repeated.

"Yes. My approval is one thing. But you need to meet your sisters. Asad's wives and make yourself worthy. Come with me. It is time you met them."

The smile fell from Goodiva's lips. She couldn't object, but her entire body went cold. She stood and followed her mother in-law out.

Chapter Twenty-Nine

Goodiva wasn't exhausted, but she was mentally drained. She walked into her empty villa and dropped her purse at the door. She rested her back against it. Defeated, she let go the deep breath of anxiety she carried all day. Nothing in her life before she met Jaxon Price could have prepared her for the past six hours.

In a haze of mixed emotion, she began to undress. She pulled off her niqāb and clothing and stripped bare. What started as a pleasant visit became awkward, tense, and grueling under the watchful eye of his mother. She met all three wives. All beautiful, all young and all fiercely proud of their title and position in Asad's life. The first wife announced she suspected she too was pregnant since Asad's return to her. That announcement rocked Goodiva to the core. Fatimah translated but by the whispered giggles and constant stares she knew the young girl left some things out. From that moment on the pregnancy celebration was for the both of them instead of just Goodiva. She couldn't conceive her life for the next five years being divided between these women. Asad's mother never stopped watching her. In fear, she retreated back to her villa, to her room, where she could lock herself away and forget the dreadful day she had. Instead of her familiar retreat, she was greeted with so many purple and yellow roses she was startled into laughter.

"What in the world? This is insane."

A dress was on the bed for her. A card was on top of it.

"Are you kidding me?" She read a message that said 'I'm waiting'.

She looked around, half expecting to see him. He wasn't there, but her heart pumped with adrenaline at the prospect of him being close. She took the dress and went inside the bathroom and showered and changed. She was in love with how light and sheer the dress was. The layers flowed enough to cover her. The sleeves were long and wide, the splits were on both legs, but only seen when she walked. She could only straighten her hair and pull it up into a ponytail.

There was a knock on the door before she could freshen her makeup after brushing her teeth.

She opened it to find a female servant she hadn't met.

"I am told to come bring you. He is tired of waiting."

Goodiva grabbed a scarf and draped it over her hair, then tucked it around her neck. She was escorted to a car. The driver didn't take the road. Instead he circled the sand dunes around the vista and drove into the night desert a short distance. She saw torches of light. When the door opened, she could not believe her eyes. Before her was a large blanket with colorful pillows. Five-foot-tall torches were erected at every corner of the blanket. A food platter with a colorful assortment of fruits, bread, dates and cheeses with falafel and meats were all-present. Jaxon waited for her. He wore an all-white thobe and even a white half-mask on his face.

Goodiva covered her mouth and smiled. She'd never imagined something so beautiful. The driver came over to help her walk up the sand to Jaxon, and he came down to receive her. He cupped her face in his hands and kissed her. The moon was full. The stars were everywhere, and the desert night was pleasantly warm.

"Hi," he said.

"Hungry?" he asked.

"Yes! I am. Very."

"Good." He walked her over to the blanket and helped her lower to the pillowed comfort he arranged around their dinner. Jaxon stretched out next to her. She ate everything from his fingers without question.

"So, how was it? Meeting her?" he asked.

"Nothing like I expected."

He nodded. "Yeah, for me too."

She stared at him as he poured her something to drink. Where should she begin with her questions? There were so many. "I don't understand something."

"What is that?" He passed her a cup.

"You said you ran away and then met the doctor whose name you took."

"True," he nodded.

"But Fatimah said you have been here many times. You lived here for a year once. You kind of made it sound like you never come here, or you don't have a relationship with your family."

"I left a lot out."

"No kidding."

He smiled. "Armand's father was my uncle, my mothers' brother. He would bring us as kids up until his death."

"Really? He was a scorpion?"

"He converted to Christianity when he fell in love with Armand's mother. No, he was not a scorpion. He didn't believe in any of the principles my jin did. But he loved his father. Armand and I visited. When we did I never saw my mother. She was remarried and her husband wanted nothing to do with the son of Fikrit It's very complicated. After my uncle died we stopped visiting jin. Me and my cousin created a different life than all of this."

"Okay."

"Is that all that happened today?" he asked.

"No," she said and plucked some cheese from the fruit tray. She sat upright, but he was stretched out on his side propped by his elbow. He peered up at her and waited. She knew she had to ask the questions, but she truly feared his answers.

"You met my wives?" he asked.

"Yes."

"And?" he asked.

"They're beautiful women but they all consider themselves more important than me. Fatimah said they are angry that I'm pregnant. In fact, your first wife announced that she is pregnant."

Asad began to choke. She watched him as he coughed up what was lodged in his throat.

"Well?" she asked.

"She's not. Trust me."

"Right, I'm to keep trusting you. When your story changes every day."

He drank from his goblet.

"Okay. Fine. Here it is. I hated every moment of it. I can't be married into a situation like that. I thought I could, but I can't do it. They were planning my wedding without any input from me. And your wives have all the say. It's crazy!"

He reached over and took her hand. "I only want you."

"But you married them. Three years ago!"

"Two," he said.

"You've slept with all of them!"

"Before I found you again. Yes."

She shook her head and pulled her hand from his.

"What happened when we were not together, I can't change. But nothing has happened between me and them since I've returned. I swear," he said.

"I'm feeling sick," she said.

"As soon as you become my wife, I will divorce them."

"I don't believe you. I don't even know who you are. It's evident you're becoming someone else. I don't know if I can do this. Not for years."

"Do what?" he asked.

"All of this. Queen said I should come home."

"You've been speaking to your friends?" he asked.

"I'm not a prisoner. Right? Right?"

He glared at her.

"Yes. I spoke to her. And she warned me about you."

He looked down into his goblet. "Can I at least have the chance to ask before you say no."

"Ask what?" she sighed.

He pushed up. He pulled her up. He kissed her and took her to the very top of the sand dune. She was so fixated on the stars in the sky she didn't see the oasis in the desert awaiting her.

"What is this?"

"Careful where you step," he said, taking her down the dune. The tent that had been erected was something out of a movie. She couldn't believe how wonderful it looked. Torches lit the perimeter of the tent and inside. Jaxon swept her up in his arms and carried her inside like a bride. The incense burning, the large pillow soft bed, canopy drapes, mixed in with the beautiful colors of red, purple, yellow. The gold overwhelmed her senses.

She was stunned speechless. And when he put her down on her feet, she placed her hands to her mouth to keep from crying out her thoughts. Immediately Jaxon went down on one knee. He held up a ring box: a large pear-shaped diamond sparkled against velvet.

"Goodiva Michelle Johnson, will you do me the honor of being my wife, my only wife, for now and forever?"

"Only wife?"

"Yes."

"Only wife?" she asked again.

"I swear on my own life. If you'll have me."

She dropped to her knees in tears and he pulled her in. He hugged her tight and she cried against his shoulder, clinging to him. She pulled off his mask and tossed it away. She held his face, the good and the bad side of him. His kiss swept in and made her the happiest she'd ever been.

WHEN SHE WOKE SHE WAS surprised to find him snuggled up close to her. She turned and touched his jaw. She kissed his brow and then he opened his eyes.

"I love you," she said.

He turned over to his back and dropped his arm over his eyes. He smiled.

"What time is it?"

"How would I know? There are no clocks," she chuckled.

He lowered his arm and looked around as if just realizing where he was. He sat up on his elbows.

"The sun is up."

"Yes it is," she said.

He pulled down the cover and placed his hand on her belly. "My daughter. Is she awake?"

"Daughter? I thought we needed a son."

"No. I will have another you," he said and kissed her stomach.

"I don't feel her yet. It's too soon, I think."

"I can't wait until you grow. I want to see and be there for all of it," he said.

She rubbed the back of his head and nape. He laid his head on her belly and they relaxed. "You really are doing better here in Dubai."

"Dr. Twelve has a new serum."

"A cure?"

"Not exactly. I'm stronger every day that I take it."

"And your anger?" she asked.

He frowned. "What anger?"

"You were different at Mayfair, paranoid about me, and angry."

"No. I wasn't," he dismissed the comment.

"Okay," she mumbled. "So, uhm, this serum."

"Yes?"

"You may not need our baby's stem cells?"

"Maybe. We will see how I respond over the next nine months," he said, and kissed her belly. "Soon it will be too hot to stay in this tent. We need to leave."

"Will you leave me again? For how long?"

"I'll try to come back tonight. After the wedding you will move in with me. And you'll never leave my side, ever," he said and kissed her belly, breasts, neck, and then mouth. "You are my Goddess."

"And you are my Romeo the Asshole," she chuckled.

He got up. She had to grab the sheet to keep him from pulling it away with him. He put on his clothes and picked up his phone. He paused to read the text messages and sent one of his own. He paced for a moment before picking up her dress. He handed it to her. "I'll be back. Get dressed for me, okay."

"Everything okay? You seem worried."

"It's fine. Change in plans. I'll take you back to the house."

"What? You're leaving?"

Before she could finish dressing, he walked out. She couldn't help but feel disappointed, but after the night of love he showered over her that would be selfish. Goodiva put on her sandals and went out of the tent. To her surprise a man was on the ground holding the side of his face. Asad stood over him with clenched fists. Had he struck him? Why? Asad barked at the other men in Arabic. He must have sensed she was among them. He glanced over his shoulder at her. She covered her hair with her scarf, but the wind was strong. He returned to her and smiled. There was a car to take her back. He said nothing on the drive back to her villa, not until he walked her to the door.

"We will move the wedding up." He took her hand and kissed the large diamond he gave her. "I want you with me always. I can't take it much longer."

"How soon?"

"Two days, my jin isn't well. He's getting worse. I want to do it before we lose him."

"Is everything okay?" she tried to look around him to the men who waited for him.

He kissed her. "I'll call you later."

"Be careful."

"Always," he said with a sweet smile and patted her on the butt before he turned and walked away. She went inside smiling and twisting her engagement ring.

"I'VE BEEN WAITING FOR almost two hours," Armand said.

Asad closed the door behind him. "I saw you at the ceremony stalking me. Did you enjoy yourself?"

"Hell no!" Armand barked. He glared. Asad glanced over at three of his cousins who accompanied Armand, and they all turned and left. When the door open and closed again, he nodded for Armand to go over to the outside balcony of the three-story home that belonged to their *jin*. Since Asad's arrival he was under constant surveillance by the orders of the crown prince. Though his jin's wishes were clear, many of the royals did not trust Asad's sudden allegiance. And now he had Armand to deal with.

"What the fuck are you doing here?" Asad said through clenched teeth. "I sent you home."

"I went home. And then..." Armand took a deep breath and exhaled. "The NSA was waiting for me. They put me on a plane and sent me back here, with another message for you."

Asad shrugged and waited. Armand looked so distressed he feared his cousin would crack, and that was a problem.

"Say it!" Asad demanded.

"Ahmed is dead, Dr. Eleven is dead, Hutch is in custody and Dr. Twelve, the last of those weirdo doctors, has been kidnapped from Switzerland. They think you had the Scorpions take him and bring him here. Is it true?"

"I don't know what you're talking about."

Armand eyes stretched. "You made a deal with the CIA. You told the crown prince about their operation. Why the fuck would you do that Jaxon?"

"Don't call me that," Asad seethed.

"You put a target on all our lives. Why? I've lost everything. The media is calling me a terrorist! A fucking terrorist! I'm a Democrat, for fucking God sakes. I voted for Bernie Sanders."

Jaxon smiled.

"You find this funny?"

"No. None of it is funny."

"Then why are you doing this!"

"The NSA lied to you and me. The CIA lied."

"What is going on?"

"They told me there was no cure. That I had to have a child to get rid of this blood cancer they gave me. Remember that lie?"

"So? Yes, I remember."

"Funny how much better I feel lately," Asad said.

Armand glared at him a moment longer. "What? Are you saying there is a cure?"

Asad refused to give any answer, but his blank stare was all he needed. Armand paced. "What is this new plan of yours? Are you seriously going to change into one of them? Become one of them? For what? Why? You weren't a killer. You aren't your father."

"I don't know. I kind of understand the Scorpions. Uncle told us to shun this life and this world. I want to belong in it." Asad shrugged. "I am what every one of you have made me."

"I tried to save you! I love you. As a brother. That disease is making you insane. Don't you see? The crown prince will never trust you. No matter what. And marrying her publicly, renouncing your wives! It's going to blow up in your face. Including my life! If that doctor you kidnapped has cured you, then take her and just go."

"I'm not cured. I still have diabetes and something bad in my blood. I may not live to see my child become a teenager. I need to make sure she and my child are safe. With or without me. I want my son to have honor, a legacy—"

"You sound like grandfather!"

"He is not a demon. He's our blood and he has shown me that I have a purpose," Asad reasoned.

Armand let go a deep sigh. He paced the floor with his hands to his head.

"Go on, what else aren't you telling me?" Asad asked.

"They can't touch you now. But if you give them Goodiva and the child, they will consider it an act of trust. I'll take her back to America. Let them protect her, and they will finish Dr. Eleven or Dr. Twelve's work. They'll make sure she is hidden from the family." Armand lowered his voice as best he could. "They'll help you get rid of the crown prince and take the title."

"I don't need them for that. She's already mine. All of this is mine. And my child belongs to no one but me."

"Listen to reason, this is a good offer."

"You tell those bastards that Dr. Twelve will take good care of me." He took a step toward Armand. Armand stepped back into the balcony railings. He looked behind him at the drop. "You tell them that I am Prince Asad bin Abdullah. Jaxon Price is a dead man buried in Seattle. Tell them my will be done."

"You can't do this. We're talking about the American government. Don't be fooled. They are already here," Armand whispered. "They will destroy us."

"It's done."

"No. No. No. No. No! Please Jaxon! The plan was to come home and bury that evil fossil and then get the information that they needed on the royals. Put someone else more benevolent in power."

"That's me, I'm the most benevolent," Asad said.

"You're killing people. You're turning into them! I know what you've been up too."

"I'm doing what is honorable. I have only dealt justice to enemies of the prince."

"Jaxon!"

"Asad!" he seethed.

Armand put up his hands in surrender. "Fine. Asad. Remember what father showed us, what he taught us when he brought us here as kids. He told us to never take the Scorpion. Ever. It's poison. We are never to be these men."

"I think you should relocate to Australia until this blows over. Contact Dander. You remember him? He worked with Hutch. He lives in Australia. He'll protect you."

"Are you really going to marry her?"

Asad smiled. "She's already my wife in my heart. We have begun the process to make it legal. She going to give me the golden child, our child. And she will be by my side."

"She knows what that means? What you're asking her become?"

"She knows."

"Then she's a stupid bitch or..."

Asad grabbed Armand by the throat and nearly tossed him over the balcony. Armand fought, but Asad kept him pinned into a back-breaking bend.

"What have you done!" Asad shouted.

"Nothing! What are you talking about?"

"Have you betrayed me? Why are you provoking me? Why! Have you told anyone about the things we've planned. The things we've discussed. Anyone?"

"No. No, no, I swear. Jahul questioned me when I landed. Who she was, and if you would seriously become the Scorpion. I didn't say a thing."

Jaxon let him go. Armand coughed and spit up the saliva he choked on. He held the balcony and looked at his cousin with horror. "Has that disease rotted your brain? Has it?"

"I'm warning you, stay out of my way. Go back to America. Tell them whatever story you want about me, but stay out of my way."

"Or what? What will you do Jaxon? Kill me?" Armand laughed. Asad turned and walked out. Armand glared after him, but he knew not to follow.

THE MASSAGE RELAXED her. Goodiva lay in a deep peace with a towel wrapped over her. She had always found a way to escape into her imagination. More than Queen and Delilah ever could. And this life Jaxon had brought her into was the closest she'd ever come to what she could dream, if she ignored everything but her feelings for him.

"Miss? Ma'am, ma'am, please wake."

She was shaken. Jasmine gave her a polite smile. "You have a visitor. Very important."

"My doctor?" she asked and sat up.

Jaxon had mentioned a new doctor would come see her later in the day. The servant smiled and walked out. Goodiva got up from the massage table and put on her slip dress and a Kimono to cover her, with a sash tightly tied around her waist. She walked out of her massage room down the hall to the living area. She appreciated the home visits, but she really wanted to go to a doctor's office and do an ultrasound. She was approaching ten weeks.

When Goodiva went to the front of the villa, she was unsure of who her visitor was until he turned around. "Hi," he said.

"Ah, hi," she replied.

"Is it a bad time? Were you resting?" he asked.

"No. It's uhm, I'm okay,"

Armand walked out of the sunken living area to the pool. She had no choice but to follow. Armand took a seat on the edge of a lounge chair. His eyes commanded she do the same. She did so out of courtesy.

"How has your stay been so far?" he asked.

"Fine."

"Have you met the family?" he asked.

"Yes."

"All of them?"

"Not your grandfather," she said. "But yes, I think so. Your family is so big I can't be sure."

He didn't smile. In fact, he rolled his eyes.

"His wives? What about them?"

She blinked at the question. She didn't want to think of his wives. She didn't feel the need to talk about the ladies with Armand. "Why are you asking about that?"

Armand stood. He walked to the edge of the pool and stared at the bottom. "He's been lying to you. All of this is a lie. A mirage. Like that little dinner date he took you on in the desert."

"I think you should leave," she said.

Armand glanced to her.

"Now. I think you should leave now."

"I'm here to help you."

"I want you to go!" She stood. "I mean it!"

"He isn't marrying you. And if he is, it won't be the kind of marriage he told you." Armand took out his phone. He pulled up an image then handed the phone to her. "Take it. Look at it."

Goodiva stared at the phone and then him.

"Take it!" He shouted at her.

She took the phone. There was a video waiting for her. She hit play. Asad was there with other men. He smiled and laughed with them. The first wife she had met before came over to bring him something to drink. He pulled her into his arms and brought her down to his lap. He hugged her. He kissed her. Goodiva felt as if she were having heart spasms at the sight of their affection.

The video ended.

"That was a party two days ago. To celebrate him and the child you're carrying. His wife, his first wife threw it."

"She's pregnant?"

Armand chuckled. "No. Your child is her child. Especially if it's a boy."

"What?" Shocked Goodiva flashed back to the awkwardness of her visit with the wives. How Fatimah edited her translations for her. The first wife wasn't saying she was pregnant in the sense that she too carried a baby. She was celebrating Goodiva's pregnancy as if it were her own. She was mocking her, because she would be the mother of Goodiva's child.

"She's happy, to have him home and a child to raise. You are just the incubator."

"You're lying," Goodiva said feeling herself grow weak.

"I'm not," Armand assured her. "My grandfather is dying. He has named Asad as his successor. And the crown prince is giving Asad a ranking title for the secret security service under him. They are called Scorpions. And he will lead his cousins and men into whatever darkness my family chooses. In a few days he will be unstoppable. He already is."

"But he loves me," she said.

"He wants the baby you're carrying."

"That's not true. He has found a cure, he's doing better."

Armand shook his head. "No. He's healing, but not doing better. That poison they give him is changing him. Making him a madman. Like his father was. The only true cure he can get is the one you're carrying. And then you will disappear into this life." Armand looked around at the plush villa and its luxury. "Much better than the cellar, but the same prison."

She shook her head in disbelief.

"I don't believe you."

"He told you that the CIA, the NSA, the American government are all trying to protect him. That he was working for them. He isn't. Remember Dr. Eleven? Have you seen him lately?"

Goodiva looked up into Armand's eyes. "He left. I have Dr. Twelve now."

"Left. Sure. If that's what you call it," Armand chuckled. "He's dead. Ahmed is dead. He's one of them now. It's why his mother has accepted him back into her life. It's why he keeps you here locked away from his wives as some dirty little science experiment. How did they treat you? Were you welcomed graciously by my aunt? Is she excited to plan your wedding, your future? Did she ask a lot of questions about your baby?"

"Shut up," she said and sat down.

"Don't be stupid!" Armand hissed at her like a snake. "Dr. Twelve was kidnapped and brought here. The American government knows that Asad is not going to keep their agreement. Your life and my life are in danger. But we can change that. Together."

"What kind of deal do you have in mind?" she asked, still not believing what she was hearing.

"Tomorrow, we get on the plane I've arranged to take you from here and we get the hell out of Saudi Arabia. We go straight to DC. You can be safe, they will protect you and the child."

"No. No. I can't go back. They'll use my baby. Just like he will. Oh God, I'm going to be sick." She ran to the bathroom and threw up. Deep in her heart, she knew that Jaxon couldn't be trusted. After all, he did kidnap her. He put her through hell with his blackmailing schemes. But she believed that an even greater part of him loved her. She needed to believe in his love.

"I have it all arranged. You just need to get in the car that I send for you. If you don't, I won't wait," Armand said from the bathroom door.

"Why? Why is he doing this?"

"I dunno. We spent our life rejecting this bullshit and now he's back and he wants it all. I don't know. Maybe it's the disease. It made his father crazy. Maybe it's the accident. He wasn't the same after it. Maybe it's you. Maybe he thinks this is the only way of keeping you. I don't fucking know him anymore. But I know he can't be stopped here. Ever. And this palace he put you in will be the prison he visits you in. Believe me."

"Then why are you helping me?"

Armand smiled. "I got my reasons."

Goodiva shook her head in disbelief.

"Seven o'clock tomorrow evening, a man will come for you. He'll come right in the front door and tell you that he's here to bring you to the doctor. You take your purse and your passport. That's it. I'll be waiting. If you're not at the airport by eight o'clock I'm out. Good luck with this bullshit."

Armand turned and left.

She didn't bother to ask him more questions. She feared the truth.

Chapter Thirty

Goodiva sat alone with the phone in her hand. Not since Armand dropped his missile of truth on her had she spoken to Asad. And nothing made sense. The video could mean anything. He was possibly playing the role he told her he would play until they were married. He could still be working undercover for the government to infiltrate his family. Wouldn't he have to be this person to do so?

She checked the time again. In thirty minutes, a driver would arrive. He would offer to take her to a doctor's visit. She didn't know what to do. Her fingers began to text a message to Asad, and she stopped. Instead, she dialed him.

"Hello?" Asad answered on the first ring.

She didn't say anything. She couldn't.

"Goddess? Are you okay?"

"Hi. Yes. I'm okay.

"I'll see you tonight," he said, and she could hear the smile in his voice.

"Oh, what time?" She wiped her tears from her cheeks."

"Late. Don't wait up. I'll be there," he promised.

She looked around the vista he brought her to. Every time he visited, she felt as if it were paradise. And it was then she remembered how it felt in his cellar. The isolation, the waiting for him and his affection. Armand was right. She had chosen one gilded cage for another.

"Do you love me?" she asked.

He said he did, in Arabic and then in English.

"I love you too. I would have never trusted you and come here if I didn't. But I love the baby. I didn't want a child before Asad, and now all I want to do is protect my baby. That's what important. You understand?"

"Do you need me to come over now? Are you okay?"

"No. I'm fine. Just my hormones. I just wanted to say...I love you. And I wish...I wish so many things. I wish I never went to Twixt's house that night. That we never had that accident that changed you. I wish I could do it all over."

"You won't have to wish much longer. I promise you."

"Okay, see you later tonight," she said.

She ended the call first. She sat there for over twenty minutes thinking of every moment she shared with him. From the moment they met to their night in the desert. She thought of him when the door opened and closed. A man walked in.

"Miss Johnson. I am here to take you to your doctor's appointment."

It was the message she knew he was sent to deliver. It was seven. It was time. She stood and wiped her tears. Armand told her to bring just her passport, but she had her little attaché case with her MacBook. Her entire life of music and dreams was on it. She wouldn't leave it behind. She picked up the case and purse before she started toward the stranger. She could have faith. She could send the man away and trust in Asad. Be patient for love. Why should she take that big of a risk? Nothing in her life ever went the way she hoped. And her child's life was now at stake.

"I'm ready," she said.

ASAD SAT AT THE TABLE with his cousins. He listened to very little of the conversation. All he thought of was her. The night before, he made his vows to her that he intended to honor the rest of his life, she was happy. He saw it. She believed in him. No woman in his life ever had.

One of his men entered the room. The Scorpion made eye contact with him and walked over to the table of men. He leaned in and whispered in his ear. His cousin had decided to take his advice and leave. He was to fly out soon. What was interesting in the news delivered was his cousins final destination. He had told Armand to go to Australia. He'd arranged protection for him and financial security. Instead he was headed to America. In particular he was headed to D.C.

Asad frowned.

Why D. C.?

Jaxon nodded to the crown prince and excused himself from the table. He removed his phone and with his thumb he turned on the tracker. He could see the GPS tracker on her phone and it was still in the villa. She was there. She was waiting for him. But something about that call with her didn't feel right. He used the tracker to track her computer. Goodiva spent most nights with it in bed with her. He knew she'd be on it now.

He stopped walking.

The computer was on the move. She was headed somewhere. And he had a good idea where.

"Mother fucker..." he said. Several looked his way, including the crown prince. He didn't give a shit. He had to get to the airport fast.

"YOU'RE LATE. I'M GLAD I waited," Armand said and grabbed her forcefully by the arm.

"There was traffic. Let's—"

He stopped. He looked out past her to the distance and her head turned. Six large dark SUV's sped toward them. "Go! Up inside the plane! Now!"

She went up the short ladder. Armand argued loudly with someone in Arabic. She expected him to follow. She was certain he would. But instead the ladder to the plane went up and the man that brought her was the only one inside with her.

"What is happening?"

The plane began to taxi slowly away. She leaned into the window to see Asad get out of the SUV. He was looking directly at her. As the plane made the turn to run its way to the clouds, Armand had his hands up speaking with Asad. Men in all-black robes had guns on him.

"What is happening! Stop the plane! Stop!" she yelled.

The man who accompanied her said nothing. They jet sped off like a rocket and they lifted to the sky. She lost sight of them at first. But when she was able to look down again, she swore she saw Armand laid out flat on his back and Asad holding the gun.

Minutes Earlier

"You have to let her go!" Armand shouted over the engine of the jet speeding away.

"Stop the plane!" Asad shouted to his men. Men hopped in a SUV to chase the jet, even though he knew to do so would put her in harm's way. They raced to get to the side of the plane or in front of it. It was a losing battle. He turned on his cousin. "What have you done?!"

"I had to. I had to," Armand reasoned. "I want my life back. I'm not like them. You're not like them. We don't belong here!"

She was almost gone. Asad could sense the jet would shoot up into the clouds any moment. A sense of panic seized him. Never in his life had he felt more lost and desperate. He shook his head to his men that were preparing to bring the plane down with a missile launcher. He took a gun from one of their hands.

"Asad...be reasonable. This could work in our favor. We can turn this around. You know we can."

Asad shot him. His cousin. His flesh and blood. The man he considered closer than a brother. The closest he ever had to family. Armand's eyes stretched in shock and horror. He touched his chest just before he fell back, and even then he cried out in disbelief. Asad had never killed a man with his own hands, but for weeks he'd sat by and ordered the deaths of men sentenced for crimes by the crown prince. He reasoned that it was for the life he wanted with her. When Armand fell dead before him, he knew his cousin was right. The man he thought he was had died in that moment. He looked up at the jet lifting to the sky and his heart broke into a thousand pieces. He almost turned the gun on himself the pain and loss was so great.

What had he done?

He turned and walked away. She was gone.

12 Hours Later

The plane had touched down once to refuel, and then they were traveling. She had no idea to where and no way to communicate with anyone. The man sitting next to her never spoke a word. And it was the longest flight of her life. When they landed, Homeland Security boarded. The officer demanded she stand. Terrified, she feared arrest or worse. They didn't put her in handcuffs. They did escort her off the jet to a waiting car.

"What is happening?"

"Your passport," the officer requested.

She handed it over. He looked at her picture and then looked at her. He looked at the picture again, and she assumed her identity was confirmed. Her laptop bag was searched, and her laptop taken away from her.

"Hey! What are you doing?! Why are you detaining me?"

"We want to ask you some questions."

"I want a lawyer. I won't answer any questions without one," she said.

The agent looked at her for a moment. "That won't be necessary."

"I want a lawyer! The last time I checked, this was still America, and I am entitled to one."

"The laws favor national security. You will be questioned, and then a lawyer."

"I want a lawyer. You asshole. I mean it. Fuck you and the law. I want a lawyer."

She was ignored the rest of the trip. Taken to a building she didn't recognize, she was then escorted by two men to an elevator and a floor with no pictures on the walls, no numbers on the doors. It was an empty white hall. Goodiva didn't want to cry. She couldn't help her emotions. The tears kept slipping down her cheeks. Why did Armand send her here? What had she done? She trusted him, and she may have put her baby and her own personal freedom in jeopardy. She was so confused and scared.

A short woman dressed in a dark blue suit approached in an official manner. "Mrs. Johnson?"

"Miss," Goodiva corrected her.

"Yes, apologies. I'm Deputy Director Spencer. Nice to meet you,"

"I want a lawyer," she said.

"Of course. Who?"

"Delilah Montgomery, she lives in Falcon Cove, Colorado. I won't speak to anyone unless she is here."

The director nodded to the man to her left, and he walked away. "Don't be upset. You've done nothing wrong. We just have questions. Please, come with me. Are you okay? Do you need something to drink? Eat?"

"I'm pregnant," Goodiva said and the tears came. "I need to eat."

The woman nodded and put her hand to Goodiva's arm. "It's okay. We'll take care of you."

Goodiva was mentally and emotionally drained. She had so little energy she didn't bother to object. She was taken to a room that had a sofa and chairs with plenty of food to eat. It wasn't what she expected from these agents. She imagined a jail cell would be her next stop.

The director left her, but two agents remained near the door. She ate and cried. She tried to relax and calm herself. It was hard. And then the door opened, and her heart surged. Queen and Delilah came rushing in. Goodiva stood in shock. There was no way they could have arrived so fast. The embrace happened and nearly knocked her over. She wept hard in Delilah's arms as Queen held on to them both.

"I'm sorry. I'm so sorry."

"Are you okay? Are you?" Delilah held her face. "Are you pregnant? They told us you were pregnant. Is that true?"

Goodiva could only nod.

"Oh my God Shelly. What happened to you?"

"I don't know. I don't know anything anymore."

"It's okay sweetie. Calm down. It's okay," Queen reassured her. "Sit. Please."

Delilah was slow to let her go. She sat and was given tissues to wipe her face. "How did you know I was coming back? How?"

Her friends exchanged looks. Goodiva didn't understand any of it. She looked at them both for an explanation, but nothing came. Queen stood. She glanced to the director and the agents. "We need to talk to her alone."

"We'll need to speak with her," the woman in the blue suit said.

"I understand. But she's been through hell. I should bring her up to speed on what all of this is. Then she will meet with you. Full cooperation."

"No I won't!" Goodiva said. She looked to Delilah. "What is going on? What do they want from me? And why are you here?"

"Please, give us an hour," Queen asked.

The director nodded and had her people escorted out.

"Is he with you?" Delilah asked.

"Who?" Goodiva asked.

"Armand," Delilah said.

Shocked, Goodiva didn't know how to answer. She looked between her friends and then to Delilah for an explanation. "What have you two done?"

"Let me explain it to her," Queen said. She sat forward on the chair so she could reach Goodiva's hands as she sat on the sofa. She took them both into her hand. "We were worried. We knew something had happened to you in Mayfair. And we knew Jaxon Price had everything to do with it. Then you left. And all of it came to light. My contacts brought me in on a government operation with the Saudi royal family."

"They said you were in Saudi Arabia with dangerous people. That you were pregnant and at great risk. And that's how we met Armand. He told us everything. How you were drugged and kidnapped. How they forced this pregnancy on you. And how you were now being held in Saudi Arabia against your will."

"That's not how it happened at all," she began.

"Are you defending that asshole!" Delilah seethed.

"Dee, stop. Stop okay," Queen said. She turned back to Goodiva. "We had to get you back. Armand agreed to work with the government. To get you on a plane. He said he'd convince you to leave. And he did. Jaxon Price isn't who you think he is. He's a terrorist. And he's dangerous."

"He is not a terrorist!" Goodiva stood. "He didn't want any of this. He...he is just trying to deal with his family. And he's sick. You don't know what you are talking about."

"The intelligence agencies know his family very well. They know more than you do on this demon!" Delilah said.

"I can't believe any of it. I believed him," Goodiva said through her tears.

"Who Jaxon?" Queen asked.

"Armand. He told me that Jaxon was trying to trap me. That my baby was in danger. I believed him. But all along he was just working with you. Meddling in my life!"

"What!" Delilah stood. "What did you say? Meddling? Is that what you think this is? Do you know how many nights we both cried and worried over you? How hard we fought to get you back home."

"I didn't ask you to do any of this!" Goodiva wept.

"We had a pact, damn it!" Delilah shouted. "Ten years old. The three of us. We made a pact. And even now I'm the only one trying to hold us to it."

"Dee...not here," Queen warned. "They're listening."

"That's what people do when they love you Shelly!" Delilah said. "How dare you turn on us? How dare she!" Delilah said to Queen. Goodiva watched as Queen walked over and tried to calm Delilah down. She hugged her. She whispered in her ear. She turned and looked at Goodiva with anger, not understanding.

"If we are wrong, if this was all a big misunderstanding, why did you get on that plane? Why did you come back?" Queen asked.

"He's not a terrorist. I don't know what he's doing over there with those people, but it's not a plot to kill...." She stopped herself. She closed her eyes. She recalled the death of Armand. It was the last thing she saw. "I don't know what's happening to him, but he's not what you think he is. He's sick. He's confused."

"There's a name for what you are going through. People who are kidnapped and tortured suffer the same kind of trauma. Some even think that their abuser is the victim. You need help sweetheart."

"Shut up!" she shouted at Delilah. "Stop it! The two of you!"

She wept. Delilah came over to her and stooped. "I'm sorry. My life is in ruins right now Shelly. Everything has fallen apart. The only thing I've had, I've always had, is you two. You and Queen. I'm only trying to help you because I love you. I love you so very much."

Goodiva hugged Delilah and cried.

They cried together.

"HAVE YOUR FRIENDS EXPLAINED to you who I am?" Director Spencer asked.

Goodiva glanced to Delilah and Queen. "Yes."

"Good. First, know that you are not in any trouble. We consider you a victim in all of this. We have Armand Al Jabar's statement. He told us what you've been through."

"He doesn't know anything about me," Goodiva mumbled.

"We know he's dead. Do you know that?" the director asked with narrowed eyes focused on her. "He died saving your life."

Both of her friends gasped.

"Did the man you knew as Jaxon Price pull the trigger?"

"I didn't see anything. We were on the plane. It was taking off. I didn't see anything," she said through her tears. No matter what they thought Jaxon was capable of, she would not tell them a damn thing to incriminate him. She just wouldn't do it.

The director reached into her leather binder and removed several large 8x11 glossy photographs. She placed them one by one on the coffee table. Goodiva frowned at the men she saw before her.

"Have you met any of these men?"

She shook her head no.

"Are you sure? Please take a closer look," director Spencer asked.

"I don't have to. I was never in the presence of these men, or any other men."

"Explain," the director said.

"No," Goodiva responded.

"Shelly, talk to her. Tell her what you know," Delilah said.

"I don't know anything."

"How about this man?" the director asked as she put an image of her boarding a plane with Dr. Eleven in front of her. "Do you know him?"

Goodiva stared at the image.

"And this man, have you ever seen him?" the director laid another image before her. It was a photograph of Dr. Twelve, the man that Armand said was kidnapped by Jaxon. The doctor who was giving her exams during her pregnancy.

"They are doctors," she said.

"Good," the director replied. "And?"

She shrugged. "They both met with me about my pregnancy."

"So you saw them both in Dubai?" the director asked.

Goodiva's eyes watered. "Yes. I saw them both separately in Saudi Arabia."

The director seem pleased. She then brought out other images. Goodiva didn't know the people. She did her best to remember those she met with Fatimah, but that meeting was for the ladies only. Only armed escorts were around them. And that image on Armand's phone of Jaxon smiling with men, she didn't see their faces. All she saw was his.

"I'm sorry, but I don't know anything. I arrived in Dubai and they drove me through the desert to Saudi Arabia. To my own private place. They had servants and doctors, and that's all. The first man to visit me other than Jaxon was Armand. He told me all these horror stories. How they would take my baby and experiment on my child for its blood. That you would do the same thing."

The comment seemed to make the director uncomfortable. Delilah and Queen noticed as well.

"What was he like, Miss Johnson?" the director pressed on.

"Who?"

"The new prince. The man you thought you knew?"

"He was a man who had his life ripped and torn to shreds because of an accident. Then a sudden illness that has put an expiration date on his life. Do you know anything about that?"

Director Spencer picked up all the images and put them in her folder. She smiled at Goodiva. "Prince Asad bin Abdullah has just buried his grandfather. He has now taken the role as the leader of his family clan and personal confidant to the crown prince. He was never Jaxon Price, the man you thought you knew."

"If you hadn't have given him that cancer—"

"He has betrayed this country and he has betrayed you!" the director shouted over her. "I am sorry Miss Johnson, but whatever stories he told you about government conspiracies to make him sick so we could use him are false. He is a terrorist. A threat. If he ever tries to contact you, report it immediately. Understand?"

She nodded that she did.

The agents left. Delilah came over and put her arm over her shoulder. Goodiva shook her head and cried. "They're lying. He's a monster because they made him one."

Chapter Thirty-One

"You awake?"

Goodiva wasn't. After a moment she opened her eyes to the sound of her friend's persistent voice. The bed was too large for just her. The guesthouse had two bedrooms. Delilah told her she would turn one into a nursery. With a full kitchen and television room, it was cozy enough to be her new home. The seclusion was what she desperately craved. She had to admit after a few days staying there it felt comfortable.

Delilah stood by the bed holding a tray of food. For the past two days Goodiva had asked her friend not to cook for her, not to show up unannounced, not to expect anything from her. She needed privacy to heal. The stress of their questions and assumptions was too much for her to handle at her current stage in her pregnancy. The doctor that she was forced to see in DC before they left warned against it. She only agreed to return to Colorado and stay on Delilah's ranch because she had nowhere else to go. She didn't even have clothes when she returned to America.

"Yes, I'm awake," Goodiva said.

"I made your favorite. Oatmeal with brown sugar, butter, pecans and strawberries."

"Thank you," she smiled.

"Also, some warmed tea, milk and honey with just a splash of cayenne. Trust me. It helped a lot when I was pregnant."

"Yuck," Goodiva gagged.

"I got another surprise for you," Delilah teased.

Goodiva sat up against her pillows and let her friend put the tray across her lap. She was famished. Yesterday she could barely keep anything down. She spent most of the day backsliding into her fits of tears and depression. She ached physically over the loss of Jaxon and his love. Even after all she'd seen and learned, she missed him crazily. Delilah hurried out the room. Goodiva ate her orange juice and tried her tea with milk. It was actually good. When her friend returned, she felt calm.

"Ta dah! It's your laptop. Queen got it back from those agents. It's all good." Delilah grinned.

"Wow!" Goodiva gasped. "Thank you so much! I didn't think I would ever get it back."

"Here it is," Delilah placed it on the bed next to her. "How do you feel?" she whispered.

"Better," she lied.

"You look good sweetie," Delilah said, and moved Goodiva's hair from her face. "I'm just so glad to have you here with me. So much has happened since you left."

"Is he who I think it is?" Goodiva asked as she ate.

Delilah smile faded.

"Who?"

"The white man I saw outside my window playing with Noah. I've seen him at least three times. Is he living permanently with you?"

"Maverick. His name is Maverick."

Goodiva frowned. "First or last name?"

"First. Maverick Lennon. He's Noah's biological father, and yes since the quarantine he's been living here."

"Really?" Goodiva dropped her spoon back into her oatmeal bowl. Delilah gave her a brave smile, but she could see the tears form in her friend's eyes.

"He's the donor that was used to inseminate me. I know you heard the story."

"Are you sure?"

"That I was inseminated with his sperm? Ah, pretty much."

"No. But are you really sure he's the donor."

"One hundred percent positive. The courts and DNA testing certified it."

"What the hell is he doing here then?"

"He wants custody of Noah. And the courts were willing to hear a joint custody agreement."

"Then I'll say it again, what the hell is he doing here Dee?"

"My compromise. I invited him to move in with us. I have to figure this out and not have a judge split my baby in half. What I won't do is have my baby taken from me for weekend visits or holidays and given to a stranger. No way in hell!"

"Dee? This compromise is risky. Moving him into your home. It's…I don't know. It's crazy."

"Tell me about it. Just forget it for now. He's not the devil. He had his own tragedy. A long story. I can't go into it. I just can't."

"I know the feeling," Goodiva mumbled.

"You do, don't you?" Delilah smiled.

"Life is complicated. It just always feels that way with us three."

"True," Delilah said. "I feel bad Shelly. You're pregnant. We've barely even talked about it."

"No. It's okay. I haven't exactly been open and receptive with sharing the news. I'm sorry. I was selfish, insensitive, obsessed with Jaxon Price ever since that night we had that accident. You needed me and I wasn't here Dee. You've been going through hell. I feel like I should be apologizing a hundred times to you."

"My problems are not your fault. I know what he did to you."

Goodiva sighed. "Yes. He did those things, but he did them to protect me. You want to know a real truth, my deepest secret?"

"You're telling me your secrets now?" Delilah smiled.

"Not just my secret. Government secrets, family secrets, it's all crazy."

"I'm listening."

"What the government didn't tell Queen and you was that Jaxon's father was once a spy for this country."

"Spy? I don't believe that."

"He was under US government protection and allowed to do those horrible things he did at that clinic for research. For some type of blood cancer they made in a lab as a weapon off of his rare illness. And this government, not the Saudis, gave that same disease to Jaxon after he had his accident. That's how all of this started. He's not a terrorist, Dee. He's their golden goose that got away. They brought me back to trap him into the deal they wanted him to make when they let him leave this country with me.

They're using me, my baby and even you and Noah. All of this is the government. It's racist, it's scary, it's institutional and everywhere."

"Shelly? Stop. You're sounding crazy."

"I don't know what Jaxon is becoming now, but I know that this started because of the same people that are talking about honor and country." She dropped back on her pillow and released a deep sigh of exhaustion. "It's hard to believe. I can't make you believe me. But I know it's the truth. I swear."

Delilah nodded. "I believe you, honey."

"You do? You just called me crazy."

She nodded. "I did. Because I judge people. I always do. I pass judgement and I sentence them. And I've been wrong about so many things, all the way back to Charles. If you say the government did this, then hey maybe they did."

Goodiva smiled.

"I wouldn't have believed you if I hadn't seen what could be done to a person because of lies and secrets. My poor baby boy. The things Charles put me through to conceive. Making me think it was my fault. Blaming me when I wasn't pregnant. The mind games. And now this? His family has trashed me everywhere. He left me with... so much heartache Shelly. All I know is that I wanted you back with me. I wanted you home and safe."

Goodiva moved the tray from her lap and Delilah crawled over to her. She kicked off her heels and allowed Goodiva to hold her.

"What is going to happen?" Delilah asked with a burdened sigh.

"I don't know," Goodiva sighed. "All I know is my baby boy is a miracle. And a lot of powerful people are watching me, waiting for my child to be born."

"I'll never let anything happen to you," Delilah said.

"You can't stop it. It's not my baby they want. It's his blood."

"Seriously? His blood? For what?"

"The blood in his umbilical cord. If they take it, then they control Jaxon. If I give it to him then...he lives and controls me. I left him knowing that without me he will die. That's the second time I've left him to die, Dee. I don't know what that means. If he will ever forgive me. I...Dee...I..."

"This sounds crazy," said Delilah.

"It's bad."

"That's okay too. I know a good doula. We can deliver the baby here. We will protect you both."

"Whatever, I'm okay either way. I trust you Dee. I always have."

"Well, first we get you up out of this bed and dressed. I have brought in some clothes for you. Amazon delivered your panties and bras."

"You don't know my size?" Goodiva laughed.

"I peeked. I got you girl. We have a doctor's appointment. We need to meet with my doula to see if you like her."

"I'm not ready to leave here. I'm not sure it's safe."

"It's safe. And we have Maverick."

"What? Who cares about him?"

"He's a decorated cop out of New York. Queen would like him, if he hadn't arrived in town to destroy my life. Anyways, I confided in him."

"Why? He's your enemy."

Delilah didn't answer. She walked away. Goodiva found her behavior interesting. Something was going on with her friend that she wasn't sharing. "He's more than capable of escorting us around town today. I need to be seen in public with him. The scandal is a problem for my business, for me...the gossip is destroying everything. So, get dressed, okay? Today we start focusing on you living again."

"What about the Montgomeries? I heard they're trying to invalidate the will."

"They won't be able to. Yes, they are trying. And treating my baby as a pariah." She shook her head. "I'll explain it all to you later."

"Okay. I'll get showered."

Delilah kissed her forehead and then left. Goodiva closed her eyes, trying to summon the strength to stand. It wasn't easy.

"It's okay sweetie," she said and rubbed her stomach. "We're okay."

Goodiva reached for her laptop. She missed the MacBook in the deepest way. The idea that the government had kept it for over a week did give her anxiety. All of her thoughts and dreams were inside. She could only imagine what they did and how invasive it was to her privacy. When she opened it she found the laptop remained fully charged. She was relieved. She connected to the Wi-Fi first. And then she checked her email. She had over 1000 unread messages. More than fifty percent of them were spam. She scrolled through each subject line, searching, and searching. In her heart, she feared he was there. But wouldn't the agents have seen the email too?

The green light to the laptop blinked on. Shocked, her fingers went stiff mid-type. She sat back and stared at the web camera. Her Facebook app connected. A call was placed and a connection established. All of it controlled by an unseen hand. Goodiva lifted her fingers from the keyboard and sat with her hands raised. Her mouth gaped in shock, but she waited. The Instant Messenger window opened with a Facebook live image. It was Jaxon. He wore his mask but was without the traditional clothes she'd last seen in. He had to be using his cell phone by the way he moved, and how the video of him kept jumping. He kept the phone lowered in his hand. He was walking. He looked down at her.

"There you are. My Goddess. I found you."

Goodiva looked around the room, expecting Delilah and Queen to run in and accuse her of contacting him. She expected the government agents to swoop in to arrest her for daring to be so bold. No one came. It was again, just him and her. Her eyes returned to her laptop screen.

"I miss you, do you miss me?" he smiled in that sly manner that made her stomach flutter with excitement.

"No." She closed the laptop. She shook her head in disbelief, how could he reach her from so far? How could get past all of them and reach her? She was alone, but the hairs on her arm stood on end. She felt as if he was in the room. She glanced at the television and feared he could see her. Goodiva eased out of bed, weak from mental exhaustion. She took the laptop and put it in the bag it came in. She placed it in her dresser and closed it.

"I won't do this again. Do you hear me?" she spoke to the dresser drawer. "Let me go!"

Six months later

Queen laughed. She laughed so hard that everyone at the table joined in. It felt good to see her happy. After the hell she'd been through, they all wanted nothing but happiness and peace for Queen. Delilah stood and raised her glass. Tonight was a night of celebration. Queen had solved a five-year-old case. The serial killer had nearly destroyed Queen's life and his connection to them all was still being investigated. However, the bad had finally gone from Falcon Cove. Goodiva could never believe in the power of the undying strength of the love she, Queen and Delilah shared. But she was a believer now.

"I want to make a toast. To Detective Queen Douglas, the woman who has always been our champion and to the girl who was our protector. I am so proud of you, of all of us, but especially you Queen. Thank you for loving me, saving me, and believing in me. Friends for life," Delilah said.

"Friends for life!" Goodiva cheered.

The men at the table raised their beers in a toast. Goodiva sipped her apple juice as Queen and Delilah danced around to the music that Queen's partner played. The serial killer that had for years haunted Falcon Cove and their lives was dead, and the case was solved. But even in the celebrating Goodiva knew that her friend Queen had been forever changed.

Goodiva hadn't felt the baby move all day. She was two days away from her delivery date. She rubbed her belly and tried to shift her weight in her seat. She drank the cold apple juice and got no response. She expected a kick or wiggle. Nothing came. Her heart began to race a bit. She was more than paranoid. Confined to bedrest the last four weeks of her pregnancy, she had been extra careful.

"Hey?" Queen said and hugged her neck.

"Hey!" Goodiva said.

"Come with me," Queen said.

"Oh? Okay." She accepted her hand and allowed her to pull her up from her seat. The others looked over with concern.

"I got her, I got her," Queen assured them. Goodiva smiled. With her arm around Queen, they walked out of the dining room to the living area. She was helped to a comfortable seat on the sofa with pillows behind her back. "How's that?"

"Feels great, thank you girl."

"It's any day now. You scared?" Queen asked

"No. Just ready to meet my baby," Goodiva said.

"You still don't know what you're having?" Queen asked and brought over her laptop bag.

"No. I told you, I don't want anyone to know. What is that you got?"

"I want us to finish our conversation about Jaxon Price."

"You mean Prince Asad?" she corrected her friend. Queen gave her a sad smile. A lot had happened in Saudi Arabia since she fled. Queen often kept her up to date. She turned the laptop around so Goodiva could see the news story. She read it aloud:

Prince Asad Abdullah al Saud stepped up in his family after his grandfather's death and the unexplained sudden death of his cousin Armand Al Jabar. Two weeks ago the crown prince arrested at least fifty of his cousins and uncles under Prince Asad Abdullah's direction. The men were being held with charges of treason and conspiracy against the royal family. The media suspected that the charges were false, and it was the crown prince neutralizing any claims to his throne and power. The masked Prince Asad had been a valued and trusted officer of his secret service forces.

"He's the man isn't he?" Queen asked.

Goodiva shrugged.

"I had a visit from our friends in the Department of Defense," Queen took the laptop back. "Have you been in contact with him Shelly?"

Goodiva frowned. "No."

"Are you sure?" Queen asked.

"Why would you ask me that?"

"You're the queen of keeping secrets, that's why," Queen said.

"Ah, you're the Queen, remember?" Goodiva joked.

"I'm serious. His activities are accelerating. We have intelligence that he is once again focused on you."

"I don't know what that means?" Goodiva said.

"It means they think he knows you're ready to give birth. They think he's plotting something."

"I don't want to discuss him. I just don't."

"My contacts have given me more information. Something is happening in Saudi Arabia." Queen pulled out documents. "Here, you can read this tonight. This is everything I could put together."

"I don't want to know. He's out of my life." She shoved the documents back at her friend.

"I'm not sure he is Shelly," Queen said.

"Why not? I told you I'm not in contact with him."

"He's unmarried now."

"So?"

"His wives have all been cast out. Publicly humiliated. He's a man with a mission."

"So what?!"

"They believe he's going to come for the baby after it's born. Or you both. Read this, tell me if anything sounds familiar or if there is anything that seems out of character for him."

"No," she said.

"Shelly—"

"I don't know his character anymore. The man I knew is dead. And I don't think he cares about me or this baby. Not the way you guys think. You said he was cured."

"He's saying he's cured, but how do we know for sure?" Queen asked.

"Well he's still alive. When he was with me that disease was killing him. He couldn't have lived this long if it weren't for something," she sighed. "All I want to focus on is a healthy delivery. Okay?"

Queen gave her a sad smile. "You're so strong."

"So are you Queen. So is Dee. We're strong together. We always have been."

Queen hugged her neck and kissed her cheek. She put the papers back. "Fine. I'm worrying and overthinking things again. Tonight's a celebration."

"Exactly!" Goodiva laughed.

"Let's party!"

WHEN THE PARTY ENDED Queen and Delilah escorted her back to her guest house. They were all too tired to talk over the events of the past few weeks. They just prayed together and over her baby. She saw them to the door and then locked down her little cottage for the night. She went inside of her room where she found her laptop sitting on her bed. Goodiva let go a deep sigh. She glanced to her phone and checked the time. It was two minutes to midnight.

Midnight was their time.

She went to the bed and turned on her laptop. He had to have been waiting. He appeared the moment she signed in.

"You're early," she said.

Asad smiled.

She smiled.

"How is my baby?" he asked.

She turned the laptop around and stood before the bed. He could see her. She was certain. She pulled her dress up over her head. She only wore her panty underneath. Her large belly dropped into view under the swell of her oversized breasts.

"You're so beautiful," he said.

Asad reclined in his chair with a half-smile. Over the long torturous months he'd watched her change in so many ways, but this was his favorite. Her hair was longer now. He loved it that way. Her stomach was so round he could barely see any part of her body because of it.

"I'm ready to pop," she grinned.

"I see," he chuckled.

It took a month after she escaped him for him to finally get her to speak with him. And when she did, it took him even longer to win her heart back. He never gave up. And she never gave in to the pressure of her friends and the authorities. Their life had reverted back to a time where they couldn't be together. But he felt closer to her each day as the birth of his child approached. She pulled on a silk robe and then picked up the laptop to sit in a chair.

"They suspect us again. I think they know we're communicating," she said.

"Fuck them. It doesn't matter what they think they know."

"You keep saying that. It does matter. Everything matters now."

"I want to be there," he said. "Right now. With you."

"I want you here?" she said.

"When you give birth. I want to be there."

"We talked about this Jaxon. I have a high risk pregnancy. I have to give birth in the hospital. There is no way. Besides, you can't enter the country. It's impossible."

"Nothing will keep me from you and my son. Anything is possible." He sat forward. "Play me some music."

She grinned and nodded. "What do you want to hear?"

"Anything, that reminds you of me."

She nodded and punched in a song to him. Rhianna's soulful voice crooned to him. He winked at her. He relaxed and listened as she complained about her weight, her heartburn, her gas, and pelvic cramps. She showed him more of her stretch marks that were now on her breasts. All of it made her so real and vulnerable to him.

"I have to go. I'm tired. I need to sleep," she yawned.

"Tomorrow? Midnight?" he asked.

"Yes. Yes. Midnight. Love you so much Jaxon. Bye."

And then she was gone. Asad lowered the lid to his laptop. She was the only one in the world he allowed to call him Jaxon to his face. Alone in his room, he stared in the dark. He didn't care about the power, or the position he held. He didn't care about the risks, or the dangers in his life. He had only a few days of this existence left. And he intended to use them wisely.

Two days later

Goodiva's voice screeched in loud agony. The paramedics loaded her to the stretcher. She fought to keep Delilah with her. "No. Please! You promised! I can't go by myself. They'll take my baby! Please God no!"

"You have to calm down," Delilah said, and squeezed her hand. "The baby is in distress. The doula and everyone agrees. We have to deliver the baby in the hospital."

"No, don't let them take me. It's not safe!" she wheezed.

Delilah was forced to let her hand go. She was lifted and put in the ambulance. A medic began to check for the fetal heartbeat as the ambulance sped out of the Montgomery ranch. It all happened fast.

"Miss Johnson. Miss?"

She opened her eyes as another painful contraction hit her.

"Breathe, breathe in and out," she was instructed. "Nice and slowly."

Goodiva's lids fluttered. An oxygen mask helped her through her breathing, and it worked. The paramedic told her she was doing well. She didn't believe him. From the ambulance into the emergency room, her fear mounted. She was taken to another room and put on a bed with her feet in foot pedals.

"Jaxon," she said weakly. She didn't mean to. But she needed him so desperately. It was time. And he didn't even know it. The doula arrived before Delilah and Queen. The doctor spoke to her before he was between her knees, reaching out his gloved hand and shoving it into her vagina. She cried out with extreme discomfort.

"I'm going to have to section her," the doctor said to her doula or the nurse—Goodiva wasn't sure. "You made a good call bringing her in."

She then heard the doctor tell a nurse to get her to STAT C in the OR. There were so many nurses and doctors around her at once she wasn't sure what was happening.

"My baby? Don't let them take my baby from me," she pleaded.

"Your baby is in breech. We are going to do a cesarean," her doula responded in a calm voice that chilled her. The woman walked at her side while she was pushed down the hospital hall.

"Delilah, I need Dee," she wheezed through her tears. "Please! She knows what to do. His cord. His umbilical cord. Don't let them take it."

Wheeled into a room flooded with bright white lights, she almost gave up hope. She and Jaxon had feared only one thing, and that was a delivery among strangers. He fretted over it night after night when they talked in secret. He warned her of the people who wanted their child and the things they would do to their baby. She promised she'd keep their baby stay safe, no matter what. All hope was lost if Delilah and Queen didn't get there in time. Goodiva heard a doctor say, 'Give me a seven'. After that, she was unable to make anything out. She prayed hard.

DELILAH AND QUEEN ARRIVED at the hospital together. Queen spoke to the hospital officials while Delilah sent rapid texts to update Maverick of what was happening. He stayed behind with Queen's partner Quinn and their son Noah. Delilah was so nervous her hands kept shaking.

"She's going into surgery and she wants you there Dee. They will do a cesarean. The doula said the baby's head is positioned wrong. They consider it some kind of breech birth," Queen said with tears on her cheeks. "This is what she was afraid of. What she knew would happen."

"Is the baby okay?"

Queen shook her head no. "Hurry! Go!"

"Okay, okay," she gave Queen her phone and went with the nurse.

"We knew this could happen," Delilah mumbled to herself. "God please protect her."

Delilah changed into sterile scrubs. She walked into a room of about eight people. She didn't understand why there were so many. When she gave birth there were only four. Who were all the people?

"Ms. Delilah, come," Marteen the doula waved her over. Goodiva was laid out on a surgical table in the center of the room with a large lamp over her. A sheet was held up across Goodiva's neck and blocked her view from the doctors opening her up.

"Oh God," Delilah felt weak at the sight of them cutting her friend. What looked like red cottage cheese was bubbling up from the surgical slice into Goodiva's lower abdomen. It made her weak in the knees.

"Sit here," Marteen said.

There was a plain metal stool by Goodiva's head. Her dear friend looked pale with fear and wept in her silent way.

"Hey? Hey, no, no, don't cry. It's okay," Delilah whispered in her ear. "I'm here."

"Who are these people?"

"Doctors, nurses, they're all here to protect the baby," Delilah assured her.

"No they aren't. Jaxon warned me. It's time. They've come to take my precious baby away."

"What?" Delilah blinked in shock.

"Please save my baby. They will take my baby."

"Sweetheart, no one is taking the baby. You're confused. Jaxon isn't here."

"No, no, no, no," Goodiva moaned. "He said they would do it. This is how they will do it."

"It's okay. I swear," Delilah said.

"Stay with my baby no matter what happens to me. I'm telling you, they will take my baby. They will. You have to give him to his father. Jaxon is the only one who will take care of him."

"No one is going to take the baby. I promise."

Then it happened: a loud cry. The baby was held up and brought over the curtain.

"It's a boy!" Marteen announced.

"You hear that? It's a boy! Not a girl. You hear Shelly?" Delilah asked.

"Yes," Goodiva nodded with her tears clouding her vision. "He's beautiful."

Delilah stood. At that moment another person in scrubs entered the room. For some reason his arrival seemed odd. He looked directly at Delilah with a mask covering his mouth and nose. The doctor made the cut and the baby was handed to nurses.

"Go with him!" Goodiva said.

"Okay," Delilah followed the newborn. She turned to see the doctors working on Goodiva. Something was taken out of her—possible the placenta and umbilical cord—and put into a container.

"Wait, what are you doing?" Delilah demanded.

The baby wailed and the doctors were working to sew Goodiva back up as if Delilah hadn't spoken. The others were tending to the baby. Delilah went after the man in scrubs who had a container with the placenta and umbilical cord, but was stopped by Marteen.

"Come with me. The baby will be taken to be examined and she wants you there."

"Who is that man?"

"What man?" Marteen asked.

"The one who took stuff out of Goodiva. The placenta I think. The umbilical cord I think."

"What?"

Delilah pushed Marteen aside and rushed into the hall. The man in the scrubs was gone.

"BABY."

"Hey?" Queen said. "You awake?"

"Where is he?" Goodiva asked.

"Right here," Delilah walked in closer to the bed so she didn't have to turn her head. She placed the sleeping infant right next to Goodiva. She felt weak, but strong enough to move her arm.

"Hi, hi, sweetheart. It's me. I'm your mama," Goodiva said. Her baby boy opened his eyes and looked up at her. "It's me, Mama. My miracle boy."

"He knows," Delilah said. "He's so sweet. He hasn't opened his eyes or even cried. Look at him now."

Goodiva kissed his brow. "He has so much hair. He's such a hairy little angel," she laughed.

"That's why you had heartburn so bad," Queen said.

"I love him so much. I didn't mind it at all," Goodiva said.

"What will you name him?" Queen asked.

"Yeah, what should we name the little guy?" Delilah asked.

"Jaxon," Goodiva said.

"What?" Delilah glanced to Queen with concern.

"He's Jaxon. That's his name."

"Ah, Shelly, that might not be a good idea."

"I don't care. This is our son. And I want him to have the better part of his father. His name is Jaxon."

The girls nodded their respect for her decision. She didn't care about anything the moment her baby looked into her eyes; she knew it was her destiny to be his mother. She kissed his nose and smiled. "Jaxon Prince Johnson. That's who you are. My son."

Epilogue

"Is he asleep?" Delilah whispered.

"Finally," Goodiva said and took a seat at the table. "The christening was so beautiful. Thank you so much Dee."

"He's a month old. I had to drag you into the church," Delilah shook her head.

"I told you his father is Muslim and we shouldn't have... never mind. I'm glad we did it. I am." Goodiva raised her glass. She clinked it with Delilah's. Her friend drank from her private stock and she envied her so much, but breastfeeding was the only choice for her little man.

"So, how is it? You and Maverick?"

"Let's not talk about it," Delilah blushed.

"You two seem to have resolved the issue of custody. That's a good sign. Right? What aren't you telling me?" Goodiva teased.

"You think I keep secrets now?" Delilah scoffed.

"Yes. You do."

"No one keeps more secrets than you Shelly." Delilah leaned in. "I know you are still communicating with your Saudi Prince."

Goodiva blinked but didn't respond.

"Why Shelly? After all this time. And what he's done. Why would you be in contact with him."

"I'm not."

"Don't lie to me." Delilah said.

"Fine. I won't lie. He's the father of my child. Our child. And I...I'm not crazy. It's complicated."

"Promise me you won't let him near that precious baby," Delilah said.

"How would I? He's not coming to America, and I'm sure as hell not going wherever he is. No need for promises Dee. It's over between us. He and I both know that."

She heard her son cry out. Goodiva frowned. "He's up already? I just fed him."

"It's because you hold him all the time. The boy can't stand the smell of anyone but you," Delilah laughed. Goodiva went for her son. He slept in the living room in a bassinet that Delilah kept there for him for when they visited the house. He was wailing and red with fury over being put down.

"Hush sweetie," she said and picked up the baby. "Hush."

She rubbed his back, and minutes later he was calm again.

"He okay?" Delilah asked as she sipped her wine, watching from the arch of the entrance to the living room.

"Yea, it's late. I'm going to take him home and go to sleep."

Delilah walked over and kissed her cheek, and then kissed his forehead. "Come back for breakfast. Maverick is making pancakes."

"He is, is he?" Goodiva laughed.

"It's just breakfast. Besides, Noah loves his pancakes.

"Thanks Dee. For everything."

"I love you sis, always. And the christening today wasn't just a blessing for your son, but for you too. You can start over. Do and become whatever you want. He's safe now. You believe it, don't you?"

Goodiva gave her a smile and nodded. "I do. Goodnight."

She went back to the guest house alone. The night was warm and humid. It was unusually dark. She glanced to the sky and saw nothing but clouds, no moon. She hurried to her cottage and went inside. Her son didn't bother to stir.

Goodiva switched on the lamp light near the door. The rest of her place was dark. "Alexa play 'After All' by Al Jarreau," she said.

"'After All,' the extended version, by Al Jarreau," Alexa responded.

The music began at a soothing tone. All through her pregnancy she serenaded her baby, and even now certain songs kept him calm. He was like her in so many ways.

She began to hum along, walking to the room next to her bedroom. Queen had done all the painting and Delilah decorated it in *The Lion King* theme. She loved the crib. She sang along with Al Jarreau while changing his nappy. Her son sucked his fist but didn't open his eyes. He was so tired. When she was done, she turned him over and patted his back soothingly. Al Jarreau's voice soothed them both. She had another hour before she would secretly connect with his father. Tonight, she'd bring the laptop into his room and let Jaxon see him asleep. Often, she let her boy sleep with her in bed, but Delilah had been on her about trying to put him in his crib.

The song ended abruptly. Confused, she looked back to the door. Then Alexa spoke.

"'Betcha By Golly Wow' by The Stylistics," Alexa said.

She hadn't requested the song. The beautiful melody filled her home. She picked up her son and held him protectively. She went to his closet and got the gun she kept hidden there. Russell Thompkins sang of catching falling stars. She quietly left the room with the gun extended.

'Betcha By Golly Wow' continued to play. She only had to step out of her son's room to confront the person who had requested the song, but her legs felt immovable. She had her son to think of. Who could it be? What would they want? Could she pull the trigger in time to protect him? Determined to do exactly that, she steeled her nerves and stepped out of the room. Jaxon stood there in his half-mask waiting for her. At first that's what she thought. But how could she be sure? Without asking he knew her confusion and prepared for it. He removed his all-black keffiyeh and placed it on the countertop in the kitchen. He removed his mask.

"Goodiva?" he said.

She dropped her gun and ran for him. She nearly crushed her son in her arms she hugged him so tight. He held her to him and kissed the top of her head. Baby Jaxon began to cry. Laughing through her tears, she stepped back. He looked down at his son and smiled. She handed him over.

"My son," he said.

"He's beautiful Jaxon. Isn't he?"

Jaxon nodded. Tears slipped from his eyes. "He's everything."

"How? How did you get in here? How are you here? There's security and..."

"I brought him," Queen said. She walked out of the master bedroom. Goodiva looked at her in disbelief.

"You did what?"

"I'll leave you two to talk."

"But Queen?" Goodiva said.

She smiled. "It's okay. I understand."

"Thank you!" Goodiva hugged her friend. Queen let her go first. She kissed her cheek and left. She turned to see him sitting in a chair and holding his son calmly. Their boy often cried when in the arms of others, but he seemed relaxed with the Stylistics singing and his father rocking him.

"How is this possible?"

"I made the deal," he said, not able to take his eyes off his boy.

"You made what deal?"

"I gave the government what they want. I don't care what it means. I couldn't live without you anymore. Without either of you."

Goodiva went to him. She got on her knees. "The stem cells, our son?"

He glanced at him. "I lied Goddess. I'm the King of lies. I made the deal after I saw my cousin die because of the sickness in me. That's how you got the laptop back. How we were allowed to talk. All this time I've been working for them inside of the family. I gave them our sons cells and my own. Because it doesn't matter anymore. All I want is you and my boy to be with me, for however long I have left. I'll give them anything for that chance. I told you. I'll never let them take you from me."

"You're not healed are you?" she asked.

"No, but they will give me enough to live. To be a slave to their agenda."

"No Jaxon. Please. I don't want you to suffer because of us."

"It's not suffering for you Goodiva. It's the best feeling in the world to have you both belonging to me again."

"I love you so much," she kissed him. "So very much."

He looked down at his son. "I won't leave the country without you. But if I don't return to Saudi Arabia, my family will discover what I've done, and they will come for us. For all of us. If I don't return the American's won't protect us either. So I either die here with you or we try to find away somewhere else."

Goodiva touched the scarred side of his face. "You're taking too many risks. You could lose everything."

"I have nothing without you. Don't you see that Goddess? You're all I ever wanted."

"You're all I want," she smiled. "Forever."

She kissed him and kissed her son.

Later that Night

After all of the countless nights enjoying his body, she didn't expect him to ask for consent. Maverick had the largest penis Delilah had ever seen. Of course, that was not surprising: the only other man she'd ever slept with was her husband. He turned her over, bringing her with him. She sat up and looked down at the man who had unexpectedly stolen the deepest part of her heart. Was this love? Or survival? Delilah could no longer tell. But this was something she needed. She lowered herself onto him and took him into her deeper and deeper.

Maverick's lips parted She could see his chest compression as he took in a deep drag of breath. It was a lot to be on him in such a needful way. She was uncomfortably full, but her body adjusted quicker this time. And then she was seated fully. She too let out a deep breath of relief. He opened his eyes and stared at her just as she began to move, as if she were some wondrous creature he'd never seen before. Her hands were flat to his chest. He gripped her hands and held them both down to his chest while thrusting his pelvis as she worked and whirled her hips.

The gentle rhythm at first wrung a whimper from her lips. "Yes Maverick, oh, oh, oh, yes."

A smile hinted at his expression and she went full throttle. She moved faster and faster, catapulting other emotions with her sexual hunger toward a catalytic ending.

The room filled with light. It blinded her. Maverick flipped her over and pinned her to the bed. Startled, she cried out. They could hear the whipping sound of a helicopter.

"What the fuck is that?" he said and sprang from bed.

"Noah!" she cried out. He dressed fast and got a gun she didn't know he kept. She'd have to ask him about it later. "Noah," she said again as she pulled on a robe.

"Stay here!"

"No! I have to get to him!"

He didn't have time to argue. He was out the door. She turned to see her mother with her son in her arms. "Take him in the room. Stay hidden!"

Delilah didn't know why she issued the warning to her mother. It was possibly pure instinct. But she did. And then she raced downstairs after Maverick. Someone was on her land. Goodiva was trapped in her cottage.

When she arrived in the foyer, she stopped in startled fright. "Queen? What is it? The light? Is it the police?"

"Put the gun down Maverick," Queen said.

"What are you doing here?" Delilah said as she tied her sash tighter.

Queen's eyes watered with the threat of tears. "She's leaving."

"What? No. No."

"I'm sorry. She made her choice Dee," Queen said with tears in her eyes.

"Noooooo!" Delilah ran for the door. Queen tried to stop her, but Delilah had strength she didn't know she had. She raced out of the house with Maverick catching up with her halfway across the lawn.

"Shelly!" she screamed in pain. She could see her walking toward the helicopter. A man dressed like an Arab sheikh, in all black. He wore half a black mask to his face stopped. He held baby Jaxon in a blanket in his arms. Goodiva was with him. Her friend stopped.

"Don't do this. Please! Don't do this!" Delilah screamed and wept. She fought Maverick with all her might.

Goodiva looked to Asad and then her. She let down her baby bag and her luggage handle. She walked to Delilah. Maverick let her go. Delilah met Goodiva halfway. She embraced her weeping. "Don't do this Shelly. Don't go back with him. Please don't leave me. I love you so much. Please don't go. I can't lose you. Please stay. Please!"

Goodiva held her and cried. She rubbed her back. She didn't say a thing while Delilah wept. Soon Queen joined them and they all hugged.

"I love you too Dee. So very much. Thank you for everything. I owe my life to you."

"No! God please don't take her. Please God!" Delilah wept.

Goodiva held her distressed friend by the face and made her look at her. "I wish I could tell you so many things. I wish I could explain it. I can't. You have to let me go Dee. Trust me. I love him and we belong together."

"He's a monster," Delilah wept. "A terrorist."

"No, he's a man. Flesh and blood. And he's done everything I've asked of him, and more." Goodiva looked back at Asad, who stood waiting with her son. "I'm going to be okay. I promise."

"Queen! Make her listen!"

"She's going to be okay," Queen said.

"You did this. You brought him here!" Delilah shouted at Queen. "You did this!"

"Hey, stop." Goodiva grabbed Delilah by the arms. "Learn to let go Dee. Trust Maverick. Trust yourself again. Trust us, the both of us. You don't have to protect us anymore Dee. You have your own life. Live it. With Maverick and Noah."

"Maverick? I don't want him."

Goodiva smiled. "You may not want him, but you're already in love with him. Stop putting yourself last Dee. Okay? Promise me."

Delilah shook her head. "Where will you go? Where will you be? Who will you be?"

Goodiva smiled. "It's a secret. For now. But I will always love you. And someday I'll be back."

They hugged again. Delilah had no choice but to let her go. Goodiva hugged Queen. "Take care of her Queen."

"You call us, if you can," Queen said. "Take care of you."

"I got this," Goodiva said. "Bye."

Delilah watched as her heart was crushed. Goodiva rushed back to her prince. He gave her the baby and then took the luggage and baby bag and followed her. She boarded the helicopter, and he did so as well. Its long blades began to turn, and they whipped up so much wind the women were forced back from the force. Delilah bumped into Maverick. He put his arms around her and hugged her. She didn't ask for it. She didn't need him. She wanted her friend. But she allowed it, because in that moment it was all she had.

The helicopter lifted up to the dark clouds and then into the sky before it flew away.

"She'll be okay. I can't explain it, but I know it. And you know I would never let her go if she wasn't," Queen said.

"I won't forgive you for this." Delilah shrugged off Maverick's touch and stormed back to the house. She could hear them talking about giving her space. She ran the rest of the way into the house not sure how much more heartbreak she could take.

"YOUR FRIEND DOESN'T want to let you go?" Asad said.

"Change is hard for her. It was like that when I moved away with my family. But she has a new future. She just needs to accept it." Goodiva dropped her head on his shoulder.

"As you have accepted me?" he asked.

"Can we trust them?" She looked up at him in reference to the men in fatigues accompanying them.

"The real question is can they trust me?" he gave her a sly smirk.

Goodiva giggled. "Betcha by golly wow..." she sang. He chuckled and sang the song with her. "You're the one I've been waiting for, forever...." Goodiva closed her eyes and believed in their love. It was the best feeling in the world. She had her family, and everything she could dream.